A TIME
OF
TROUBLES

To my great friend Denn
will much love and affectan -
Dale
Nov 15, 2019

The books of the *Itan – Legends of the Golden Age* series by Oladele Olusanya are:

Book 1, Gods and Heroes,

Book 2, A Time of Troubles,

Book 3, A New Age, and

Semimotu and Other Stories

Visit www.oladeleolusanya.net for more details.

A TIME OF TROUBLES

ITAN—
LEGENDS OF THE
GOLDEN AGE
— BOOK TWO —

OLADELE OLUSANYA

Library of Congress Control Number:		2019910883
ISBN:	Hardcover	978-1-7960-4947-3
	Softcover	978-1-7960-4946-6
	eBook	978-1-7960-4945-9

Print information available on the last page.

Rev. date: 07/30/2019

To order additional copies of this book, contact:
Xlibris
1-888-795-4274
www.Xlibris.com
Orders@Xlibris.com
781025

CONTENTS

*To the patriarchs of my family, Solesi of Ikenne (1850–
1954) and Emmanuel Jonathan Odusanya, "Baba Mamu"
(1876–1954), whose exploits are herein recorded.*

And in memory of my son, Ayodeji Kehinde Olusanya (2012–2016)

Igba ogun l'ode ile Yoruba
Ni a fi ta mi leru
Ti a di mi ni okun
bi eni nde ekute ninu oko;
A ta mi sinu oko eru
bi eni nta agbado loja.
Esan ni oruko mi, sugbon nisisiyi,
nwon fun mi ni oruko Potoki—
Eni ti a ta leru, ti a gbe lo si ilu Brasiili.
Bawo ni ajo mi yio ti ri?
Ibo ni olugbeja mi wa?
Ha! Isoro ati iya nla nbe ni oko eru.
Igba ibanuje ni eyi je
fun gbogbo awa inago
lati ilu karo o jire.

'Twas war that came
upon the land of the Yorubas
that made me a slave,
I was tied up like a bush-rat,
And like a basket of corn
I was sold in the marketplace.
Esan is my name—
though now they call me a name in Portuguese—
He who was taken to the land of Brazil against his will.
What would become of me?
Would I ever see my native land?
Ha! What pain and suffering it is
to live in the land of bondage;
And a sad time it is for all "inago" people
From the land of "karo o jire."

-Lament of the Yoruba Slave Child Taken to the Land of Brazil.

A Century of Strife

THE STORIES OF the Old Woman tell of an era in which the Yoruba people descended into what she called *igba inira*, the "time of troubles." This was in the nineteenth century, according to the method of counting time by the white man, when the golden age of the Yorubas described in *Gods and Heroes* came to an end. It was a period that was intimate and contemporary to the Old Woman, for she was born in that century of strife. She bore witness to the stories of discord, war, and slavery that marked that age.

Like those earlier tales of ancient Yoruba gods and heroes, these stories belong in the tradition of the *arokens*, the ancient storytellers of the Yoruba people that the Old Woman epitomized. Many of these are tales I heard as a child from my grandmother, who herself was a protégé of the Old Woman.

My grandmother Efunyemi was born in Ikenne-Remo in Ijebuland in the final years of the nineteenth century. She regaled me as a child with stories of her famous father, Solesi of Ikenne, who, as a young teenager, went to war as a drummer boy in the Remo army in 1862. According to my grandmother, Solesi was captured in that war and taken to Ibadan. Throughout my childhood, I was intrigued by these stories, including the dramatic tale of Solesi's escape back to Ikenne and his becoming a great chieftain in his hometown. I also heard stories of my grandmother's marriage into the polygamous household of Odusanya in Ijebu-Ode, and of the involvement of her husband in the wars and other momentous events of that era.

My interest in this troubled, but stirring epoch of Yoruba history was revived later in life when I read Rev. Samuel Johnson's *History of the Yorubas*, which has been compared to Edward Gibbon's *Decline and Fall of the Roman Empire*. From that time, I determined to tell these stories in my own voice.

In writing about this era in my epic tale of my family and the Yoruba people, I knew I would have to lay bare the answers to many of the riddles that had intrigued me since my childhood. Who was the warlord that took Solesi to Ibadan? How did Baba Mamu fare as he journeyed to see peace come to Kiriji, a place as distant from Ijebuland as my childhood imagination could conjure? And how did those strutting *oyinbo* soldiers, administrators, schoolteachers, and priests come to impose their rule over our people from their own country thousands of miles away across the sea?

I knew I had to tell the story as it happened, leaving nothing out. I would follow the precepts of the Old Woman and her protégés as I did in *Gods and Heroes*. Thus, *A Time of Troubles* is filled with scenes of war, suffering, and loss, but also of love, redemption, and the search for happiness by ordinary men and women who try to make sense of the tragedy and calamity around them. There is also a story of Agbako, the old Yoruba demi-god of retribution and nemesis of mankind.

On these pages, we meet the major historical figures who played pivotal roles in the history of Yorubaland of that era. These include the British colonialists who helped establish the Colony of Lagos, men like Governor Carter, Consul Campbell, and William "Red Beard" McCoskry. We learn about the famous obas, Kosoko, Akitoye, and Dosunmu of Lagos; influential native-born merchants like Balogun Kuku of Ijebu-Ode, Madam Tinubu of Abeokuta, and Captain J. P. L. Davies of Lagos; and the warlords Ogunmola, Kurunmi, and Ogedengbe, who made their mark in the various theaters of war that bedeviled that troubled age.

All the battles described in *A Time of Troubles* took place, more or less as described—from the Battle of Osogbo, the destruction of Owu, and the defeat of Kurunmi of Ijaiye, to the battles fought by the upstart city-state of Ibadan leading to the Kiriji War, and the Battle of Imagbon, fought by the Ijebus in 1892, the pivotal event that paved the way for the imposition of British rule over Yorubaland.

In writing this book, I must admit that I have taken the stories of the Old Woman and my grandmother, and turned them into a novel—what the experts would call a "historical novel." It is genre descended from Walter Scott's *Ivanhoe*, which was my favorite English novel growing up and a book that used an evocative period of European history to transport the reader wih riveting scenes and timeless characters derived from the imagination of the author. Along the way, my tale departed quite a bit from the traditional Yoruba story that the Old Woman told children by moonlight. For what I have done is to utilize the power of poetic invention to make this my own unique story of Yorubaland in a time of war. It is a device of which I know the Old Woman would approve, though it may not follow strictly her own ideas of traditional storytelling.

As with the other volumes of the *Itan*: *Legends of the Golden Age* series, the cover images and chapter illustrations of this book are original art compositions by me and Dipo Alao, my friend and artist of the Osogbo school. And each chapter is preceded by an original verse in Yoruba translated into English. Thus, this book can be viewed as a creative endeavor that provides vignettes, not just of history, but of the enduring arts and culture of the Yoruba people. These are the stories of how those ancient traditions survived that century of strife that we now call the "time of troubles."

CHAPTER 1

Eko akete, ilu ogbon
To ba duro ko sora,
Ko si yangi;
Eko o gba gbere,
Eko o gba gbere rara o!

Eko stands aloof,
The island that teaches wisdom to fools.
When you stand in the streets of Lagos,
Look to yourself and beware;
For Eko does not care,
Eko does not care for you at all!

—Traditional song of Lagos.

A New City by the Sea

AS THE EMPIRE of the Alaafin disintegrated, many Yoruba city-states followed the example of Ilorin and declared their independence from Oyo. These included the Egba, the Egbado, and even the Awori in faraway Badagry on the coast. With warlords running the newly established Yoruba towns set up by fleeing refugees, at Ibadan, Abeokuta, Ijaiye, and Ago d'Oyo, it was a time of anomy and civil dislocation throughout Yorubaland.

The war chiefs and their war boys went on a rampage. They took over whole towns and subjected their population to their capricious rule. They sent messages to towns and villages to pay ransom, or else they would be attacked and devastated. Towns and villages that did not comply were surrounded, sacked, and pillaged for booty and loot.

The greatest prize to be had were slaves, which were sold at great profit at the slave markets of Lagos and Badagry. There now developed a brisk and profitable commerce in this commodity among the towns and villages of the forest communities where the Yorubas found themselves concentrated after the forced migration from old Oyo. This was because no Yoruba chieftain or important personage of that time thought that the comforts that made life bearable could be complete without the help of slaves to do household chores for his wives, work his farms, and even fight his wars.

As a grim symbol of the culture of the time and of a people in anomy, the institution of slavery became a corrupting and debilitating influence at every level of society and in every town, village, and hamlet of Yorubaland. For the merchants at the coast had made a compact with white men who came across the ocean in great ships to buy the men, women, and children that their people sold for money. These slave traders sent constantly to the hinterland for a steady supply of the commodity that was the source of their wealth.

The procurers at this end were the warlords in whom was incited a greed and avarice for war that was no longer fought for ethnic pride or political alliance, but for undiluted personal gain. The greed of the warlords drove them to wage war solely to capture slaves from among their own people.

In exchange, they received ornaments of brass, silver, and gold to adorn their many wives and concubines. They received bags of cowry shells to purchase luxuries that hitherto were unknown to them. As they sold more slaves, they acquired more bags of cowries, with which they purchased even more luxuries and horses and weapons of war with which to capture more slaves.

This constant state of war displaced whole populations. The very foundation of society was shattered. The sanctity of life was constantly breached. Women were ravished in the sight of their husbands, and their babies slaughtered or carried off at the point of the spear. Kings, rulers, and warlords debased their subjects, and the old gods were dishonored.

As this century of troubles progressed, the slave trade intensified until it became a wholesale commercial enterprise. The central town of Ipomu near Ile-Ife became the major slave market in the hinterland. On the coast, it was Lagos or Badagry.

Yet the most influential and wealthy slave merchants were from Ijebu, that part of Yorubaland that straddled the trade route between north and south. At the height of the slave trade in the mid-nineteenth century, the Ijebus were the middlemen and major local beneficiaries of the slave trade that decimated the land, though very few Ijebus themselves were sold and bought as slaves. Many Ijebu merchants and chiefs became very rich and powerful from dealing in slaves.

A Balogun of Ijebu of that period was said to have boasted to a white missionary in Lagos thus:

"There is no slave market on the face of the earth where a white man or an Ijebu man can be bought or sold."

Our story begins at the brutal scene of a slave raid on a defenseless village in the Yoruba hinterland. It was a spectacle that the comfortable merchants and middlemen in slaves in Lagos rarely saw or tried to imagine.

The scene was a small hamlet, now destroyed and completely wiped off the face of the earth, which, in the middle of the nineteenth century, lay astride the road between the towns of Ofa and Oje, not far from the bigger Yoruba towns of Ijaiye and Ibadan.

As told by the Old Woman eighty years later, it is the story of a brutal attack by marauders on Itanku, a village that was sparsely defended. This story was told to the Old Woman as an eyewitness account by the nine-year-old boy from Itanku named Ogungbayi, who escaped and survived the attack. His father was an elephant hunter who was away on a hunting trip when their village was attacked by slave raiders. The boy's mother and three siblings—two sisters aged ten and twelve and a boy, a toddler of four—were captured.

Their village, Itanku, was a place noted for its rich dark soil and harvests of *agbado*, the yellow corn that was sold by its farmers to surrounding towns like Ijaiye and Ibadan for a comfortable profit. In its heyday, it was a quiet place of rest, its peace broken only by the occasional quarrel of gossiping women and the chatter of playful children.

But the day came when the *Baale* or village head, a farmer named Abijo, was sent a message by Iba, the leader of a group of war boys from Ibadan. Abijo and his vilagers were ordered to pay a ransom of one hundred baskets of cassava, sixty drums of palm oil, and sixteen male and female youngsters to be delivered by a certain date, to prevent their village from being attacked and burnt.

The villagers could not comply. The Baale sent desperately to the nearby towns of Ofa and Oje. But no one came to their aid.

*   *   *   *   *

The slave raiders came just before dawn. They came by foot and on horseback. There were three grown men or war captains leading a heavily armed group of fifty war boys. The oldest of them was a battle-hardened veteran thirty-five years of age. To the others, whose average age was nineteen, he was old. They called him Iba or Baba. They were part of the army of Bashorun Oluyole in Ibadan, a detachment of mounted warriors who normally fought with the *seriki*.

There had been a lull in the incessant wars that Ibadan fought with its neighbors in those days. And it was understood that at such times, the fighting men could supplement their livelihood and hone their fighting skills by embarking on slave-catching operations, especially those directed at small villages and hamlets that were not under the protection of Ibadan.

First, the war boys arranged themselves at carefully spaced intervals to surround the entire village. They were careful not to leave any gaps through which anyone might escape. Then five of them went in with lighted brands to set fire to the thatched roofs of the huts.

Thus, the first inkling that the sleeping inhabitants of Itanku had of their fate was the smell of burning thatch and the acrid smoke that choked them in their sleep.

They ran out into the waiting arms of their captors. Those who resisted or came out with weapons—mainly cutlasses wielded clumsily by men who were farmers, not warriors—were cut down mercilessly. Abijo, the Baale, was the first to fall, shot in the chest by a young war boy wielding a musket.

Then the war boys went from one burning hut to the other as the sounds of gunfire and the wailing and moans of the wounded and the dying filled the air. They searched and brought out those hiding inside their huts or those who could not come out by reason of infirmity or age. Infants and toddlers were killed off instantly with spear thrusts through the chest. The war boys knew they would not be able to feed them.

Many of the women, particularly the attractive young maidens, were raped on the spot. The three older warriors kept untouched one maiden each for themselves. These three were stripped half-naked and tied to a tree, to await the pleasure of the men at a later time.

After Ogungbayi ran off undetected, he hid behind a bush and watched what was happening to his family. He could see his mother and two sisters already fettered with ropes around their necks, wrists, and ankles. They huddled on the ground as the barrel of a musket carried by one of the war boys hovered over their heads.

Ogungbayi could not see his younger brother, the toddler, Ogunbi. He wept bitterly. All the people he had known all his life, apart from his father, who was away on a hunting trip, were now prisoners of this desperate and heartless band.

He watched as one of the captured young women, who was yet to be fettered, broke away and made for the bushes. She did not go far, as Iba, the oldest warrior, came after her. He easily caught up with her with his long loping strides.

Iba grabbed the maiden from behind with one hand. With the other hand, he struck her on the side of the head with a great blow, which felled her. Then he pounced on her as she lay wailing on the ground, her voice raised in a loud shriek. Ignoring her distracting cries, he tore away her *iro* with one swift movement. Crouching over her, he sank his teeth into her exposed breasts. This brought an even greater howl from the maiden. And now she displayed a strength that surprised the old warrior. He could not subdue her or keep her still so he could ravish her in peace. In this, he was helped by one of the war boys, a teenager who could not have been older than thirteen years.

His name was Mutiu. Because he was small in stature, he was known as Mutiu Kekere, *Little Mutiu*. Sometimes they simply called him Kekere.

Barely a teenager, Mutiu was a mere slip of a child. He had a smooth, almost beautiful, oval face with doe-shaped eyes and closely cropped curly hair. He was the smallest in the group, but he was one of the deadliest. Few dared to cross him, known as he was for his viciousness and violent outbursts. Though he was one of the youngest, all the men feared him. Part of the reason for this was that he was the son of the late *seriki* of Ibadan and therefore was protected in high places.

From a young age, Mutiu had shown himself to be a renegade. Following the footsteps of Mufu, his equally depraved elder brother, Mutiu had left his highborn family at an early age to cast his lot among thieves and vagabonds.

His brother, Mufu, had died violently on the streets of Ibadan five years earlier. It was in a fight over a woman who had been betrothed to him. But his brother's death had not deterred Mutiu from pursuing a career in the business of violence and death.

It surprised no one that Mutiu ended up in a slave-raiding gang. His brother had been a slave catcher too. Although he was nominally an Ibadan war boy, Mutiu had no appetite for conventional war. He had no desire to defend his hometown, Ibadan, from its enemies. All he cared about was to follow his gang on slave raids and other exploits for personal gain. These frequently involved drunkenness, rapine, and murder.

In pursuing these exploits, Mutiu imagined himself as honoring the memory of his slain brother. In his peculiar, if depraved, way of reasoning, he thought Mufu would have understood. The musket Mutiu carried everywhere he went was the same musket that belonged to his brother Mufu and which, according to eyewitness accounts, had been the instrument of his untimely death. This musket had been given to the young eight-year-old Mutiu by Taju, his brother's protégé, who had been at the scene of Mufu's violent death.

Mutiu Kekere was mean and vicious. And he was totally without conscience or remorse. Many of the older men thought he was mad, and they avoided his fits of anger.

This boy, Mutiu, now stepped up. With a vicious sweep of his two arms, he slammed the butt of his musket against the side of the girl's head. She lay still, stunned.

But this was too much for her young husband, who was watching the scene while he was held from behind by two of the marauders. He broke free and leapt at the old warrior, who was bent on ravishing the girl. The angry villager rained heavy blows with his fists on the crouching figure of Iba, who at that time was trying to pull down his *sokoto*.

But this was the last thing the enraged husband would ever do in this life. There was a loud bang, followed by the smell of gunpowder and a puff of smoke from a musket shot. At point-blank range, Mutiu, the teenage war boy, had shot the husband in the head with the same musket with which he had brained the dead man's wife.

As they watched Iba rape the still, unresisting figure on the ground, a madness took over the boys. It was the fever and insanity of war, which sometimes took over the most rational of young men in the thick of battle.

One of them, Taju, a tall muscular lad of eighteen, ran to Iba, his body trembling with heat and lust.

He tapped the old warrior on the back and said roughly, "Iba, get off. You've had enough."

Then with his two strong hands, Taju gripped Iba by the shoulders. He heaved the older man up and tossed him aside. Then pulling down his own *sokoto*, he fell on the still, unmoving maiden. Twelve of the boys took their turn ravishing her, among them Mutiu.

But when they had finished and their eyes cleared, only a few of the men and boys experienced any satisfaction or joy at what they had done. They were ashamed and avoided one another's eyes. It was then that they noticed that the figure on the ground lay quite still in the same spot, unmoving, with no sign of life.

"She is dead," said Iba, his senses returning to him.

His voice was low and subdued. It was devoid of his usual brash warrior's impudence. Now there was a hint of remorse and regret.

He lifted the body, walked some distance with it, and tossed it into a smoldering pile of flame and smoke. This was an unidentifiable structure next to one of the burning huts. It could have been a granary for corn, but now it was covered with burning debris.

Someone noticed the body of the husband who had died trying to protect the honor of his wife. His body lay on the ground next to the very place where his wife had been brutally raped. His head was a mass of blood, tissue, and bone mixed with sand. Crawling ants had gathered, and flies buzzed around the gory mass. One of the boys pulled the corpse feetfirst and dumped it beside his wife in the burning pile.

In the end, the village of Itanku was completely destroyed. This little-known place in the heart of Yorubaland, which was loved by its inhabitants for its dark rich soil and harvests of corn, would now be known only for it brutal extirpation—its very existence erased from the minds of men. The habitation of its captured and slaughtered inhabitants was left in smoldering heaps of ash and burning thatch.

A thick brown smoke hovered over the desolate village as a band of vultures gathered to feast on the bodies of the dead. And as the attackers began to drive their fettered captives before them into the bush, the shrieks of these scavenger birds filled the air, marking the village as a scene of death.

The men looked up. There was no light in the sky. A veritable darkness had descended on the village at noon. For as the vultures circled overhead and the smoke thickened and wafted toward the clouds over the burning village, the light from the sun was cut off. A brooding shadow lay like a fatal canopy over the gruesome scene.

Many of the men of the village who had offered resistance to the marauders still lay wounded on the ground. They were all killed, one after the other, before the slave raiders moved off. Their throats were slit. Two war boys held down each injured man while a third wielded a sharp curved knife, stepping aside as blood gushed from the severed neck artery. The war boys had no need for captives who could not walk unassisted. Many of the elder people in the village were left inside the burning huts to perish.

The young Ogungbayi, aged nine, was the only person in the village to escape. He hid out in the bush for five days; but he witnessed the entire scene of horror, brutality, and rape that engulfed his village on that fateful dawn.

Those of the villagers who survived the attack were tied together with stout ropes and leather straps. A few iron chains for the necks and wrists were also produced. Then they were quickly herded into the bush. There, in a nearby clearing in the forest, waiting for the war boys, was a group of slave dealers. There were twelve of them, shrewd, weary-faced merchants and battle-hardened former soldiers. They were heavily armed with muskets, swords, and daggers. Two of them were turbaned Hausas on horseback.

The exchange of goods was swiftly made. The captives were handed over to the slave dealers. In return, the warriors received two crates of guns and ammunition and twelve heavy bags of *owo eyo*, or cowry shells, the currency of the day.

There was talk among the men of how much they should keep and how much to take back to Ibadan. Apparently, they had to report back to Oluyole, the Bashorun at Ibadan, who received a cut from whatever loot and booty the war boys got from their activities, either in war or unsponsored brigandage and slave-catching capers such as these.

As Ogungbayi watched from his hiding place in the bush, he heard other names mentioned—Ogunmola, Ibikunle, and Latosisa. These names belonged either to the leaders of the group or other war captains in Ibadan whose palms would need to be greased by the war boys.

After this transaction, the war boys went back to the farmlands that surrounded the burning village. They began to cut down the ripe corn on the stalk and dig up the yams in the earth waiting for the harvest. The boys from Ibadan were hungry. They had an army to feed.

The slave dealers also wasted no time. They hastened to be on their way. Quickly, they counted the captives. There were seventy-six in all, twenty-five grown men, forty women, and eleven children above six years of age.

Working in a very rapid and efficient manner, the slaving party produced heavy iron shackles for the wrists and ankles and wooden locks and fetters for the necks of the captives. They quickly shackled the captives together in groups of seven. Then they pulled them to their feet, shouting at them to start moving. They took care that those in the same conjoined group were of roughly the same height, but they did not separate the men from the women. And with a shout of command in Hausa from one of the turbaned horsemen, the convoy moved and headed south in the direction of the coast.

"Yala!" the Hausa leader shouted again as they moved off.

But the very next day, when they had barely left the burning village behind, the slave convoy was apprehended by a war party under the command of a rising young war captain and native of the nearby town of Ijaiye. He and his group of warriors had been attracted by the smoke from the burning huts and the cries of kites and vultures circling overhead, those opportunists and sensors of death.

They seemed to have appeared from nowhere. One moment, the convoy was trudging along a narrow bush path, the captives in the middle and the armed guards on both sides and to the front and back of them. The next moment, there were armed horsemen on both sides of the long chain formed by the slave convoy, leveling muskets and arrows at them. There must have been at least two hundred of them.

One of the slave convoy guards reached rashly for his gun. There was a loud boom of a musket, and he lay dead on the ground, a great bleeding wound in his chest. The rest of the slave detail kept their hands to themselves.

There were so many of these intruders that they looked like an army, which indeed they were. Many of them rode horses, but most were on foot, armed with bows and arrows. The horsemen carried heavy lances and spears, and many had muskets strapped to the flanks of their horses, which on closer look could be seen to be the small ponies favored by the warriors of Ijaiye.

It was clear that this was a well-trained, disciplined group of warriors. They were from Ijaiye, and they were heard addressing their leader as Kurunmi.

The Ijaiyes were known to be the best fighting men in Yorubaland, after the Ibadans. They gave no quarter and never retreated in battle. Under the leadership of their young leader, Kurunmi, who had already made his mark in military circles for his success against the Fulanis in Ilorin, the discipline and heroism of warriors from Ijaiye were well-known.

Hearing the name of Kurunmi, the slave dealers knew what they were up against. They did not attempt to resist. They had no desire to give Kurunmi's men an excuse to shoot them down.

The Ijaiye horsemen came nearer. They completely ignored the slave dealers and went straight to the captives. They looked at each man, woman, and child with great interest. Then their leader jumped down from his pony. He was quite young. At that time, Kurunmi could not have been older than twenty-nine years of age.

"Are there any of you here," he loudly addressed the shackled captives, "who are from Ile-Ife?"

A few of the captives shouted back in the affirmative. These were closely inspected. Their facial marks were examined. And they were asked to speak a few words to see if their dialect and accents matched those of Ife.

These lucky ones—and there were just twelve of them—were separated from the rest. Their shackles were removed, and they were placed on the backs of the horses of a few of the riders.

All the while, the slave band had kept quiet, fearful of antagonizing this superior force. But now with part of their lucrative cargo slipping out of their hands, one of them, a Yoruba man with Offa tribal marks, spoke up.

Inwardly, the man from Offa was seething. He was barely able to contain his anger and indignation. But outwardly, he tried to be reasonable. He turned to Kurunmi.

"But we have paid good money for these people you are taking away," he blurted.

"How are we going to get our money back?"

There was a pause as Kurunmi looked at him. The Ijaiye leader appeared to be deciding on a reply. He paused for a moment. But then he turned away, totally ignoring the question. He strode back to his horse, which was eagerly champing on a bit of turf.

Kurunmi mounted the horse. He steadied himself as he held the reins. But the horse kept its head down. It was reluctant to leave the juicy piece of grass it was munching. Then sensing the tug of the reins from its impatient rider, the horse sprang on its hind legs and gave a soft neigh.

Kurumi steadied the beast with a pat on the side of the neck, and the horse put its front hooves down. Then with a movement of his upraised hand, the Ijaiye leader motioned to his men.

Those who had dismounted swiftly jumped back on their horses. They tried to form a rough military formation. But with the thick bush, shrubs, and trees close around them, their efforts were only partially successful. Then without a word and as suddenly as they had appeared, Kurunmi and his men rode away.

What had happened was that Kurunmi, the young war captain of Ijaiye, had a commission from the Ooni of Ife, who was alarmed that slave catchers from Ibadan, Ijebu, and Egbaland were taking as slaves men, women, and children of Ife. This was in spite of a solemn agreement by the leaders of the various Yoruba city-states that citizens of Ile-Ife, the spiritual capital of Yorubaland, should be immune from capture and sale as slaves in any part of Yorubaland.

The Ibadan warlords and their war boys were especially notorious for flouting this agreement. Lately, this had caused friction between Ife and the young Kurunmi of Ijaiye on the one hand and Ibadan under Bashorun Oluyole on the other.

The remaining captives wailed and cried. They pleaded in vain for the Ijaiye horsemen to rescue them too. But their pleas fell on deaf ears. Kurunmi's men simply told them it was only people from Ile-Ife that they were authorized to release.

As they rode off, following the command of their leader, the Ijaiye men were quiet and orderly. The last the slave group saw of them were the backs of the dozen rescued men and women as they bounced up and down on the horses that bore them to Ijaiye and freedom.

For the remaining captives, the nightmare had only begun. The march to the coast was a horror none of them could ever have imagined.

The slave party kept a brutal pace. Those who tried to slow down the group by their weakness or weariness, or those who straggled, were mercilessly whipped. Their guards had them hidden in the bush during the day and made them travel all night. There was little food for the captives and an even more limited supply of fresh clean water. If any of the captives were pressed and wanted to relieve their bowel or their bladder, they had to do so standing up. The captives were not given water to wash their bodies or clean their teeth during the fifteen days it took them to get to the coast.

Three of the captives drowned at the crossing of the Majidun River near Otta. The other captives suspected that these men and women drowned themselves deliberately to escape the horror and deprivations of a life of captivity.

None of the captured villagers had any idea where they were headed. There was whispered talk among the guards, which was interpreted by the more sharp-eared among the captives that they were to be taken in great houses that moved over the waters to the land of white men across the great ocean.

In the end, sixty-one men, women, and children among the captives from the village of Itanku reached the coast at Badagry in that year 1845. These captives who had survived the forced march through the forest, which was even more gruesome than the horrors of their capture and the destruction of their village, ended up in a slave market on the island of Topo, off Badagry.

The children were immediately bought by various private individuals from Lagos to be used as domestic help in their households. Six of the more attractive of the young females were bought by a trader from Ikorodu. They would be resold as domestic servants and concubines to rich merchants in that bustling and newly important town.

The rest were sold off to the captain of a waiting American ship in a mass auction organized under the auspices of a noted Ijebu slave dealer from Lagos.

This merchant was a young man named Odumosu. He was an agent and partner of the notorious Madam Tinubu, an Egba woman of considerable power and influence then living in Lagos.

*   *   *   *   *

The boy Ogungbayi, who escaped capture during the invasion and destruction of his village, Itanku, got away and joined a group of young refugees he met hiding in the bush near the town of Oje. They were three boys a bit older than him, but all were barely in their teens.

They all had one thing in common. Their parents and families were dead or had been captured by slave catchers. They had no homes to return to. The four of them made their way south by foot along narrow forest paths, passing through abandoned farms and dense tropical bush.

The boys survived by picking fruits and digging up roots along the way. They set traps for small animals and shot many others with crudely made slings. One of them managed to steal a bow and a sheaf of arrows from beside a sleeping warrior after sneaking into a war camp on the border of Egbaland. With these bow and arrows, they shot rabbits, bush rodents, and birds, which they ate with delight.

They scrounged, scavenged, and stole food from farms and hamlets along their way. They kept off the main bush paths. And every morning, they kept the rising sun on their left shoulders so that they went due south. In the evenings, they made sure the setting sun was to their right. They slept in trees at night to avoid detection by any passersby and to escape predatory wild beasts.

One of the boys said he had been told that the activities of slave raiders were less in Ijebuland. And indeed, in that age of upheaval and dislocation all over Yorubaland, Ijebu towns and villages were relatively prosperous and safe. The boys' plan, therefore, was to cross into Remo from Ibadan territory. They avoided the Egbas. Anytime anyone came toward them, the boys hid in the bushes and listened carefully to the speech and accents of the passersby.

In this way, they reached Remo. One of them died from the bite of a poisonous snake near Ode Remo. Another drowned in the river Olu near Ogere when he was carried away by a strong current.

Ogungbayi ended up in Ikenne. He tasted the water of the Uren river and decided this was the place for him.

His friend Adejuwa, the oldest of the group, who had the bow and arrow and was the wisest and cleverest of the four, went on alone. He declared that he would not stop until he got to Lagos. He wanted to be a servant to a white man on that island, where many had gone before him to make their name and fortune.

The stories of our family tell us that the boy Ogungbayi was apprenticed to a hunter in Ikenne. He prospered and lived to a comfortable old age. He was the grandfather of a prominent friend of my grandmother Efunyemi in Ikenne.

This girl's name was Iwalewa. Later in life, she became a well-known seer and priestess of Ogun in Ikenne.

*   *   *   *   *

Around the time that Osogbesan came back to Ile-Ife, contemplating the astonishing rise of Ibadan from the ashes of the old Oyo Empire, another town in Yorubaland had begun to make an impact on the story of our people. This town was located four hundred miles from old Oyo.

It was on the coast of the great ocean, not far from that sandy beach on which Obari and Aarin were said by the Old Woman to have met the god Olokun.

This town was on an island that was part of a sparsely inhabited region of lagoons, creeks, sandbanks, and small islets that formed the coastline of what white men called the Gulf of Guinea, a great indentation of the coast that bordered the broad Atlantic Ocean on its eastern, tropical shores.

The island had a harbor that attracted seamen who came in great ships from foreign lands. Soon, it became a great center for trade and commerce.

Our people called this place Eko, a name said to have been derived from a Bini word. But the Potoki, or Portuguese, who were the first white men to see it, called it Lagos, which in their language meant the "place of the lagoon." That name, Lagos, stuck. It was used over the next centuries by natives and foreigners alike.

Our stories tell us that white men, starting with the Portuguese, had been coming to Lagos even before the time of Oba Esigie of Bini. They traded with the local indigenous people. They brought beads, salt, guns, and gunpowder, which they exchanged for native woven cloth, ivory, and animal hides.

Then they discovered slavery. The coast around Lagos and nearby Badagry soon became known to the Portuguese seamen and merchants as *a costa dos escravos*---the Slave Coast. But in the beginning, very few captives, who were mainly criminals and prisoners of war, were sold by our people. These unfortunate captives were taken in great ships across the water to the land of the white men.

Then in the early years of the nineteenth century, Portuguese ship captains discovered the American slave ports of Savannah, Charleston, and New Orleans. These sea captains became attracted by the huge amount of money to be made from the sale of their human cargo at these American ports. They resolved to feed the insatiable thirst for these unpaid laborers, who were now making many Southern plantation owners very rich. In short, the transatlantic slave trade became very profitable. By 1812, foreign ships began to transport slaves in large quantities from the port of Lagos to America.

The Ijebus were the first Yorubas to arm themselves with guns bought from the white men. They became the most ardent and successful slave dealers among the native population. Former Ijebu merchants who sold cotton and palm kernel became traders and middlemen in this new lucrative line of business.

Our people took to dealing in slaves like duck to water, and many of them made a fortune. It was this class of Ijebu traders whose ranks one of our ancestors, Odumosu, joined later in life.

According to family legend, Odumosu made a lot of money as a slave trader, though he later abandoned it to go into timber, native clothes, and imported goods. He even dabbled in agricultural produce and briefly harvested kola nuts on his own farm in Igbobi on the Lagos mainland.

*　　*　　*　　*　　*

The story of Odumosu began inauspiciously enough in Ijebu-Ode. Later in life, he claimed he was the son of the Awujale Fusengbuwa of the Tewogbuwa ruling family. The story he told was that his mother was thrown out of the palace as a result of an intrigue by the other wives of the king who banded against her.

Odumosu also said that he was the second of a set of twins by his mother and that the first twin died in infancy. The family narrative is not very clear on this point.

But we find him at the age of fifteen paddling a canoe that ferried people from the river Yemoji down to the lagoon at Epe. There, these passengers disembarked and made their way to the ports at Ebute Ero and Ebute Elefun on the island known as Eko.

Most of the people that Odumosu ferried were traders who went back and forth between Lagos and the Ijebu waterside. To Lagos, these merchants took their loads of palm kernel, yam and cassava. On the return trip, the canoe was loaded down with bags of sugar, salt, fine beads, and shawls of foreign manufacture. These were brought from Europe and Asia by great ships moored off the Lagos harbor.

Odumosu worked for a master who owned the canoe. But he made a good living. At the end of each day, he was paid ten cowries. This was the equivalent of sixpence of the white man's money.

Every day, he carefully added this to his collection in a leather bag, which he kept hidden in a hole inside a tree in the bush. He dreamt of saving enough to purchase his own canoe. Odumosu was an ambitious young man. He planned to go into business for himself after a few years.

One day, Odumosu agreed to take two men to the lagoon at Epe. But from the first, they aroused his suspicions.

For one, they offered to pay double the asked price for their passage. Second, they insisted on being alone with Odumosu in the canoe. They did not want any other passenger. This was why they were paying double the price for the trip. And they paid their passage up front, handing over a small bag of cowry shells to Odumosu before he cast off.

Odumosu untied the mooring to set the canoe adrift. He gave the fare to his master before they departed, and his doubts left him. Odumosu settled his guests into their seats, a pair of planks placed across the bow of the canoe. He then stepped inside the shallow water. He pushed off, his muscles taut and straining. Then, he jumped inside the canoe as he began to tread water and started rowing down the middle of the Yemoji.

The river became wider as other tributaries joined it. The riverbank was lined with dark, green vegetation and great leafy trees that cast a shadow over the water. Soon, they entered the broad lagoon. Now Odumosu had to focus his attention on carefully maneuvering the canoe because the undertow was stronger here. However, the current carried them in the right direction. They drifted westward toward the great jetty at Epe.

Odumosu knew these waterways like the palms of his hands. He had no need of maps that the occasional European he had as passengers, who were mainly missionaries, talked about. But even if he did have a map, it would be useless to him. He did not know how to read or write. The white man's strange markings and drawings meant nothing to him.

They could now see the bustling jetty ahead on the right side of the broad lagoon. But instead of allowing him to coast straight ahead, the two men asked Odumosu to head for the opposite bank and let them out.

This was a strange request. For it meant his passengers would need to walk for at least another hour before they reached any human habitation or any pier from where they could hail any of the big boats that went to Lekki, Ebute Meta, or Ebute Ero.

"Surely, they cannot be thinking of robbing me," Odumosu said to himself.

He had nothing of value on him. And his two passengers had already paid their fare before they left Imagbon. So they could not be trying to get off without paying.

Odumosu did not give this odd request a second thought. He turned his canoe's stern and pushed off toward the sandbank. He concentrated on his maneuvering.

For a moment, he thought he heard the two men whispering. Still, he paid no attention. Then there was a soft sound, and he sensed rather than saw a movement behind him. He started to turn, but it was too late.

All he heard was a swish. He felt something hard hit him on the back of the head, and he fell into pitch darkness.

When Odumosu came to, his head ached. He tried to touch the back of his head, where most of the pain came from, but he found he could not raise his arms. He was bound hand and foot.

It was dusk, but the light of a waning moon allowed him to see as he looked around him.

He looked up and saw a big white canvas sailcloth filling with the wind. He was in a small sailing boat.

But where was he? What had happened? Where was his canoe? Where were his passengers? Who had tied him up, and where were they taking him?

The boat rocked violently. He became seasick and almost vomited.

Then he knew. They were no longer on the lagoon. Somehow, they had crossed the sandbar, and they were on the open sea.

He felt sick—this time not from the motion of the boat. He was a captive, bound for those slave ships he had heard so much about. He would never see Ijebu again. Odumosu wept. Tears of bitterness and rage, for his carelessness and stupidity, coursed down his cheeks.

Then suddenly, in the darkness, he heard a shout, then the boom of a gun, and the boat rocked more violently. There was the sound of men grappling. He heard someone shout in a strange nasal language, and then there was a white face looking down at him.

He was to piece together what had happened later. He had been kidnapped by slave catchers who worked as agents for a Portuguese ship that lay at anchor off Escravos in the Bight of Benin. They were paid to supply the slave ship with men and women they captured in the coastal areas from the Ijebu waterside to the mouth of the Benin River.

These men were taking Odumosu in a boat along with other men and women they had captured. They were headed for the big ship moored in deep waters. But they had been accosted by a British naval boat from the HMS *Bournemouth*, which patrolled these waters for the purpose of intercepting boats and ships that attempted to carry slaves from the Bight of Benin to the New World.

The year was 1825. It was the height of the transatlantic slave trade. Odumosu was lucky. A few hundred yards to one side or a few minutes earlier or later, and their boat would have been missed by the Royal Navy patrol.

The men who controlled their boat were arrested. They were taken aboard the HMS *Bournemouth*. There, they were clapped in irons and put under guard in the hold.

As Odumosu was to learn later, the British monarch had declared, a few years earlier, that slavery was banned throughout the British Empire. These waters were controlled by his sovereign majesty, King George, the Third. Those men now cooling their heels in the hold belowdecks would answer to British law whatever their nationality.

Odumosu and the other freed captives were taken to the island of Lagos, where they were set free. Had they been freed when they were already on the slaving ship or on the high sea, the jurisdiction would have been beyond the hands of His Majesty's consul in Lagos. Then they would have been taken to Freetown in Sierra Leone, in the Lion Mountains, eight hundred miles away along the Guinea coast.

It was in this way that the fifteen-year-old Odumosu, an illiterate orphan boy from Ijebu who paddled a canoe in the Ijebu waterside, was transported to the island of Lagos.

*   *   *   *   *

The Lagos where Odumosu was deposited in that year 1825 was the most important city on the Guinea coast, which stretched from Gambia in the land of the Wolof to Calabar in the east.

It was a busy seaport with a sheltered harbor. And its deep waters could accommodate the biggest ships of the great maritime nations of the world. The island was a commercial hub and had become something of an international melting pot.

On its streets, one encountered English, French, German, and Portuguese government representatives, adventurers, sailors, missionaries, and merchants. These Europeans jostled on the jetty or bargained at the storefronts with important-looking native chiefs and their well-appointed wives and concubines. The women were weighed down with the latest European finery and jewelry imported from London, Lisbon and Paris, brought to them courtesy of these merchants and those big ships moored in the harbor.

Here, on the most fashionable street on the island, called Broad Street, the consul of His Majesty, the king of Great Britain, was accosted by a Lagos socialite. She briefly escaped the arms of her mulatto husband, a handsome freeborn Negro from Cuba, to greet His Majesty's representative.

Across the wide street, a "white-cap" chief, who was a counselor to the oba of Lagos, walked with the dignity and pomp that his high position demanded. He was draped in a great white robe tied over his left shoulder, and several heavy ruby-red coral beads hung down his neck. He was escorted under a great umbrella held over his head by a retinue of no fewer than twelve fawning slaves and his three wives.

And down the road just before one reached Idumota, in a darkly lit warehouse, a furtive conversation went on between a slave dealer from Ijebu and the captain of a Portuguese ship anchored off Escravos, who bargained and haggled over the price of a soon-to-be-delivered cargo of slaves.

The most important and powerful personage in this social mélange was not His Highness, the Oba of Lagos, but the representative of the king of Great Britain. He was the consul appointed from the Colonial Office in Whitehall, London. Backed by a small retinue of bureaucrats and military attachés, it was he who provided protection to the island through the presence of the ships of the powerful British Navy in the harbor and off the coast of Lagos.

The British government had declared that the portion of the Slave Coast around Lagos was in its sphere of influence. So, by putting pressure on the local chiefs, backed by the presence of the navy, the consul and his staff kept rival European powers—France, Germany, Portugal, and the Netherlands—from having any significant influence or participation in local trade. The British Consul prevented the other

Europeans from signing treaties with the local chiefs that would diminish British influence in Lagos and the Yoruba hinterland.

Odumosu was deposited right in the middle of this power hierarchy. On the recommendation of the subaltern of the marine vessel that had rescued him, he was taken in as a servant by the British Consul in Lagos.

* * * * *

Odumosu lived with the British Consul to the Bight of Benin and Biafra, the Right Honorable John Beecroft, for three years in the "boys' quarters" attached to his official residence at Onikan. The consul was a kind and generous man. He arranged for Odumosu to be taught to read and write in the English tongue.

Odumosu showed aptitude, and soon, his master moved him to the administrative office of the British consulate, which was housed in an imposing building of Portland stone overlooking the race-course. There, he worked as a clerk on a monthly salary of two shillings. He took notes and dictations, and learned how to balance ledgers and accounts.

During this time, Odumosu's services were also employed in the writing and translation of various documents compiled by the English representatives in Lagos to help all manner of travelers, adventurers, soldiers, and merchants from Europe who had business to conduct on the coast and hinterland of Yorubaland.

Thus, Odumosu was involved in arranging supplies and letters of introduction for Clapperton, then the Lander brothers, when those adventurers departed from the coast to travel to the hinterland. He helped furnish Reverend Hinderer with provisions when he went off to establish one of the first Christian missions in Yorubaland in Ibadan.

Odumosu read with dismay the dispatches between London and Lagos regarding the fall of Ilorin. As a result of this event, he found himself now reexamining his status as a child of Yoruba, heir to the legacy of Oduduwa, not just a person born in Ijebu. Odumosu became a Yoruba patriot. And it made him sad to hear the pitiful news from the interior of the Yoruba states in turmoil.

His Ijebu accent and dialect changed. He began to speak the cosmopolitan Yoruba of Lagos, which was understood by everyone on the island, even those from the hinterland. For by this time, this Lagos Yoruba had become the lingua franca among the various African groups who made Lagos their home. These included Awori émigrés from Badagry, Fon from Porto-Novo, Asante from the Gold Coast, and Mende from Sierra Leone.

One day, one of the English merchants on the island, Mr. George Ollivant, came to the consulate office. Hearing high praises of the talents of the young native clerk, he offered Odumosu a job to work under him.

From his vantage position as Ollivant's purchasing clerk, Odumosu came to know a lot about the goods and merchandize that passed through the great warehouses owned by foreign companies and a few rich native merchants in Lagos. These buildings were located along the jetty on the harbor side of the Lagos Lagoon, which some people had started to call the Marina.

Odumosu made up his mind that he too would become a great merchant. He vowed that he would own one of these warehouses one day. Encouraged by his European, Saro, and Brazilian friends, he left the employ of Mr. Ollivant and became a small trader.

Odumosu's thoughts and actions were now those of a man bitten by a bug—the bug for making money. Becoming wealthy became the chief thought and pursuit of his waking hours. And it haunted his dreams at night.

Odumosu started by renting a small store in the center of Lagos Island off Broad Street. He bought European goods that were now increasingly sought after by the more affluent of the local population.

He stocked his store with fine ladies' dresses from England, along with combs, toiletries, scissors, knives, and other household items that he obtained from a Dutch merchant who owned a big warehouse on the wharf. He sold these to the heads of rich households in Lagos, who would send their servants and slaves to his store.

Then he opened a produce store in a lower section of the island at Ita Balogun, not far from Idumota, where he sold palm oil, yam flour, and cassava flour from Egbaland and Ijebu to these same households.

Odumosu was now the owner of his own commercial enterprise and was richer than most of the native inhabitants of Lagos. But he found he was not satisfied.

He had been on the island for barely ten years. He already owned two stores and had acquired a plot of land not far from Idumota for his private residence. Yet he chafed and worried. He had sleepless nights. For he hankered after the big money.

Odumosu became impatient and unsatisfied anytime he took a walk by the harbor and saw the big warehouses owned by the very wealthy local merchants and trading houses from Europe. He soon found that the richest of these merchants, both native and European, were those who dealt in slaves. Their great warehouses on the wharf were merely a front for the conduit of their less savory line of business.

These men held slave auctions in Ikorodu, Epe, and Badagry, even at Ebute Meta on the mainland. The presence of British naval ships off the Lagos coast had lately become a problem. So they contrived to send their human merchandize to Portuguese, American, and Brazilian ships waiting off the coast at Badagry, Escravos, and Porto-Novo.

But these men made sure they were not seen conducting this side of their business in or around Lagos Island. They were all neighbors of the British consul in Lagos, and they did not want to cross him. Everyone knew that the consul frowned at this line of business and had sworn to stamp it out.

Spurred by greed, Odumosu dreamt of becoming a trader and middleman in slaves like those rich and powerful men. It did not occur to him that it was ironic that it was he of all people who now wanted to be a slave dealer. He, a former captive, who would have been a slave on an American cotton plantation if not for the armed intervention of the British. It did not bother him unnecessarily that it was such a person as himself who now wanted to circumvent the British and profit from trading in these unfortunate captives.

And it is doubtful if he thought philosophically about his desire to embrace an activity that kept a human being under the ownership and control of another person against his will, often in inhuman and degrading conditions. Odumosu's rationale, if he thought about it at all, was that he was chasing his dream of wealth and social position. He wanted a life of luxury.

"I am an Ijebu man," he said to his *omo Eko* friends, who were perplexed by this insatiable itch. "And Ijebu men like to make money."

"What is wrong," he asked them, "with trying to be rich?"

He only wanted to be like those rich and powerful European merchants and middlemen. It wasn't him who took these slaves captive in the first place. He would simply be the middleman who made sure that they found a willing owner. If he didn't do it, someone else would. Turning his nose away in disgust would not help the enslaved person.

He also reassured himself that he had frequently seen slaves treated very kindly by their owners, who were his rich friends in Lagos. Some of these domestic slaves, he told himself, lived better than the starving families who straggled into Lagos with nothing on their backs after being displaced by the wars in the interior.

And Odumosu did not want to think about what happened to those captives taken on the long journey across the sea to America. Nobody really knew what happened to them when they got there. And really, he did not want to know. He thought only of himself, and of his dream and fantasy of great wealth. It was true that one could make a living buying and selling palm kernel, clothes, and household utensils in Lagos. But in that day and age, the real money was in slaves.

But it was not until he met the powerful woman who was the most prominent slave merchant in Lagos at that time that Odumosu was able to achieve his peculiar dream. And it was by a sheer stroke of fortune that Odumosu made the acquaintance of this woman, for when they met, she was the wife of the reigning king of Lagos.

Within a few years, this remarkable woman would become the stepmother of another king, Oba Oluwole, and the sister-in-law of yet another, Oba Akitoye, whose story would become interwound with that of Odumosu. This was the person who changed the course of Odumosu's life and fortunes after he met her by chance in his small store in Ita Balogun in 1835.

It came about this way. Odumosu was trying to sell a consignment of palm kernel, which he had brought by ferry from Ikorodu. One day, he received a message from one of his agents that at a certain time the next day, an important merchant would come to his store and buy them off him.

When he was told that this merchant was a woman, Odumosu scoffed. But when he heard her name, he sat up. A jolt of excitement shot through him. The woman merchant he was going to meet on such short notice was Efunporoye Osuntinubu. She was popularly known as Madam Tinubu. Everyone in Lagos knew her story.

*   *   *   *   *

Efunporoye Tinubu was born in humble circumstances in the Egba town of Abeokuta. After various stints selling kola nuts and other odds and ends, she drifted to Badagry, the great port and slave market.

Somehow she made important connections. Soon, she joined the group of influential merchants who controlled the sale of captives brought from the hinterland to the ship captains who took this human cargo across the sea. She became rich, powerful, and well connected. Everyone now called her Madam Tinubu. Then she moved to Lagos.

Odumosu knew that this Madam Tinubu moved in rarified social circles on the island. He could not have dreamt of meeting her on the streets, not to talk of being personally introduced to her.

Madam Tinubu had just relocated to Lagos from Badagry, but she still managed to remain a kingpin in her lucrative line of business. She received hefty commissions from connecting the slave traders from the hinterland with the Portuguese and American captains who shipped the cargo across the ocean.

The story that Odumosu was able to piece together later was this. After the death of her first husband, a wealthy Egba prince who had introduced her to the slave-dealing business, Efunporoye had married a prince of Lagos named Adele, who that year had been made the new oba of Lagos.

She had arrived in Lagos earlier that year with her second husband, the new oba, with great fanfare. Her lifestyle of conspicuous display of wealth soon became known, envied, and admired by everyone on the island. There was a story that she needed the services of two hundred slaves to serve her guests at the installation ceremony of her husband, Oba Adele.

And despite being the wife of the king, Efunporoye had continued her slave-dealing activities in Lagos.

Using her connections at the palace, within a short space of time, she had come to know all the important European merchants, sea captains, and foreign government representatives who lived in or passed through Lagos. Soon, they were all vying for her favor, her counsel, and the access to deals that she only could provide.

Madam Tinubu was the person to go to when any foreigner in Lagos wanted access to commerce and trade routes. She was the person to be contacted if treaties needed to be signed with local chiefs not only in Lagos but in Abeokuta, Badagry, Ikorodu, and points farther off in the hinterland. She was said to have a finger in every pie, especially those pies that made a lot of money.

Now he, Odumosu, was being presented with the chance of his life. He was to meet face-to-face with this powerful magnate and be given the chance to make a good impression on her. He knew that the future of his business plans depended on this meeting.

The next day at the appointed time, Odumosu watched with awe as this beautiful and powerful woman, the *olori* of Lagos, made her regal entrance into his store and into his life.

Madam Tinubu was attended by a retinue of five servants, all female, and a male bodyguard. She was a beautiful tall woman—as tall as Odumosu, a man of more than average stature. She was dressed in a costume of fine damask cloth of light blue and maroon. This dress was in two pieces, a wrapper tied around her waist that reached down almost to her ankles and a top that looked like a blouse without sleeves. Her shoulders and arms were bare.

Not so bare, thought Odumosu. For she had thick bangles of copper, gold, and silver that covered her wrists and forearms. And she had gold rings on almost every finger of both hands. Around her neck was a single necklace of expensive red coral beads attached to a pendant of radiant gem that Odumosu was sure was diamond. This adornment reflected all the colors of the rainbow as she moved her neck. Odumosu noticed that Madam Tinubu had no makeup on her face. But her skin, which was as dark as ebony, glowed like polished wood.

On her head, she had a great head tie of fine silk in two separate colors that fringed the head. This she allowed to flow behind her like a great cape. It reminded Odumosu of a woodcut he had seen of Queen Victoria. There was no doubt that this magnificent Yoruba woman had copied the style of the young British queen.

On her feet were sandals fringed with silver and gold, completing the picture of a woman of wealth, power, and great allure. Odumosu had never seen anyone like her in his life, not even in cosmopolitan Lagos. And he had now lived in the great city for close to ten years.

Odumosu overcame his shyness and temporary confusion at being confronted by this remarkable specimen of beauty and wealth. He bowed and moved closer to meet the impressive lady and her retinue.

Quickly, he called one of his servants to get a chair. With a bow, he presented his visitor with it.

"My name is Odumosu, and I am the owner and manager of this humble store," he said smoothly in English. "I hope your ladyship would allow me the pleasure of attending to you myself."

He was surprised when she bowed in return and gave him a curtsy. It was just the slightest hint of a bending of the knees, but a curtsy nonetheless. Then she extended her soft, delicate heavily ringed hand to be shaken.

Odumosu thought he was going to swoon when that soft, perfumed hand touched his. But he managed to go through with this piece of social etiquette. He even smiled with contrived composure as he looked directly at his visitor and customer.

The face he saw was oval and perfectly formed, with haughty eyes, a well-formed nose, and full, sensual lips. It was a face of physical comeliness, determination, and intelligence, but also one that spoke of lust and desire. It was a face that a king or a prince would throw away a kingdom for. Odumosu thought that she looked very young, not older than a teenager, but he knew that they were about the same age. Odumosu was then twenty-five years old.

Efunporoye Osuntinubu, the young and beautiful wife of Oba Adele of Lagos, looked back at Odumosu and smiled. She appeared to be enjoying herself. She cocked her head slightly to one side as if she expected him to start a conversation.

It was a gesture that said to Odumosu, "Yes, I am listening to you." It told him that even though she was an important and wealthy personage, the wife of one of the leading kings in Yorubaland, she was humble and would let him, an ordinary manager of a small merchandize store, treat her as an equal.

From the beginning, Odumosu could see that he had made a good impression on his august client. When she shook his hand, her touch lingered. She looked directly at his face and smiled.

She told him that she would buy all the consignment of palm kernel he had in his store. In addition, she needed food supplies for her household, which she would like him to provide. Apart from her residence at the palace of the oba of Lagos, she had her own personal dwelling in a fashionable square in the center of the island.

She asked him to call her Efunporoye, not *olori* or Madam Tinubu.

Odumosu, for his part, made sure that all the samples, bags, and crates of produce she wanted were brought to the feet of the great lady by him, the proprietor, himself. He made sure that all the best specimens in his store were produced.

In the end, he was pleased with himself. He knew that he had a good deal going, because not only did his illustrious client buy more in quantity than she had earlier indicated, she paid extra, asking him to regard the excess as a gift from her.

After her business was completed, Odumosu noticed that she gave him a squeeze when she shook his hand again and said goodbye.

Efunporoye came to Odumosu's store many times in the next few weeks, always giving him a gift and always making him feel honored and appreciated.

They became great friends. Some people whispered that they were lovers, though she was the wife of the king. Whatever it was, Efunporoye was soon asking the advice of Odumosu about her own business deals. Without either of them realizing it, they had become business partners.

With personal introductions by Efunporoye, Odumosu soon met the most important merchants and warehouse owners that dealt not only in palm kernel, the king of the cash crops at that time, clothes, salt, and imported European goods, but also in firearms and slaves.

Under his partner's tutelage and instructions, Odumosu began to supervise private slave deals.

He conducted, at great profit for himself and his partner, massive auctions in slave markers in Ebute Meta, Badagry, Epe, and Ikorodu. In exchange for the slaves, he obtained crates of firearms and ammunition brought by French, Portuguese, and Dutch ship captains from Europe. He sold these to the Ijebus, Egbas, and Ibadans, who sent their agents and middlemen to him from the hinterland.

Odumosu began to make more money than he could count. He built his own mansion close to the great building in which Efunporoye herself lived when she was not at the palace with her husband, the oba.

That district of central Lagos, where she made her home and popularized, was named after her. Everyone called it Ita Tinubu. It quickly became the most fashionable section of the island, next to the Brazilian quarter around Campos Square.

*　　*　　*　　*　　*

Luck ran out for Odumosu and his partner, Madam Tinubu, barely two years after they had started their very lucrative partnership. Oba Adele died suddenly in 1837, making Tinubu a widow for the second time. But Efunporoye showed her mettle as a master organizer and manipulator who knew how to play the political game for high stakes.

She moved swiftly. She used her influence to install her late husband's son, Oluwole, who was very close to her, as the new oba of Lagos. Thus, she continued to enjoy the influence and protection of the *iga*.

But Odumosu was shocked when Efunporoye told him she was going to remarry. Her third husband, the new oba's military chief, was a man named Yesufu Bada. He was a Moslem from one of the leading families of Lagos. He was said to be descended from the Bini chief, Bazuaye.

But personal tragedy continued to dodge the steps of the enterprising Madam Tinubu. Oba Oluwole himself died, presumably from an accidental cause, before he had spent three years on the throne. But Odumosu could only watch with fascination as the unfazed Efunporoye now arranged for her former brother-in-law, Akitoye, an Egba prince, to take the throne.

In this way, Odumosu and Efunporoye continued their charmed lives of business and political dominance in Lagos as they consolidated and expanded their business empire.

But things changed drastically and suddenly for Odumosu in 1845, exactly ten years after he had gone into the slave-dealing business with Efunporoye.

One day, he was summoned to the British consulate. Since a new consul had just been appointed from England, Odumosu assumed this was one of the usual courtesy visits as the new consul got to know the important personalities in town. He was therefore shocked at the brusque and businesslike tone of his host at their short meeting.

Without much of a preamble, this is what the consul said to Odumosu, "I want to remind you that since 1833, Her Majesty has abolished slavery in all the waters, lands, and territories controlled by the British Crown."

In case Odumosu had forgotten, the consul reminded him that this included Lagos Island and all its surrounding islets, creeks, and lagoons. Also, Epe and Badagry, for that matter. He then made it clear that he would begin forcefully to impose sanctions on all those in Lagos who chose to flout this law, including, and not limited to, the threat of exile.

"I am aware," the consul continued, "of a consignment of slaves that you, Odumosu, and your partner, Madam Tinubu, obtained recently from the hinterland and sold in the slave market in Topo Island off Badagry.

"You were able to do this with the connivance of the Portuguese."

Well, he had news for Odumosu and his fellow dealers in slaves, the consul said. The British had plans to take over from the Portuguese the fort at Topo, with its protective guns and cannons. They would then have unbroken jurisdiction on the waters between Badagry and Lagos up to Epe and Escravos in the Niger Delta.

Odumosu was not a dull or obtuse person. It was being made very clear to him that the trade which had made him very rich in the last ten years was being closed to him by this blunt British official. His exciting and profitable livelihood had suddenly become very risky.

Odumosu had always known that the British Navy was determined to thwart the activities of the slave ships and the Portuguese and Brazilian slave merchants who swarmed over Lagos and profited from this pernicious commerce. But he and the other slave dealers had always found ways to continue with their business.

But now that the new consul was a man of such determination, things had become so much riskier indeed. They would no longer be dealing with amiable and conniving officials, who winked at their activities and looked the other way.

Odumosu went home and had a counsel with Efunporoye. He was scared. He wanted them to stop their slave-dealing ventures.

But he could not convince Efunporoye. She, confident and unperturbed as ever, assured him they would still have the protection of the Portuguese and the French, who were in competition with the British. She told him confidentially that there were advanced negotiations at that very moment between some of these other foreign governments and important chiefs in the hinterland, notably the Egbas, to sign a treaty that would allow them to continue the slave trade.

Not everyone was as puritanical as the supercilious British, she said. Efunporoye convinced Odumosu to continue dealing in slaves. But his heart was not in it.

For the next deal that he arranged with an Egba slave trader, he had to travel with his consignment on a long and dangerous journey to the French port at Porto-Novo. He was almost caught with his heavy bags of cowries as he came back into the territory of the consul. After this, he began to have second thoughts.

When he got back to Lagos after the trip to Porto-Novo, Odumosu had a dream. He was in a strange land that he could not recognize. Yet it seemed familiar. He could see that there was a sea in the distance and jagged mountains rising behind him. He was in a large cultivated field in which a strange crop grew, neatly arranged in rows stretching to the far distance. Though he did not know it, these were coffee plants. He was alone in the middle of this plantation.

Then a woman came toward him. It was Efunporoye. She had on a European dress and a sun hat. Her walk and the sway of the hips were typical of her.

Odumosu went toward her to greet her. As he drew nearer, he could now see the face; and with some shock, he realized it was not Efunporoye.

This lady was the most beautiful being he had ever seen. She looked like Efunporoye the way he knew her when they first met. But her skin was very light, like that of a white woman, and she had the slim nose of a European.

She came up to him and took his hand. When he looked into her eyes, he noticed that the irises were a strange silvery hue with flecks of grey, through which he could see the reflection of his own face. It was like the glassy surface of the sea in calm weather. He remembered his days as a canoe boy in the creeks round Epe and the wonderful feeling that would come over him when he came in view of the wide blue sea. He had such a feeling now, and it calmed him. It was like the whisper of heaven on a turbulent world.

"Peace. Be still," it said.

He felt at peace, and this creature was the source of it. He knew without being told that she wanted him to walk with her.

And as they walked along, she said softly to him, "Slavery is an evil thing. You should have nothing to do with it."

She looked at him with a moist tenderness in her silvery grey eyes, as if she was sad and might break down and cry. Then abruptly, she withdrew her hand from his and walked away.

He did not attempt to go after her. And as her figure receded in the distance, he awoke from his dream.

* * * * *

After this, Odumosu's conversion was complete, revolutionary and irreversible. Not only did he decide to stop all his involvement and activities with trafficking in slaves, he became an ardent abolitionist.

He attended meetings of like-minded people on the island. He became friends with the consul and other British officials who had made it their goal, both personal and official, to help put an end to the slave trade.

Odumosu now devoted himself to the mundane and safer old commerce that he had neglected while he flourished in the trade with slaves. He began once more to make money the hard way.

He sold palm kernel and woven native cloth to European merchants who exported them to Europe from the port in Lagos. In return, he obtained European finery and iron implements for the household, farm, and field, including muskets for hunting and gunpowder and firearms for warfare. The latter included breech-loading rifles, which he sold to Ijebu middlemen.

Among these merchants was a rising young chief from Ijebu-Ode named Kuku, who sold some of the guns the Ijebus did not need to Bashorun Oluyole in Ibadan.

In his new line of business, Odumosu lost a considerable fraction of his income. He had to work harder, and the profits were slower in coming in. But he was happy. He finally built his big warehouse on the wharf. And he was invited by the rich and influential Brazilian merchants on the island to join their exclusive chamber of commerce.

He moved in the highest social circles among the native-born Lagosians as well as the expatriate European community. Soon, he became recognized as a valued friend of the principal European representatives on the island and as an informal adviser to the British consulate, his former employer. In particular, the vice-consul, Benjamin Campbell, became his good friend.

Thus it was that Odumosu was asked to be a go-between the British and an old acquaintance he had known through Efunporoye.

This was Oba Akitoye, who had been deposed by another former Lagos king, Kosoko, who was now installed as oba.

Unlike the amiable Akitoye, Kosoko was despised by the consul and the rest of the British establishment. This was because as soon as he ascended the throne, he proved to be an inveterate ally and enabler of slave traders. He became a thorn in the side of the British in their desire to stamp out the slave trade in the Lagos territories once and for all.

Odumosu was summoned to the British consulate office near the race-course. John Beecroft, the consul, was a former seaman who had found time to educate himself in the classics. He often quoted liberally from English literature.

To Odumosu, Beecroft expressed himself in Shakespearean terms. He declared that Kosoko possessed "multiple villainies of nature of the most vile kind," which to him was to deal in slaves.

"What we want from you," the consul told Odumosu as soon as he had settled him down with a small glass of brandy, "is to carry a confidential message to an important man now in exile in Badagry. He is no other person than Akitoye, the former oba of Lagos. The message is that we, the British, with the blessing and approval of London, would help Akitoye regain the throne of his fathers if he agreed to help us stamp out the slave trade."

Odumosu looked at the consul with awe and trepidation. He remonstrated. Why would the consul think that it was he of all people, a genial man and a simple man of commerce, who would be the one to bear a message of such import?

"Kosoko, that scoundrel," the consul added, without appearing to listen to Odumosu's reservations, "has refused to sign such an agreement. We need someone who knows Akitoye. And that person is you."

He continued, "In fact, my spies among the local population have informed me that Kosoko is in touch with French officials who are trying to get him to sign a treaty with France that would cede the island of Lagos and all its territories to France."

In return, Beecroft informed Odumosu, his face now looking stern, that the French government would not only allow Oba Kosoko to continue the slave trade in Lagos but also pay him the princely sum of five hundred British pounds a year.

And this was how Odumosu became a negotiator on behalf of the British.

*   *   *   *   *

When Odumosu reached Badagry, he found that Akitoye was on Topo Island, where he was being guarded by a detachment of the British Navy, who had just seized that island from the Portuguese.

The old slave market had been shut down, and the Union Jack flew on top of the fort, which had been built there half a century earlier by the Portuguese.

As he walked down from the gangway of the ship that brought him from Lagos, Odumosu could see great iron guns—he later was to know they were called "cannons"—that looked up into the sky. Some pointed toward land, but most of them faced the sea. As he learned later, this was to deter any brazen seaborne Portuguese attempt to regain the port.

To get to the fort where Akitoye was housed, Odumosu had to walk some way along the beach. Odumosu would later say that the beach at Topo was the most beautiful place he had ever seen in his life. He was mesmerized by the blinding white sand and tall coconut trees which waved lazily in the wind. Small crabs scurried busily around his feet. And once or twice, he allowed the incoming waves from the blue-green ocean to wash over his feet.

"There is no such virgin beach on Lagos Island," Odumosu said to himself. In Epe maybe, or the Lekki Peninsula.

Odumosu felt like a child. If he had no pressing business at hand, he would gladly have stayed on that serene island for a whole week. He would loll in the sun and eat coconuts and boiled crabs.

But he soon got down to business with Akitoye. He repeated the confidential message from the consul. The British would help Akitoye regain his crown if he agreed to sign a treaty abolishing the slave trade.

Odumosu's mission to Akitoye was successful. The old king agreed to everything proposed. Odumosu was convinced he would keep the bargain. He had always known Akitoye as an upright and decent man.

That same day, Odumosu went back to Lagos on the same ship, provided by the British Navy, that had brought him.

When he reported the news to the British consulate, the consul could see the light of achievement shining brightly in the eyes of his confederate. Beecroft looked with warmth and admiration at this former slave dealer turned abolitionist, a most unlikely ambassador indeed to the cause of British interests.

What Odumosu had brought back from Topo Island to present to the consul was an oral agreement between Kosoko and the British government, which both sides agreed would later be put in writing. It called for the British to bombard Lagos.

The British would force Kosoko out and install Akitoye as oba. Power would be shared between the new oba and British administrators at the consulate acting on orders from Whitehall. But both sides would know who the real master was. It was the British monarch, Her Imperial Majesty, Queen Victoria. Pax Britannica was coming at last to this corner of the Dark Continent.

The two men, Odumosu and Beecroft, discussed the fear expressed by some at the consulate—that some of the Lagos princes who were loyal to Kosoko might balk at the return of Akitoye. Some of these princes considered Akitoye to be an Egba prince, not a true Lagosian. His mother, after all, was from Abeokuta.

It was therefore agreed that a delegation would be sent to these princes. Their agreement would be secured with what the consul euphemistically referred to as "blandishments." Odumosu did not think he had to ask Beecroft the nature and price of these inducements.

* * * * *

On a cloudless day in late December 1851, Odumosu looked out of his house in Ita Tinubu. There was a commotion in the street. He saw people pointing, shouting, and running toward the waterside. The British were coming.

Odumosu knew this of course and was prepared for this day. But still, he came out of his house. His heart thumped with excitement as he went toward the direction people ran or pointed to. Soon, he got to the Marina. Now he could see a convoy of warships flying the blue-and-white ensign of the British Navy steaming in across the harbor.

But they did not stop. As Odumosu and the crowd standing on the piers watched, the ships went around the southwestern tip of the island to enter the broad lagoon. There, they would be within sight and cannon shot of the oba's palace.

Odumosu now turned around and made for the northern side of the island until he stood not very far from the oba's palace, the Iga Idunganran. He saw that the big warships were already anchored in the calm waters of the lagoon.

He watched as a delegation of naval ratings, led by a lieutenant in crisp white, was rowed ashore. Odumosu was surprised to see that the lieutenant was black-skinned like himself.

"How did an African get to become a lieutenant in the British Navy?" Odumosu asked himself.

"Could he be from Lagos?"

Later, Odumosu would find out the name of this naval officer. He was James Pinson Labulo Davies, a Saro from Freetown, who was born in that town to freed slaves of Yoruba descent. His parents had been emancipated on the high seas from a Portuguese slave ship by a warship of the British Navy.

This Lieutenant Davies was the first African to become an officer in the British Navy. On that day. Odumosu could see that he wore his white naval uniform with pride and aplomb.

Timing their steps to the staccato beat of their military drums, Lieutenant Davies and the other sailors of the naval delegation from the British warship marched directly to the Iga Idunganran.

As Odumosu would learn later, Oba Kosoko was given an ultimatum, which he flatly refused.

The delegation went back on board. The ships began to fire their big guns. Most of the destruction was wrought on dwellings on the southwestern corner of the island. The gunners had been instructed to be careful not to damage the oba's palace itself.

Panic and pandemonium broke out, particularly in that section of the island which received the brunt of the rocket and cannon fire. And in the midst of this carnage, many islanders whose dwellings were not hit came out to watch. These spectators were awed at the destructive power of modern warfare brought to their doorsteps.

For many years after this, stories were told of the many ears that were deafened, some permanently, by the loud swooshes and booms that shook the island. These came from rockets that flew up in the air and landed with a spectacular explosion of flame, dust, and debris.

Rubble piled up everywhere. For those in the neighborhoods where the cannon balls landed, escaping the bombardment and fleeing to safety were the only things on their minds, not fight or resistance. And even if they wanted to fight, what weapons did they have against the big guns of the British? What could they do against projectiles that brought death and destruction from such a great distance?

What little resistance that was offered came from die-hard Kosoko supporters, who had most to lose if their benefactor would cease to be king, and his guards from the palace. These few stalwarts tried to defend the island using old ceremonial cannons that they did not know how to fire. Small, pitiful firearms were wielded by young men with very little practice. Lagos had never gone to war in anyone's lifetime, and few men on the island had ever fired a shot in anger.

As the big guns continued to fire, many hundreds of dwellings were leveled into dust, burying many of their inhabitants in the rubble. Soon, the whole island lay under a cloud of smoke and debris. The gods of war, as usual, stood firmly on the side of those with the big guns.

This Bombardment of Lagos, as local journalists later called this unequal military engagement, lasted three days. The engagement was fiercer than the British Navy had anticipated.

It was only after this aerial blitz stopped that British sailors and marines, with muskets and howitzers, came ashore. They swiftly dispatched the few local fighters who tried to put up a fight. By this time, most of those who supported Kosoko had put up their weapons. Most of them found somewhere to hide while many fled in canoes rowed across the lagoon and creeks that surrounded the island.

Local agitators, who had been instructed beforehand, now came out into the streets. Some of them had been commissioned by Odumosu acting on behalf of the British consulate. They waved banners and sang songs critical of Kosoko. They stirred up the people to come out into the streets in a riotous rebellion against the king.

With this mob at his heels threatening to burn the palace down, Kosoko was deposed a second time. He fled into exile in Epe in a canoe rowed by two of his slaves. His three wives and the little property he could take with him were all he had on board.

Odumosu was one of the islanders invited by the British captain, a bearded naval officer named Jones, to come aboard his ship, the HMS *Bloodhound*. There had been seventy-five casualties among his men, including fifteen dead. Odumosu found out that one of the wounded sailors was the dashing black lieutenant, Davies, who had been wounded by a loose piece of shrapnel when one of the big guns on his ship misfired.

Akitoye, Odumosu's old friend, was on board. He had been brought by boat from Badagry. He and Odumosu greeted each other warmly. Each man was pleased with the part he had played in bringing about this turn of events.

When the bombardment finally came to end, Akitoye went ashore to the welcome of a great crowd of people and chiefs—at least those who had not fled with Kosoko. He went directly to the Iga Idunganran, where his reinstallation as oba was conducted by the priests and white-capped chiefs.

Odumosu had made sure that these important kingmakers had gifts sent to their houses the night before, courtesy of the consulate and local allies of Britain.

True to his promise, within a month, Akitoye affixed his mark to a treaty with the British queen. It barred the slave trade forever on Lagos Island and its surrounding territories.

Odumosu would always remember that day. He celebrated the occasion in his house with his friends, relatives, and servants. He opened a rare bottle of a bubbly white wine imported from the Champagne region of France. It was New Year's Day, 1852.

One of his friends, James White, Esquire, a handsome mulatto who had emigrated from the West Indies and had affirmed his Africanness by marrying a Yoruba lady, asked Odumosu's guests to keep quiet while he made a speech. They could see that he was tipsy from a bottle of English port sent from the consulate. He slurred his words and stammered quite a bit while he tried to make his short speech, which indeed he had rehearsed earlier.

To those who strived to understand White's alcohol-hampered speech, this is what they heard:

"Today, E-E-England has performed an a-act which the grateful children of A-Africa shall long r-r-remember. The r-r-root of the slave trade is torn out of the s-s-soil of Yo-Yo-Yorubaland forever."

Later that year, White wrote those same words in a long, well-composed article for an abolitionist newspaper in New York in the United States of America. That newspaper article was brought back to

Lagos and was joyfully read and circulated among the local abolitionist group that included Odumosu and his friends.

* * * * *

But Odumosu and other Lagosians, as they now called themselves, found that their former king, Kosoko, would not stay away quietly. From his exile in Epe, he continued to foment trouble in Lagos. He sent his spies and agents to provoke open agitation and organize street protests against Oba Akitoye.

Fighting broke out in the streets. There was an attempt on Odumosu's life. Doubtless, those who supported Kosoko and desired his return were not happy that Odumosu had deserted his old calling and was now working with the British and the new oba to permanently end the slave trade.

Odumosu had been warned by his own spies. He was not at home. But the newly installed glass panes in the window of his downstairs parlor were broken by a thug wielding a club.

Kosoko did not succeed in retaking Lagos. But his agents poisoned Akitoye, thus ending abruptly the reign of one of the most peaceable kings of Lagos of that era.

And what happened to Madam Tinubu, Odumosu's old business partner and sister-in-law of Oba Akitoye?

After she and Odumosu parted ways when Odumosu decided to abandon the slave trade, Madam Tinubu persisted in her proslavery activities. It was an enterprise that had made her very rich and powerful. She saw no reason to change her line of business so late in life.

Besides, she convinced herself, she had powerful connections that went above the head of a mere British consul. She was the intermediary between several European governments and powerful native merchants, warlords, and potentates on the Slave Coast from Badagry and Lagos to Abeokuta and the hinterland.

She was the confidant of many princes on Lagos Island, including relatives of her late husband Oba Adele. She also had a powerful ally in the Alake of Abeokuta. She was held in high regard by Portuguese, German, and French merchants and government agents, who needed and respected her services, connections, and advice.

She asked herself, "What do I have to fear from the arrogant and meddling British?"

With characteristic arrogance, she told Odumosu, when he tried to remonstrate with her, "I am an *omo Egba*, a proper daughter of Yorubaland. I was born into a family of kings. I am not afraid of any *oyinbo* man, even if he calls himself a vice-consul."

"I have dealt with more powerful men than him," she added.

Now, she was referring to Odumosu's friend Benjamin Campbell, the vice-consul, who was the most vocal of the officials in the consulate in speaking and acting against the unrepentant slave dealers like Tinubu who remained on the island.

Odumosu could only shake his head. Prior to this speech from his former business partner, he had no knowledge that Efunporoye, though the wife of a former king of Lagos, was born into a royal family in Abeokuta.

By now, Efunporoye had made up her mind to engage in a public feud with Campbell, who soon after this, was elevated to the position of consul. But this was where Tinubu made a costly mistake. For Campbell was even more stubborn and tenacious than she was. He was the epitome of the pugnacious British bulldog.

Tinubu was wealthy and cunning. And she had powerful friends in high places. But what Campbell had on his side was not just his own dogged determination. Backing him was the full power of the British Empire, with its army of dedicated officials supported by the force of a navy that was the mightiest in the world.

Campbell swore a solemn oath to himself that he would use whatever it took to vanquish his stubborn adversary. For Campbell, it was not just the moral issue of fighting slavery and confronting those who were its agents and profiteers. As a progressive, he believed that the continuation of the slave trade in that day and age was an affront to the conscience of a civilized world. But more important to him as an Englishman, Campbell viewed his fight with Madam Tinubu as a question of the just use of power to affirm the superiority of the British sovereign over petty native potentates.

Like his predecessor, Beecroft, Campbell had a love for Shakespeare. He remembered some lines from the bard that provided him with the apt imagery and metaphor he needed. He told those who listened to him that he was determined that, even if he had to use "bare-faced power," he would "sweep this arrogant slave dealer aside." The antagonism between the two was a duel to be fought until one of them was rendered hors de combat.

Campbell was also a romantic. He had a fondness for the Middle Ages, when knights in armor engaged in jousts and duels and, as moral champions, went forth to slay evil dragons and put wrong to right. He was the knight errant in shiny armor who had come to slay the fire-breathing dragon that threatened the peace of the countryside around the royal castle. Dragons and slave dealers to him were the same.

And in the end, Campbell prevailed. This particular combat ended when Campbell called in the power of the British Navy. He invoked the threat of British gunboats to force Tinubu into exile in Abeokuta in 1856.

The consul, of course, was emboldened by the proven success of that earlier "gunboat diplomacy," in which he had also played a part, concerning Oba Kosoko, another notorious slave dealer. In both instances, the outcome was the disgrace and exile of a powerful native who had dared to oppose the representative of Her Majesty Victoria Regina, Queen of Great Britain and Empress of India.

But after he had dealt with Madam Tinubu, the consul faced another crisis, to which he again appealed for advice from his friend Odumosu. For news came out of the Iga Idunganran of the sudden death of Oba Akitoye. This event was said by many to be the result of poisoning by agents of the exiled Kosoko.

On the advice of Odumosu, the consul speedily consulted the Lagos white-capped chiefs, who chose as their new king the son of the old one. Thus it was that Prince Dosunmu, whose name would be notoriously misspelled by the British as "Docemo," was installed as the new oba. He was the eldest son of Akitoye.

But Dosunmu was not as staunch an opponent of slavery as his father. Odumosu and other local progressives watched with dismay as the old Portuguese and Brazilian slave traders came back to Lagos and engaged in their old business with impunity. They had been waiting in the shadows for this opportunity.

These "miscreants," as the consul called them, brazenly held a slave market at Ebute Meta, on a jetty across the lagoon from Lagos Island.

Odumosu and his local abolitionist friends were outraged. But they did not simply get angry. They swung into action. They sent petitions and wrote appeals to the Colonial Office in Whitehall. And the British Parliament responded. It swore to put an end to slavery along the Guinea coast, especially in Lagos, once and for all.

"This would be achieved," the Prime Minister, Lord Palmerston, declared in a grand speech in Parliament, "even if we have to formally annex Lagos and take over its administration from the oba and his native cabinet."

And so once again, the Royal Navy sailed into action. On a hot afternoon in August 1861, a British naval squadron entered the deep waters of Lagos harbor, having sailed past the breakers and the gap in the sandbar.

A deputation of sailors and officials was lowered in a boat. They came ashore to see the king at the Iga Idunganran. An ultimatum of either compliance or abdication was given to Oba Dosunmu.

For three days, the king vacillated. But in the end, he realized that he was in no position to confront the British. He had few friends and supporters even among the princes in his advisory council.

According to what Odumosu heard later, Oba Dosunmu's lack of viable options was made clear to him by the interpreter who accompanied the blond lieutenant who had come to the palace at the head of a naval platoon loaded with howitzers. The king would either sign the papers of abdication, the interpreter assured him, or he would find himself blown into oblivion along with his palace with the naval guns that were pointed at that very moment at his palace.

After the forced acquiescence of the Lagos monarch, Commander Beddingfield came ashore. It was he who commanded the West Africa Squadron of the British Navy from his flagship, the HMS *Prometheus*. Accompanying him were other senior British officers, including the designated acting governor of the new colony, the Irishman McCoskry.

With Dosunmu deposed, papers were signed with the native council. Lagos was formally annexed as a territory of the British Crown. Oba Dosunmu packed his belongings, and trailed by his family, he became yet another oba of Lagos forced into exile by the power of British "gunboat diplomacy."

Power now rested firmly in the hands of the British colonial administrators. Lagos was a Colony of Her Majesty, Queen Victoria.

* * * * *

The Right Honorable William McCoskry, Consul of Her Majesty for the Bights of Benin and Biafra, was now the Acting Governor of the new Colony of Lagos.

A week after the abdication of Oba Dosunmu, McCoskry was installed in a newly refurbished colonial mansion on the Marina not far from the race-course. It was evening time. McCoskry stood beside a desk in his study. It was on the ground floor of the two-story building, which for the previous five years had been the residence of the British consul on the island.

Through the open window that opened unto a flower bed of hibiscus and bougainvillea, McCoskry could hear the buzz of grasshoppers and the noise of frogs and toads as they cried to each other in the dark in their age-old mating call. The window had been left open because the air was warm and cloy. It was a typical night in the tropics. And McCoskry was used to the climate, having been a merchant and swashbuckler who had traded all over the Guinea coast from Freetown to Calabar.

Unlike previous consuls appointed from England, McCoskry was a businessman and an adventurer, not a career diplomat in the service of the Colonial Office in Whitehall. He felt almost like a mercenary, and sometimes he acted like one. In his business dealings over the years, he had driven a hard bargain with native middlemen and European ship captains alike. This was how he had become comfortably rich. And today he could say that he had reached the apogee of his life ambition. He was the first colonial governor of Lagos, even if only in an acting capacity.

McCoskry stroked his bushy red beard with his left hand. He chuckled to himself as he remembered the nickname given to him by the natives of the island. They called him "Apongbon" – "Red Beard" in their native Yoruba.

Later, a street on the island would be named after him, Apongbon Street, though it would be in a disreputable part of town that had once been used by the islanders as a refuse dump. It was in the extreme southwest corner of the island where the waters of Lagos harbor swept around the island to merge with the expansive lagoon, a vast shimmering glass that stretched farther than the eye could see, to the shores of Ikorodu and distant Epe.

But Apongbon Street was in the future. This evening, the bearer of that name, Apongbon "Red Beard," was more concerned with his own health. He had a deep fear of tropical illnesses. He had once come down with a severe attack of malaria, which had almost killed him. He was therefore morbidly afraid of the bite of mosquitoes. This was despite the fact that since the early 1850s, he and other European travelers and missionaries on Lagos Island regularly used quinine, obtained from the bark of the South American cinchona tree, to combat the effects of malaria. Before moving into the building, McCoskry had made sure that there was a mosquito screen installed in all the downstairs windows.

Now he made a mental note that he would need to send for his wife, Sara, from Belfast. She would help with the servants and improve the quality of the food. She would also be indispensable in the social circles that would invariably spring up among the European expatriates in the new colony.

McCoskry turned and took in a view of the large room, with its bookshelves and small writing desk in the corner. On a whim, he bent forward and took up a small book from his desk. It was the collected works of the poet Shelley. For the past fifteen years, he had carried it with him everywhere he went. The old leather cover was old and worn, and quite a few pages were missing.

He opened the book randomly. He came to a well-used page and read a few lines.

> *My name is Ozymandias,*
> *King of kings,*
> *Look upon my work, ye mighty*
> *And wonder!*

McCoskry closed the book and put it back on top of the desk of polished dark brown mahogany wood.

Yes, he was British. And he and his countrymen were masters of the world. Their monarch, a woman, was queen of Great Britain. But really, she was empress of the world, the new king of kings. She was more powerful than the emperors and shahs of ancient Persia. And she controlled more territory in her dominion than Alexander the Great or Genghis Khan.

McCoskry's compatriots were not just great poets, he reminded himself. They were the best soldiers and sailors in the world. And they made darn good merchants and colonial administrators too. As one of those businessmen and administrators, although he was actually from the province of Ulster in Northern Ireland, McCoskry was very proud of the solid British stock he came from.

*   *   *   *   *

One morning soon after this, the Union Jack was hoisted high from a flag post at the battery at Ebute Elefun not far from the palace of the oba. Young fresh-faced Royal Navy ensigns stopped and saluted the proud symbol of their great empire "on which the sun never set."

Civil servants from the Colonial Office in Whitehall, newly arrived on the boat HMS *Surrey*, sat on park benches on the Marina and munched their lunch of turkey sandwich wrapped in sheets of ledger paper. They could hear native-born boys in the nearby grammar school on Broad Street, through an open window, recite a poem by Lord Byron.

> For the sword outwears its sheath,
> And the soul wears out the breast,
> And the heart must pause to breathe,
> And love itself have rest.

It was a British dawn, and British values proudly and firmly held sway over Lagos Island.

Odumosu was also very proud of this day. He relished the part he had played to make it come to pass. He told himself that this was a day to be remembered in history.

Later that evening, Odumosu stood on a jetty in Lagos harbor. He watched the British warships fire their guns in celebration. He was surrounded by a crowd of native-born islanders. It was a happy crowd, mostly of young people. They laughed, shouted, and pointed over the waters to the big ships and the yellow flames that spat from time to time from the mouths of the great guns. Their faces would light up briefly as the guns fired and rockets lighted up the sky.

What Odumosu thought he saw in those dark-skinned faces that beamed all around him was a mixture of hope and excitement for a bright new era.

But was it innocence or naïveté?

*   *   *   *   *

The day of the formal annexation of Lagos by the British was celebrated the next year, 1862. Odumosu was invited by the Governor. He was given an honored place reserved for the gathered dignitaries, few of whom were black-skinned natives of the island.

The common people of Lagos—women and men, servants and children—stood around and gaped at the fineries of the European ladies and the uniforms of the pompously mustached colonial officers. Their red-and-white military attire, epaulettes, gleaming medals, and high hats made the children giddy just to look at them. The crowd also admired the rich robes of the Lagos merchants and the gold and silver ornaments that adorned the ears, necks, and wrists of their opulent wives and concubines.

The most famous Lagosian of her day, Odumosu's old partner, Madam Efunporoye Tinubu, had come back briefly from exile in Abeokuta. She explained to Odumosu that she had been allowed by the British authorities to return to visit her relatives in Lagos.

She had done very well back in Abeokuta, she told Odumosu. Using her wealth and influence, she had become the Iyalode of the Egbas.

"One day, monuments will be erected and streets will be named for me in my native land," she said to Odumosu. "Let the colonial masters in Lagos scorn and reject me. I am a leader of my people."

Efunporoye assured Odumosu that she was treated like a queen in her native Abeokuta. Then, abruptly she turned away from him to acknowledge a young woman who knelt to greet her in the middle of the crowd. And that was the last time that Odumosu would see or talk to his old friend and partner.

Odumosu went to sit in his "reserved" section. He removed his hat and loosened his tie. Fastidiously, for this great occasion, he wore a European suit. He felt cool as his face was fanned by an evening breeze that came in from the harbor. Its coolness brought a momentary sense of peace and serenity that soothed the disquiet he felt despite his joy at seeing this day.

He looked up. What he saw was a clear blue sky, with a few fluffy clouds drifting lazily inland from the sea. He noticed the new British flag of the Colony on a huge flagpole by the pier. He admired the fluttering red, blue, and white ensign of the foreign queen who was now his sovereign.

Odumosu's thoughts were mixed. Peace and prosperity had come to Lagos and the rest of the Colony. But it was still a time of troubles for his Yoruba people in other parts of their ancient land.

Even now, the Ijebus were fighting the Ibadans, who had besieged a town of the Ijaiyes, allies of the Egbas, intending to destroy it or take its inhabitants captives to be sold into slavery.

Up in the north of Yorubaland proper, the Fulanis, those uncouth *gambaris*, held great swaths of land that once belonged to the Oyo Empire. They had driven away men and women who had considered this the land of their fathers going back a thousand years.

The old capital of the Oyos had been in ruins for three decades now. It lay empty and unpopulated, its people fled or sold into slavery. Reports came to the coast that the old citadel had become a sad and desolate abode of ghosts, never to be rebuilt for human habitation.

"The sun is setting over our ancient Yoruba civilization," Odumosu said gravely to himself.

As was his wont during times of great import and internal discomfiture, Odumosu found it reassuring to hold conversations with himself.

"Is it possible," he asked himself, "that it is these pale-skinned strangers from a foreign land, with their clipped accents spoken through the nose, who will be the deliverer of our people?"

Would the salvation of the Yorubas come indeed from English missionaries, khaki-clad soldiers, and white-uniformed sailors alighting from the same gunboats that had lately shelled the homes of the people they intend to govern?

And would the leaders of the Yoruba people learn from the British and develop a passion for rule and order?

If all these would come to pass, Odumosu said to himself, he was an optimist and would gladly say bye-bye to the old ways.

"But is this really the future?" he asked himself again.

Odumosu barely heard the rambling speeches given by the invited dignitaries from the dais erected in the open air at the end of the jetty. The hum of the restless crowd of native islanders and the polite clapping from the seated guests were vague, distant noises to him.

"Would there come a time when educated and civic-minded native-born Lagosians run our government, be teachers and principals in our schools and chaplains in churches where we can sing hymns in our own language?" he continued his soliloquy.

"Can businessmen like me one day operate independently and export our produce free from the control of white men?"

Odumosu considered himself to be a clear-eyed rationalist. He believed it was the white man's superior military, technical, and administrative machine that had won the day. Not his religion borrowed from Jews, who themselves were heretics. Nor was it the supercilious morality of the missionaries who waved their Bibles in people's faces and burnt effigies of the pagan gods.

He, Odumosu, a former slave merchant, genuinely believed that the establishment of the colony, which had succeeded in ending the slave trade, was a good thing for Lagos.

"And it would be a good thing for the rest of Yorubaland too," he told himself.

He allowed himself a vision of the future. He saw British suzerainty and law replacing the barbaric rule of the chieftains and warlords who now controlled much of the Yoruba hinterland.

Odumosu looked around him. He noticed that most of the Yorubas in the crowd wore European attire like him.

"The ways of our ancestors are dying all around us," he said to himself with some sadness, which was odd since he welcomed the changes wrought by the coming of the white man. He was honest enough to admit that he was one of those who benefited from those changes.

Odumosu continued his reflections. The age of the ancient Yoruba heroes, of men and women who were deified after they left the earth, was a thing of the past. Warrior leaders like Oranmiyan, Esigie, and Obanta, who founded dynasties for their people, were no more. Their golden age had ended long ago.

What the new times needed, he told himself, were people like him—practical men with the sense to shape a new, hopeful future for the Yoruba people. They would be traders and administrators, teachers and clerks, judges and physicians—individuals who found inspiration in the learning of the white man.

Odumosu could not but reflect that the passing of the old ways also signaled the demise of the old gods of Yorubaland. They had not been able to save Lagos from falling into the grasp of the white man. Nor would they save Abeokuta, Ijebu-Ode, Ibadan, or Oyo either.

As for the god of the Europeans, Odumosu went to church with them on Sundays. He went through the reading of the Lord's Prayer and the Apostles' Creed. But he admitted to himself that he went to church mainly to get close to the white men who held the reins of power on the island and to gain the connections that helped his businesses flourish.

So did he have a god?

He had read some of the European philosophers. Most of them were atheists—Voltaire, Jean-Jacques Rousseau, even the young Nietzsche. But Odumosu preferred to think of himself as a freethinker. Or a skeptic.

"Why should I worry about things that I will never know or understand?"

He told himself that there were more practical issues that demanded his attention, like maintaining his household, running his businesses, and paying his servants and workers on time.

Odumosu did not realize in time that the ceremony had come to an end. The last speaker had left the podium, and people were getting up to leave. Finally, he too stood up.

But he stayed briefly to greet an acquaintance who grabbed his hand in a big handshake. After a few minutes of exchanging pleasantries, Odumosu freed himself.

He said "O daro" to his friend. Then he turned away from the jetty and started the short walk back to his two-story abode in Ita Tinubu.

CHAPTER 2

Omo Eko la wa
Eru Oyinbo kan ko le ba wa.
Nigbati alaiye ti de ile aiye
Lati ma gbadun ile yi,
Ni awa ti nje oba.

We are sons of Lagos,
We are not afraid of any white man.
From the beginning of time
Since the owners of the world
Came to rule this earth
Have we lived as kings.

Omo Eko

I N THE YEARS following the establishment of the colony in Lagos, so the family stories tell us, Odumosu's financial empire grew. He imported silk from England, stockfish from Norway, and coffee and corned beef from Brazil and Argentina.

He traded native cloths woven in Offa and Ilorin in his shop in Ita Balogun to natives and Europeans alike. He brought kola nut, palm kernel, and groundnuts from the hinterland and sold them at a comfortable profit to retailers in Lagos.

He even planted a farm to grow and harvest his own kola nuts at a place on the mainland near Yaba, which he called *igbo obi*, later to be known as Igbobi. Prices were going through the roof due to the blockade of the trade routes by the war between Ijebu and Ibadan, and Odumosu knew that Lagosians who turned to farming would reap great profits in the years ahead.

To launch his farming ventures, Odumosu borrowed money from his rich Brazilian friend, Da Silva. His Saro friend, Captain J. P. L. Davies, the former naval officer who was now retired, had also become a wealthy entrepreneur. It was he who introduced Odumosu to the cultivation of cocoa and even leased him part of his land in Agege for this purpose.

But Odumosu never got the hang of cocoa farming. He thought the village of Agege was too far. The intense cultivation and constant attention that this king of "cash" crops demanded took him away, more than he wanted, from his business interests on the island. He therefore gave up cocoa farming.

*   *   *   *   *

Among the indigenous population of the island, the upper echelons of the Lagos elite in Odumosu's day were controlled by three groups.

First were the omo Eko, whose ancestors were born on the island. Many of them were actually from Badagry and Abeokuta. But quite a few could trace their distinguished origin from the white-capped chiefs of the old Awori dynasty of Ogunnire and the noblemen who followed Chief Bazuaye from Benin. They maintained a hold on the local administration from the oba's palace, the Iga Idunganran.

Odumosu himself was not born in Lagos, but in Ijebuland. But he was accepted as a member of this group as an *omo Eko*. His influence in the community and his association with previous obas, such as Akitoye and Dosunmu, had cemented his credentials. This was further enhanced by his nickname, Omo Eko.

And how did Odumosu get this name?

What Odumosu told his friends was that it originated with his old friend. Efunporoye Tinubu, who, during her fight with Vice-Consul Campbell, declared impudently that she was an *omo Egba*, a proud child of Egbaland; therefore, she was not afraid of any oyinbo man. After this, Odumosu, when talking with his friends turned this into a pun.

He would say, "Omo Eko le mi. Eru oyinbo kan ko le ba mi." I am a child of Lagos. I have no fear of any white man.

The second group of influential Lagosians were the Saro. These were freed slaves from Sierra Leone who boasted English surnames like Cole, Johnson, Crowther, and Macaulay. They were the educated elite who dominated the professions, law, education, priesthood, accounting, and the bureaucracy that served the British colony. They were educated at the CMS Grammar School in Freetown. Many of them had been to England, and they let everyone know it.

One of the most prominent Saros in those days was a man who dominated Lagos social and financial circles like a colossus. He was Captain James Pinson Labulo Davies, or JPL, as many of his friends called him. He and Odumosu became very good friends. It was he, who, as a young lieutenant in the British Navy in 1851, had participated in the Bombardment of Lagos, which led to the deposition of Oba Kosoko. Davies had been wounded in that action, after which he retired honorably at a very young age from the West Africa Squadron of the British Navy.

He became a merchant seaman and rose to become a captain in the mercantile navy. He sailed all over the Guinea coast and beyond—to Conakry, Calabar, and the island of Fernando Po.

Once, in a feat that tasked his skills as a mariner, he took his crew round the Cape of Good Hope to trade a shipment of molasses with the Cape Dutch for Guinea corn and turkey from Gambia. This dangerous voyage dismayed his financial backers back on the island. And it almost cost him a full mutiny of his native crew, who feared he was taking them to the end of the world.

Where a profit was to be made, there Captain Davies sailed his ship. He made a lot of money, which, after he retired, he now augmented with his many commercial activities on land. He had his finger in every profitable pie. This ranged from warehousing on the wharf to farming cash crops in the native lands north of the Colony, in Igbobi, Ikeja, and Agege.

Davies was a close associate of two other prominent Saros in town. One was the exuberant and energetic educator Thomas Babington Macaulay, who was about his own age. He had been named after the famous Englishman and abolitionist Thomas Babington, who, with William Wilberforce, had helped found the Church Missionary Society in London in 1799.

Odumosu came to know Davies as a true philanthropist who believed in the education of the native population as the way for the future. It was he who had given his friend Thomas Macaulay the sum of fifty pounds sterling as seed money to start his Grammar School in 1859.

The other Saro friend of Captain Davies was the middle-aged Ajayi Crowther. Odumosu knew him as a former slave and cleric who had translated the King James English Bible into Yoruba. He had lately become the first African bishop of the Church of England for the Niger diocese.

With Bishop Crowther, who was also Thomas Macaulay's father-in-law, J. P. L. Davies formed a lasting association for the public good. Together, they established various societies and programs to benefit their fellow black-skinned Lagosians. They established a social and philanthropic club, which they whimsically called the Academy. Davies was the first president.

The two men were the vanguard of the small intellectual circle of native-born educated men on the island. Their other Saro friends and collaborators in this group included prominent Lagosians with English surnames like Forsythe, Randle, Cole, Blaize, George, Johnson, Vaughan, Thomas, and Willoughby. These Saros, all men of education and substance, were known and befriended by Odumosu.

But it was the third group, the Brazilian émigrés, who held the purse strings of the business community. They were ex-slaves who had obtained their freedom in Brazil and had booked a passage to Lagos.

Such a person was the man they called Esan, who was about twenty years younger than Odumosu. Despite the difference in age, the two men became close friends due to their partnership in various business concerns that brought great profit and satisfaction to both men. Esan's other name was Da Rocha. This was the Portuguese surname he brought back from the land of Brazil.

Esan was born in Ilesha in the heart of Yorubaland before he was captured by slave dealers after his parents had sent him to Lagos to get an *oyinbo* education. He was sold into slavery and transported to Brazil. After buying his freedom, he had arrived in Lagos with his wife and infant son. He possessed little else apart from the proverbial shirt on his back.

But he had gone into moneylending, and he soon made a great fortune that was the stuff of legends. Esan told Odumosu he was planning to build—on a street named Kakawa, not far from where Odumosu lived—a mansion that would be "fit for a king."

Esan's remarkable rags-to-riches story was told in the popular songs of the day. It was said that he himself had written some verse in Portuguese about his time as a slave boy in Brazil. This was later translated into Yoruba and English.

Igba ogun l'ode ile Yoruba
Ni a fi ta mi leru
Ti a di mi ni okun
bi eni nde ekute ninu oko;
A ta mi sinu oko eru
bi eni nta agbado loja.
Esan ni oruko mi,
sugbon nisisiyin,
nwon npe mi ni omo Da Rocha—
Eni ti a ta leru,
ti a gbe lo si ilu Brasiili.
Bawo ni ajo mi yio ti ri?
Tani yio je olugbeja me?
Sugbon iponju ati irora ko le po titi

Ki omo onile ma rele.
Emi yio pada si ile baba mi
Lati ko ile giga ti o lokiki
ni ile karo o jire.

'Twas war that came
upon the land of the Yorubas
that made me a slave,
I was tied up like a bush-rat
and like a basket of corn
was displayed for sale in the market;
Esan is my name,
though now they call me Da Rocha—
he who was taken to the land of Brazil
against his will.
But no matter how hard the struggle
Or how perilous the voyage home,
I will return to the country of my birth
To build a mansion fit for a king
in the land of "karo o jire."

This poem, which was called the "Lament (or Song) of the Yoruba Slave Child Taken to the land of Brazil," was printed in an early edition of the *Anglo-African*, the first newspaper of its day among the indigenous population of Lagos. It was read avidly by the literate sons of the land, a select group that comprised less than ten percent of the native population of Lagos Island at that time. They were mostly Saros and Brazilians.

With their education, European connections and business acumen, Esan and other Brazilian émigrés on the island speedily accumulated wealth, attaining along the way a high place on the social ladder.

Over the years, these men and their families became associated with property and entrepreneurship on Lagos Island. Their Brazilian-Portuguese surnames—Da Silva, Da Rocha, Gomez, Pereira, Campos, and Da Costa—came to have an exotic Latin ring that exuded substance and wealth.

Odumosu did his best to associate with these expatriates from Brazil. And his affiliation with them paid dividends, both in his business and personal life.

*   *   *   *   *

In 1862, Odumosu made his first and only trip to England. It was to be present at the wedding of his friend Captain J. P. L. Davies to his second wife, Sarah Forbes Bonetta. Davies's first wife, a Spanish lady named Matilda, had died nine months after their marriage.

His new fiancée, Sarah, was a beautiful black girl of eighteen who lived in England. She was originally from Yorubaland, having been born in Egbado province. Her birth name was Aina. Her father was a chief of Oke Adan. When she was five years of age, a hostile force of Dahomeans led by their infamous female "Amazon" warriors attacked and burnt down her town. They killed her parents and took Aina as a young child into captivity.

But the Dahomean king took a fancy to Aina, conscious perhaps that she was the daughter of a great chief. This was the great King Ghezo, who ruled over the Kingdom of Dahomey from 1818 to 1858. Ghezo brought up the young Aina in the royal household as the personal slave and attendant of his favorite wife, Kadija. Though she was a slave, Aina's beauty and her natural dignified carriage caught everyone's eye.

When Aina was about twelve years old, an English ship captain in the service of Queen Victoria went on a mission to the court of the Dahomean king to negotiate a trade agreement. Part of his mission was to persuade the king to stop, or at least to ameliorate, the practice of slavery in his kingdom.

The name of the English naval officer was Captain John Forbes. His ship was the *Bonetta*. Forbes, like others before him, was struck by the beauty and noble carriage of the young slave girl Aina. He persuaded King Ghezo to free her and to let him take her away.

Thus it was that Captain Forbes of the good ship *Bonetta* took Aina to England.

The beautiful young African girl, a former slave, became the toast of London. The *Evening Standard* carried her story. And no less a personage than Queen Victoria, hearing about her, adopted her as a protégé.

And why did Victoria, Queen of Great Britain and Empress of India, behave so kindly and with such genuine affection toward this poor, orphaned African girl? Was it perhaps because the queen herself was aware of the black African blood that some said ran in her veins?

Whatever it was, this African ancestry of the famous queen was not common knowledge at that time. It was certainly not acceptable to society in mid-nineteenth-century England. For this was a time when the idea of the perceived superiority of the white race reigned supreme in the minds of most people in England. Especially was this so among the favored, rich, and pampered upper classes of which the queen was the head.

But the facts were these, as Captain Davies, who related them to his friend Odumosu, found out from a secret, but impeccable source close to the palace in London. The queen's grandmother Queen Charlotte was a German princess before she married George III in 1761. As a princess, Charlotte's royal pedigree was unimpeachable. Both her parents, Charles Louis Frederick, Duke of Mecklenburg-Strelitz, and Princess Elisabeth Albertine of Saxe-Hildburghausen belonged to two well-established royal houses of Europe. But mixed in her lineage, the source told Davies, was the blood of a Portuguese noblewoman of African ancestry. This was Margarita de Castro e Souza.

According to Davies's source at St. James's Palace, early portraits of Princess Charlotte did indeed show traces of her African facial features. But these were downplayed in subsequent official portraits after she became queen of England. And initially, it was said that some of the courtiers at St. James's Palace did not like Charlotte when she became queen. They disparaged what they considered her rather dark complexion and broad nose. Some even said she was ugly.

But in reality, Charlotte was tall, slim, and stately. She bore very well on her well-proportioned body and shapely head the elegant silk dresses, elaborately embroidered bodices, and feathered hats of that fashionable era. She soon won the hearts of the people of England with her charm and intelligence.

And once she had learned the English tongue and could communicate with ease, Queen Charlotte displayed a warmth that was rare in other members of the royal family. A lady of good taste and quiet, refined manners, she became the epitome of that fashionable era that would be called "late Georgian" in England.

Perhaps because she was aware of her own origin as the descendant of a black woman, Queen Charlotte became actively opposed to the slave trade. She loved good works, especially those that benefitted the lower classes. She was the benefactor and founder of the Kew Botanical Gardens in London. And she was the person who introduced the Christmas tree to England.

She patronized music and the arts, as well as many charitable projects for the poor. Queen Charlotte's Maternity Hospital in London was named for her. And Mozart, the Austrian-born musical prodigy, dedicated a whole opus to her when he visited England in 1765.

When she first met George III, having been brought over by land and sea from her small duchy in Germany to wed the young twenty-two-year-old English monarch, Princess Charlotte neither spoke nor understood a word of English. In fact, the couple had never cast eyes on each other until that moment. But Charlotte soon became a witty and fluent correspondent not just in German but in English. And she charmed not just her husband but the English people, a nation so notoriously hard to please.

Later in life, Queen Charlotte would remark with wry amusement that she had been met, wedded, bedded, and dispossessed of her virgin maidenhood by her husband at the age of seventeen years, all in a single day and night.

When Odumosu heard this story, he could not, with his usual astuteness and eye for history, coupled with the advantage of hindsight, but be impressed by the grace and artful dignity with which this remarkable lady sat on the high throne of state in St. James's Palace beside her husband as queen of England.

Odumosu learned that there were many triumphs in Queen Charlotte's life. But there was great sorrow, and disappointments too. Many of these were deep and personal.

For it was during her husband's reign that the rich and profitable colonies of North America, which became the United States, were lost forever to the English Crown. And within a decade of that loss, her friend and fellow queen consort, the younger, and some would say more beautiful, Marie Antoinette was beheaded by the people of France for the ruinous profligacies of her court.

After Marie Antoinette and her husband, the hapless Louis XVI, were arrested and kept under guard at the Tuileries Palace in Paris,

Odumosu was told that Charlotte, in anticipation of their escape, prepared one of the British royal residencies, the Holyrood Palace in Edinburgh, Scotland—the reputed birthplace of Mary, Queen of Scots—for the safe haven of the deposed queen and king of France.

"It is not true," Marie Antoinette had written to Queen Charlotte, "that I said, 'Let them eat cake,' when my counselors told me that the poor people of France were dying from lack of bread."

Marie Antoinette was eventually not able to make it to this sanctuary. But her brother-in-law, the Comte d'Artois, who managed to escape the Revolution and sailed to England, was permitted to stay at Holyrood for several years, on the personal intercession of Queen Charlotte.

Other tragedies followed, as Davies related to Odumosu. For soon after this, Charlotte's husband, George III, slowly became blind, deaf, and mentally incapacitated from a pernicious illness, which no one, including the best physicians in England who were summoned to the court, had a name or cure for.

Odumosu could never decide if Queen Victoria was influenced by the purported African ancestry of her grandmother Queen Charlotte in her kind treatment of his friend's fiancée. What he knew was that with the encouragement and protection of Queen Victoria, Aina, the former slave girl, converted to Christianity. She became an adherent of the Church of England.

And when she was baptized, Aina's native name was changed. She adopted the English name Sarah, which was then quite fashionable in London. On the suggestion of Queen Victoria herself, she added the name of her benefactor, Captain Forbes, as her middle name, and that of his good ship *Bonetta* as her surname.

Perhaps watching the grand ceremony of the wedding of his friend Captain Davies to his beautiful fiancée, Sarah Forbes Bonetta, in a small chapel in Windsor Castle stirred dormant romantic feelings in Odumosu. All he knew was that, after this, he too wanted to marry and settle down.

And thinking of his friend's good luck in marrying a beautiful bride who was a protégé of Queen Victoria, Odumosu began to dream and romanticize of a marriage partner who would not be from Lagos Island or the Yoruba hinterland. Like Sarah Forbes Bonetta, she would be a grand lady with an exotic name from a foreign background.

This was how, from one of his Brazilian business connections, Odumosu made the acquaintance of a young lady, a mulatto, whose family owned a coffee plantation in Brazil.

Her brother, Jose da Silva, a black Brazilian whose grandmother had been taken to Brazil as a slave from West Africa, had emigrated from Brazil to settle in Lagos.

*   *   *   *   *

Jose da Silva considered the enlightened island of Lagos, where he saw black people from many parts of the world thrive in business and commerce, to be one of the few places in the world that the progeny of a slave could, with pride, call home. Here, among freeborn people of his own race, he could hold his head high and not feel inferior to any white man.

Back in Brazil, Jose's father, who was a white settler from Lisbon, had become rich from the cultivation of coffee. He owned a fair-sized plantation just outside Rio de Janeiro. But his wife, Jose's mother, was a mulatto, a half-caste. Her mother had been an African slave brought over from the Slave Coast.

From an early age, Jose knew what it was to have dark looks cast at him on the streets, and to feel the hurt of racial animosity. The reason he had left Brazil was because he had fatally wounded in a duel a man who had used a pernicious racial slur to refer to his sister.

Jose, therefore, loved it in Lagos, where there was an unprecedented mingling of people of many races. Unlike the Portuguese *coloniale* in his native Brazil, he thought the white English expatriates he met on Lagos Island were relatively color-blind.

Many of his omo Eko friends in Lagos disagreed with him on this opinion. These were native-born Lagosians and Saros who knew firsthand the supercilious and hypocritical attitudes of British colonial administrators and merchants on the island.

Jose himself did not appear to have been a victim of this racial divide that existed in Lagos. His business dealings with the English merchants on the island were always cordial and beneficial to both parties. And he did not visit their consulate much. His Lagosian friends however thought Jose was naïve. And they told him so.

Many years later, when Jose had become more conditioned to the realities of the racial divisions on an island where the British colonial administrators were the top dogs, his friends told him of the case of a young Saro doctor, John Randle. This was a man Jose himself would come to know well when, years later, Randle married the first daughter of Captain Davies and Sarah Forbes Bonetta.

Randle was one of the first Africans to qualify as a physician from Edinburgh. But he resigned his position in the colonial medical service in Lagos because he was paid half the salary given to *oyinbo* physicians with whom he had the same qualifications.

At this time in our story, Da Silva had become a good friend and business associate of Odumosu. They loved and trusted each other like brothers. Da Silva, therefore, introduced Odumosu to his younger sister, Constantina, who was still living in their family estate in Brazil.

Once introduced, Odumosu and Constantina courted across the sea. They wrote love letters to each other which took six weeks to go halfway around the world across the Atlantic and back.

Inspired by his new love across the sea, Odumosu became romantic. He ordered books from England. And he perused volumes of English literature, seeking the right words and quotes to woo his lady. There was no public library then on Lagos Island. So from a bookstore in the Strand in London, he sent for and purchased a complete set of the plays of Shakespeare, a volume of Shelley, and several books of poems by contemporary English writers.

He spiced his letters to Constantina with verses from the newly published sonnets of Elizabeth Barrett Browning.

> *How do I love thee?*
> *I love thee to the depth*
> *my soul can reach.*
> *When out of sight.*
> *I love thee to the level*
> *of every day's most quiet need.*

Then he tried Shakespeare, expressing his feelings in the words of the young Juliet to Romeo:

My love is bounteous like the sea.
The more I give, the more I have for thee.

Constantina wrote him back in kind. She too knew some Shakespeare, which she had read in Portuguese. She took his hint and paraphrased Juliet.

My love for you is constant,
like my name Constantina.
I will drop everything, my love,
And come to thee at the end of the earth.

Although Constantina was a young girl in love, she was still a devout Catholic. Her parents were dead. Her brother was in exile three thousand miles away from home. And she loved a man she had never met, who lived thousands of miles away across the ocean.

"Who can I turn to for advice and counsel?" she asked herself on many lonely nights, when the ache of her love for a man she knew only through letters threatened to overwhelm her.

"Am I blinded by infatuation? Is my love real? Or are my feelings the feverish emotion of a lonely maid starved of real friendship?" she often asked herself.

"Is my passion simply overheated?"

Superaquecido was how some of her friends had described her feelings, when they read her letters to her lover across the sea. They laughed at her innocence and ardor.

Now that her father was dead, her uncle, Filipe, her father's brother, ran the plantation. But Constantina was not very attached to him. She had no other close relations close by.

So one day, she put on her shawl and, as a supplicant, went to the church in the monastery of São Bento, which was in Rio. She was driven there in a horse-drawn carriage owned by her uncle.

She knelt at the niche by the shrine of the saint, lighted a candle, and put her palms together in front of her face. She did not say any prayers. She knew the saint would hear her words straight from her heart and give her an answer.

And the answer came that night. Floating above her bed was the face of the saint, San Benito. It was the same image of the icon depicted in the monastery's stained glass window. The face spoke to her, its lips unmoving, but she heard its voice clearly.

The voice said to her, "Va com ele, minha filha. Go with him, my child."

Constantina made up her mind to go with her heart and the advice of the saint. And immediately, she felt at peace. It was a serene feeling that bore her gently aloft to a safe and secure place where no harm could befall her. For weeks afterward, she hovered delicately in a high region among the clouds, supported in the thin air by her love and the certainty of the blessing of heaven.

Soon after this, she and Odumosu became formally engaged through the medium of the seaborne mail, which had been the courier and go-between of their love. He mailed to her a package containing a silver engagement ring set with stones. They were high-carat diamonds of an exquisite cut that he had ordered from Jermyn Street, London.

Constantina received and accepted the ring with tears in her eyes. She slipped it on the fourth finger of her left hand. It was a perfect fit, again a sign of the approval of their match by the agents of heaven. Now she made plans for the long sea voyage from Brazil to the Guinea coast. She would join her love at last, and they would live as one forever.

At last, the day came when Constantina left her native land, never to return. She boarded a ship from the harbor at Rio de Janeiro at the mouth of Guanabara Bay.

As the ship passed through the point known as the Pão de Açúcar, or Sugarloaf Mountain, Constantina took a last look at the mountain peaks of the Serra do Mar. But she had few regrets about leaving her native land.

She was leaving behind a land and family heritage tainted by slavery and racism, to be with her beloved brother and the man she loved.

The voyage was unremarkable. All her thoughts were of seeing her brother once more after fifteen years.

She admitted to herself that she had jitters about joining the man of her dreams whom she had never seen. It was true that he had charmed her with his wonderful letters across the sea. But would he be the man she thought he was?

Six weeks later, Constantina disembarked at the port in Lagos to the arms of her brother, Jose. Her fiancé leaned back and beamed.

Odumosu tried to hide his inner agitation. It was no easy thing to be at the seaport to welcome a betrothed lover one had never met or seen.

But from his first look at her, Odumosu saw that Constantina exceeded his highest expectations. And as he looked at her more closely, he realized with a shock that Constantina looked very much like his old friend Efunporoye Tinubu as she had been twenty years earlier when he had first met her.

The two women shared the same height and the same slim hourglass figure, which was vigorously highlighted by the Victorian tight-bodiced dress that Constantina wore. Both Efunporoye and Constantina had the same oval face, if one discounted Constantina's light mulatto complexion, the European cast to her nose, and her high cheekbones. They even had the same soft giggle, which enchanted and did not mock the listener, and the same way of tilting the head to one side to encourage conversation. They had the same haughty, impish, laughing eyes.

Constantina was tall, almost as tall as Odumosu. Her olive skin was flawless, as if it had never been touched by the sun. And her doe-like eyes made his heart race.

As he came nearer, Odumosu looked deeply into those eyes. He saw silvery, light-gray irises through which he saw his own reflection. It was the glassy, calm surface of a sea that would never experience a storm.

And yes, he was calmed by the sight of those eyes. His agitation disappeared, and he was at peace, as in a dream.

And now he knew.

She was the lady in the dream. The one who had convinced him to stop trading in slaves. She had been sent to him to change his ways. To clear the path for her to be part of his life.

Odumosu had never imagined that anyone could be so beautiful, so pure, and so feminine. He silently congratulated himself on his exceedingly good fortune in landing such a beautiful lady, who would now be part of his life. For she would soon be his wife.

He moved forward, cleared his throat, and extended his hand to the exotic, beautiful creature who was his betrothed. At the same time, he looked again at that strange and yet familiar face. His eyes shone with tears of joy and gratitude.

"How do you do?" he greeted her in the formal English of that time.

At first, Constantina was taken aback and said in Portuguese, "Ola, como vai?"

Then she realized that she was in a new land, where no one, except perhaps her brother, would ever speak her native language to her. She collected herself and became once more the charming lady.

"And how do you do?" she replied softly in perfect, but Portuguese-accented English.

Leaning forward, Odumosu planted a light kiss on the proffered cheek of his fiancée. Then he took her hand and led her down the jetty.

"Voce e muito gentil, meu querido. You are very kind, my dear." She found herself saying to him in Portuguese.

What she wanted to say was "Eu te amo muito. I love you very much." But she knew she had to act the part of the lady. She had to restrain herself. At least when they were in public.

She too was happy with her choice. Her fiancé was the way she had imagined him. In fact, she had seen him once in a dream, and this was exactly how he looked.

There were many things she would like to say to him. But it would take some time before she would be able to express her thoughts well enough in the English tongue.

"Thank you, thank you," Odumosu replied joyfully in English and clasped her hand tighter in his.

*   *   *   *   *

The nuptial ceremony between Constantina and Odumosu was celebrated at the new Roman Catholic mission on Oil Mill Street in Lagos.

The church was a walking distance from his home on Campos Square, which had been named after one of the old Brazilian captains of industry who had settled on Lagos Island. It was in this exclusive section of Lagos that Odumosu had built his new mansion, next to that of his friend Jose. Odumosu had the house built in the Brazilian style, then in vogue in Lagos, complete with balconies overlooking the street. These were decorated with wrought iron balustrades imported from Rio de Janeiro.

After the ceremony at the Church of the Holy Cross, guests were entertained at a lavish reception in Odumosu's magnificent new dwelling. And on the Monday following their nuptials, the *Lagos Weekly Times* ran the story of the wedding under the headline "Omo Eko Marries Brazilian Beauty."

The *Weekly Times* was the weekly newspaper that had replaced the daily *Lagos Times*, which was now defunct. It was published by one of Odumosu's business friends, Richard Beale Blaize, a Saro. The piece about the wedding was written by one John Payne Jackson, a journalist and intellectual who had emigrated from Liberia and who now moved in the same social circles as Odumosu.

And indeed, the marriage ceremony of Constantina to Odumosu would be remembered for years afterward by many Lagos socialites as one of the best-attended society events of their time.

After this, Odumosu became a nominal Catholic to please his bride. He made a point of going to Mass with her every Sunday until the day he died and she became a widow.

Theirs was a marriage made in heaven, or at least in the realms of dreams. It happened exactly as Constantina had seen it in one of her dreams in Brazil. And her dream had come true. For she had crossed the ocean to the ends of the earth to be with her love. And they were together at last, two hearts that would beat as one till death did part.

In the years ahead, Odumosu and Constantina did their best not to shatter this happy illusion, which was their enduring reality. It had been created by their rich and creative imagination, high hopes, and the kindness of the gods.

With his connections to the Da Silva family, Odumosu became a resident of two worlds. In one, his old familiar life continued as he mingled with his native-born Lagosian friends in his warehouse and stores. Many of these men had come over from the hinterland, especially Abeokuta and Ijebuland, to escape the wars and turmoil of the times.

But when the day's business was done, Odumosu came home to a house where Portuguese was spoken. He basked in the beauty of a splendid mansion that was right in the middle of an exclusive section of the city that would later be termed "the Brazilian quarters." He learned a spattering of Portuguese to please his wife and to rib his friend and brother-in-law, Jose.

In 1880, when the time came to finish the new Catholic cathedral, the Holy Cross, which was built on the site of the small church where he and Constantina were married, Odumosu used his influence to make sure that it was a cousin of his wife, Lazarus Burges da Silva, who molded the ornate floral masonry at the front and side entrances and the high vaulted ceilings of the new cathedral.

The couple also brought in a cabinetmaker from Brazil, one Balthazar dos Reis, to carve the woodwork on the altar. It was this craftsman who put the flourishes on the bishop's throne and the pulpit that would be admired for decades after they were completed. This new cathedral was the first of its kind in the whole colony to be so magnificently decorated in the baroque European style of an earlier century.

In later years, that house in Campos Square where Constantina and Odumosu lived and raised their five children would be celebrated as one of the original "Brazilian" houses that were much admired by historians and architects of the next century.

Odumosu called his wife Tina or "darling." She called him Baba Tunji, after his first son, Adetunji, following the Yoruba fashion.

Constantina learned to speak fluent Yoruba. But she retained many of her Brazilian ways. She always wore a hat when she went out. And she continued to wear her European dresses, which she kept at the height of fashion every year.

Her fashion tastes shifted, for inspiration and guidance, from Rio de Janeiro to London. In this, she followed the example of the European ladies in Lagos, the wives and daughters of the British expatriates in the Governor's entourage. But she also wore the brightly colored "up-and-down" print blouses and wrappers that were favored by well-to-do Aganyi women from the Gold Coast and Saro ladies from Sierra Leone.

Odumosu himself mellowed and blossomed under the influence and attention of his sophisticated foreign-born wife.

Always a snappy dresser, he grew even more dapper and cosmopolitan in his carriage and manners as he aged. He cultivated a grand, well-maintained mustache in the manner of the English gentlemen of the late Victorian age. His speech was full of British idioms and literary turns of phrases. His diction was crisp, almost Etonian.

When they passed him in the street, people looked in admiration at Odumosu, a mustached old man in a buttoned-up suit from Regent Street, London. And they remarked on his intelligence, humanity, and wide range of interests. Perhaps not quite the Renaissance man, for he was born two centuries too late and several latitudes too close to the equator, Odumosu, in his later years, was nevertheless the picture of a true Victorian gentleman of the tropics.

Constantina and Odumosu led a good life. Theirs was a marriage of love, which was a rarity in those days. It was marked by external gaiety and inner contentment. Their house in Campos Square was a place of mirth and laughter, of tea parties at five o'clock in the evening, and of soft sonatas by Mozart played by their children on the grand piano in the parlor downstairs.

Their three boys were educated, first at the new CMS Grammar School located in Cotton House on Broad Street and then in England.

Their house, with its baroque European interior and Brazilian-style balustraded balconies and windows facing the outside, was constantly being painted and repainted, especially just before the New Year festivities. This was the time of year when a group of children of Brazilian émigré parents donned colorful costumes and masks, which they called *caritas*, and pretended they were having a *carnaval* in the old Brazilian style.

Sadly unkept and neglected by later generations of the Odumosu family, this grand house of the late nineteenth century fell into disrepair. It was pulled down one and a half centuries after it was built to make way for a nine-story building that was leased to a state-owned insurance company.

*   *   *   *   *

Odumosu's joy, in the early years of the Colony in Lagos, that slavery was now banned throughout their British territory, was dampened by the knowledge that Portuguese ships moored off Badagry and Porto-Novo were still making a not-so-secret traffic in the forbidden trade. These ship captains received their cargo from Yoruba middlemen who went over the water to them in boats and canoes.

But Odumosu knew that this traffic too would stop. In America, the war between the States would soon end, and he had no doubt which side would triumph. And in Brazil, that bastion of slavery and racism, the emperor was being heavily pressured by liberal elements in his own cabinet. It was widely expected that he would soon declare an end to slavery throughout that vast land.

The worldwide march of the progressive ideas of the abolitionist movement was inevitable, fueled by the desires and actions of men like him. Soon, Odumosu assured himself, slavery would cease to exist throughout the world.

He knew that negotiations were going on at that very moment for the British, Germans, and French to carve out colonies out of all the native lands along the Guinea coast to their mutual satisfaction. The French—despite their duplicitous assurances to several local chiefs, particularly the Egba—had already agreed to ban slavery in their own colonies once the agreement was signed. Later, this exercise would be referred to as the Scramble for Africa.

It did not take long for the news to reach the rest of Yorubaland that the ownership and commerce in slaves had been banned in the Lagos colony. Domestic slaves in the Yoruba hinterland heard about this edict, and many escaped to make it to Lagos.

The Egba chiefs, who had been allowed some autonomy in their own land by the British, now complained that their household slaves were running away to freedom in Lagos while the authorities in the Colony did nothing to stop them or send them back.

But many people in Lagos felt that the Egba chiefs had only themselves to blame. After all, it was these same chiefs who had welcomed the Christian missionaries to Abeokuta. They had allowed them to build churches and schools where the English language was taught, as well as the scriptures, catechism, and the Apostles' Creed. Some of these native chiefs even sent their children—the stubborn and unruly ones, they admitted privately—to be trained in the white man's schools.

And now, with the rapid anglicization of so many institutions in Lagos, many old traditionalists, not all of them uneducated idol worshippers, began to feel that they would need to put their foot down somewhere. Or else, they told themselves, the ancient culture and traditions of the Yoruba people would be completely swept away.

The changes were coming too quickly. And it was the elite on Lagos Island, in whose ranks Odumosu belonged, who led these changes. Soon, the abandonment of Yoruba traditional values and the wholesale embrace of the white man's religion, language, dressing, even courtship and marriage, spread to the rest of Yorubaland.

This was especially true in Abeokuta, where the influence of missionaries had come the earliest. Then it spread to Ibadan, Ife, and Ondo, finally reaching Ijebuland.

Old pagan priests, *ogboni* cultists, and Sango worshippers, who stayed with the old Yoruba religion, wrung their hands and rued the day that their obas allowed white men to come into their towns to preach and build schools.

Women no longer came to consult the *babalawo* when they became pregnant. When the time came to deliver their babies, they did not call the native midwife with her calabash of herbs and *agbo* to tend to them. And when their children fell sick, they took them to the mission dispensary.

Parents no longer gave their children names that honored the ancient gods of their fathers, like Efunyemi, Esubiyi, or Awosanmi. Instead, they gave them Hebrew-derived names from the Bible. The most popular of these were David, Samuel, and Sarah.

And as Odumosu saw with some amusement, the Christianized section of the population of Lagos now began to manufacture newfangled Christian alternatives to standard Yoruba names. Thus, all around Lagos, children were christened and addressed as Oluwajoba, Oluwatosin, and Oluwagbemiga.

The parents of these children, and the priests who encouraged them, said these names were in honor of Oluwa, the Christian god, who they said was the same Olorun Olodumare of the Yoruba pantheon.

But the pagan priests were not amused. One of these traditionalists complained to a coreligionist as they attended their monthly *ogboni* fraternity meeting at Ebute Ero.

"This is a new god from a foreign land, where men speak through their noses and allow a woman to govern them as queen," he said.

"They have come to our land to conquer us. They want to eliminate our language and sweep our old gods away." He hissed in disgust.

"Nothing good would come out of it," his friend agreed.

Odumosu was not a party of this school of thought. He was sure that the adoption of Western education and, by extension, the technology of white men would be the fuel that would ignite the flame of progress and achievement for his people.

He did not however think Christianity as a religion was essential to this process. For by this time, Odumosu had separated in his mind the Judeo-Christian theology of the *oyinbo* missionaries from the technological and industrial marvel presented to the world by England and other Western European countries.

In fact, many of Odumosu's friends turned to the East and saw the Moslem religion as an alternative to Christianity, which they equated with colonialism and the odious doctrine of racial superiority. In an article published in the *Lagos Weekly News*, Edward Wilmot Blyden, a Liberian who was born in the West Indies, argued that Islam was a more natural fit for Yorubas and other African people.

Some of Odumosu's other friends even advocated a wholesale return to the Ifa religion and the worship of the old Yoruba gods.

But what everyone agreed on was that it would be healthier if their people did not imbibe every aspect of the European culture presented to them by their *Gesi* schoolteachers and priests.

Odumosu and his friends made these points as they debated in one of the progressive, intellectual clubs that had now sprung up all over the island,

"We Yorubas, especially in Lagos, need to keep the wholesome aspects of our ancient culture, including courtesy and diplomacy, and respect for elders. "And we need to be united as a people."

Odumosu spoke these words to his fellow members at a meeting of the Lagos Mutual Improvement Society, of which he was treasurer.

"One nation for all Yoruba people, as in the old Oyo Empire. And down with the Colony!" Yakubu Grillo, one of the more radical young men at the meeting, shouted.

The meeting of the society took place in Ita Faji, in the upstairs parlor of one of their rich sponsors, the publisher Richard Beale Blaize. The voice of Grillo, the young man, was so loud that Odumosu feared his words could be heard through the open window by passersby on the street below.

Grillo was one of those radicals who refused to stand up at the singing of "God Save the Queen."

"Nihilists," the older men called him and his group.

"But can we ever again be united as one people?" Odumosu asked no one in particular. He knew that this question could not be answered by anyone present at that meeting.

Odumosu recognized that the time of troubles was not over for the Yoruba people beyond the coast and everywhere else outside the Colony of Lagos.

At that very moment, a bloody internecine war that fueled the terrible evil of slavery, which he and the other abolitionists abhorred, raged in the heart of Yorubaland. But men like him hoped for an era of peace and enlightenment throughout Yorubaland that would replace their century of darkness, slavery, and strife.

When the meeting ended, Odumosu came out into the street into a pouring rain. He stepped carefully, trying to avoid the stagnant puddles. He grimaced as he thought of the mud that would cover his highly polished black shoes by the time he got home. He tried to maintain his dignity, and dry state, under a broad black umbrella which he held tightly in one hand.

A passerby hurried past, clutching his own black umbrella. He made to avoid Odumosu. But he looked up and, despite the heavy rain, recognized the philanthropist and abolitionist. Raising one hand in a gesture of respect, the man saluted Odumosu, using his nickname, "Omo Eko,"

Despite one hand clutching his own umbrella, Odumosu removed his hat with the other hand. He dipped his head slightly in the direction of his greeter and said in Yoruba, "O se. Maa gbadun." *Thank you. Enjoy yourself.*

Indeed, everyone he met cherished Odumosu's humility, friendliness, and good humor. His selflessness in behalf of great causes was well known. He was the symbol and epitome of the surprising story of their island, the new city of the Yorubas by the sea.

A veritable denizen of Lagos, he was their Omo Eko.

CHAPTER 3

Arakunrin yi ja ogun ni Oshogbo,
lati rà ọlá awọn eniyan rẹ pada.
Jagunjagun ni lati Ile-Ife.
Iyawo re, Aarin
jẹ omo jagunjagun ilu Ibadan;
Eyi ni idi ti o fi dimo oko re
lori esin ti a npe ni Jagun.
Bayi ni wọn se gun esin yi
lati Ibadan de Ikenne,
ilu eti odo Uren.

He fought at Oshogbo,
to redeem his people's honor,
a warrior from ancient Ile-Ife.
She was a war captain's daughter
from brash new Ibadan.
But a tragic fate pursued them,
And so it was that she clung
to her newlywed husband,
And on the brave steed Jagun
they rode through the night,
to succor in Ikenne,
beside the sacred river Uren.

The Warrior from Ife

AFTER THE FALL of old Oyo, the city of Ile-Ife tried to reclaim its exalted status among Yoruba city-states. But it did not have the military force to back its ancient standing. It was at this time that the city of Ibadan came on the scene.

Ibadan, located on the southern edge of the savannah, was established as a war camp around 1929 by displaced soldiers who had fled the debacle of the fall of Oyo, their ancestral home and capital of the ancient empire of their people. These warriors were joined by refugees and adventurers. Soon, this settlement became a fortified garrison town manned by the most accomplished warlords and warriors of Yorubaland.

Ibadan was the place where intrepid warlords and their war boys now engaged in stirring battles to defend Yorubaland against the marauding Fulanis. For after destroying the ancient Oyo capital, the emir of Ilorin enjoined his men to invade and put to waste the rest of Yorubaland.

Thus it was that this new town of Ibadan assumed the role of protecting other Yoruba towns from conquest by the Fulani army from Ilorin. Ibadan became the new city of heroes.

*   *   *   *   *

In the year 1829, four years after Odumosu arrived in Lagos after being rescued from slavery, the boy Solaru was born in the Iremo quarters of Ile-Ife. His parents were Osolarin and Osoyemi. They both came from distinguished families of Ile-Ife. His uncle was the great Osogbesan, Afonja's former aide-de-camp.

According to the story handed down to us from the Old Woman, Solaru's two parents perished during the *shopona* epidemic that swept through Ile-Ife in the year of his birth. It was Osogbesan's beloved wife, Tiwalewa, who breastfed Solaru after the death of his parents, thereby ensuring his survival. His uncle and aunt later adopted him after their own son died after being thrown from a horse.

A child born in an age of conflict, Solaru grew up with a mind infested by the spirit of war. As soon as he was old enough, he wanted to leave home to seek warlike adventures that would win him laurels and glorify his family name.

Solaru listened to all the war stories told by his uncle, Osogbesan, a former *eso* of the Oyo Empire. His favorite stories were about his great-grandfather Osolemisi, who, a hundred years earlier, had defeated an army of the great empire of the Asante at a place called Atakpame. Solaru wanted to be a hero like his famous ancestor.

Osogbesan told the boy many stories of old Oyo. Solaru mourned the two kings Oluewu and Eleduwe, who fell in that last battle before the walls of Ilorin. Sorrow filled his heart any time he remembered the abandoned capital city of the great empire of his people. And he longed for war for the redemption of his people.

As he looked around him, Solaru could see that the glory of Oyo, the pride of his ancient Yoruba people was no more. And his native town of Ile-Ife was a supine shadow of its former self. But as he looked southward, he saw in the new military stronghold of Ibadan a place where a young man could pursue his dream of military glory.

He listened attentively, therefore, as Osogbesan told him stories about Ibadan.

"The town of Ibadan was called Eba Odan by its early settlers because it lay in an area bounded on one side by the forest and on the other by rolling grassland," Osogbesan explained.

"With time, this name was contracted to Ibadan."

According to Osogbesan, Ibadan remained a city of warlords, men renowned as much for their quirky personalities as their outstanding military valor. In particular, Solaru loved to hear the story of Lagelu, the founder of Ibadan.

"Lagelu was already one of the greatest warriors of his generation before he established the war camp of displaced soldiers at Eba Odan. He was born here in Ile-Ife. He is a kinsman of your aunt, Tiwalewa," Osogbesan told Solaru.

"His nickname was 'Oro a pata maja'," he added.

Osogbesan told Solaru the story of how Lagelu and his men were once forced out of the settlement when they were attacked by a strong band of renegade soldiers from Oyo.

"The excuse for this war was that in a dispute in the market, an *egungun* from Oyo had been inadvertently disrobed and his face exposed to public view by men from Ibadan.

"Lagelu and his men took temporary refuge in the hills surrounding the town. In their hideout, they survived on *oro*, lime, *igbin*, snails, and *eko*, a gruel made from cornmeal. This is the origin of their *oriki*, which says 'Ibadan omo a j'oro sun.' *Ibadan, the people who eat lime for supper.*"

These stories of Lagelu and those who came after him, related by the old warrior Osogbesan to his adopted son, had become part of the contemporary legend of the Yoruba people, especially in the heartland in places like Ile-Ife. Solaru soaked up these stories of the founding fathers of Ibadan like a sponge.

"After Lagelu died, the leadership of Ibadan fell on the shoulders of a man called Maye. Then came Oluyedun, who styled himself Aare Ona Kakanfo, although everyone knew that this old honor no longer held its former prestige or power. He was followed by Lakanle. After Lakanle came Oluyole, who is the current leader of Ibadan."

According to Osogbesan, Oluyole's mother, Agbonrin, was a daughter of the great Alaafin Abiodun. Thus, Oluyole had always been very conscious of his noble pedigree. So when he was chosen as leader of Ibadan, he did not want to be a mere Baale, a title he considered pedestrian. It was an affront, he said, to his image as a warrior and grandson of a famous Alaafin.

"Oluyole wanted nothing less than the position of Bashorun. And he got his wish. For this ancient title was bestowed on him by the new Alaafin recently installed in the new capital of Ago d'Oyo."

Osogbesan explained that this Alaafin was an old comrade of Oluyole.

"His name is Atiba and he is a prince of old Oyo. He is a son of Alaafin Abiodun by one of his younger wives. After the old man died, it was said that his wives were treated badly by the king who succeeded him. This was Alaafin Aole," continued Osogbesan.

"Atiba's mother therefore left Oyo. She took her young son to her hometown of Akeitan. When Atiba grew up in Akeitan, he became close friends with the Oja family, who ruled the nearby village of Ago. Ago, at that time, was known as Ago-Oja in honor of its founder, the warrior Oja."

Osogbesan told Solaru that this Oja was the elder brother of Elebu, who was treacherously killed while he clung to the branches of a *gbinigin* tree beside the Ogun River during the Gboko campaign. This was on the day the Ilorin cavalry was routed by a combined Bariba and Oyo army under Eleduwe.

"During that conflict, Oja's family had allied with Ilorin. Prince Atiba, who also lived in Ago-Oja at the time, went along with his friends Oja and Elebu to that war. But he was saved from perishing in the river Ogun by his uncle Yesufu, who carried him across the swollen river on his own horse."

Solaru was intrigued. "Why did Atiba, a prince of Oyo, fight on the side of Ilorin against his own emperor, Alaafin Oluewu?" he asked.

Osogbesan's answer came readily.

"Atiba had spent many years as a young prince in Ilorin under the protection of the Kakanfo, Afonja. He therefore had a warm relationship with the sons of the Yoruba chieftains who controlled Ilorin at that time. This was why he fought beside the Ilorin war captains who were the friends of his youth. They were all Yoruba, not Fulani."

Osogbesan continued the story.

"And as I can remember, Prince Atiba had a falling-out with Alaafin Oluewu before the Gboko campaign. It was said that he was publicly insulted by Eleduwe, king of the Baribas, who, though brave, was haughty and condescending. So Atiba and the Alaafin were not the best of friends. Thus, Atiba could not resist his chance to humiliate Oluewu by joining forces with Ilorin."

Osogbesan then told Solaru that after the deaths of Oja and his brother, Elebu, their family's line of succession to the leadership of Ago-Oja came to an end. It was then that Atiba saw his chance. He made himself leader of their small farming community of Ago. Though Atiba was not born in the town, his pedigree as the son of an Alaafin gave him prestige in the eyes of the people of Ago. They welcomed him as their new leader.

"The people of Ago were rewarded for their choice. Not only did Prince Atiba adopt Ago as his hometown, but he also wanted Ago to be the new capital of a reconstituted Oyo Empire.

"But Ago-Oja was very small. It was little more than a hamlet. To make it the befitting capital of his new empire, Atiba compelled hundreds of the inhabitants of many of the surrounding towns and villages to leave their homes to move into Ago.

"He also convinced many of the old Oyo nobility and priesthood, who had fled to towns like Kishi and Igboho, to join him in Ago-Oja."

After this, it was not difficult for Prince Atiba to convince the Oyo Mesi to declare him the new Alaafin.

"I knew Prince Atiba then. He was passionate in his mission to revive the glory of Oyo. And within a short time, he had succeeded in turning Ago-Oja into a fair-sized town. People began to refer to his new capital as Ago d'Oyo—*Ago becomes Oyo*. Later, we all called it Oyo-Atiba, in honor of the new Alaafin."

When Solaru repeated Sogbesan's stories to his friends, he said to them, "Bashorun Oluyole is going to restore our lost heritage as Yorubas. We as young men have to go to Ibadan to help him fight the Ilorins."

Solaru told his friends many other stories about Oluyole that he learned from his uncle Osogbesan. He told them that Oluyole, despite his earlier falling-out with Alaafin Oluewu, was one of the Oyo princes who fought valiantly with the Oluewu in that last battle against Ilorin.

He also told his friends about Oluyole's distinguished lineage. Apart from his mother being a daughter of the famed Alaafin Abiodun, Oluyole's father was an Oyo war commander who fought under Alaafin Majotu.

But Solaru's "*baba*," Osogbesan, was not keen about his protégé's desire to go to Ibadan to fight under Oluyole or any other warlord. He did not like the stories of depredations and atrocities that now came to his ears regarding Ibadan war captains. Osogbesan thought many of the new leaders in Ibadan were uncouth. They were ill prepared to be the new leaders of the Yorubas.

He told Solaru, "These men lack the upbringing that come from tutelage by palace tutors, priests, and eunuchs that, for ages, gave members of the old Oyo nobility their refined manners and sense of honor."

According to Osogbesan, the warlords in Ibadan used their power to pillage and burn indiscriminately in the name of war. They fought their incessant battles, not to make Yorubaland safe, he said, but to become rich from the capture and sale of slaves.

Osogbesan gave Solaru the recent example of the town of Abemo, whose leader, Ayo, ran afoul of Kurunmi, a friend of Oluyole and leader of nearby Ijaiye.

Kurunmi had taken sides with a man called Lahan, who was Ayo's rival for the leadership of Abemo. To help Lahan, who had lost control of the town to Ayo, Abemo was attacked by an army sent by Kurunmi and his friend Oluyole. It was a sad and heartless story that Osogbesan told.

"Men, women, and children of Abemo who managed to survive the assault on their town were captured and sold into slavery."

Thus, to Osogbesan, the assumption by Ibadan of the mantle of leadership of Yorubaland was a dark time indeed for our people. As he saw it, it was the latest chapter of the "igba inira" that had been set in motion by the curse of Aole.

Osogbesan did not want his adopted son to have anything to do with the warlords in Ibadan. But in the end, he relented as he confronted the realities of the time. He realized that he could not stop Solaru from going off to become a warrior.

Osogbesan had to admit that Solaru was skilled and brave. And he wanted to be a hero. After all, it was he, Osogbesan, an *eso* of Oyo, who had trained the young man in horsemanship and the art of war. Solaru would give a good account of himself. And if he survived, he would come back to Ile-Ife laden with glory and honors.

Thus, the day came when Osogbesan gave Solaru his blessing to go to Ibadan. Then he asked Solaru to break the news of his departure to his aunt.

When Solaru went in to see Tiwalewa, he realized with some shock that his aunt was now an old woman. The once erect and beautiful maiden of Ife was stooped and gray-haired. Her vision was poor, and she was hard of hearing. Her face was full of wrinkles that crisscrossed her dark skin like tanned leather. And her eyes, which alone retained some of the sparkle of youth, were tired and sad.

Tiwalewa knew she might never see her nephew and adopted son again. She hugged Solaru and held him close. And in tears, she whispered in his ears the ancient prayers and incantations that would vouchsafe his safety and survival.

* * * * *

The Ibadan in which Solaru arrived in 1840 was a heavily fortified war camp despite its pretensions of being a typical Yoruba city.

At first glance, the town appeared to possess all the trappings of a Yoruba metropolis of that age. It had its priests, high chiefs, and the council of state that advised the ruler. It had its Oja Oba, the king's market, and the Iyalode, the most important woman in the town. But the ruler in Ibadan, unlike other towns of Yorubaland of that period, was not an oba or Baale. He was Bashorun Oluyole, who held both civil and military power in his hands.

After Bashorun Oluyole, next in power and influence in Ibadan was a man named Elepo, who, Solaru was told, was the greatest military tactician of his day. But for reasons of his own, Elepo had declined the title of Balogun. The Balogun title had therefore been given to Oderinlo, who held this title when Solaru arrived in Ibadan as a would-be military recruit. Lajumoke was the Otun Balogun while Opeagbe was the Osi Balogun.

Solaru was assigned to the cavalry force headed by Chief Ogunrenu, who as *sarumi* was commander of the mounted warriors. Solaru was delighted to learn that this Ogunrenu also hailed from Ile-Ife. In fact, Ogunrenu was a distant kinsman of his own late father, Osolarin, brother of Tiwalewa.

The first thing that surprised Solaru on entering Ibadan was that though the town had many city gates through which one entered and exited the city, the town walls were neither formidable nor well maintained. Solaru was aghast.

"How can this be the fortress city that would defend Yorubaland, if its own defenses are so shoddy?" Solaru asked, greatly perplexed.

As taught to him by his "baba," Osogbesan, the conventional wisdom of warfare was "breach the walls and take the city."

But his new Ibadan friends sat him down and explained the situation to him. "We can sneer at our enemies. For we have nothing to fear. We in Ibadan are the *idi ibon*, 'the butt of the gun.' We are the ones who fire at the enemy. Our foes do not have the power or audacity to fire back. Nobody would dare attack Ibadan.

"No enemy can come close to our city walls, not to talk about entering or sacking Ibadan."

"Ogun o ko wa ri. Awa ara Ibadan iseru enikankan. *War has never carried our city. We in Ibadan have never been slaves to anyone.*" They recited this parable of their famous town of warriors.

After this confident reassurance about the might of their city, Solaru slept better at night.

"Ko si babanla eni to to be—*Nobody dares attack Ibadan.*" Solaru would hear that bold statement many times in the coming months.

Solaru came to learn about this famous Ibadan panache and military ethos, which combined bravery in battle with an arrogant nonchalance. Before long, he became an *omo Ibadan* himself, and he too started to feel and act the same way.

He began to wear his *fila ode*, or hunter's cap, at a rakish angle with the top bent over his left eyebrow. He learned to carry himself with a swagger. He walked with his body tilted to one side with a panache copied from his friends, who were born and bred in Ibadan. And before many weeks had passed, even his speech pattern took on an Ibadan lilt.

But Solaru also learned that this Ibadan of Bashorun Oluyole could be a dangerous place for a young man. The narrow streets bristled with heavily armed warriors at every corner. Since all the young warriors, encamped in different locations all over the town, did not feel they were ready to go abroad if they did not have several weapons stashed on their bodies, quarrels led to fights. And these fights frequently led to bloodshed.

Before he went out, Solaru, therefore, made sure he had a large knife prominently tucked into a band around his waist. He also carried a sheathed short sword at his side. This was his *ida*, an adaptation of the saber, which he was trained to wield as a warrior on horseback.

Solaru soon showed Ogunrenu, his commander, that he was cut out to be a fine fighter on horseback. He was one of the best recruits that the seasoned commander would see in his career in Ibadan. The years of training under Osogbesan showed. It was clear to everyone that the young Solaru possessed a natural aptitude for war. His fearlessness and apparent disregard for danger marked him out as a born warrior. He soon earned the appellation *jagun-jagun*, or warrior.

When he first arrived in Ibadan, Solaru was called by his comrades Omo Ife. This was said in a half-joking, deprecating way. After all, people from Ile-Ife were not conspicuously known as fighters. But when Solaru began to distinguish himself as one of the best fighters among the young recruits, he became known as *jagunjagun omo Ile-Ife*—the warrior boy from Ife.

Much later, he was simply called "Jagun Ife." After this, everybody forgot his given name. His very close comrades, such as Ogunmola, called him "Jagun."

This Ogunmola was about the same age of Solaru. He was born in the town of Iwo, which was a short distance to the north of Ibadan.

Ogunmola was a heady, restless youth. Short in stature, he was stocky and strongly built. His strength was proverbial. He never backed down from a fight, and he fought everyone bigger than he was. He was the clear leader of his group of cavalry recruits.

Ogunmola took an immediate liking to Solaru, whom he called "Omo Ife." Solaru, in turned, called him "Omo Iwo." Ogunmola, however, insisted that everyone else call him "Bashorun." He told his friends that he would be Bashorun in Ibadan one day.

Ogunmola explained to Solaru that he had been the war boy of some of the most powerful commanders in Ibadan soon after he had arrived in town. Men like Ibikunle, Opeagbe, and Oluyole were his mentors and protectors. He had accompanied these older Ibadan warriors on many raids to capture slaves. He was well rewarded for these activities. He had a stash of bags of cowry shells stowed away in a secret hiding place. Ogunmola confided to Solaru that not only would he become a great warrior and be made Bashorun, but he would also be a very rich man.

Solaru and Ogunmola knew that they were young warriors in an Ibadan army that would soon be sent to war against Ilorin. They were all eager to prove their worth. They promised to kill many Fulanis in battle. They would cut off the beards of these *imales* and bring them back as souvenirs to Ibadan.

Irugbon ara Ilorin
la nlo ja fun.

It is to pull off the beard of Ilorin men
that we are going off to fight.

They sang this song with glee as they trained with the rest of the young recruits.

Ogunmola, though he was the same age as Solaru, was a seasoned fighter from his slave-raiding escapades. He ascended the ranks without difficulty.

Solaru, on the other hand, had to prove himself, especially since he was not from Ibadan. However, the many hours that his uncle, Osogbesan, had expended on his training served him well. And when his commander discovered that Solaru was very good with horses, he became one of his favorites.

*   *   *   *   *

It was at this time that Solaru met the maiden Aarin, who was the daughter of his commander, Ogunrenu.

One day, Solaru was sent to Ogunrenu's house with a message from the deputy, Ojokolu. Ogunrenu was not at home, but his daughter was. Solaru found himself delivering his message to a beautiful young teenage girl, who looked at him impudently and asked him what he wanted. The two young people were not far apart in age, and they fell to talking.

The girl asked one of her slaves to get Solaru a calabash of water to drink. She invited him into her father's spacious front parlor, where she gave him a low stool to sit on while she sat cross-legged before him on a mat spread on the hard-packed clay floor.

But Solaru preferred to stand, being the military recruit that he had trained to be in the previous few weeks. He was in his commander's house. And he was technically on duty since he had brought an official message for him.

Not wanting him to tower over her while she sat on the mat, the girl also got up from her sitting position. She now stood beside Solaru while she waited for him to deliver his message. And this was how Solaru, the young warrior from Ile-Ife, made the acquaintance of the daughter of his commander, Ogunrenu, and fell deeply in love for the first time in his life.

From the moment she opened her mouth to speak to him, Solaru was delighted that the girl did not effect the Ibadan dialect. Like him, she spoke the classic speech of Ile-Ife. And he noticed that she carried herself with a refinement that reminded him of the highborn royal princesses of Ile-Ife he frequently saw but had never the chance to speak to when occasion took him to the Ooni's palace in Ile-Ife.

For a girl of fifteen, the girl was tall. She was slim, light-boned, and very beautiful, more so than any maiden of Ibadan or Ile-Ife that Solaru had ever seen.

He noticed that her skin was dark, with a bluish hue that seemed to glow in the soft light that came through the open window of the front parlor, where they stood and talked. And when she moved her face toward the light from the open window, Solaru saw that her eyes were bright and expressive, with strange light-brown-colored irises that looked back at him with curiosity and a little amusement.

Solaru knew the stories of the descent of the people of Ile-Ife from Oduduwa. This, he knew, was the ancient progenitor of their race, who, it was said, came from a land far away in the East. He found himself staring at the girl's face for a long time. And as he did so, he thought of the Nubian ancestry he thought he detected in those light-colored eyes and delicate well-formed cheekbones.

When Solaru saw the daughter of his commander for the first time that afternoon, what he beheld at close quarters was the profile of a goddess. Inwardly, the young warrior bowed low at the shrine of a deity personified in the form of the beautiful maiden who stood before him.

And as he stood there, Solaru took in all the features of that remarkable face. On both cheeks were three thin vertical facial marks, which were delicately crafted and strangely attractive. Almost invisible until he looked very closely, the scars were so light that they were almost the same tone as the rest of her skin. Solaru knew that those three lines on each side of the girl's face were known among the Yoruba people as *pele*. They were very fashionable at that time among the highborn families of Ile-Ife.

Solaru himself had no marks on his cheeks. His parents had died before they could decide on which type of facial marks they would give him. And now he said to himself that he had never seen such a beautiful rendition of Yoruba facial marks on anyone in his life.

It soon became obvious to Solaru that the girl was conscious of his gaze. He was fascinated that she did not look away. With bold impudence, she stared back at him. And in doing so, she created a strange and uncommon interaction between the two young people. For in the culture of their people, girls at that age were taught to be shy.

Solaru did not mind. And he himself did not look away. Instead, he asked himself, "What does she think of me?"

Unperturbed, looking slightly amused, the girl peered back at Solaru. While appearing to be listening to his words, she had cunningly drawn him closer, daring him to be the first to look away.

And as Solaru continued to look deep into those strange light-brown eyes, he knew she wasn't just the deity at whose shrine he silently worshiped. His profane thought was: *This goddess is human—and could be possessed!*

He found that he wanted this young girl more than he had ever desired anything in his life. And he made up his mind there and then. This girl, whose name he could no longer remember, would be his wife. He would stay by her side and be with her forever.

Meanwhile, the girl, Aarin, not wishing to continue to stand facing the young man, insisted that Solaru take the stool while she sat on the mat beside him. And so Solaru sat down. But he found that though he was no longer looking directly into the eyes of the beautiful young maiden, his closeness to her made his heart beat fast. The longing and desire that came over him made him dizzy. But he managed to steady his thoughts.

His head cleared, and he found his tongue. And as soon as he had delivered the message for the sarumi, which the girl dutifully promised to forward to her father, Solaru did not waste time before he began to ask his own questions.

He asked again for the girl's name, though she had given it to him when he first came into the house. Then he boldly asked her if she was promised to someone. He knew that arranged marriages were common in Ile-Ife and Ibadan.

His disappointment was keen when Aarin told him that she had been promised to another man since she was a child. This was young Mufu, son of Chief Toki, the late *seriki* of Ibadan. His family were allies of Bashorun Oluyole. She told Solaru that he and Mufu were about the same age.

Confused and disappointed, Solaru could only mutter vague words and phrases that he hoped passed for conversation. His thoughts whirled and made him ever more confused and dizzy.

After a while, he said "O dabo" and made his exit.

*   *   *   *   *

Solaru spent the next few weeks in emotional turmoil. He was in love with a girl he had only seen once, and he knew he had to marry her. *But how would he accomplish this feat?*

Aarin was the aristocratic and very beautiful daughter of one of the most highly placed chieftains of Ibadan. Obviously, any suitor who would show his face at her father's door would need to have singular qualifications and accomplishments.

Solaru told himself he was highborn himself. After all, he was the nephew and descendant of *esos* of old Oyo. And he was kin to the Ooni of Ife. But he was in another man's town, he was an orphan, and he was penniless. But his instincts and self-confidence told him that the *orisas* of his clan were on his side. His *ori* clearly wanted great things for him, starting with betrothal and marriage to this strange beautiful girl.

And soon enough, Solaru had another chance to visit his commander's house when his group of young warriors was invited to the sarumi's compound to witness an animal sacrifice in honor of the god Ogun.

Later, Solaru would not remember the details of the rituals of that day. He could not pay attention. His mind was elsewhere, distracted by images of light-colored eyes, Nubian cheekbones, and long shapely limbs that were at that very moment quite close to him in another part of that compound.

But Aarin was nowhere in view. She was ensconced somewhere inside the house with the other womenfolk while the rituals to the god of war went on outside in the large front courtyard of the sarumi's residence.

The ceremony to propitiate the god Ogun required many animal sacrifices. A bull, then a dog was slaughtered. But the ceremony went by Solaru's eyes in a blur. The priest of Ogun was a sleepy old man with a sorrowful voice and slow movements. He almost put Solaru to sleep. But although Solaru paid little attention to the details of the ceremony in front of him, his mind was awake, fixed on the images of Aarin which flickered before him.

He made his plans craftily. He would not leave that house that day until he let Aarin know his feelings. He would boldly woo her. And despite her being promised to another young man, he would convince her father to let him, a poor orphan soldier from out of town, take her hand in marriage.

When the ceremony was over, Solaru managed to get away from his comrades. He slipped to the other side of the house close to a window of a large room, where he knew the women usually gathered to gossip. Peering in, his heart almost skipped a beat, for he saw the object of his emotions.

He caught Aarin's attention and, not speaking, beckoned to her to join him outside. There was no one around this side of the compound, and they would be alone.

Aarin herself did not need much bidding or convincing. She too, despite her outward haughtiness, was quite taken by this brash, but dashing young warrior. She had thought of him a lot since that fortuitous visit two weeks earlier when he had met her alone at home.

She had tried to find out as much as she could about him. She liked what she heard. Her father, Ogunrenu, liked him and spoke of him as one of the more promising of his new recruits.

Aarin got up, her heart beating fast. Not quite knowing what she planned to do, she gave some excuse to the women around her— something about some chore in the backyard. Soon, she found herself outside, standing before the young warrior from Ife.

She looked at him gravely, scanned his face carefully and gave him a slight inquiring smile. She was eager to hear him talk. Meanwhile, she would keep her own feelings in check while she heard him out. Her smile was the shield that would guard her own emotions.

Solaru knew this was his chance to convince her. It was now or never. He knew this might be the most important talk he would ever give in his life. But he had a lot of faith in himself. He knew he could not fail.

First, he looked at Aarin and tried to convey the earnestness of his feelings. Then in a low soft voice, he began to speak to her of his great love for her. Then the calmness deserted him, and his words came out in a torrent. As he spoke, his voice shook with passion and desire.

Aarin understood him clearly. His passion stirred something in her. And she was afraid that she might not be able to keep her feelings in check or manage the depth of her response to this bold declaration of love made to her face. For what she felt was a deep tenderness for this young man. It was an emotion that she had never felt for anyone in her life.

There was something else there too—a grown-up feeling, as if she was a mother and this young man was her child.

Aarin's mother had died when she was an infant. Even now, she could not make any sense of why she had lost a loving parent or where her mother had gone.

Was she now trying to act the part of the mother she never knew?

OLADELE OLUSANYA

Aarin felt as if she was a grown woman—and a mother. And like a mother, she wanted to care for this young man whom she hardly knew.

"A woman is like a mother to a man," a voice inside her whispered. And she understood.

With no sense of shame, she realized that she had completely forgotten Mufu, the young man to whom her father, in a foolish act of being beholden to an old comrade, had promised her.

At that moment, the intensity of her own feelings became clear to Aarin. She wanted this young warrior. And as these feelings came to her, she remembered her dreams.

Aarin had always had dreams since she was a child. Even though no one had ever explained them to her, she knew that her dreams connected her with the ancient wisdom of the gods of her people. She cherished this link every time she went to sleep next to the old woman, the nurse who slept next to her on her sleeping mat.

But she did not always have to be asleep to have those dreams and visions. Sometimes she would be sitting down at home or be engaged in some household chore when she would go still. A vision would pass before her eyes. Time speeded up. And the events of many years would pass before her in the blink of an eye.

In those dreams and visions, she had powers that belonged to someone else, in another time and another place. And she lived, in these dreams, in a quiet and peaceful land beside a slowly moving river, where the future was already past, and the past was yet to come. Her connection with that river was something she knew was old, as old as the time of her people in the land of *karo o jire*. She was a seer who had been given the gift to look forward and backward in time, and tell stories filled with knowledge and truth.

Now as she stood before Solaru, Aarin's eyes fogged over, and she had one of her visions. Only this time, she was no longer a child. She was a grown woman, a female with adult desires and skills that were no longer spiritual. Images of lust and passion came before her. She beheld scenes of sensual abandon that were shocking to her, a virgin fifteen years of age. And she saw that she was no longer alone in that beautiful valley beside the gently moving stream. She was with the young man who was standing in the real world right before her.

At first, she was a deity whom the young man had come to propitiate with sacrifices that he placed before her in a covered bowl. But then she became transformed into a sculptured figurine of the quintessential Yoruba maiden who knelt with a carved calabash at a holy shrine. And she knew that her sacrifice as that young maiden would be her body offered on the altar of that young man's passion.

The scenes changed. She and the young man now lived in a house together. He went out to hunt. He caught fish and tilled the soil. He brought back things for her. She cooked, washed, and took care of him. They were man and wife.

In one scene, she stood naked in front of him as the young man cupped his hands around her bosom and caressed her. She surrendered herself to his embrace as he gently laid her down and did things to her. And even though she had no experience of such things, she knew they were things a husband did to his wife.

Her vision went away, and Aarin found herself standing in front of the young man beside a wall in her father's compound. She looked at his face and listened to his voice, which came to her clearly as he continued to talk to her of his desire for her.

Aarin knew she was a child of the quiet, lovely place of her former dreams, where power was given to her to see ahead and into the past, and to tell the destiny of men. But she was also the woman with adult desires of her newer vision. She knew that standing before her was the young man in that vision who had done those things to her. And what was more, though those things had shocked her, she had wanted them.

Now as she stood before him, Aarin could feel Solaru's maleness reach out to her. It melted her resistance as her own female desire struggled to be let out. She wanted to be swept up by this young man and be held close to his body. She wanted him to cup her bosom in his hands, right there in the open, as they stood together in her father's compound, as he had done in the vision.

She knew now that Solaru was the man destined for her, not Mufu. He was the one who would take her away from her father's house to his own home. And henceforth, only two people would really matter in her world—she, the fifteen-year-old daughter of Ogunrenu, the *sarumi* of Ibadan, and this young man standing before her, the warrior from Ile-Ife. She *knew* that he would eclipse everything and everyone else in her life, even her beloved father.

Aarin moved closer to Solaru, and she could feel her skin tingle from the warmth that came from his body. His passion and her own desire came together. They coalesced into a fog that swirled before her, obscuring her vision. She could no longer see the young man, but she could feel his power. And she knew that her own face, as presented to him now, was the picture of a weak and helpless maiden submitting to a strong man. Her smile, which was her shield, was gone.

But then, despite the fog that blinded her and the certainty in her mind that this young man was the man destined for her, Aarin paused. A voice in her head had begun to ask questions.

Clamorous and insistent, the voice asked questions of her that she had no answers for.

"What do you know of men?" the voice asked.

"And what do you know of the acts carried on behind closed doors that make a couple man and wife?"

Aarin's thoughts crystallized. Suddenly, she was sane and rational, no longer fettered by unthinking desire. She realized that she and Solaru were little more than children. What did she know of him except that he was a young, and presumably brave, warrior in her father's cavalry unit? And that she had seen a vision of him in a daydream?

Not having a mother, the little that Aarin knew of the world was gleaned from observations of her own father and the limited knowledge imparted to her by the old woman who took care of her. This woman had been her mother's faithful slave when she was alive. When her mother died, she had taken over complete charge of her. Thus, Aarin had always been alone, isolated, and protected. She had never played secret childhood games with children her own age.

She realized she was only a girl and that she was still very young. There were many things she did not know. And through the fog that threatened to submerge her calm rationality and native common sense, the voice in her head now spoke to Aarin of her dead mother.

"What would your mother expect you to do?" the voice asked.

At this, Aarin felt her face and eyes begin to rise above the fog. Wilfully, she struggled against the sensual impulses that threatened to overcome her. And with a strength that she knew came from her dead mother, she pulled herself up until her head and upper body were completely above the fog.

She was determined now to be rational, proper, and decorous. She would be the daughter that her mother would be proud of. She would not allow an immature and girlish giddiness to overcome her resolve.

"Shame on you," she scolded her dark and selfish desire as it strove to push her head back into the fog. "I am going to do the right thing."

"I have my reputation to maintain," Aarin said to the dark phantom of her desire. She was the chaste unmarried daughter of a great chieftain of Ibadan. There was a proper way of doing these things according to the traditions of her people.

"My father is a respected war captain of Ibadan," she continued sharply, as her stubborn desire hovered around the borders of her consciousness, trying to force its will on her.

"And my mother was the daughter of a prince of Ile-Ife, descended from a long line of Oonis. I am not going to bring shame on myself, my family, and my parents."

With this, Aarin's head and body emerged completely above the fog, which now swirled futilely about her feet and ankles. She felt her emotions return to normal.

She held up her hand and asked the young man standing before her to stop talking.

In a calm voice that came from the mother she never knew, Aarin talked to Solaru earnestly and rationally. As she did so, her mother's voice became her voice. It spewed forth a wisdom that was beyond her own power and reasoning. As it spoke, the voice was stern and unemotional, though Aarin could not completely hide the softness and tenderness that came from her own part of it.

As she spoke, she reminded Solaru that they hardly knew each other.

But the young man simply pressed on with his plaint. Now even more urgently, he promised that he was going to marry her. He would take her back to their ancestral hometown of Ile-Ife, away from uncouth and uncivilized Ibadan.

"How are you going to do this?" she asked him coyly.

Her confident smile had returned. The height of her passion had passed. The fog had cleared.

"You know that my father has already promised me to Mufu, the son of his dear friend, the late seriki Chief Toki," she added.

Solaru had no reply to this. What he felt was a pang of distress and a heightened ache of desire for her. He said something that she could not catch. On an impulse, she reached out and touched his face. As her soft fingers lingered on his cheek, she heard him sigh.

No words passed her lips, but it was a touch that said "Next time we meet, I will be yours. And it will be with the blessing and sanction of my father."

Aarin felt the young man's body stir. The muscles of his face came alive and vibrated to her touch. Somewhere in his temple, her finger felt a throbbing, which she knew came from the rapid beating of his heart.

She knew she could not trust her own heart not to start beating fast too. And she did not want the fog of desire to return.

She withdrew her hand before he could attempt to hold her or tempt her further. And as swiftly as she had come, she left him standing there by a wall in her father's compound, and she was gone.

Over the next few weeks, Solaru was disconsolate. Outwardly, he practiced his military exercises and took part in war games with his companions. Many of his fellow recruits remarked that he had become even more hard, more tenacious, showing the traits of a true warrior. But his very close friends like Ogunmola noticed that he was quieter and more introspective. He no longer joined or laughed at their bawdy jokes and crude youthful camaraderie.

Solaru's every waking thought was of the girl Aarin. Now even more determined, he worked on his plans to win over her father and make him change his mind regarding the choice of a son-in-law.

For in his heart, Solaru *knew* that the gods had fated Aarin and him to be together.

*   *   *   *   *

It was at this time that news reached the military command in Ibadan that a large force from Ilorin had attacked the town of Osogbo, which was an ally of Ibadan.

Osogbo was an ancient town of the Yorubas, which had long been one of the important city-states of the Oyo Empire. Its king, the Ataoja, was descended from one of the grandsons of Oduduwa. The town was famous for the shrine of the goddess Osun on the banks of the river of the same name, which flowed close to the town. Legend had it that this was the very place where Osun, wife of Sango, had achieved her apotheosis, transforming herself into the goddess of the river.

The Ataoja—threatened by the overthrow of his town walls and the enslavement of his people by the Fulani army from Ilorin—sent a powerful embassy to Ibadan asking Bashorun Oluyole to send an armed contingent to relieve the siege with which, at that moment, the Ilorins had invested his ancient town.

Thus it was that within a few months of arriving at Ibadan and just three weeks after he met Aarin, Solaru, the young warrior from Ife, found himself marching with his fellow newly conscripted warriors to Osogbo to fight the Ilorin invaders.

His eyes shone with excitement, and his heart beat loudly in his chest as he marched out of the Ibadan city gates. His good friend Ogunmola was by his side.

The two comrades talked lightly of pulling the beards of devout *imale*, which was what they called the Fulani Moslems who now controlled the old Yoruba frontier outpost of Ilorin.

"If the *imales* from Ilorin are foolish enough to invade a town that is a friend of Ibadan, then they deserve what is coming to them," said Ogunmola. He was a firm believer in the superiority of Ibadan over any force on the face of the earth.

"Surely," he continued, "these Fulanis from Ilorin must be rather dumb. Hadn't they heard that no one can bother Ibadan or its friends without paying a price for his insolence?"

But although Solaru and his friend Ogunmola had volunteered for the cavalry, there were very few horses to go around. And the few that were there had been apportioned to the captains, commanders, and their personal contingents. Solaru and Ogunmola, therefore, found themselves marching off to their first battle in a cavalry unit as lowly foot soldiers.

The march from Ibadan to Osogbo took the Ibadan contingent through the towns of Iwo and Ede. They passed abandoned farms and empty villages from which the inhabitants had fled on the first rumors of the approach of the Fulani invader.

After they crossed the Oha stream, a tributary of the Osun, they found themselves in a land of lush green vegetation and giant *iroko* trees with vines and creepers that snaked around their trunks like the intricately woven braids of a new bride.

They did not enter the town of Osogbo itself. That ancient town dedicated to the goddess Osun was barricaded on all sides, its walls manned by ancient warriors with fearful eyes. All the young men were outside the city walls, armed with whatever weapons they could find to face the Fulani, who were encamped within shouting distance of the defenders.

For the defenders and their allies, the odds for success were slim. Everyone knew that the Ilorin army was the better trained. The Fulanis had superior forces in foot soldiers. They also had a mounted cavalry, of which the Osogbo defenders had none.

To prove their point, carefully and methodically over the previous few weeks, the Ilorin invaders had tightened their siege around the city like the stranglehold of a great wrestler matched against a weak and inferior opponent.

To get into their positions as defenders of the threatened city, the Ibadan men had to fight their way through a line of Ilorin foot soldiers. When at last they arrived at the barricades thrown up around the positions of the Osogbo men, after having lost three men in the skirmish, the Ibadan commander held a hasty conference with the Osogbo chieftains. The result of this council of war was that Solaru and the others found themselves deployed behind the northern and eastern barricades, where they faced Fulani horsemen whose vague forms and movements they could discern in the waning evening light.

It was then that their commander told them the portentous news from the intelligence gathered by the Osogbo spies. Solaru and the other Ibadan men were surprised but not alarmed to learn that that the Fulanis were expected to launch a great cavalry attack the very next day.

How appropriate, they said to themselves with characteristic Ibadan insouciance, that they had arrived in time to take part in the great battle that had been expected since the Ilorin army had arrived to lay siege to the city of Osogbo nearly a month before.

On this eve of the battle, which thrust itself on the new arrivals like an ill-opportune guest, Solaru and the other men from Ibadan gathered in the great tent of their commander, Ogunrenu. They would be fortified with one last harangue as they prepared for that fateful dawn.

They had no time to rest or stretch their legs after their tiring march from Ibadan. They knew that all of them would see the sun rise the next day, but many would not see it set. This thought focused the minds of these men and boys. Their physical weariness disappeared like a mild irritation that dared not show itself in the presence of a great malady that was laying waste the body of a strong man.

Several of the men brought out their fetishes—gourds, ostrich's feathers, amulets, and *ados* secured around waists and arms. The brave talk of war and glory during the march to Osogbo now turned to sober thoughts of death. The older ones among the men talked about the mysteries of war and dying.

What happened to a warrior if he fell in battle? What lay on the other side of that mythical river betwixt the land of the living and the dead?

If any of them died, would he be taken up to the sky to the abode of the gods to be with Ogun, the god of war? What exactly took place in the afterlife?

Those who loved a good life imagined a place where they would drink palm wine with their old comrades and tell stories of ancient battles at the feet of Ogun all day long.

Would there be women there?

One of the old warriors explained that there was no day or night in *orun*, heaven.

Solaru found that, surprisingly, he was not afraid of the coming battle. He too had become philosophical. It was as if nothing could be more normal than for a group of young men to be talking casually about the possibility of their own death.

"How can we know where we are going after this life when we do not really know where we came from? Many of you talk of life after death. For myself, I believe in life *before* death." Solaru found himself making this statement aloud, made bold by the gravity of the moment.

"I will survive tomorrow," he added with youthful finality.

No one said anything. But they all looked with surprise at the young man. Solaru continued his soliloquy. He went on talking, as if to himself. It was as if he did not know or care that there were other men in that place who could hear him talk and comment on his views.

"And I will marry my *ololufe* Aarin when we return to Ibadan. I will have many sons. And I will grow old to become a great chief."

Solaru stopped and looked around. He was surprised at himself. He had made this declaration more to reassure himself than to join in the discussions of the other men, most of whom were much older than him.

His close friends, who were also there at the meeting in their commander's tent, knew Solaru as a young man of few words. They were astonished at the depth of feeling that had come out of the mouth of their comrade. Solaru was the only one who knew that what he had said aloud was something he had not really thought about until that moment. It had come out of him spontaneously and unbidden.

Solaru told himself that this was the moment of truth. The outcome of the battle the next day would be either of two things. It was either he came back to the Ibadan camp on his feet, or he was carried off the battlefield on his back, feet-first, a corpse. And he knew clearly what his choice was. Heaven, the home of the gods, may be the place for dead heroes. But he, Solaru, loved this life. He wanted to live. He wanted to go back to Aarin.

Solaru's commander, Ogunrenu, now made a speech. When he spoke, his voice was loud and bold. But his talk was neither boastful nor jingoistic. It was not a wishful or philosophical rambling. There was nothing in his speech about heaven or gods or martyrdom. It was simply a reasonable and rational appeal to the patriotism of the men.

Hearing Ogunrenu speak, Solaru was reminded of his "baba," Osogbesan. He almost forgot that this man was the father of the girl he loved, his future father-in-law. That night, Ogunrenu was simply the war captain who tried to inspire his warriors. He spoke on behalf of their commander in chief, the great Bashorun Oluyole.

Solaru listened intently as Ogunrenu told the men that the survival not only of Ibadan but of the entire Yoruba people lay in their hands.

"Shitta, the emir in Ilorin, on instructions from the Fulani king, the sultan of Sokoto, had boasted that the aim of their campaign in invading the lands of us Yorubas is not simply to capture or destroy Osogbo.

"The Fulani army intends to go on from here to raze Ibadan to the ground as they did old Oyo. If their wish is granted, they would dishonor our wives and daughters and sell our sons into slavery.

"Then they would go on to capture all the other Yoruba towns from the country of the Egbas and Ijebus all the way to the coast of great Okun in the land of the Ilajes and Aworis.

"They have promised, if we do not stop them, to dip their holy book into the sea."

The men hissed. The universal outrage was palpable in that large dimly lit tent of their commander.

"Not if we can help it!" Ogunrenu said at last. His voice was a hoarse shout.

Then all the men, including Solaru, pulled off their caps and shouted in response, "O ti o. Nile yi ko!"

"No," they said to one another, "not in our land!"

* * * * *

The battle of Osogbo the next day was, for the young Solaru, the defining event of his life.

The Ibadan auxiliaries under Chief Oderinlo, the Balogun, had drawn up their forces for the defense of Osogbo so that they were placed to the south of the embankment that separated the two armies. Solaru noticed that this battleground, located in the farmlands just outside the town of Osogbo, was a country of dense bush, small trees, and shallow streams. The ground was muddy from a recent rain.

That night before the battle, the countryside all around the quiet and nervous men seemed peaceful, calm and ordinary. But Solaru knew it was a deceitful prelude to the death and destruction that the older warriors assured him the next day would bring.

The men from Ibadan went to their battle positions. Each man was given orders by his captain to choose a place where he would stay on alert throughout the night before the order for battle was given at dawn. There would be no sleep for anyone.

Solaru found that the two enemy camps were so near that he could hear the preparations in the Ilorin camp. He could even discern the enemy warriors' speech patterns. He was able to recognize and distinguish the few Yoruba phrases from the sonorous Hausa and Arabic accents of the Fulani commanders as they gave their men their last instructions.

Solaru listened to the neighs of the Fulani horses with some trepidation. He wondered what he would do if an Arab stallion galloped at him the next day, seeking to trample him underfoot. Though he was trained as a cavalryman, he had been given no mount. In this battle, he was a foot soldier, at the mercy of the sabers of the mounted Fulani and the hooves of their horses.

Solaru shuddered. But he said to himself, "We are better trained than those ignorant *imales*. And our commander, the sarumi, is more experienced than any indolent Fulani prince."

And so it proved to be.

When the orders were given and the battle was joined the next morning, Solaru and the defending Ibadan auxiliaries stood their ground in the face of charge after charge by the Ilorin cavalry.

The Fulani horses were hampered by the unfamiliar forest terrain. Their riders could not wheel and maneuver as they were used to, and they could not use their lances to much effect. The hooves of their horses got trapped in the undergrowth or were stuck in the marshy ground.

Trapped in that great maelstrom of blood and mud that was played out in the Osun river valley on the outskirts of Osogbo in the year 1840, the great Fulani army lost many men and horses to the arrows of the Ibadan archers stationed on the high ground overlying the valley in which the battle raged below. Yet on the Ibadan side, the casualties were light.

The Osogbo foot soldiers and their Ibadan allies kept themselves hidden. They crouched behind the bushes, from where they made sudden deadly sorties with arrows and swords aimed at the bewildered Fulani horsemen. They shot horses down from under their turbaned riders and hacked men to death as they fell.

Within a few hours, it became clear to both sides that the tide of battle was in favor of Ibadan and their Osogbo hosts.

The Ibadan commander in chief, Balogun Oderinlo, now gave the order for a massive counterattack. Drumbeats took up the signal, and the men responded with a great roar.

"Ibadan, Oyo, Bashorun, Alaafin!" the Ibadan men shouted, giving their battle cry.

Solaru ran with his comrades as the foot soldiers around him leapt up, swords in hand, to dash across no-man's land, which separated them from the dreaded Fulani cavalry. They attacked the Ilorin positions across this open space as Ibadan archers, stationed in the hills above them, kept up a deadly volley aimed at the opposing Fulani. These bowmen rained down darts that kept the Fulani cavalry at bay while the Ibadan men and boys darted across the battle line. Many Fulani horsemen and their mounts fell under this relentless volley of arrows.

Solaru rushed forward, brandishing his *ada*. He soon found himself tangled in a mass of men and horses. At first, he found it difficult to distinguish friend from foe. But he found out that many of the Fulanis wore long turbans. By these, Solaru was able to tell whom he should strike at.

Hardly knowing where he got the strength, Solaru leapt up and dragged a Fulani cavalryman from his horse. He had seen that the horse was struggling in one spot, its legs stuck in the muddy marshy ground.

The fight was a blur. For Solaru, it was an out-of-body experience. Surely, it was not him, but someone else, who struggled in that life-or-death combat with an enemy who would kill him if he did not dispatch him first. All Solaru remembered was his foe's black turban, a bushy beard, and wild, frightened eyes that glared at him as the fallen rider struggled to disentangle himself from his horse and confront his attacker.

Solaru gave his foe no chance. His two arms held out in front of him like an implacable instrument of death, he plunged repeatedly with his sharp-pointed double-edged *ada* at the abdomen and chest of the prostrate Fulani until the man lay still. Then he turned swiftly round, seized the frightened horse by the reins, and pulled it to safety. The horse, captured in battle, was his.

Solaru did not attempt to mount the horse. He simply dodged all the weapons and missiles thrown at him. He maneuvered himself and the animal to the safety of a tree far from the maelstrom of the battle. There, he tied the horse up. Then crouching on his knees, he unslung his bow and sent arrow after arrow in the direction of any turbaned warrior he saw.

At the end of that fateful day, victory was claimed by Osogbo and its Ibadan allies. The siege of Osogbo was raised, and the vaunted Ilorin cavalry put to flight, never again to venture south into Yorubaland.

*   *   *   *   *

When the men in Solaru's company regrouped after the battle at the designated meeting place, they greeted one another with shouts of glee. But they mourned their dead and missing.

Everyone congratulated the young warrior Solaru on his capture of the magnificent beast. It was then that he was able to inspect the horse. It was an Arab stallion, jet-black in color, with a blaze of white on its forehead.

But now that he had survived his first battle, Solaru was full of conflicting emotions. He was happy to be alive. But he felt no elation at the thought of the man he had killed and whose horse he had taken.

He realized now that though he was a good soldier, he was not a born killer. He had no stomach for blood, or the glory achieved through the death of another human being, even if that person was a foe, an enemy of his country and people. He began to wonder how far he would make it as a warrior if his sensibilities were so fine. He should be rejoicing like his comrades around him, but he was sad.

The battle was winding down. Solaru could hear the groans of wounded men and the loud protests of prisoners who were being fettered and otherwise ill-treated. It all seemed so unreal, not quite what he had thought war would be.

Through the dust, sand, and blood that smeared his face and tainted his vision, Solaru tried to assert control over his reasoning and his emotions. He tried to lift his tired and confused spirit above the disillusionment that threatened to overwhelm him. He knew he would need to ground himself in reality in order to preserve his sanity. To do this, he would need to envision and plan the future that awaited him when he returned to Ibadan.

He had survived his first battle. He had killed an enemy. He was a hero. Now he could go home. He could go back to Ibadan to claim the beautiful Aarin as his bride.

"This is no more than my due," Solaru said to himself.

He and his fellow warriors had turned the tide of the conflict with Ilorin. They had prevented the proud Fulani from marching through Yorubaland to "dip the Koran in the sea," as their commander had said they would if they were not stopped.

He, Solaru, *Jagun Jagun lati Ile-Ife*, was a valiant warrior in the great vanguard army of the Yoruba people. He would bask in his moment of glory and claim the spoils of war and honors due to a hero returning home.

Surely, he told himself, he was no less deserving than others of the prize he sought—the hand of the beautiful daughter of the *seriki* of Ibadan. He was a youth with promise in the new dispensation that would be ushered in by this victory. He should be as well favored in this regard as the sons of the *baloguns* and *sarumis* of Ibadan. His pedigree was just as impeccable as theirs. For was he not born in Ile-Ife, the cradle of his race? And was he not a descendant of *esos* of Oyo?

He had proved by his valor that he was brave and victorious in war. The two hundred *orisas* of Ile-Ife would ensure that he was lucky in love.

*　　*　　*　　*　　*

A week later, the victorious Ibadan contingent—under their Balogun, Oderinlo—returned to Ibadan.

Solaru rode into town on his warhorse, which he had named "Jagun." This was a play on his own nickname, *Jagun Jagun Ife*. He was a good horseman due to his training under Osogbesan. It did not take him long to make the horse trust him.

Apart from this warhorse, the only war booty that Solaru brought with him from the battlefield at Osogbo was a strange musical instrument that someone had abandoned in the Ilorin camp.

Rummaging with his comrades in a tent of the enemy the morning after the battle, they had found it under a pile of arrows. And Solaru had claimed it as his war prize. It was a *goje*. This was the name it was called in Hausa. The Yorubas had no other name for it.

Solaru found that this goje was little more than a sound box. It had thin wires strung from one end to the other, which gave different pitches of sound when he plucked them. He knew that the goje was used to give rhythm and melody to the percussion beats of drums, but he did not know how to play this instrument, which was unknown in his native Ile-Ife. But he was sure he would learn.

Solaru was glad that Aarin would see him ride into town like this—a mounted warrior and a hero. Her hand in marriage would be his real prize of war. Aarin had told him that her full name was Aarin-ni-imo, which meant "in the middle lies wisdom." To Solaru, Aarin's name was a message. He would seek the middle ground in his pursuit of his life with her as his wife. They would live a life of humility and quiet moderation.

Solaru knew that his prospects, regarding his bid to claim Aarin as his bride, had improved considerably. He was now a war hero. He would boldly confront Aarin's father—his commander, Ogunrenu—with a declaration of love for his daughter, and ask for her hand in marriage. He would marry Aarin and take her back to Ile-Ife to live with him.

He planned his strategy and followed it carefully. First, he sent to his "baba," Osogbesan, in Ile-Ife. He knew that Osogbesan's wife—his aunt, Tiwalewa—was kin to Ogunrenu. Then he asked courteously for permission to speak with the sarumi himself. But he did so only after Osogbesan had sent his own delegation from Ile-Ife with suitable presents to his future in-law.

After this, Solaru occupied his mind with the formulation of clever ruses that allowed him to visit his commander's house and speak to Aarin at every opportunity. Since Aarin's mother was dead, the old woman, the nurse of her infant years, was her guardian and constant chaperone.

This woman was a former slave who had taken care of Aarin since she was an infant. She had nursed Aarin as a baby with her own breasts after Aarin's mother died. Luckily, the old lady took a liking to Solaru and connived at the meetings and dallying of the two young people.

Aarin herself now spoke to her father. She was an only daughter, and her father doted on her. She told him, on her knees and with tears in her eyes, that she had never loved Mufu, the man promised to her.

Their arranged engagement had been a mistake, she declared flatly. She detested that young man, who she said was good for nothing. He was a drunkard and he kept bad company. He was not to be compared to Solaru, the warrior from Ife and hero who had won her heart.

"I would rather die than marry Mufu," Aarin said at last to her father. Her chin jutted out, and her eyes blazed with defiance. The light-colored irises glistened with tears.

Aarin's father was now forced to confront his own doubts about Mufu. And reluctantly, he admitted his error in judgment. He confessed that he too had become disappointed at the way Mufu had turned out.

"He was once a promising youth," Ogunrenu said sadly. "But after his father, Toki, the old seriki died, he fell on evil ways."

It was common knowledge all over town that Mufu spent his time in the company of disreputable young men who drank palm wine all day long when they were in town. And it was said that they lived a life of violence and thuggery when they were outside Ibadan.

Ogunrenu had heard people say that Mufu and his friends were involved in the business of catching and selling slaves. They never lifted their hands to defend their city. They played no part in the stirring battles fought by war leaders like him, Ogunrenu, and their compatriots to save Yorubaland from the threat of Fulani conquest and domination.

It was no easy thing for Ogunrenu, an upright man and a warrior, to admit his error. It was even harder for him to break his word and renounce Mufu's claim to his daughter. But once he made up his mind that this was the right thing to do, he went about it with a will.

Ogunrenu employed the services of the priestess of Olokun, who produced a credible oracle that Mufu was not fated to marry Aarin. In fact, the priestess declared that a great tragedy would follow such a union.

The betrothal between Aarin and Mufu was therefore annulled. In atonement, sacrifices were made to Orisanla and Olokun. A large number of presents were also sent as compensation to the head of the old seriki's family, who was Mufu's uncle. After this, Bashorun Oluyole himself was brought in to smoothen things over between the two families.

It was only then that Aarin was formally betrothed to Solaru and the day for their marriage rites fixed.

* * * * *

The day came at last. In a simple ceremony, Ogunrenu took his daughter's hand and gave it to Solaru. The bridal price—twelve baskets of yams, three drums of palm oil, and forty heads of cowries—had been brought from Ile-Ife. Solaru and his bride wore matching *alare* cloth woven in Iwo.

The traditional rituals of matrimony performed that day for Solaru and Aarin followed the old traditions of Yorubaland, harking back to a happier time before the fall of Oyo and the advent of the time of troubles.

The ceremony went like a dream for Solaru.

"Could this really be happening to me?" he asked himself. Could he, an orphan from Ile-Ife, truly be laying claim to the most sought-after maiden in Ibadan?

His aunt, Tiwalewa, was too ill to make the journey. But Solaru was pleased to see his "baba," Osogbesan, beam at him as he and Aarin drank a portion of fermented palm wine from an intricately carved calabash. Then he listened to a long blessing from the priestess of

Olokun, who predicted a long and happy union for the couple. They would be blessed with many children, she said, both male and female.

It had been agreed by both families that the bride would follow her husband to his hometown of Ile-Ife, which, in fact, was her own hometown too. In the meantime, the sarumi gave them a small house to live in Ibadan until they moved. Solaru was a warrior in the service of the Balogun of Ibadan, and he still had certain military obligations to fulfill.

Soon, the ceremony came to an end, and Solaru went to the house prepared for him and his bride. It was already dusk, and the tropical night was closing in. The house was dimly lit by an oil lamp. This was a hollow vessel of baked clay filled with distilled palm oil and a cotton wick, which was placed on a wooden stool in the front room.

Aarin, his bride, would be escorted here later. As he waited, Solaru longed for his bride with the now-familiar ache in his loins.

Soon, he told himself, Aarin would be with him. And they would be alone together for the first time in their lives. He would do with her what he had dreamt all these months, and the ache in his loins would at last go away.

Solaru's thoughts were a jumble of happiness, anticipation, and doubts. He felt joyful and fulfilled that he had won the mysterious and beautiful young woman he had promised himself the first time he saw her. But now that all his scheming and planning had borne fruit, he was nervous and fretful. The duties required of a man on the marital night scared him. He had to perform the final ritual of the *igbeyawo*, the taking of his bride's maidenhead.

"Am I up to it?" he asked himself.

Solesi *knew* what was expected of him. But would he be able to fulfill this manly role?

His mind turned in many directions, propelled by a dozen different thoughts. His confusion was fueled by his own ignorance and the mystery with which his people, the Yorubas, cloaked even the most mundane of human acts.

Solaru knew that men and women copulated before they had offspring. He had seen his horses do it. But he knew that what happened between a man and a woman on the marriage night went beyond that. It was not just a physical act. It was an emotional bonding that would make two strangers *oko* and *iyawo*. He knew he loved Aarin. But how was he to express his sacred love by profaning it with a coarse carnal act?

Of course, he was not totally ignorant. Once, in Ile-Ife, when he was just thirteen years old, a young girl the same age as he had allowed him to touch her under her short *iro*. But nothing further had happened. Solaru did not know what to do, even as the girl spread her legs, giggled, and edged him on.

What had saved him was that they had heard a noise, and both of them had scrambled to their feet. The girl hastily arranged her iro and stood up. It was the girl's mother, who had stumbled on them in the back of the hut.

Nothing close to this had happened to him after that. He had not succeeded in losing his innocence. To prepare himself for this night, Solaru had consulted Sule, an old Oyo cavalryman who had marched with him to Osogbo. Sule was married and had three wives. Therefore, Solesi surmised that he knew everything.

Sule tried to explain to Solaru the things he needed to know, leaving no details out. At the end, he also gave Solaru an aphrodisiac. This was a powdery substance in a small gourd with a stopper made out of compact sponge. As Sule explained to Solaru, this was to save his honor in case his manly strength failed him in the hour of need.

"Such things do happen," Sule said vaguely to Solaru. Then he gave him a sly wink.

Sule then proceeded to give Solaru arcane details of what he knew about a woman's anatomy, especially the areas that would concern her husband the most.

Female circumcision was practiced throughout Yorubaland in those days. But the practice was not standardized. It varied from town to town and from family to family. And it often depended on the whims and skills of the *olukola*. Sule explained to Solaru how some women were cut badly. And then they were not so good in the marriage bed.

Solaru knew that Sule could speak on this matter with some authority. Not only had he married three wives, but in his soldier's life, he had had his pleasure with scores of women in many lands—concubines, *ales*, and slaves—from Ogbomosho and Ikire to Offa. Sule's opinion, as he expressed it to the very attentive Solaru, was that the best women to enjoy were those whose parents had the good sense to leave them intact in that most important area.

As Solaru now waited for his bride, he remembered that he had almost died of longing as the nuptial ceremony went on earlier in the evening. He could not take his eyes off the beautiful form of the young woman beside him who would soon be his wife. The shape of the two mounds bulging through the *alare* iro, which was tied decorously above the breasts, tantalized him. His body twitched with anticipation and desire.

Meanwhile, the women of the household of Ogunrenu were engaged in the important ritual of accompanying the bride, Aarin, to her husband's house.

As they went along the narrow streets, wending their way slowly and ceremoniously, the women sang out joyfully to one another and to passersby.

"A nmu 'yawo re ile oko. We are taking the bride to her husband's house," they cried out from time to time.

Aarin's face was covered with a length of *aso ofi* in the form of a veil as they walked the short distance from her father's compound to the house prepared for the couple. Aarin knew she looked radiant, beautiful, and happy. But inside, she was going through her own questions and doubts.

Would the rejection of Mufu lead to recriminations or even an attempt of revenge by his friends and family?

What bad luck might come to her and Solaru from this former betrothal being cast aside?

And would there be another price to be paid by her family?

For how could this state of affairs, which was now known to every commoner and chieftain in Ibadan, not affect her father's position and influence in the councils of state? Her father, after all, belonged to the same high social circles where Mufu's late father had held sway not so long ago as the much-beloved seriki of Ibadan.

Would people not say that her family had done a dishonorable thing by breaking their word to Mufu and his family?

Aarin remembered that the current seriki was a kinsman of Chief Toki, Mufu's late father. He held seniority over her father in the ruling hierarchy in Ibadan. Her father was merely the sarumi, who traditionally was ranked below the seriki.

And on whose side were the Balogun and the Bashorun? How about the priests of the other deities and shrines? Everyone knew that worshippers of Olokun like her and her family were not popular in Ibadan. And what of the opinion of the townspeople and the gossip of the women?

This was the day of her marriage. It was a day she would remember till her dying day—the day she, a maiden, went to her husband's house to lose her virgin status forever. This should be the most important day of her young life. But her happiness was clouded by a sense of confusion and loss.

Would she be able to bear the loss of the old life she had led in her father's house? How about the happy innocence of her childhood, which would never come back?

She knew she loved Solaru. But she had a feeling that her love for him was ethereal and immeasurable. It belonged not here on earth, but high up in the clouds—in the realm of the gods. Could this kind of love ever be expressed or measured in simple physical terms?

All through the ceremony, while the priests and priestesses chanted prayers and her father pronounced his blessings on her, Aarin had felt she was not really there. She saw herself floating above the scene and peering down strangely at herself in her rich wedding clothes.

She had felt the same way earlier in the day when she was bathed and dressed by the women and servants of her father's household. They had put on her a rich and heavy woven cloth of *alare*. The *iro* was wound around her body and carefully tucked in above her breasts. Around her neck, they placed a necklace of red coral. Her hair was elaborately plaited and decorated with pieces of bronze, copper, and silver ornaments. These were gifts and heirlooms she was told had belonged to her dead mother, who had been the granddaughter of an Ooni.

Aarin had listened as the women of her household talked gaily about the auspicious predictions of the priests and priestesses. They gushed at the bridal gifts brought by her husband's family from Ile-Ife and the ones given to her and her husband by her own illustrious father, the sarumi of Ibadan.

But all Aarin thought was that she did not want any gifts. She herself was the gift and sacrifice that would be laid down this night for her husband, Solaru, the warrior and hero from Ile-Ife.

The physical side of the relationship between man and woman weighed heavily on her. Since she had attained puberty, Aarin had been aware of the effect she had on boys and men. She was conscious of the looks that they cast at her when she went to fetch water from the stream. It made her feel feminine and wanted in a very adult way. But she could also not help feeling that she was a fetish that men ogled and lusted after. She remembered the way Solaru himself had openly desired her from the first day they met.

It was a wonder how her body had transformed in the last three years since she started seeing her *ikan osu*. The way her body filled out—not just at the breasts, but in the hips and buttocks—astounded her. And she had allowed herself to follow the dictates of her new body in a way she hardly understood. She had learnt to walk in a new way, swaying her body and hips at the behest of that poorly understood urge that was the power of her sex.

But what about the other, spiritual side of her being that she had been aware of since she was a child? Young and old said she was beautiful. But Aarin wondered if any of them knew of her inner strength, the ageless wisdom and power vouchsafed for her by the gods. What did they know of the visions and dreams that gave her a knowledge that surpassed anything they knew here on earth?

In the days leading to her marriage ceremony, Aarin had listened to the other women of her household talk—crudely, it seemed to her—about what happened on the marriage bed. They told jokes regarding men's body parts, using euphemisms and sly insinuations.

Ojikutu, the friend of her childhood, who had been married for only three months, came by. She had tried to offer a graphic description of what had happened to her on the night she went to her husband's house. But Aarin had tactfully shut her down.

For Aarin thought she already *knew* what was required of her as a woman to please her husband. She had touched herself several times in the past. She knew that sense of heaviness that built up in her pelvis, making her legs weak and her eyes dizzy. She had experienced that great wall of water that rose into her head and burst like a waterfall, flowing down to create a wetness between her thighs. It was like dying and coming back again.

She knew how to bring this on. She had done this to herself when she was alone several times since she was thirteen years of age. Aarin, therefore, felt that her body was tuned and prepared for this day.

She knew all she needed to know. *What did she have to fear?*

She was ready for her husband, Solaru, to do the things to her that would make the water break over her head and send ripples to her feet. After all, he had already done those things to her in her dream. The hour had come for her to please him in real life.

*　*　*　*　*

At last, Aarin and Solaru were alone in the hut allocated to them by Ogunrenu. But they avoided each other's eyes as each confronted the strangeness of their being together alone at last. They knew there was no going back. This was what they wanted, the fulfillment of their dreams and passion.

Aarin and Solaru undressed shyly and slowly. Then they lay next to each other. Aarin's naked body now touched Solaru's for the first time. And although Solaru tried to remember all the lessons he had been taught by Sule, he found himself unprepared for the reality that confronted him. Though they lay close together, they did not speak or look at each other. There was a distance between them that was borne of ignorance, shyness, and modesty. Neither knew what to do, or how to do it.

After some time, Solaru found some courage. Reaching out, he touched Aarin. He found two soft mounds that were pleasant to his touch. Gently, he moved his fingers over them. Slowly, Aarin warmed to his touch but still she made no sound.

Some natural instinct now moved him further. He let his hand wander to the belly, then down to the beads around Aarin's hips. What he lacked in knowledge and experience he made up for with the natural instinct given by the gods to all men for the procreation of the race.

Solaru's fingers moved away from the beads. Emboldened, he touched and caressed the soft hair below them. Miraculously, he found a slippery knob that made Aarin twitch and moan. She reached out and began to touch him too. Then with both arms clasped around his torso, she pulled him to her.

The touch of this maiden, his wife, the softness of her breasts, which now pressed against his chest, and the silky hair that he had encountered in that most unlikely of places—all were new to Solaru. For the previous few months, especially during the Osogbo campaign, he had known only the hard life of the warrior. Backbreaking exercises, the harsh routine of the camps, and the long march as they went out of Ibadan to seek the enemy were his only experiences. The surprisingly soft body of his wife and his own hardness which pressed against her, compensated for it all.

But he found that when he came to the threshold of that citadel that he had been told was his, entry was denied. The challenge was thrown, but he could not summon the password. Solaru tried to remember what he was supposed to do. But breaching that ancient wall, devised by Obatala when he fashioned the first woman, proved more difficult for Solaru than pulling down the Fulani cavalryman from his horse at Osogbo.

This revelation astounded Solaru, but it did not deter him. He got up, his youthful torso silhouetted by the moonlight streaming in from the half-open shutters. The hut had wooden shutters fitted by local workmen with ingeniously devised hinges, which he had left half open to let in the breeze.

In the half darkness, Solaru reached out and took out the jar that he had been given by Sule. He rubbed the oily content on himself. Then he poured the powder from a small gourd into his palm and swallowed it. Then he drank from a flask that Sule had also given him. The liquid tasted sweet, but pungent.

Solaru breathed heavily as he went again to his bride. Now his strength astounded him. And as he prepared to breach the defenses that had proved impregnable at the first call to battle, he was happy he now knew the password.

He heard a voice in his head sing to him. It was a martial ditty that was timed to the rhythm of his movements.

> *Iwo ni ida*
> *Oun ni yio dio mu;*
> *Bo si nu koto*
> *Lati wa dukia re.*

> *You are a sword*
> *and she is your scabbard;*
> *Descend into the cave*
> *And find her treasure.*

Aarin felt her body tense, then soften as she sensed her husband's movements within her. She tried to respond. But the pain she felt overpowered her capacity for pleasure and fulfillment. It was a deep, searing pain that was more she could ever have imagined.

Still, she clung to her husband, for her instinct for pleasure overcame everything else. She dug her nails into his flesh. Suddenly, something gave way. There was a sensation of warmth, then a throbbing, which began in her loins and lower abdomen. Then it was in her chest, her neck, and her head. A wave crashed and washed over her, followed by another wave. She cried out. *It was the dying and coming back again.* Aarin felt faint, and she passed out.

When she came to, she found herself next to the young man, her husband, who clasped her in his arms. His rhythmic breathing told her he was asleep. She had tasted his sacred offering. And he, she knew, had accepted her sacrifice.

Was it this way with her own mother on her wedding night? Aarin would never know. Her mother was not here to be asked. How about her friend Ojikutu, who had gone into her husband's home three months ago? And how about the gods? Was it this way with Sango and Oya?

Aarin wondered if she would get pregnant and have a child. Would she have many children and bathe them in the stream as gentle waves washed over them?

She felt the warm pulsating body of the youth next to her. She would always love him. She would follow him everywhere he went. She would call him *oluwa*, lord, and *olowo ori mi*. For he had paid the bride price for her. She would honor him, cook his meals, and wash his clothes. She drifted slowly to sleep, vaguely aware that part of him was in her.

Aarin dreamt. She came to a deep cave that was lit from above by a preternaturally bright light. She was clothed in white. She found herself kneeling in a posture of supplication, a covered calabash of offering held in both her hands.

She saw two beautifully carved elephant tusks balanced on a low dais in front of her. She squinted and tried to understand the scenes depicted on the ivory. But she could not concentrate. She became aware that other beings were there. They watched her, waiting perhaps for her to do or say something.

Aarin looked beyond the carved ivory tusks. In a half circle facing her, seated on ancient carved stools, was a group that she instantly recognized, though she had never seen them before.

There was Obatala, the great *orisa* himself, and Orunmila, the great seer. She recognized Ogun, dressed as a hunter, and Sango with his double-headed ax held on his knees. But there was another being—a majestic unmoving figure cloaked in white, who sat apart from the others. It was Olokun.

None of the seated figures talked. They remained silent and solemn. They looked kindly at Aarin. It was the figure in white who spoke. Although his lips did not move, she heard clearly his words.

"You are a not a mere mortal woman, Aarin-nimo." Olokun said her full name. It sounded strange to Aarin since no one had addressed her that way since she was a child.

The voice continued, "For you have been favored above other men and women by the gods and elders of your people. You have been given knowledge and wisdom to know many things that are closed to other mortals.

"You will go on a long journey. You will settle in a land beloved of the gods. You will be a great seer among your people. Women who have been barren will have children because of you. And in your old age, children will come to you, and you will tell them the stories of your people."

Aarin woke up but fell asleep again. And immediately, she went into another dream. This time, it was the old dream of her childhood. She was in that quiet and lovely land in the middle of which flowed a gently moving stream. She had the power to predict the future and to look back in time. She possessed the *ase* to tell the destiny of men.

Aarin was still asleep and dreaming when Solaru stirred later and gazed at the sleeping girl beside him.

Was this the maiden he had married that very day? They had both lost their innocence, and they would never be the same.

Through a haze, as the potion he had drunk began to recede in its effects on him, Solaru congratulated himself. He now knew what the gods wanted him to know. He had accepted the sacrifice of his betrothed's maidenhead. He had tasted the knowledge that brought pleasure and power. *But why had the gods hidden this from him for so long?*

He saw a rope hanging by the bed. He looked up and noted that the roof of the hut was open to the sky. The rope went up into an endless void. Solaru grasped the rope and held it taut with both hands. And he began to climb, steadily, carefully, hand over hand, never looking down. He was like a skilled palm wine tapper climbing his tree.

Soon, he reached the seat of the gods high among the clouds.

The face of Orisanla came before his eyes. The deity smiled at him and spoke to him in a low voice that was full of majesty and compassion. While the great god spoke, Solaru lowered his head and made obeisance. He prostrated as the deity blessed him.

After this, he went down Obatala's rope back to his bed and the waiting arms of his bride.

*   *   *   *   *

Just after dawn the next morning, Solaru woke up beside the beautiful maiden who was his wife. He touched her and was thrilled as she murmured and stirred. In the half-light of the dawn that now filtered in through the half-open shutters, he studied Aarin's face as she turned toward him and opened her eyes.

And although it should have now been very familiar, the strange cast of that Nubian face was still a surprise to him. Those light-colored eyes, which sparkled in the dim light and threw his own reflection back at him, filled him with love and made him hold her close to him.

Aroused, they had their pleasure again. Aarin now responded with a passion that matched her husband's, though she was still in a drowsy, half-sleepy state. She held him tightly and pressed her body into his. At the height of her passion, she cried out, and her voice was husky with fulfillment. What Aarin felt was the waterfall break over her head, sending ripples to her feet. She felt herself die and come back again.

Afterward, she spoke softly to her husband in a whisper. She murmured to him in her half-wakeful state.

"My lord, *olowo ori mi*. Ma fi mi sile," she said. "Don't leave me, no matter what happens."

"I would never leave you," he replied. But he wondered what she meant.

Solaru got up and dressed. There were many things for him to do that morning. He had to get permission from the Balogun to go back to Ile-Ife with his bride. But first, he had to go to the house of Aarin's father, where there was yet another ritual he had to go through.

Joy and pleasure coursed through his body. He had never been so happy in his life. He whistled a tune from a song he knew as a child.

> *Yokolu, yokolu,*
> *ko ha tan bi?*
> *Iyawo gboko lu le,*
> *oko suke.*

> *Yokolu, yokolu,*
> *is it not over now?*
> *The wife threw the husband on the ground,*
> *The husband developed a hunch on his back.*

Solaru did not know why he remembered that ridiculous song. And he did not care. He knew it could never apply to him and Aarin. He would love Aarin forever. And she would never fight or quarrel with him.

He told himself that he just wanted to hum a tune that reminded him of the happy times of his childhood when he was comforted by the warmth and love of his aunt, the compassionate Tiwalewa. He had learned that song from her.

Of course, he would never quarrel with Aarin. He whistled the tune again. Then he burst out laughing.

*   *   *   *   *

Mufu was in his forest lair not far from the town of Oje near Ijaiye when the news came to him of Aarin's impending marriage to Solaru. He had been in the bush with his gang of slave catchers for three months. Their mission had been very successful.

Just two weeks earlier, he had led his men on a raid into the Egba territory of Odo Ona. They had surrounded and burnt down two of the villages in the dead of night. They captured its inhabitants, whom they sold as slaves to middlemen who were Egba men from the newly reestablished refugee settlement of Owu in Abeokuta on the Ogun River farther south.

From these two raids, Mufu kept for himself a young slave girl, with whom he spent several nights of concupiscent indolence. He spent his days drinking palm wine with his comrades. He told himself that life was sweet, for he never had it so good.

If at this moment Mufu thought about his hometown of Ibadan, it was with a sense of distance and distaste. He did not care for the false, often-paraded patriotism of the people of that town. All he knew was that he was going back to Ibadan one day to claim his betrothed, Aarin. But he hardly knew her.

In the meantime, he intended to make a lot of money in the slave-catching business. He already had hundreds of bags of cowry shells, the currency of the day. They were stowed away in a secretly dug pit on a farm he had bought in Eleiyele, just outside Ibadan. This farm brought in harvests of kola nut and was managed exclusively by slaves under a supervisor, an old warrior who had been wounded in the thigh and had retired from warfare.

Mufu thought with clarity of what he would do when he returned to Ibadan. He would be a very rich man. And he would show all those supercilious chieftains and counselors who had deserted him and his younger brother, Mutiu Kekere, after their father had died.

He would marry his betrothed, Aarin, and make her his *iyale*, or first wife. After that, he would pay the bride price on two other maidens from the best families in town. The Bashorun would have no choice then but to make him one of his high chiefs. Perhaps even seriki, like his father before him.

It was in the middle of these daydreams that a horseman rode in at full gallop. The rider, who was one of Mufu's point men in Ibadan, reined in his horse, jumped off his mount, and, panting as if his chest would burst, blurted out the news.

While Mufu was consorting with his slave girl in the bush, his betrothed had been married off to another man in Ibadan. And not even a real Ibadan man at that—this wife stealer was a renegade son of nobody from Ile-Ife.

Mufu's blood burned in his veins as he thought of the perfidy of Ogunrenu, Aarin's father. How about Aarin herself? Of course, he told himself bitterly, one could never trust women. They were ready to lie with any man once the right price was paid for them. Slaves, wives, or concubines—what was the difference? They were all the same.

Mufu cursed his *ori*, his luck, his people, and his gods. He railed at the injustice that had afflicted him all his life. He remembered the untimeliness of his father's death, after which his mother and the other wives of his late father were claimed by his uncle, the old seriki's brother. He thought bitterly of the state of penury and loss of social status that had befallen him and his infant brother, Mutiu, who was now eight years of age.

He remembered the disdain that the people of Ibadan had showed toward him for what they considered his disreputable way of life—the very life he had been forced into as the only way to survive. *What did they expect him to do?*

Mufu made immediate preparations to go back to Ibadan with two of his comrades. Bitterly, he swore to have his revenge. He would kill the scoundrel Solaru, that ingrate from Ile-Ife who had dared to come to his town to take his bride.

He had heard about this Solaru, how he carried himself as if the town belonged to him, acting the hero just because he was in the Ibadan cavalry that had gone to fight the Fulani in Osogbo. Mufu hated and despised this presumptuous young warrior and others of his kind who looked down on people like him.

After he had dispatched the impostor, he would make Aarin's father give her back to him. He knew with certainty that before he left Ibadan, either he or the despicable wife snatcher, Solaru, would be dead. And he was sure in his heart whose body it was that would be covered, at the end of the day, by the soft red-brown clay of Ibadan.

So when he arrived in Ibadan after two days of hard riding, Mufu made straight for the compound of Ogunrenu.

He was lucky. He had hardly turned the corner from the main town thoroughfare to enter the Lagelu quarters, where Ogunrenu's clan lived, when he saw his enemy sauntering down the hill in the other direction, carrying himself as if he was not aware of his guilt and perfidy.

Leaving his two companions, Mufu ran toward Solaru. He unsheathed his knife and unleashed a bloodcurdling yell that issued from his throat like the sound of a rabid hound. So sudden was this attack that the crazed figure was almost on Solaru before the latter realized something was amiss. But hearing the yell and a shout from a passerby, Solaru turned around in time. He raised his arm and dodged swiftly to parry the blow that was aimed at him from behind.

Mufu missed his aim, and the knife clattered to the ground. With a howl of fury, he launched himself bare-handed at Solaru. Stooping, he seized a large piece of rock from the ground and swung with all his force at Solaru, catching him fully in the center of the face.

Solaru could not dodge the blow this time. He cried out in pain as he felt his nose cartilage break with a crunching sound that seemed to go straight through his skull. His face was bloodied. But his senses became concentrated with the fear of death and the wish to survive.

Solaru turned to face his foe. The two young men grappled. Each of them knew that this was a do-or-die affair. One or both of the two would be dead before this struggle was over.

Revenge and the cold desire for the death of a hated rival burned like a furnace behind Mufu's eyes. His rage spewed forth like a bilious smoke that clouded his vision, his reasoning, and his judgment.

What Solaru had going for him was his love for his new bride. The will to live for Aarin spurred him. He had visions of the idyll that awaited them and the happy little children frolicking at the back of the big thatched-roof hut that they would have together. Surely, love would triumph over hatred and revenge.

Meanwhile, the intertwined destiny of the two protagonists paced on the sideline. It was a strange lone figure, which, mouth agape, watched their combat closely and with great interest, as it waited for its moment to intervene and end the fray. For it held in its hand the instrument of the death of one of the two combatants. It carried a loaded musket.

Mufu was a wild and scrappy combatant. But Solaru was the better fighter of the two. Skillfully, with the cold and deadly efficiency of the trained fighter, Solaru steadily gained the upper hand. Soon, he had Mufu pinned to the ground.

With the weight of his own body as leverage, Solaru held his opponent's head in his two hands. Systemically, he began to pound it like a musket ball into the dust. Soon, he hoped, his opponent would pass out; and he would make his escape.

But the two companions who had come with Mufu did not stay idle for long. Seeing that their leader was being bested in this deadly fray, one of them—a lanky teenager named Taju, the one who carried Mufu's musket—came close and stood over the two combatants. He lifted the musket and leveled the long-barreled muzzle over the fighters, aiming at the dead center of Solaru's back.

Solaru turned in time and saw his danger. In the twinkling of an eye, using all his strength, he threw his body to one side, instantly exposing the chest of his opponent. At the same time, there was a loud boom that was so close to his ears that Solaru felt he would be forever deafened. There was a spattering of blood all over his clothes and his face and eyes.

Solaru looked down and sideways at his opponent. Mufu lay spread-eagled on the ground, a great red wound in the center of his chest. It was a crimson stain that slowly spread across the front of his light cream-colored embroidered dashiki.

The brown eyes, which a moment ago were full of the fury and desperation of combat, were dull and gray. They bore the faraway look of one looking at the world from a distant place.

*   *   *   *   *

That night, as she lay beside her husband, Aarin sobbed disconsolately. She bewailed their fate and her misfortune in being the cause of the death of the young man who had been betrothed to her.

Even though she did not love Mufu and hardly knew him, she felt a great emptiness in her stomach and a deep sorrow for his young life cut short. She tried to imagine the anguish of his old mother, whom she had often helped with minor chores.

Would she, Aarin, now carry a sense of shame and guilt among her people for the rest of her life?

But she knew that Mufu had been responsible for his own death with his insolence and foolhardiness. It was his implacable desire for revenge against her and Solaru that did him in. Doubtless, Mufu, with the help of his friends, would have killed her husband had he not been killed by his own firearm wielded by Taju, his friend.

Solaru could not sleep. His mind kept turning over the events of that fatal day. He knew that the story Mufu's friends had put out was that it was Solaru who had fatally shot Mufu after grabbing the musket from Taju. Solaru knew he was not guilty of murder. But could he have done anything differently?

Confused and exhausted, he went into a slight doze. But he had a nightmare in which the Bashorun pronounced his doom—a sentence of death.

"A life for a life," Oluyole intoned gravely as Mufu's two lying companions, his old mother, and younger brother, Mutiu, glared at him with implacable hatred and nodded their heads in agreement with the judgment of the Bashorun.

Solaru found himself bound hand and foot, waiting to be slaughtered like the sacrificial bull whose immolation he had witnessed in Ogunrenu's compound at the festival of Ogun.

He struggled violently. He was desperate for life and freedom, and the love of his newly married wife. He knew Aarin waited for him. His fetters came loose, and he made a run for it.

It was then that he woke up, covered in sweat, his heart pounding in his chest.

What was he to do?

And as he lay in the semidarkness beside the maiden for whose love he had paid a great price, the same voice that spoke to him in the Sky the previous night came to Solaru.

It was a voice that seemed to come from deep inside him. And though he knew that the message came from his deity and protector, Orisanla, there was a cadence now to the voice that he knew to be that of Osolarin, the father he never knew.

"You are not safe here, my son," the voice said.

"The family of Mufu will come after you," it continued. "They will try to kill you. And they will take your bride from you and sell her into slavery."

The voice continued, "In their eyes, you have defiled Aarin because she was meant for their son. You have not only wounded their family honor by taking the woman meant for them, you were also the cause of the death of their son. Even though the people of Ibadan, including the Basorun, will say you are blameless in the death of Mufu, his family will not rest until they get their revenge.

"You must leave Ibadan, my son. But you must not go back to Ile-Ife. Your enemies will seek you there. And you will only endanger the family of your guardians—Tiwalewa, your aunt, and Osogbesan, her husband. You must go to a faraway land where no one from Ibadan will look for you or ever find you.

"You must ride tomorrow at dawn on your horse, Jagun. Aarin-nimo, your bride, will ride behind you as you fly to safety and succor. You will go like Sango's lightning toward the south to a land where your destiny awaits you."

Then the voice blessed him with these words:

> *Like a storm*
> *that blows across Yorubaland*
> *from the great ocean of Olokun*
> *to the sandy banks of Odo Oya,*
> *you will sweep all obstacles aside.*
> *No one will stop you, my son.*
> *Like the deep currents*
> *that run in the river Ogun,*
> *you will slip through the traps of your enemies.*
> *Like the wind that even*
> *the mighty iroko tree cannot stop,*
> *you will pass through*
> *the outstretched hands of those*
> *who pursue you.*

And it happened as the voice of his father said.

The very next morning, before the break of dawn, Solaru took his bride, Aarin, by the hand. Running lightly on unshod feet, they made for the stables. They said goodbye to no one. No one awoke. No one challenged them. And no one stood in their way.

Solaru untethered the mighty horse and led it out of the stable. He stopped to put on his riding boots with its bronze spurs.

It was the festival of Oloolu, and there was a curfew from dusk till dawn throughout Ibadan. No one was about. He laid the saddlebag on the rump of the horse and tied it securely, making a double loop with expert fingers. On a whim, he had placed the small *goje* he had brought from Osogbo in the bag along with the other essential items he thought they might need for the journey.

Then he mounted the great horse and placed Aarin behind him, lifting her up easily with his strong youthful arms. She clasped both her arms around him and clung tightly to Solaru as the great warhorse whinnied and raised its forefeet high in the air.

Aarin knew she loved this young man desperately. She would go with him to the ends of the earth. But perversely, even at this desperate moment when their lives were in danger, all she could think of was that she couldn't bear to share him with someone else.

Solaru was impatient. Freedom beckoned. And a new life. He drove his spurs deep into the horse's flanks. The mighty horse sprang up. And with a great leap, they were off.

Houses and streets, bushes and trees flashed past them. Solaru avoided the main city gate that went south out of the city, choosing instead a little-known portion of the city wall that had fallen into disuse. The horse easily made the jump. Too late, Solaru saw the sole sentry who had been sleeping at his post, his head bowed in a sitting position. But before the guard could bestir himself, they were gone.

Jagun bore them swiftly toward the south. The valiant horse ran as effortlessly as the wind. People stepped back and gazed as the wonderful beast sped by, its hooves hardly touching the ground. All they heard was the *kutupa kutupa* as the horse's hooves hit the hard-packed earth of the forest path.

Three days and three nights they rode, stopping only twice to drink from a stream. Where they were bound, they knew not. But the horse knew, directed as it was by the gods.

And when at last they stepped into a strange clearing, early the fourth morning, they saw dew on the leaves and shafts of sunlight breaking through the tree branches. And they heard, for the first time, the cadenced accents they were to know later as those of Remo. They were on the outskirts of the town of Ikenne close by the river Uren.

Aarin, half-asleep on the horse behind Solaru, to whom she held on tightly, opened her eyes. She looked round. And she liked what she saw.

She was happy that they had come to this place. It was a land she knew from her childhood dreams and those ancient memories that represented the collective past of her people. She knew it would be a quiet and lovely place, through which flowed a gentle river. For it was not just the place of her dreams—it was the land of her future.

The voice now came again, softly, in Solaru's ears.

"You have arrived," the voice of his father whispered to him. "You are in the land destined for you."

*   *   *   *   *

They were happy in their new land, and Solaru prospered. Hearing his story, the people of Ikenne called him the "Warrior from Ife." And learning that his family came from that same Iremo quarters in Ile-Ife from where the people of Ikenne were said to have come, according to their old legends, the people and their oba showered him and his bride with favor and attention.

And even if they did not believe that Solaru was an *orisa* himself, so princely was the bearing of this young warrior and so beautiful and radiant was his bride, Aarin, that the people of Ikenne referred to the couple as *omo orun*, "children of heaven." Indeed, they had appeared suddenly among them, as if dropped from the sky. They loved them like a gift from the gods.

Solaru was given a large piece of land near the river Uren by the oba of the town, who was known as the Alakenne. He was also given a dozen slaves to work the land for him.

And so it was that Solaru became a successful farmer even though he had never farmed in Ile-Ife or Ibadan. The Warrior from Ife ceased to be a warrior or a fighter. He abandoned his weapons of war for an *oko* to till the soil and an *ada* to cut down the low shrubs and weed the wild grass. And the fertile earth of Ikenne, nourished by the sacred river Uren, brought forth its fruit for his harvests.

But no fruit came forth from the conjugal labors of Solaru and Aarin. Many years passed, but Aarin did not get pregnant. The priest of Ifa was consulted. The babalawo cast his *obi* on his *opele* on an *iko* mat spread on the earth floor. He prescribed concoctions for Aarin to drink in one gulp, magical kola nuts to chew, and a strange chant to be muttered by the riverbank in the dead of night.

But she remained barren. This cast a pall on the relationship between Aarin and Solaru, although perhaps they continued to love each other.

Inevitably, the day came when it was said to Aarin by the other women of the town when they went to wash at the Uren, that Solaru had a concubine, a maiden who was now betrothed to him in Shagamu. She was the daughter of the Akarigbo.

The gossiping women gave Aarin details of this liaison, which were complete and convincing. They told her of the day Solaru had gone to Ofin in Shagamu to ask for the hand of the maiden to be his second wife in the ancient rite of *itoro iyawo*. They listed the names of the friends who had gone with Solaru to Shagamu. They wove envious tales of the wealth and majesty of the maiden's father, who was Olofin, the owner of Ofin, the ancient palace in Shagamu, the seat of rule and authority in Remoland.

Finally, they told Aarin the name of the maiden herself, Efupitan, and of her remarkable beauty. Seeking to stir her envy and jealousy, they told her more than she wanted to know. This maiden was younger than Aarin, they said. And even though she was still living in her father's royal palace in Shagamu, she was already expecting Solaru's child.

There was a bitter quarrel that night between Aarin and Solaru. There were tears, shouting, and angry denunciations. At first, Solaru uttered an unconvincing denial. Then as the altercation wore on, he uttered the cold and damning admission. And although Aarin berated him and clawed at his face with her sharp fingernails, he remained calm and simply held her hands.

After this, Aarin moved out of Solaru's compound and out of the lives of his friends and their adopted family in Ikenne. She vowed never to go back. She could not forgive her husband's lack of faith.

What had happened to their young love? What about the heady promises he had made to her?

Where had it gone, the excitement of their marriage night? And that perilous flight from Ibadan, when she had clung to him as the brave horse Jagun bore them to Ikenne and freedom?

What had happened to the youth who had chosen her for his own when she was barely past puberty and had loved her with such joyful abandon and unsparing devotion?

Why indeed were men so fickle?

Aarin felt abandoned and lost. Trapped in her pride and innocence, she felt keenly the powerlessness of her sex. She felt wounded and betrayed, and her heart ached.

She remembered what an older woman had once told her. This woman had told her that marriage in Yorubaland did not mean the same thing to men and women. In men, she said, the passion of youth invariably cooled as they confronted the aging of the mate who had come in the flush of youth to their marital bed.

"It is not just my own experience," the old woman had told Aarin. "It is the universal truth for all women."

"Men are fickle. They cannot bear that the firm pubertal breasts of the maiden they married as a youth would sag or that her body would be less firm or responsive to their caress."

Aarin knew that the taking of the bride's maidenhood by her husband on the marriage night was a sacred ritual throughout Yorubaland. It was enshrined in the lore of the land—a theme inculcated into the minds of girls since their childhood as a worthy goal to look forward to. They were told that in this sacrifice lay esnhrined the very morality of the clan.

"But the sacred blood spilled by women when they lose their virginity is an offering that merely feeds the pleasure of men," that same woman had told Aarin.

"So, what do men sacrifice?" Aarin asked bitterly.

Aarin knew that her people placed a premium on childbearing. Every bride was made to understand that it was the very essence of womanhood and the reason for marriage. A barren woman had her value as a wife diminished. And it was common among her people for a man to look for a second wife when the first could not have a baby.

She now remembered, with bitterness, those songs she heard from the women of her father's household as a child in Ibadan.

Kila o ba fowo ra, lai s'omo.
Omo l'ere aiye,
Omo ni iyi, omo ni gbe ni ga.
Bi ina ba ku, a fi eru boju
Bi ogede ku, a fi omo ropo.
Ni ojo ti a ba ku,
Omo ni o gbehin wa.

Of what value are riches
without a child.
A child is our dignity.
He is our reward in this world.
He is the one that makes us proud.
When the fire dies,
it covers itself with ashes.
When the banana tree dies,
it replaces itself with new buds.

*When we die, it is our children
that live after us.*

That word *agan*—"barren"—struck Aarin like a lance. It transfixed her, piercing her sense of individuality and worth. It removed from her the very essence of her womanhood.

Her inability to get pregnant and have a child had decreed her useless to her husband. But did this mean she would be worthless to society? With grim determination, through her tears and the ache in her heart, Aarin decided this would not be so.

*   *   *   *   *

At first, the people of Ikenne said Aarin had gone mad. But she knew this was not so. She was a child of her old dream in which the destiny of men and women had been put into her hands. There was a plan for her, and she knew what to do.

The only thing Aarin took out of the dwelling she had shared with Solaru was the *goje*, that musical instrument of the Hausas that she had learned to play skillfully.

She had a hut built for herself on the edge of the bush near a grove along the path that led to the Uren. From that time on, she lived alone and knew no man. And without any training, she became a devotee of Olokun, the universal sea-god of the Yoruba people, and of Uren, the river goddess of Ikenne. She wore a white robe and shaved her head. She fasted for months. She became so weak that she was barely able to keep herself upright as she puttered around in her hut.

The spirits of Olokun and of Uren came into her. And she was filled with wisdom and the knowledge of the future and of the past. She remembered the dreams of her childhood, which had come to her as she slept beside the old woman, the nurse who took care of her in Ibadan after her mother died. Now she understood. She had been brought to live in that same quiet and lovely place of her dream beside the gently flowing river.

Like the woman in her dreams, she was a seer who had been given the power to see what had been and what would be. She saw things that other humans could not. She heard animals move in the forest far away. And she saw birds whirl about in the sky even when she was inside her hut.

Her vision extended beyond the ken of normal men and women. She saw the past and the future. She knew and told stories of the heroic golden days of her people as if she was there. For indeed, *she was there*. She had lived the past, and the past was in her.

Alone in her hut, as she played the goje softly to herself, Aarin summoned the spirits and memories of the past, even those that had existed long before she was born. These spirits came into her, giving her knowledge and wisdom.

She became the repository of the history, through the ages, not only of Ikenne and Remo, but also of Ibadan, Ile-Ife, Oyo, and all the towns and city-states of our people. A living *aroken*, Aarin became the source of the fables and legends learned by the children of Ikenne, who, many years later, would sit in a circle around her feet as she told stories to them on moonlit nights.

Her fame as a prophetess spread. People from all over Ikenne and beyond came to her with their troubles. In particular, women who were barren sought her help. And because of her intercession with her deity Olokun, they became pregnant and were able to have children.

"Agan a di olomo. *The barren will not long remain childless*," she told these women firmly and with complete faith in the power of the deity.

And though she herself never had a child, her own reproductive failure, decreed by Olokun, was transmuted into joy and success for others. With the power given to her by her deity, she assisted other women to achieve this act of personal achievement and redemption.

As Iya Olorisa Odo, priestess of the river, Aarin interceded on behalf of her supplicants in an ancient grove near the sacred river of Ikenne, which became her shrine. And when she prayed in this shrine, she did this not only in the name of Olokun, but also of Uren, goddess of the river.

And indeed, it was the goddess Uren that Aarin became chiefly associated with by the people of Ikenne. As they knelt in her shrine, they heard the priestess address the river goddess as her mother. "Ye mi, Uren. Orisa, a f'ase soro."

"Uren, my mother," she would say, "you who speak with authority in your voice. Hear me."

When she prayed to the goddess of the river, people saw that she was imploring and firm. But she was respectful, for she spoke as a daughter to a loving and giving parent.

> *Awon to nwoju re*
> *Dawon lohun, Orisa,*
> *So won di abiyamo*
> *Nitori omo laiye, omo l'aso,*
> *Omo ni igbehin iya re.*

> *Awon to loyun sinu*
> *Orisa, je ki a gbohun iya,*
> *Ki a gbohun omo.*
> *Gbogbo awon ti o ti bimo*
> *Ma je ki omo seku mowon l'owo.*

> *The supplicants that look to thee*
> *Hear them, O Orisa,*
> *Let them conceive and bear children,*
> *Because the child is life itself;*
> *A child is the clothing*
> *that covers her mother's nakedness.*
> *And when the woman leaves this world,*
> *It is her child that she leaves*
> *to take her place.*

> *For those who are pregnant*
> *and are about to give birth,*
> *Orisa, let us hear the mother*
> *cry out in labor,*
> *and hear the wail of the baby.*
> *And those who already have children*
> *Let not their children die in their arms.*

Thus it was that Aarin, as Iya Olorisa Odo, prophesied and healed the demons of the many afflicted who came to her. Soon, these were no longer just women. Men, even great chieftains and obas, came with offerings and sacrifices to her shrine. Everyone sought the blessing and favor of the priestess of the river. Before long, she became a natural feature of the town of Ikenne, as permanent and ageless as Uren, the sacred river.

After a time, no one called her Aarin anymore. She was known as *Iya abore odo Uren*, *Iya aborisa odo*, or *Iya Olorisa*, the priestess mother of the sacred river. Later, the people of Ikenne simply called her Iya, "mother," or Iye in their Remo dialect.

But Aarin's transformation was not just spiritual. It was manifested in her physical beauty, which became even more marked after she became a priestess. Whenever they came to her shrine, people were struck by the tall, slim frame of the priestess. And when they examined at close quarters that delicate face with its almost-invisible Ife facial marks, light-colored eyes, and Nubian cheekbones, they recognized the profile of a deity. Those who knew her, and talked of her afterward, said Iya Olorisa of Ikenne remained an icon of the physical comeliness of our people, even as she grew into old age.

And indeed, Iya Olorisa knew that her unfading beauty was the manifestation in her of Olodumare and all the deities of the land, not just Olokun and Uren. She felt a closeness, even a kinship, with these gods and goddesses. Their power moved her. And their voice was her voice.

As the priestess of the sacred river, she was the guardian and protector of all the beasts, fish, and humans who thrived because of the river Uren and depended on it for their sustenance. And in later years, she became the mother of all the children of Ikenne, who called her Iya Agba, long after she had ceased to be a prophetess or a priestess. She told these children the stories of our people, and they in turn passed them to us, their children and grandchildren.

Thus, it is as Iya Agba, the Old Woman, that we know her as the inspiration and narrator of our *itan*, the stories and legends of the golden age of our people.

*   *   *   *   *

Solaru's new wife was Efupitan. She was a princess of the royal family of Ofin in Shagamu. Her father was the Akarigbo. This king of the Remos had no son. When he died, he knew he would have no male heir to carry his name. The kingship would pass to another of the Shagamu ruling families.

But the Akarigbo took a look at Solaru, who had asked for the hand of his favorite daughter in marriage, and he said to himself, "This is the son I never had."

Indeed, what the Akarigbo felt toward Solaru was the emotion that had been denied him because he had no sons. This was why the Akarigbo made Solaru a promise that after he married his daughter, he would make him his Aremo, giving him the royal title of a prince of the royal house of Shagamu.

Solaru understood that the title of Aremo bestowed on him as the son-in-law of the Akarigbo was largely decorative. It carried no real power. He could never hope to succeed to the kingship in Shagamu or anywhere else in Remo. But as Aremo, Solaru had to take a new name. He was no longer to be called Solaru. His new name was Adeuja.

People close to Solaru still called him Jagun Ife, the Warrior from Ife. But to everyone else, he was Adeuja, son of the Akarigbo. His old name, Solaru, was slowly forgotten. And so it was that even within his own family, his children and grandchildren would later not know that he had such a name.

Efupitan was already pregnant when Solaru had his rift with his first wife, Aarin. After their betrothal, the new bride moved into Solarus's house in Ikenne, which was where, in due time, she delivered her baby.

It was a boy—a strong, laughing infant that brought joy to the household. Everyone said his birth was an omen of good things to come for his happy parents. And indeed, Solaru, now known as Adeuja, saw the birth of the baby as an affirmation that this new union had been blessed by Orisanla, the great god.

Adeuja gave the child the name Osolesi, which everyone, as usual, shortened to Solesi. This name, in the tradition of his family from Ile-Ife, was in honor of Orisanla.

For despite the distance of time, Adeuja wanted his new family in Ikenne to remember that his ancestors were esos of old Oyo and counselors to Oonis in Ile-Ife. He wanted to honor the great hero of his clan, Osolemisi, who had defeated the Asante at Atapame, and Osogbesan, who witnessed the last stand of Oluewu, the last emperor of the Yorubas.

The ceremonies and festivities that attended the birth of the child Solesi were well noted by the people of Ikenne. At his *isomo-loruko*, three priests were present.

After casting his kola nuts and reading the augurs, the first priest said, "He is a child of destiny. He will be a mighty chief. He will live long in the land of his birth, longer than all his peers."

The second priest said, "He will go on a long journey. Let us pray that he does not forget the house and gods of his fathers, and that he does not bring back strange tribal symbols from a foreign land." This caused some consternation.

The third priest declared, "He will enjoy the love of strangers, especially women."

"*A se,*" everyone said in unison. *So may it be.*

The boy Solesi grew up to be loved by his father, Adeuja; his mother, Efupitan; and everyone who knew him. In particular, he was the apple of his father's eyes. Adeuja, the former warrior from Ile-Ife, loved his only son with an uncommon affection that sometimes caused an ache in his chest.

From his earliest years, the child Solesi had his ears tuned to the sounds that pervaded his father's household and his Remo town of Ikenne. He loved the singsong accents of Remo, especially the thin voice of his mother and other women when raised in song. He developed an ear for music. He loved the sounds of all the musical instruments of Remo and the traditional songs of his people, especially the *orikis* and chants that were sung to the beat of drums.

During festive events in Ikenne, young Solesi would watch and listen to the voices of the *akewis*, the oral poets and praise singers of the town as they stood in front of his father and other great chiefs of Ikenne and chanted their *orikis*. This was often performed to the accompaniment of the *gangan*, the talking drum, and *shekere*, the gourd rattle.

Solesi would never forget the first time he saw an *akewi* stand before his father, cup his hand over his mouth, and sing out in a sonorous voice the high-flowing *oriki* of Adeuja, son of Akarigbo.

> *Adeuja yoju si wa o,*
> *Baba oloye*
> *Aremo Shagamu*

Jagunlabi Ikenne,
Ikenne "ireke."

Adeuja, come out to greet us,
Great chief, person of honor;
Crown prince of Shagamu
Our powerful force in Ikenne.

Solesi listened as the *akewi* sang of his father's descent from Ile-Ife, the place he knew was revered as the mother city of the people of Ikenne.

Adeuja omo Akarigbo
Olofin ni'lu Shagamu
Jagun jagun lati Ife,
Ife omo olodo kan o tara,
Omo odo to nsan wereke,
To nsan wereke.

Adeuja, son of Akarigbo
Of the palace in Shagamu;
Warrior from Ife—
Ile-Ife of the famous stories.

Throughout his childhood, Solesi would hear the people of Ikenne, young and old, commend his father for his physical comeliness. For indeed, Adeuja retained the good looks and princely bearing of his youth into middle age. Despite his broken nose, which was the result of his fight with Mufu, the Warrior from Ife was a very attractive man. His desirability, especially among the maidens of the town, was proverbial.

Jagun jagun nwe l'odo,
Gbogbo omoge lo nowo ose.
Aja o ni jobi k'aiye to pare.
Onile, e jade wa,
Eni to sun si iyewu, e dide lori eni
Ki e ba wa ki Jagun-jagun lati Ile-Ife.

The warrior bathes in the stream,
And maidens reach out to offer him soap.
A dog will not chew kola nut
until this earth passes away.
Those of you at home,
come out to join us,
And those who are sleeping,
rise up from your mat,
Come, let us salute the Warrior from Ile-Ife.

Young Solesi was aware that his father, Adeuja, was the son of the Akarigbo. But he did not understand how his father could be a warrior from Ile-Ife at the same time. But then not everything that adults did or said made sense to him.

*   *   *   *   *

Solesi grew up to be a restless and impatient child. In this, he was like many in his family before him. Constantly on the move, he never seemed able to stand still. He learned to ride his father's horse, Jagun, before he was nine years old.

People stopped what they were doing and stared when they saw him ride that beautiful black horse with the white blaze on its forehead. There were not many horses in that small Remo town of farmers, artisans, and hunters.

At this time in the history of our people, Remo had remained serene and untouched from the conflicts unleashed by warlords and their war boys in that time of troubles. Few men in Ikenne had been to war. And fewer still could boast of the opportunity of ever having ridden a horse.

Despite being born in a peaceful corner of Yorubaland, Solesi, from an early age, wanted to be a warrior like his father, the Warrior from Ife. He played war games with his friends in the forests around Ikenne. And he learned to wield his father's old cavalry saber. He could shoot an arrow to hit his target at fifty paces before he was ten years of age. He had an unerring eye, quick reflexes, and the audacity of a born fighter.

The fact that he was small for his age never deterred him. He made up for his small stature with his quick brain and nimble body. And his laughing eyes beguiled his enemies and won him his way out of any trouble.

But the most remarkable gift given by the gods to young Solesi was his talent for music. Without anyone teaching him, he learned to play all the traditional drums of Ikenne before he was nine years old. To this repertoire, he added skills in the playing of other musical instruments, including the goje, which the priestess of the river taught him and allowed him to play.

Like his father and mother, the boy Solesi was a very attractive person to look upon. He was light-complexioned, with a soft, delicate face that drew sighs from girls and women. Solesi grew up without any tribal marks on his face. This was because his father could not decide whether to give him the Ile-Ife marks of his own ancestors or the Ijebu marks of his adopted hometown of Ikenne. His mother, Efupitan, did not want him marked at all. She and the other women of Ikenne loved the beautiful unmarked cheeks of the child Solesi, which were as attractive as those of a girl.

Solesi was a favorite amongst all the girls of his *egbe*, or age-group. Many of them promised to marry him as soon as they were old enough and could get their parents to consent to the union.

But at this time in his life, Solesi did not favor or savor the company of girls. He was the leader of his group of male friends. And he had a lot of exuberant masculine energy. What he loved to do was to organize games, races, swims in the river, and wrestling matches—anything that required physical prowess and afforded the thrill of competition.

For a small-statured person, he had a quickness that compensated for any deficiency in brute strength. He easily held his own against bigger and stronger-looking opponents. And for this, he earned the nickname Akeredolu—"the small one that achieves great things."

* * * * *

Young Solesi's wish, from an early age, to become a warrior, came to pass sooner than he had hoped for. For before he was twelve years old, war came to Ikenne.

At this time in our story, the Remos were constantly on the alert for the martial activities of their neighbor to the west, the Egbas. This was because the Remos had incurred the wrath of Egba warlords because they had opened lines of trade for supplies to pass through Remoland from the coast to Ibadan, their neighbor to the north. At that time, Ibadan was engaged in a protracted war with the Egbas. To the Egbas, the friend of their enemy was their enemy. Everyone knew therefore that, sooner or later, the Egbas would seek their revenge against Remo.

So it was that one day, news reached Ikenne and other Remo towns that an Egba army had crossed the border. Egba warriors were now said to be marauding through many Remo border towns from Ogunmakin to Ipara.

The Remo chiefs held a council of war at Shagamu, their capital, under the auspices of the Akarigbo. The decision was unanimous. The Egbas had to be stopped. And to do this, Remo had to go to war.

But Remo was a small nation of farmers and traders. It did not have enough men skilled in the art of war. A peaceful people, the people of Remo were not war-seeking aggressors like their neighbors to the west and north, the Egbas and Ibadans.

For help therefore, the leaders of Remo looked to the north, in the direction of Ibadan, their warlike neighbor and ally in the recent Ijaiye War. For even in the backwaters of Remo, everyone knew that Ibadan, the former camp of outlaws and war refugees, had become the foremost military power in Yorubaland.

But Adeuja, the former Warrior from Ife, was not happy with the coming war. Even though the Remos were going to be helped by his old friends in Ibadan, he had his misgivings.

Like his "baba," Osogbesan, who had tried to discourage him from going to Ibadan to fight the Ilorins, Adeuja discovered one strange fact. He, the Warrior from Ife, did not want his son to go to war.

When Adeuja tried to debate with himself his arguments against the war, he tried to be rational. He knew he had to put his feelings into words. And the words came to him one afternoon, in the quiet of his house.

First, he mumbled the lines to himself. Then he sang them out, in the rhythm of an old *ijala* that he had learned as a child.

> *Awon jagun-jagun atijo*
> *Nwon kii fe ki omokunrin won*
> *ki o lo si oju ogun.*
> *Ogun ko da bi iyan,*

Ogun ko da bi eko;
Awon ti ogun ti jari,
ki i fe ko tun sele mo,
Nwon ko fe ipadanu
awon omo won.

Old warriors
do not want their sons
to go to war.
For those who have been in battle,
war is a brutal business
that they do not wish to relive;
They do not want the suffering
or death of their children.

Adeuja's pacifist sentiments were not shared by his son. The boy Solesi welcomed the coming conflict with the Egbas. He wanted to be part of the action. He was only eleven years old. But his blood quickened to the beat of war drums that was now heard all over Ikenne.

Solesi thrilled to the talk of heroic and stirring deeds that now issued from the mouths of young men in Ikenne. Everyone in town had suddenly become brave and patriotic. Every young man, it seemed, wanted to fight or even die for his native land.

Like these young men, Solesi wanted to go out and fight like a true patriot of Remo. For there was warcraft in his blood. It was a trait that, through the generations, had not deserted his clan. It was an inheritance that, his father could have told him, came from ancestors who were soldiers and *esos* of old Oyo. Their heroism called to him from beyond the mist of years.

Solesi could not ignore this call. It came from brave and mighty men, who, in times past, had established Ile-Ife, Oyo, Ibadan, and Ijebu-Ode of the Awujales. They had answered the call when their time came. They had left their families to defend their land and to wreak destruction on their enemies.

Young Solesi knew his time had come. He too would play his part. He would be a hero.

CHAPTER 4

An wa ọmọ wa
Ti o sọnu lori ogun
Ti a ja pẹlu awon Egba.
"Ṣugbọn o ti lọ si Ibadan,"
ni awon ara ilu nso.
Omọde yi dara pupo.
Gbogbo awọn wundia ti Ikenne
ti won ti ni ife re,
ni nṣọfọ rẹ.

We are seeking our boy.
who was lost in the war
with the feckless Egba.
"But he is gone to Ibadan,"
many in the town whispered.
"He is a comely youth,
And the maidens of Ikenne
mourn him."

War Boy

THE SPIRIT OF anomy hovered over Yorubaland. It brought forth an endless cycle of warfare, which in the mid-nineteenth century ravaged many proud and ancient Yoruba city-states.

Like a blight, it spread across the land of *karo o jire* until it reached Remo, where hitherto there was neither war nor threat of war. The madness of war now swept into this peaceful land, whipping up the indolent hearts of its men to thoughts of violence and bloodshed.

So it was that war drums woke up the sleepy village of Ikenne and young Solesi answered the call. The young man's wish to become a fighter like his famous father, the Warrior from Ife, was fulfilled. At the first rumor of hostilities with the encroaching Egba, borne on the news of the devastation by the Egbas of the Remo frontier town of Ipara, Solesi became a drummer boy in the hastily formed Remo army. This would be his own contribution to the Ikenne war effort. Solesi was only eleven years old. But he lived in a time of troubles in an age of conflict. Thus, he was old enough to become an *omo ogun*, a "war boy."

To go to war, Solesi was accoutred like the other warriors of his time. He wore jumpers that reached to his knees. Above this was a dashiki, a short hunter's jacket. It looked very much like the cloak worn by Obari on his adventure to the sea three centuries earlier. He wore a strong belt of deerskin around his waist to which were tied or slung various accoutrements of war. And to go to war he would be barefoot, for he had no footwear.

His father, the Warrior from Ife, though skeptical of his son's rationale for going off to fight, nevertheless took him to a *babalawo* to prepare him for war.

"Gbegbe igbe soko iwaje," the babalawo chanted his ancient incantations as he prayed for Solesi's safe return from *oju-ogun*.

"You will go. And you will come back," he said.

Solesi came back home from his visit to the babalawo equipped with several amulets and charms that included dyed cowry shells, feathers of birds, and the bleached skull of a small rodent. All these were attached or sewed to his war tunic, a short dashiki dyed in *aro* to a dark-blue hue.

Strapped to his belt on his left hip was his short *ada*, which was the basic weapon of the Remo fighter of the day. Some of the older warriors also carried short throwing spears or lances. A few of the men, who were hunters in civilian life, carried the muzzle-loading musket known as *saka bula*.

To Solesi, all the bluster and talk of war around him in Ikenne were the preliminaries to the real game of war that he would soon partake in. Eagerly, he immersed himself in the spirit of the game.

With his friends and playmates, Solesi had always liked playing war games. Now he could play his part in earnest—not with make-believe actors his own age, but with grown-up warriors for whom the possibility of death was real. It was no longer a game in the bush at the back of his father's house, at the end of which he would say to his friends, "I am hungry. Let's go home."

Solesi entered into his martial role with fervor. He learned the special war song of the Ikenne war contingent. And he sang this ditty throatily as his two hands simultaneously beat an accompanying rhythm on the small drum that hung low against his belly.

> *Ko si eiye l'oju orun*
> *To le fo bi asa.*
> *A de o;*
> *A kere koro,*
> *Awa omo Ikenne.*

> *There is no bird in the sky*
> *That can soar like the hawk.*
> *Here we come;*
> *Small, but ferocious,*
> *The sons of Ikenne.*

Solesi played the small drum called *omele*. It had a leather strap that went around his neck, leaving him free to beat the goatskin leather of the drum with a pair of short curved drumsticks. It also allowed him to leave the drum, if need be, and reach for his weapon of war. He carried his short sword, which had been specially made for his small stature by Lanipekun, the town blacksmith. This was strapped to his left hip with a leather thong so that it was within easy reach of his right hand.

He also had a bow strapped to his back. His quiver of arrows hung over his left shoulder.

He was primarily a young musician in the service of the *ibalogun* of Ikenne. Solesi's job was to play his drum to stir the blood of the older men, who were the real warriors. His drumbeats in the field of battle would induce these placid men of Ikenne—farmers and hunters in peacetime—to defy the arrows and lances launched at them from the other side as they dashed forward to grapple with the enemy in the thick of battle.

Solesi practiced playing his drum every day with the other *omo onilu*, drummer boys, who were mostly teenage boys. Although he was the youngest of the group, Solesi's musical skills shone above everyone else's. Before long, he became the star of the group. And indeed, for the musically inclined, it was a thing of beauty, whenever they practiced, to hear Solesi expertly weave the rapid rhythm of his omele in and out of the heavy thuds of the big *iya ilu* and *gangan* of the older warrior musicians. It was his job to set the pace for the bigger drums.

The older men and the war captain Osoeye, the newly appointed Balogun of Ikenne who occasionally came out to watch the *omo onilu* practice, beamed at young Solesi. They were proud of his expertise with the small drum.

Although everyone else knew that he was only a drummer boy, Solesi fancied himself a real warrior. He told himself he would soon see action. He would have the chance to shoot his arrows at the enemy, and he would be shot at in return. Therefore, he carefully honed his fighting skills by practicing with all the different weapons of war he could lay his hands on in Ikenne.

He begged for several of these from the older men. Swords, daggers, and spears were given or lent to him to play and practice with. At one time, he even had a musket, which he had coaxed an old elephant hunter to teach him to load, aim, and shoot. However, it was as an archer that Solesi's skills shone the most. Although he already considered himself a great shot, he practiced with his bow and arrow every chance he had. He was keen to show everyone, especially Balogun Osoeye, what a great shot he was.

That he was an expert with the bow, there was indeed no doubt. Even his commander, Awoniyi, was known to have remarked that the boy Solesi had been well taught by his father, the Warrior from Ife.

This Awoniyi was a cynical old warrior who had gone off with his friends from Ijebu-Ode to fight on the side of Kurunmi in the just-concluded Ijaiye War. Therefore, everyone in Ikenne agreed that he knew all about conflicts and wars.

These were very happy times for young Solesi. He told himself that this was what he had prepared for all his life. He was glad that the war games he had played since he was little more than a toddler had paid off. By dint of his own expertise and preparation, he was ready to go to war to make his name. And he was certain he would come back a hero.

And what did Solesi's father, veteran and hero of the battle of Osogbo, think about all this?

In reality, Adeuja was bothered, not amused or pleased, by all the war preparation taking place in his town. And the involvement of his young son in these warlike plans did not gladden his heart. Like many old soldiers, Adeuja, the former Warrior from Ife, had grown weary of war. He did not want his son going off to fight for any warlord.

Strangely for a former warrior who had fought on the side of Ibadan, Adeuja began to talk dismissively of the skills and prowess of the fighters from that warlike town. He did not care, unlike the rest of the townspeople, for the acclaimed military might of Ibadan and the advantages accruing to Remo now that the Ibadans had consented to fight on their side against the Egbas.

In fact, Adeuja thought this military superiority of the Ibadan warlords was vastly overestimated. Besides, he had heard stories about the deterioration of social morals and military ethics among Ibadan warriors since the time he fought beside them at Osogbo twenty years earlier. In Adeuja's view, the Ibadan war machine was no longer the patriotic, well-disciplined unit that had sworn to defend the sovereignty and honor of the Yoruba people.

"The Ibadan warlords are in it for themselves," the former Warrior from Ife told his listeners.

"All they want is to lord it over other Yoruba city-states. All they are looking for, in waging their wars, are opportunities to procure more slaves for their farms and captive women for their beds.

"They are all brigands and glorified slave raiders," he concluded, the distaste showing in his voice.

While he said this aloud, Adeuja's private thoughts were conflicted. He was sad and disheartened.

He had fled from Ibadan to this valley of peace. All these years, he thought he was lucky to be far from the madness of the wars that ravaged the Yoruba heartland north of Ijebuland and Remo. He had felt safe and lucky to be far away from that insanity. But now the Egbas and Ibadans had brought their war to his doorstep.

"And they want to take my only son from me," he said sadly to himself.

Why would war not leave him in peace? Why did it insist on invading his tranquil adopted home?

Adeuja had become a philosopher. He was no longer a warrior. Thoughts of this coming war with the Egbas only served to sap his sense of security and happiness. And a sadness came over him. He thought of the impermanence of human joy and the finiteness of life itself. All humans were going to die. Why would some men want to expedite the process by engaging in unnecessary wars?

As these thoughts went through him, Adeuja realized with a shock that he was a pacifist at heart. In fact, he had been so all along. He had only gone to war in his younger days because of youthful ignorance and a naïve lack of self-examination.

And so Adeuja continued to express his antiwar sentiments to people who came to his house in Ikenne. Many of the men who heard him talk this way went away and told their wives that the Warrior from Ife had become paranoid and womanly.

The truth was that as Adeuja approached middle age, he thought more and more of his coming old age and inevitable death. He wanted his only son to be near him and to comfort him when his time came.

He never knew his own father. Perhaps in compensation for this, Adeuja desperately clung to the cocoon of his family. For only in the warm domestic nest of his wife and son did he find a sense of safety and comfort. And he realized that his only son, Solesi, who occupied the center of that world of comfort, might be cut off from him because of this war.

Sometimes Adeuja had a strange feeling that his experiences as the Warrior from Ife, hero of the battle of Osogbo, and his betrothal to Aarin may have belonged to another person—so unreal were they now. *Or were they from a dream?* All he was certain of now was that he was Adeuja, a peace-loving citizen of Ikenne and prince of Shagamu.

And he began to have dreams. They were dreams of his past. But sometimes they were deeply disturbing visions of a strange portent for the future.

One night, during this time of the great preparation for the Iperu campaign, Adeuja had a dream. The warriors, boys and men from Ikenne who had gone to war against the Egbas, had come back home. But his son, Solesi, was not among them. Adeuja woke up in fear and confusion. His body glistened with sweat. Despite the warm tropical night, he felt cold, and he shivered.

He did not want to admit it, but Adeuja had also begun to feel with a painful keenness the absence of Aarin in his life. She was the one who used to listen to his dreams and helped him to interpret them. She had been his counselor, the one who gave reassurance and support that were always rational and clearheaded. She was the great love of his life and the passion of his youth. She was the one for whom he had paid a great price to win.

Adeuja realized that he missed Aarin more than he cared to admit. He felt sad. And he blamed himself. Due to his fault, he had lost her forever almost as surely as if she had died. He missed her closeness to him and her almost-mystical prescience and sagacity, which he had taken for granted while she was his wife and companion.

Now that Aarin was a priestess and belonged to everyone in Ikenne, she was lost to him in any personal sense. He knew he could visit her shrine by the river if he wanted to, to seek the wisdom that came to her through her deities, Olokun and Uren. But this was not the same as the personal friendship, advice, and comfort he needed. He told himself that another loss like this in his life would do him in.

Adeuja felt tired and old. He knew with certainty that he would not survive the loss of his son. But he remembered the untamable fires of youth and the hardheadedness of his own teenage years. Was he not the same Solaru, who, as a young man, had pestered his uncle, Osogbesan, to allow him to go off to become a warrior in Ibadan? And now he was unhappy that his own son clamored to be allowed to go off to fight.

"It must be in the blood," Adeuja said to himself. "Solesi could no more help himself than a dog refuse to bark at the sight of a hostile stranger in his master's house."

And thus, reluctantly, Adeuja gave his blessing and permission for his only son to go with the Ikenne auxiliaries to help drive the Egbas out of Iperu.

*   *   *   *   *

The day came when the order came from the Remo commander in chief in Shagamu for the men of Ikenne to march out to meet the enemy waiting for them at Iperu. As they set out, the boy Solesi was in the front. He was in the middle of a line of drummers who led the Ikenne auxiliaries as they trudged out of the town.

Solesi would always remember that day very clearly. It was early in the morning late in the rainy season. It was just after dawn. Women were on their way to the stream to fetch water, their earthenware pots balanced delicately on their heads as they swayed their hips in rhythm. Old Kuteyi was stretching his legs in front of his hut as usual. And the sun shone just as brightly as on any other morning that Solesi could remember. There was a smell in the air of unharvested corn in the field. It was a most ordinary-looking day.

At first, the group of men and boys were quiet as they marched out of the town. They did not look back as they left the last hut behind in the town of Ikenne. Some of the men thought of the wives and children they had left behind. Would they ever see them again?

But soon, the older warriors began to talk in low whispers about the enemy they were about to face. The Egbas were feared and respected as a warlike people by the Remos.

Their town of Abeokuta had been founded around the same time as Ibadan following the dissolution of the Oyo Empire. Due to friction with the Ifes and Oyos after the Owu war, the Egbas had fled en masse to establish their famous city of refuge under the rock. They named their new town Abeokuta, which meant "under the rock." The population of the new town grew rapidly with more Egba refugees streaming in, pushed out of their ancient dwellings and towns which were located in and around the site occupied by the new settlement of Ibadan, which became their perennial foe.

But like their oppressors in Ibadan, the Egbas of Abeokuta soon became known for their propensity for war. And once their appetite was kindled, the Egbas never tired of involvement in one conflict or the other. Their constant foe was Ibadan, their old nemesis. Perhaps they never forgave the fact that the site on which Ibadan stood had once been farms that belonged to the ancient Egbas.

The men of Ikenne also talked about the Dahomeans, the fearless and warlike race who were neighbors of the Egbas to the west. One of the older men brought up the legend of the female warriors of Dahomey.

These were the famous *ahosi*, who, everyone knew, were braver than their men and even more ruthless in battle. One of the Ikenne men, a garrulous hunter with graying hair named Alabi, said that these women warriors gave no quarter and killed all their prisoners. According to him, these women had only one breast, which they exposed in battle. But woe betide any foe that attempted to strike at that one exposed breast. He would not live to tell the tale.

Alabi repeated the story of how one of these female warriors had been captured by the Egbas. She broke her chains, grabbed a sword from one of her guards, and slew him with one stroke. Then she fell on the same sword, killing herself before the rest of her captors could react.

Thus it was that the legend of the female warriors of Dahomey infested Solesi's imagination for the rest of that march to Iperu.

"What is real, and what is to be believed?" he wondered.

Solesi was only a boy. He believed the stories told by grown men like Alabi, who, of course, knew more about these things. But anytime he remembered those stories of the women warriors of Dahomey, he grew fearful. And Solesi would dream all his life about these mythical female warriors with one breast.

"Omoge olomu kan," he called them.

But soon, the warriors marching out of Ikenne had gone past Ilishan. And now as they approached the outskirts of Iperu, they heard the murmur of war camps. All the talk about Dahomey and its fearful female warriors came to a halt. Their minds became focused on the task at hand.

What would be asked of them? And what would they do? Would they give a good account of themselves when they confronted the Egbas?

The order was now given by their commander, Osoeye, for the men and boys to array in battle rank. The beating of war drums recommenced with Solesi in the lead with his sonorous *omele* setting the tone with his percussive rhythm.

The surreal sound from many drums filled the air. The men stiffened their poses and quickened their steps. Each tried to keep in step with the man or boy next to him. Solesi felt a thud in his chest, and his heart began to beat fast with anticipation and fear.

Would he live and return home to Ikenne? How would his mother react to his demise if he fell in battle?

The vision of a sword thrust into his bowel or a speeding musket ball from an Egba *saka bula* piercing his heart filled Solesi with dread. It quickened his already-palpitating heart. The prospect of a sudden and violent death in the afternoon not far from the place of his birth made him shiver.

Solesi tried to think of bravery and honor. And as he tried to still his quaking heart, he found that the beat of his drum brought him a sense of calm and comfort. Slowly, his heart quieted, finally settling into a steady rhythm that followed the beat of his drum. He would soon see action, and that would settle it.

"Would I be brave, or would I prove to be a coward?" he continued to ask himself.

Solesi's mind was a turmoil of questions. But still, he yearned for the coming action. Wasn't this what he had always wanted? The beat of the drums from his comrades all round him was a familiar sound that he knew and understood. He was surrounded by men from his own town who would protect him and perhaps die for him. He began to feel brave and comforted. He felt strong. He was going to war. He would be a man. He would survive, and he would return home.

Soon, the men reached the outer barricades surrounding the Ibadan defenses. For the men and boys from Ikenne, the battlefield in and around Iperu was a mere fifteen miles from their own home, but it was a week's march away for the battle-weary Ibadans.

As the fresh-looking men and boys from Ikenne looked at the dirty, mud-besmirched Ibadans, they realized with a shock that these strangers were the real professional soldiers, not they, who were merely playing at war. They, the contingent from Ikenne, were boys and men having an adventure not far from home.

The Ibadan contingent was encamped partly within the town of Iperu, but mostly in the surrounding forest. Their tents and camps dotted the landscape as far as his eyes could see. Solesi thought that their number was more than he could count even if he tried.

To the Remos, who were not versed in perpetual war as the Ibadans were, it was an awesome sight to meet the famed battle-hardened warriors from Ibadan. These Ibadan warriors were dressed much like the men from Ikenne. But to Solesi, they looked more warlike and fearsome than his compatriots. There was a look of weariness and desperation on their sweaty faces that commanded respect and fear.

"These are men one does not trifle with," Solesi said to himself.

This feeling was not helped by the fact that the Ibadan warriors held their bows taut, the arrows pointed at the Remos as they marched toward them. They looked ready to shoot their supposed allies down at the slightest provocation.

But then as Solesi's heart began to beat fast with fear of a confrontation borne out of misunderstanding or someone's reckless act, both sides seemed to remember that they were friends and allies. The challenge was given, and the password acknowledged. Then the men and boys from Ikenne were let through to see the Ibadan commander.

*   *   *   *   *

There he was, the celebrated warlord, Ibikunle, Balogun of Ibadan. Ibikunle was then only fifty-nine years of age, but he was very old in the business of war.

"He does not look like the Balogun of Ibadan," Solesi told himself with some disappointment.

And indeed, Balogun Ibikunle looked old and ordinary. The famous Ibadan war commander—whose nickname was Kiniun Oju Ogun, "the lion of the camps"—was dressed in a short dashiki. He wore a soldier's cap like everyone else. His war tunic was off, and his neck and beardless face glistened with sweat from the midday heat. He appeared to have just finished his afternoon meal. As they came in, one of his boys brought a bowl of water for the Balogun, which he poured over his hands. He wiped the water off on the sides of his dashiki.

Solesi saw that the Balogun was a shortish man with prominent Ibadan tribal marks. These were three horizontal lines that dominated each half of his face. He had a paunch. And the receding hair on his forehead was not quite covered by the ridiculously small soldier's cap he wore.

OLADELE OLUSANYA

No one would have guessed by looking at this meek-looking middle-aged man that he was the second most powerful man in Ibadan after the Baale.

"If indeed he is the commander in chief, where is his war tunic?" Solesi recoiled with indignation at this breach of his boyish expectation of the etiquette of war in a noted war leader of a famous warlike state.

"And where is his commander's baton?"

Solesi had expected that a Balogun of Ibadan would carry around the battlefield a baton like the Aare Ona Kakanfo, whom he had heard so much about.

In fact, at that time, Balogun Ibikunle did not just look old—he was very sick. He found it difficult to empty his bladder, and his body was swollen and heavy with dropsy.

Lately, when he appeared in front of his soldiers to address them or give orders, he had to have his lieutenant lift him bodily to mount his horse. And then they would strap him on the horse to keep him from falling off. On one occasion, at the end of a long day of skirmishes with the Egbas, his men had to cut his riding boots off his swollen legs and feet to get them off.

At that moment in the war between the Ibadans and their Remo allies on one side and the Egbas on the other, the Ibadans tenuously held on to their war camps in and around the town of Iperu. The besieged town was nominally in the hands of the Egbas, but lately, they had partially withdrawn to a higher ground to the west of the town.

The Ibadans had then moved their own men into the half of the town vacated by the Egbas. They left the remainder of their forces in a half circle to ring the town in from the south and east. For they planned a strategy that would finally dislodge the entrenched Egbas and push them back toward the border of Remo with Egbaland.

But the conflict had gone longer than the Ibadans had anticipated. More and more, it was becoming clear that this was not the quick campaign the Balogun had promised his men when they set out from Ibadan three months earlier. Their supplies in food and ammunition were running out, and morale was low. This part of Remo was not an agricultural country, and food was scarce.

The Ibadans had hoped for a quick victory so they could go home to celebrate the annual Oloolu festival, which had now come and gone. Many of them, especially the captains and warlords, had their wives, slaves, and even children with them in their camps. In those days of permanent conflict, families often followed the master of the house to battle.

The Egbas, at the beginning of the campaign, had occupied the town after they had driven away its inhabitants. But by the time Solesi and the Ikenne men arrived, the Egbas had withdrawn from most of their entrenched positions within the town.

Solesi knew nothing about military strategy. Later, he would come to recognize the advantages to the Egba commander of the strategic withdrawal, which now placed his men partially outside the beleaguered town. His men could now snipe at the enemy with their guns and arrows from the cover of the bush and the safety of the hills. If they had not moved out when they did, the Egbas would by now have found themselvescompletely ringed in by the experienced Ibadans, who would then cut their line of supplies for provisions and reinforcements.

When Solesi and the other Ikenne warriors moved into the quarters allocated to them by the Ibadan commander, they found the town of Iperu, which they knew from more peaceful times to be totally deserted by its residents.

There were no gossiping women in the village square. They saw no playful half-naked children chasing a stray dog along the narrow streets that led to the market. And not a single goat could be seen rummaging in the bush along the dirt roadways.

The center of the town around the market square had been the scene of a deadly hand-to-hand combat a week before the men of Ikenne arrived. A few stiff, bloated corpses lay around. They were blackened with soot from half-hearted attempts by the Ibadan men to burn the bodies to prevent disease.

The center of the town had been seized by the Ibadans after that engagement. So the surrounding dwellings and compounds, including the oba's palace, were now occupied by Ibadan war chiefs. But the Egbas, driven into the periphery of the town and the surrounding forest, kept up a constant harassment. Thus it was that the Ibadan commanders soon began to regret their lordly accommodation in the oba's palace.

In the days after their arrival, Solesi witnessed firsthand the deadly nature of these incessant attacks by the dislodged Egbas, who launched sorties, sometimes several times a day, to harass the Ibadans and their

Remo allies. In addition, Egba sharpshooters, hidden in trees in the small hills overlooking the town from the west, constantly sniped at the Ibadans as they moved about in their camps, picking off the men at will.

In this last enterprise, the Egbas had a deadly ally. He was a young man foreign to Yorubaland. And how did this young warrior come thousands of miles away from his home across the ocean to fight among a people whose language he barely understood?

Solesi would later hear the story of this man whose name was John Pettiford. He was a black American, a former slave, who at the beginning of the war between the States had run away from his master's plantation in South Carolina to join the Union forces in Boston, Massachusetts. On conscription into the Union Army, he knew he would become a free man by the proclamation of President Lincoln himself.

Pettiford joined the all-black Massachusetts Fifty-Fourth Infantry Regiment, which was commanded by Colonel Robert Shaw, an idealistic young white man from Boston. This was how Pettiford, a former slave, took part in the invasion of his old native state of South Carolina in a brazen attack on the rebel-held garrison of Fort Wagner, which lay at the entrance to Charleston Harbor.

Pettiford and other former slaves who had enlisted in the Union Army knew the risks they were taking by fighting with the Yankees against their former masters. If they were captured, they would expect no mercy from Southern soldiers, who viewed all freed slaves as "contraband."

Thus, in that famous battle under the guns of Fort Wagner not far from Charleston Harbor, Pettiford and the other black conscripts gave no quarter, for they expected none. They paid dearly for it. Only half of these ex-slaves returned from that battle, in which their beloved young white commander, Colonel Shaw, lost his life. Pettiford was one of the few who survived.

He emerged a hero. He had killed three rebel soldiers—the first time he would ever kill a man. It gave him a strange, savage satisfaction to thrust his bloody bayonet into the chests and bellies of those white Southern soldiers as the fight degenerated into a desperate hand-to-hand combat.

Many months later, Pettiford would tell his shipmates one night on board the merchant vessel *Pocahontas*, on which he served as a sailor hunting whales in the northern Atlantic Ocean, "I never looked at the faces of those men I killed during the war. But for all I cared, those three rebel soldiers could well be the kinsmen and nephews of my cruel former slave master in South Carolina."

Pettiford would not clearly remember afterward how he managed to survive not just the battle, but also the bitter retreat back to the North. But he knew even then that this was the singular experience in his life that would make him a man.

But before his regiment could regroup and be replenished before being sent back to the front lines, Pettiford deserted the Union Army. He threw everything he had away and buried his uniform in a forest somewhere in Maryland. He kept only his blue-gray forage cap, which he kept hidden in an old rucksack he found in a barn outside the village of Pikesville.

He trekked to Baltimore, where he stowed away on a whaling ship, which he learned was about to put out to sea. After a few days, he emerged from his hiding place.

After first giving him a flogging for embarking on his ship without permission, the captain of the *Pocahontas* put Pettiford to work on deck among his men. The ship was shorthanded due to the war, and the men were glad for any help they could get, especially from this tall well-muscled young Negro, who everyone suspected was a Union Army deserter.

Pettiford told the men on board the ship that he was a runaway slave, a "contraband." He hated the word "deserter." He also hated his slave name, Pettiford, but he kept it anyway. Only now, he insisted that everyone, especially his white shipmates, call him Mr. Pettiford.

It was in this way that John Pettiford sailed before the mast all over the Atlantic. He harpooned whales and cut them up for blubber. When at last he put to shore in Bristol, England, he told himself he was tired of life as a seaman.

His life at sea had actually been quite profitable. Not only had he saved all his earnings, but he was a free man. Most importantly, he had learned to see white men as his equal. And he had learned to read and write. He had become literate through the efforts of the boatswain, Mr. Billy, a quiet Englishman from Liverpool.

Pettiford was now able to think leisurely about his next voyage, which he was determined would be his last before he departed this world.

He was determined to get to Africa, the land from which his grandfather had been taken away as a slave a half century earlier. The legend in his family was that his grandfather spoke a language known as *Inago*.

But to get to his African homeland, Pettiford had to make another voyage by sea. Paying his way as a cabin passenger, he sailed from Bristol to Lisbon. From there, he booked a passage to the Guinea coast on a Portuguese schooner that traded along the West Atlantic seashore for native gold, palm oil, and elephant tusks.

Pettiford came ashore for good at Whydah and never went back to sea. He was determined to follow the trail of what he remembered of the tales told in his family of his Yoruba ancestral land.

By way of Badagry, he followed the British missionary Henry Townsend to Abeokuta. In this bustling capital of the Egbas, he found that the war skills he had gained at the battle of Fort Wagner came in great demand in a Yorubaland in turmoil. So it was that though he could hardly speak a word of Yoruba, Pettiford became a henchman of the Balogun of the Alake of Abeokuta.

With his military skills, he was a favorite in the Egba war camps. He would put on his old battered Union Army forage cap and smoke tobacco from a curved brown-stemmed pipe as the men gathered around him.

The Egba men stared in admiration at the calm, cool-paced audacity of their black-skinned mercenary. And indeed, he was a strange sight to behold. Pettiford always dressed like the other men in traditional Yoruba dashiki and *sokoto*, but he always had that strange old Union Army forage cap perched low over his eyebrows.

Pettiford spoke little to those around him. For he was laconic by nature. But he was an indispensable ally. First, he helped the Egbas push back the Dahomey raiders who, before then, had devastated the countryside around Abeokuta, destroying farms and carrying away men and women as captives.

Then he went to war with the Egba warriors as they confronted their old nemesis, the Ibadans—first in the disastrous Ijaiye War, where he taught the men who came with him from Abeokuta to shoot their muskets straight, and now in this punitive expedition to Remoland.

He was the only Egba warrior at the battle of Iperu with a modern functioning rifle. The other men had muskets. Pettiford's weapon was an 1853 Enfield rifle, which he had brought with him from Europe. Made by the Royal Small Arms Factory in Enfield, England, it was a single-shot, muzzle-loading rifle adapted from an older musket design. It was the most accurate long-range weapon of the time.

With this weapon, Pettiford was a deadly marksman. He found himself working mainly as a sniper for the Egbas. With the sights of his Enfield carefully adjusted, he found he could hit his target accurately up to five hundred yards, which was more than the distance any of the ancient and unreliable muskets of his opponents could reach. Besides, he was so far away that the enemy was confused. They never knew where the shots were coming from.

Pettiford's role at the battle of Iperu was to shoot down from a distance as many of the Ibadan war chiefs as he could. For this, he kept himself hidden all day long in a tree on the hillside overlooking the Ibadan positions in Iperu from the west.

His companions noted with wry amusement and admiration that even in the midst of battle, his strange blue-gray cap was always perched on the back of his head. And clamped between his teeth, they would see his old brown tobacco pipe, from which he would puff a small cloud of smoke from time to time. Then he would sight another target below and, with cool, but careful nonchalance, squeeze the trigger of his Enfield rifle.

*   *   *   *   *

Solesi watched with horror as Pettiford, the deadly foreign-born marksman, picked off the Ibadan war chiefs one by one. He learned from his hosts that many high-ranking Ibadan commanders had already fallen to the deadly sniper fire of this foreign adventurer, whose name they all knew.

Solesi learned that the casualties of Pettiford's sniping had already included the *osi balogun* and the *seriki*. Even the valiant soldier and warlord Ogunmola, the *otun balogun*, had only escaped within an inch of his life. His tall hat was blown off his head as he scrambled into cover.

Largely as a result of the activity of the deadly Mr. Pettiford, the Ibadan soldiers had now become disenchanted. They no longer had the stomach for this profitless war. After all, they were not fighting to defend their own turf or farmlands. And there was little promise of war bounty in slaves and treasures to be had, even if they prevailed and eventually won the war.

Many Ibadan warriors, some of them seasoned campaigners, began to press their warlords to take them back home to their wives and their farms back in the land of Oluyole. Soon, this pacifist sentiment and disillusionment with the war among the soldiers in Iperu filtered back to Ibadan.

The family of the Balogun of Ibadan was related to the Alaafin in Oyo. The Alaafin was still recognized as the supreme leader of the Yorubas even though his empire was a shadow of its former glory. The Alaafin was prevailed upon by the Ibadan leaders to craft a plan to save the face of Ibadan, his consistently reliable supporter and ally.

Stating that he wanted to forge peace among his Yoruba subjects, the Alaafin, therefore, sent the chief priest of Sango from Oyo-Atiba to Iperu, with a royal command for all sides to cease hostilities.

Thus, it was with some relief that Solesi and the other tired and disillusioned young warriors in Iperu heard that the priest of Sango had arrived in Iperu with a mission of peace from the nominal emperor of the Yorubas, the Alaafin of Oyo.

As Solesi listened to the older warriors talk about this message of peace, he heard them refer to the instigator of that message, the Alaafin as the foremost oba in Yorubaland.

"Iku, Baba, Yeye," they called him. There was a note of awe in their voices.

Death, Father, Mother. "What did this mean?" Solesi asked an older warrior from Ibadan. But even he did not know. Solesi was left to his own devices to make sense of this strange appellation of the Alaafin.

Regarding death, Solesi said to himself, "This is all around us on this exhausted battlefield."

"But Father and Mother?"

He remembered his own parents—Adeuja, the former Warrior from Ife, and his mother, the doting Efupitan. He was confused.

The Sango priest sent by the Alaafin from Oyo made a great impression on Solesi. He was a tall gaunt figure, with a shaven head and a face heavily scarred with smallpox. His only covering was a thin white robe tied at the waist. This left his upper torso bare. The exposed part of his body was covered with a thick paint of white chalk. His feet were unshod. And everywhere he went, he carried the emblem of his office before him. This was the wooden double ax sacred to the god Sango.

This priest was accompanied by two sullen boys of Solesi's age. They wore red robes tied at the waist, which also left their torsos bare. Their faces, necks, and bodies were painted with the same esoteric white chalk. They were acolytes from the Sango shrine in Oyo-Atiba.

Solesi wondered how these boys had managed to walk all the way from Oyo, which, in his mind, must be a faraway place indeed. It would be almost as far away as walking from the moon, he surmised. Since he did not see the priest and his acolytes on horses, Solesi assumed they had walked all that distance from Oyo to get to Iperu.

The war commanders on both sides agreed immediately to hold a peace conference, which would be mediated by the emissary of the Alaafin.

This meeting, which took place in a small house in the center of Iperu, went on for several hours that evening. News of the deliberation came back in bits and pieces to the common soldiers on both sides of the conflict, who waited anxiously in their camps. It told of how the commanders on both sides sat down, exchanged pleasantries, and talked to each other like long-lost friends. They listened politely to the messenger of the Alaafin and nodded their heads in agreement. After this, they all agreed to stop the fighting.

It was as if the madness of war was forgotten, for a few hours at least—replaced by the ancient Yoruba ethos for diplomacy and compromise. These were attributes that some of the older warriors told Solesi were hallmarks of the Yoruba people, now seemingly lost in an age of relentless war.

This peace agreed upon by all sides was remarkable news indeed to Solesi and everyone else who heard it. Just a few hours earlier, those same chieftains who had put their consent to this agreement, and the warriors carrying out their orders, had been trying to kill each other in all manner of ways with swords, guns, and arrows.

The reality was that both sides were tired of a war that had provided no clear advantage to any side. There were no victors or vanquished. Everyone was simply glad at the chance to leave the battleground and go home. They would leave the Remos to go back to their farming and trading.

As day broke, the war camps were struck, and bugles for cessation of fighting were sounded on all sides. Even the truculent Egbas seemed tired of fighting a profitless war and were ready to go home.

The captains and commanders of both armies mounted their horses and pointed their noses homeward. The foot soldiers trudged slowly behind them. And Iperu once more became a quiet and peaceful market town.

But when the exhausted Remo warriors returned to Ikenne, young Solesi was not among them. Someone said he had been captured by the Egbas. Everyone in Ikenne cursed the treachery of the Ibadan in not protecting him.

*   *   *   *   *

The truth was that Solesi had not been captured by the enemy. Despite the cease-fire, the Egba snipers were still at work even as the Ibadan warriors struck camp and prepared to leave. A ball from Mr. Pettiford's sniper's rifle had grazed young Solesi's head, and he had fallen into a swoon.

Seeing him fall, one of the Ibadan chieftains, who had been the actual target of the shot, picked Solesi up and placed him on his own horse. Not finding any Ikenne warriors nearby, for they had all gone, he had set off for Ibadan with the young drummer boy in tow.

When Solesi came to, they were already past Abanla village and were deep inside Ibadan territory. Going back home was impossible. Tears of rage ran down his cheeks.

It was the warlord Ogunmola, the Otun Balogun of Ibadan, who had rescued Solesi. He treated the young Ikenne drummer boy with kindness. He had his servant bind the young man's head wound and give him food and water.

And when he questioned the boy and got to know who he was, Ogunmola remembered his father, Solaru, who had fought with him at Osogbo. From that time on, Ogunmola treated Solesi like a son.

Years later, Solesi told his daughter Efunyemi what happened to him when they got to Ibadan. The warlord Ogunmola had the boy's cheeks carved with the tribal marks special to the people of Ibadan. This was not an abuse, as Solesi himself knew and explained to Efunyemi. In that time and age, it was a sign of distinction, indicating Solesi's acceptance as a citizen of Ibadan.

Since he had been adopted by Ogunmola, young Solesi was now an Ibadan subject and would not be allowed to go back to Remo. The understanding was that he could come and go as he pleased, but only within the walls that defined the boundaries of the city of Ibadan.

Not long afterward, the tides of war changed. Even though Remo continued to oppose the encroaching Egbas, they were no longer allies of Ibadan. The Ibadans were now fighting all the Ijebus, who now allied with Ife, Ondo, and Ekiti to confront Ibadan near the small town of Oke Mesi in yet another conflict that would be known as the Kiriji War. Being allowed to return home now became impossible for Solesi, the war boy from Ikenne.

Later, Solesi came to understand more deeply why Ogunmola had had his *onikola* give him the Ibadan tribal marks. Ogunmola had recently lost his only son. The gesture of the infliction of Ibadan marks on the face of Solesi was the warlord's rite of adoption of the captured war boy as a replacement for his son. Ogunmola wanted Solesi to accompany him to his battles and attend him as his *omo ogun*. Having the tribal marks identified Solesi as an Ibadan warrior. If he was captured in battle, he would be returned to Ibadan in exchange for whatever negotiated price or ransom his warlord was willing to pay on his behalf.

Thus it was that Solesi became a favored protégé of the famous Ibadan warlord. In this position, Solesi would remain by the side of Ogunmola for the next six years until the Ibadan leader passed away.

We do not know exactly what happened to that mercenary of the Egbas at the battle of Iperu, the deadly African American marksman John Pettiford. We know from the Old Woman that many stories were told about him. His bravery and marksmanship with the rifle were well-known. His odd, laconic, and quiet ways were also legendary. It was also true he had learned Yoruba, but he never spoke it much.

The stories that came down to us also tell us that he never took a wife. The winsome maidens of Abeokuta could not entice him with their soft eyes, their swinging hips adorned with colorful beads, or their naked bosoms, exposed when they went to the stream to bathe.

Pettiford kept to himself in the camps. Even though he was a protégé of both the Balogun and the Alake, he refused to be made a chief or a war commander in the Egba army.

And even though the Egbas learned from the English missionaries in Abeokuta that his first name was John, he insisted that everyone, especially white men, call him Mr. Pettiford. As a runaway former slave in America, he had been disrespected by white men too many times in his life. Being addressed by white men as Mr. Pettiford was his way of asserting his manhood.

What eventually happened to Pettiford is not very clear. A version of the story says he was captured by a band of Dahomey *ahosi* female warriors and tortured to death. Another said he caught malaria and died of fever in Abeokuta, cared for by an *iya olorisa* who lived on the banks of the Ogun River.

Whatever became of him, his effect on my family's history was very strange indeed. Because of him, my great-grandfather Solesi of Ikenne came to sojourn in Ibadan—a Remo boy with Ibadan tribal marks carved incongruously on both cheeks.

*   *   *   *   *

Ten days after Solesi arrived in Ibadan riding behind Ogunmola on his horse, Mapo, an event occurred that changed the status of the exiled young drummer-boy.

Ibikunle, the sick and old Balogun, the "lion of the camps," died. This resulted in immediate and far-reaching changes in the leadership of the town of Ibadan. Ogunmola was now the most powerful of the chieftains. He was asked to become Baale. This he rejected as being an effeminate title not befitting a warrior of his renown.

"Am I, Ogunmola, to become Baale, to sit at home and eat *eko* with the women while other men go to war and weave for themselves chapters of glory in the annals of our native land?" This was what Ogunmola reputedly told the delegation of Ibadan high chiefs who had come to his house to congratulate him on his elevation to the highest position in their town.

The story is told of how the Alaafin in new Oyo had then offered Ogunmola the position of Aare Ona Kakanfo. After all, the old occupant, Kurunmi, was no more, and the position had not been filled.

But Ogunmola also rejected this honor. He was already a celebrated warrior, he told the Alaafin. And if he wanted to be Balogun in Ibadan, he would. He did not think the position of Kakanfo of Yorubaland was any more distinguished than that of Balogun of Ibadan.

Ogunmola wanted something grander, the biggest prize of all in Yorubaland that was next in power and prestige only to the Alaafin. He demanded to be made Bashorun. But there was a problem. The Alaafin already had a Bashorun with him in the new capital of Oyo-Atiba.

But Ogunmola persisted in his demand, and in the end, the Alaafin agreed to have two Bashoruns. One would be in Oyo town to oversee local civil matters. The other, the more powerful position with its seat in Ibadan, would be held by Ogunmola as the military overlord over all Ibadan and Oyo forces.

Thus, within a few months of arriving in Ibadan, Solesi watched as Ogunmola, his mentor and benefactor, was installed as Bashorun.

Solesi accompanied Ogunmola to Oyo-Atiba to see his master receive from the hands of the Alaafin himself the staff of office and the great *ileke iyun*, the beads of chieftaincy, which he would now wear around his neck as the chief minister of the realm.

For Ogunmola, it was the pinnacle of achievement of a life dedicated to war and ambition. And even though the position of Bashorun, unlike in the days of Sango, did not give him the power to pass a death sentence on the Alaafin, it was still a very powerful position.

Here he was, Ogunmola, who was not even from Ibadan or Oyo, sitting on one of the mightiest of seats of the heirs of Oranmiyan. He did not come from any of the ancient families of princes and chieftains who had ruled the Yorubas for centuries. He was not even one of those in Ibadan, as scions of the old Oyo nobility, who proudly described themselves as having "arrived in town on horseback."

Of humble origin, Ogunmola was born into a small unknown family in Iwo, a small town to the northeast of Ibadan. He left his family at an early age, running away to Ibadan to seek his fame and fortune as a soldier and adventurer. At that time, not many people in Ibadan had heard of Iwo. But soon, everyone knew about him and his hitherto undistinguished birthplace.

The story Solesi later learned about Ogunmola was that he started out as a war boy to some of the most powerful chiefs and warlords in Ibadan. And he had made his mark. He had gone on their behalf on numerous raids to capture slaves and other booty. With his loot, he bought farms and became very rich.

The elevation of Ogunmola to the position of Bashorun brought a life of relative ease and comfort to Solesi, his young protégé. Ogunmola loved the young Remo boy—omo Remo, as they called him. And he protected the boy from those who would want to treat him like a captive or a foreigner.

Solesi spent many pleasant hours with the famous warrior, whose escapades were already the stuff of legend. Even though he was one of the greatest warlords that Ibadan, a city of warriors, would ever know, Ogunmola was also a great talker and spinner of tales.

A short man, he was said to have liked to wear tall hats to enhance his stature. It was one of those tall hats that had saved his life in Iperu, when Pettiford's sniper bullet had gone through it instead of through his skull. Ogunmola would also ride the biggest horses in battle.

Solesi discovered that Bashorun Ogunmola had a keen sense of the history of his land and his own place in it. He knew all the stories of Ibadan, even of events that had happened before his time. For as a young man, he had been a protégé of a son of Lagelu, the legendary founder of the town.

Ogunmola was also very boastful. He liked to talk of his battles and heroic deeds. And he described these events on a grand scale, just as he did everything in his life—with a sense of drama and ceremony. He had his own set of drummers and praise singers whose duties were to wake him up from bed in the morning and serenade him all day long. They followed him everywhere he went, even into battle.

Ogunmola's trait of colorful garrulity was a rarity among the Yoruba fighting men of that age, who tended toward the laconic. But Solesi, a lover of stories, was happy to spend many hours listening to the war stories of Ogunmola.

One day, as the Bashorun wound up one of his long stories about his escapades fighting the Ilorins, Solesi asked Ogunmola this question, "At the battle of Iperu, why were the Remos allies of Ibadan when, as I have heard, the other Ijebus fought against Ibadan?"

They had just had supper, and Solesi knew the mood for storytelling was on his master.

"It is a long story," replied the Bashorun as he leaned back against a stool covered with the hide of an antelope. He stretched his legs on the raffia mat on which they were sitting.

"I must start from the fall of old Oyo, then go to the founding of Ibadan and Ijaiye as refugee towns and the story of three comrades who became foes."

It was then that Solesi heard for the first time the story of Kurunmi and the Ijaiye War. And he heard it from the mouth of the person who played one of the most prominent roles in the conduct and conclusion of that conflict.

*　　*　　*　　*　　*

"The town of Ijaiye was founded about the same time as Ibadan after Ilorin fell into the hands of the Fulani, and our people fled south from the savannah.

"The old city of Oyo itself was later burnt and destroyed by the Fulani from Ilorin. The capital seat of the Alaafin was moved to the south to a place called Ago-Oja, later to be known as Ago d'Oyo and then Oyo-Atiba. It is the new Oyo, although it is not to be thought that it could ever be compared to the majesty of the old capital that had stood for almost a thousand years.

"The leaders in this new capital of Ago d'Oyo, especially the new Alaafin, were very close to the warlords who ruled Ibadan and Ijaiye. The three were like sister towns, all established around the same time by warriors fleeing the collapse of old Oyo.

"But at that time, this new Oyo was not strong militarily," Ogunmola explained to Solesi. "It depended for its protection on the strength of the warlords in nearby Ijaiye and Ibadan. The Alaafin needed their help to protect and defend what remained of his empire."

As Ogunmola went on with the story, he made it clear to Solesi that Ibadan was the most important and powerful of these three towns— Ago d'Oyo, Ibadan, and Ijaiye—whose leaders now managed the affairs of the former Oyo Empire.

All the three towns were occupied by refugees and members of the military establishment from old Oyo. But it was Ibadan that produced the best fighting men and war commanders of the new age. Thus, virtually all the military chieftain titles traditionally given by the Alaafin were now given to warlords from Ibadan.

"These included the positions of Bashorun and Balogun. Even the ancient title of Aare Ona Kakanfo, which had remained vacant for many years after the death of Afonja and Edun of Gbongan, was revived and given to Ibadan war captains.

"One of these transplanted warriors from old Oyo was a young prince named Atiba, who lived here in Ibadan with Oluyole, the Ibadan war chief who was my commander. Their close friend was another soldier named Kurunmi, who hailed from Ijaiye.

"They three of them—Atiba, Oluyole, and Kurumi—lived together in Ibadan as brothers. They shared a common cause fighting Ilorin. They saw themselves as doughty defenders of what was left of the Oyo Empire.

"Later, when Atiba became Alaafin in new Oyo, he elevated his two companions to the two most important positions of power next to him in Yorubaland. Alaafin Atiba made Oluyole of Ibadan Bashorun, or prime minister. He installed Kurunmi of Ijaiye as Aare Ona Kakanfo, or field marshal.

"But after the defeat of Ilorin at the battle of Osogbo by Ibadan in 1840, in which I took part as a young warrior with your father, a rivalry between Ibadan and Ijaiye began to grow.

"Those three—Atiba, Kurunmi, and Oluyole—had lived in the same camps and fought against a common enemy while they were young soldiers in Ibadan. But their views of the future and destiny of Yorubaland changed now that each occupied a position of power in his own domain.

"Atiba, as Alaafin of Oyo, was the head of the new empire of the Yorubas. Naturally, he wanted the Yorubas to be under one leadership—his own.

"Kurunmi, for his part, went back to his hometown of Ijaiye after he was installed as Aare Ona Kakanfo. But now that he was the leader in his own realm, he began to think that members of the new royal dynasty in Ago d'Oyo, now known as Oyo-Atiba, were not the true heirs to old Oyo.

"After Alaafin Atiba died, Kurunmi wanted to succeed to the throne a Yoruba prince who came from one of the old towns in the savannah close to old Oyo like Igboho, where children and grandchildren of the old Alaafins still lived.

"But Oluyole, who was now Bashorun in Ibadan, saw things differently. He saw Ibadan as the leader and protector of the new order in Yorubaland. He and other Ibadan chieftains came from Oyo. They had proven themselves to be the savior of Yorubaland after turning back the Ilorin army at Osogbo. Oluyole, therefore, felt that Ibadan should choose the leader of the Yorubas in the person of the Alaafin."

As Ogunmola explained it to Solesi, the powerful warlords in Ibadan, with Oluyole at their head, wanted their friend and ally Atiba and his family to remain in power in new Oyo. That way, they would be able to control the Alaafin and the affairs of Yorubaland from Ibadan.

These conflicting interests quickly led to a three-sided struggle. Ibadan sided with Oyo, while Kurumi opposed Atiba's plan to establish a dynasty in Oyo comprising his own line after he passed away.

"We young warriors in Ibadan at that time saw it as a quarrel between brothers—an *ija orogun*."

But what started as a quarrel over the rights of succession to the throne of Alaafin Atiba became a merciless war between brothers that broke the unity of Yorubaland.

"Alaafin Atiba was cunning. Before he died, he declared that the old rule that required the Aremo, the eldest son of the Alaafin, to commit suicide at the death of his father, should be voided. He wanted his son Prince Adelu, the Aremo, to succeed him.

"But this suggestion of the Alaafin was against the practice that had been in existence for the previous two hundred years in Oyo. Even those of us in Ibadan, who supported Atiba, had to admit this. The accepted practice was that the Aremo should die with his father."

Atiba's argument in revoking the old rule, according to Ogunmola, was that this was a new age. He argued that the office of the Alaafin, which was the supreme monarchy of the Yoruba people, needed a smooth and orderly succession of power from father to son. After all, as he pointed out, this was what had prevailed in the old days.

"And we in Ibadan, under the leadership of our Bashorun, Oluyole, agreed with Alaafin Atiba. So also did a few other Yoruba city-states aligned with Oyo.

"But many of the leaders of the other Yoruba towns—mostly in the south and east, such as the Egba, Ijebu, and Ekiti—kicked against this agreement in private. But they did not oppose it publicly until Alaafin Atiba died."

So it was that when Alaafin Atiba died in 1859, his son, Adelu, was made the Alaafin in Oyo in line with this agreement. However, his ascension to the throne was immediately opposed by Kurunmi in Ijaiye. Kurunmi refused to go to Oyo to pay homage to the new Alaafin.

The disagreement between Oyo and Ijaiye got worse when a rich merchant woman from the town of Ijanna died. Her name was Abu, and she was the *iya oloja* of Ijanna. Having no heirs, her property, by custom, was to be possessed by the Alaafin.

Ogunmola paused and had a drink from his gourd. Then he continued the story.

"But Kurunmi, in whose territory of Ijaiye the small town of Ijanna lay, claimed possession of Abu's property.

"Kurunmi's men, lying in wait, subdued the small force sent by Alaafin Adelu to enforce the royal claim. Not only that, Kurunmi seized some of the Alaafin's men as captives, after which he sent an insulting message to Oyo-Atiba that these men would only be released on the payment of a ransom of ten cowries per head. This led to war.

"Oluyole in Ibadan came swiftly to the side of the outraged Alaafin. Most of the Ibadan chieftains and we, their lieutenants, considered ourselves to be friends and brothers of Kurunmi. But we were alarmed that Kurunmi, if his arrogance and disrespect toward the Alaafin were not challenged and his ambition not thwarted, could become a thorn in the side of the new Yoruba order.

"I am afraid we saw in Kurunmi another Afonja, a rebellious Aare Ona Kakanfo, who disobeyed the Alaafin and cared little for the unity or survival of the Yoruba people.

"But the Egbas, Ijeshas, and Ijebus did not see it that way. They took the side of Ijaiye. They argued that an important old custom was being abrogated by the succession of the son of the late Alaafin Atiba to the throne at Oyo. On his father's death, they insisted that the Aremo should have taken his own life.

"To be fair to those people, even though we did not agree with the Egbas and the Ijebus at the time, what they thought was at stake was the principle of upholding tradition and the rule of law in Yorubaland."

Ogunmola paused in his narrative. He called for a servant to bring him a bowl of kola nuts. To wash it down, he drank copiously from a small calabash, which was replenished from time to time from the large gourd, or *ikeregbe*, of palm wine by his side.

Then he continued the story.

"This is how we at Ibadan found ourselves practically fighting every powerful city or king of Yorubaland.

"At that time, Oluyole was Bashorun, Ibikunle was Balogun, and I, Ogunmola, was Otun Balogun.

"The powerful Yoruba kings from Ijebu, Ilesha, and Ekiti who opposed the ascension of Alaafin Adelu did not stay idle. They swiftly mobilized their fighting men to come to side of Ijaiye.

"They sent them into the farmlands around Ijaiye to defend the town against us Ibadans. We responded by sending an army from Ibadan to attack Ijaiye.

"We were shocked that the Egbas came to fight on the side of Ijaiye against us. For their leader had recently sworn an oath of allegiance to Ibadan.

"But for the Ijebus, on the orders of their Awujale, to also come against us distressed us greatly. It was an outrage. The Ijebu king was supposed to be our great ally."

Ogunmola continued, as Solesi listened, totally absorbed in this story delivered to him firsthand by one of the protagonists in the conflict. He could see that it was the fascinating tale of a fight between brothers-in-arms.

"But I can tell you that we were neither surprised nor alarmed," Ogunmola added with a chuckle, "that the emir of Ilorin also declared war against us. This sly old enemy had always wanted to recover the territories we Ibadans had taken from him following his defeat at the battle of Osogbo.

"But as a war leader and Otun Balogun of Ibadan, I told my men and the other chieftains who gathered to discuss the situation that we should be ready to fight and to win. I told them that we, the fighting men of Ibadan, should not be afraid of any of these powerful city-states ganging up against us.

"These were my words to my comrades:

Awa ni kiniun
Ti obo nlepa
lati ja iru re je.

Oladele Olusanya

We are the lion.
They are mere monkeys
sniping at our tail.

"Deliberately, I had made my statement sound like an *ewi*."

As Ogunmola spoke, there was a glint in his eyes that, to Solesi, was like the smoldering fire of burning coal. He could see clearly that this part of the story animated his mentor greatly.

Ogunmola went on to describe to Solesi how he had brought out his short fighting sword in that war council that the Ibadan commanders held on the night before their first engagement with the Egbas.

"I showed it to the other commanders. Then I stuck it dramatically in the ground, where it stood quivering like an arrow," Ogunmola said, his eyes still blazing.

Solesi remembered an old story of Oranmiyan that he was told by the priestess of Uren in Ikenne. He thought Ogunmola's action was inspired by the story of Tunwase, the legendary companion of Oranmiyan, who had stuck his sword in a similar fashion in the sand on the eve of the founding of ancient Oyo.

Next, Ogunmola recounted how he made a powerful speech to the other Ibadan war leaders. He admitted that he tried to be as dramatic as he could.

"'I want you all to know,' I said, 'that once we embark on this war, we should expect victory or death. There is no turning back. We are like esos of old Oyo.'

"'If we turn back now, how shall we face our womenfolk at home? And how can we be sure we can defeat the Egbas and the Ijaiyes when they attack us in our homes if we cannot do so now that we have their town surrounded?'"

Ogunmola continued his story.

"I, for one, was undaunted because I knew we were lions. We would get the better of all of the enemies arrayed against us. What did we have to fear from the Egbas, who until recently were our servants? Or the Ijeshas, who I saw as jealous upstarts who would jump at any opportunity to enrich themselves at our expense?

"I reminded the other Ibadan war leaders that the Ijebus had only embraced the Ijaiye cause because the messengers we sent to Ijebu had been turned back at the border and not allowed to see the Awujale, who was our ally.

"Instead, the Ijebu king had been deceived into receiving the delegation from Kurunmi. The Awujale prematurely gave his word to the Ijaiyes. And afterward, he could not break it. The heart of the Ijebu monarch, therefore, was not in this war against us."

As Ogunmola had predicted, the military might of Ibadan proved too strong for the Egbas, whose performance was so ignominious that their war chief, Anoba, was forced to commit suicide after his forces were routed in several battles with the Ibadans.

Once again, as had so often happened in their short, but proud history, the Ibadans proved their military superiority. They prevailed mightily despite the many powerful city-states arrayed against them.

Kurunmi may have been described as the greatest Yoruba warlord of his age. But that did not count for much in the eyes of Ogunmola and the other Ibadan war leaders. In the end, Kurunmi and his allies were decisively defeated.

Ogunmola now turned fully to face Solesi as he came to the last dramatic scene of his story of the Ijaiye War. The Bashorun's brown eyes shone with pride. And now there was a chuckle in his voice as he described the final engagement that sealed the fate of Ijaiye.

"It was I, Ogunmola, who, as Otun Balogun of Ibadan, led my men to attack and capture the town of Iwawun. I did this to cut off the supplies that the starving and besieged Ijaiyes were receiving from the Egbas through that town.

"I wanted to end the war for good. I, for one, was getting tired of it and wanted to get back to my wives and my farms, which were being neglected."

He laughed and put the half-empty calabash of palm wine to his lips.

"But this is a battle I will remember for the rest of my life. I made my men rush in to take the surprised town in the darkness before dawn. The hapless defenders were still sleeping when we burst into their tents.

"I can still see images of the slaughtered Ijaiyes as we cut them down in their camps and among the tall corn in the farmlands around the town of Iwawun, where they fled. The cries of dying men filled the air. And the blood that we shed that day soaked into the soft brown earth, which hardened and cracked under our feet as we fought.

"The battle was bloody because neither side gave quarter. My men were impervious to pleas of mercy. The carnage that day was of a scale that I had never seen before or since in all my years of warfare. The Ijaiye warriors defending the town of Iwawun fought bitterly despite our superior numbers.

"But in the end, it was I—mounted on my horse, Mapo—who entered the defeated town of Iwawun at the head of my men to claim a hard-fought victory. I had my men raise the standards of Ibadan and the Alaafin in the center of the town.

"But by this time, five of Kurunmi's sons lay dead on the battlefield, including his eldest and heir, Arawole."

Solesi looked at the older man in awe.

"This was how we concluded the Ijaiye War and returned to Ibadan," Ogunmola said at last.

What Ogunmola did not add was that the victorious Ibadan warriors did not simply return to their homes in Ibadan to tend to their neglected wives and farms. After their great and stunning victory at Iwawun, the Ibadan army took a detour through the town of Ijaiye itself, completely destroying it. They slaughtered many of its inhabitants. Those who could not escape were taken captive and sold into slavery.

At the end, the victorious Ibadan army had reduced once proud Ijaiye to a place of emptiness and desolation. Ogunmola and his men destroyed and burnt down every single dwelling in the town. And they killed or carted away all its domestic animals.

This calamitous defeat, which saw the total destruction of his city, devastated Kurunmi, who alone among his commanders survived the battle. This was the city of which he had proudly boasted that no enemy could vanquish.

But as Ogunmola told Solesi, it was the death of his five sons— especially his eldest, Arawole—that broke the spirit of the old soldier Kurunmi.

According to Ogunmola, Kurunmi fought on for some time after this devastating defeat. He and the few men he still had with him harassed the departing Ibadan warriors in a bitter irregular action. But Kurunmi was now a warrior without a home to go back to, and a warlord without men to lead.

In the end, Kurunmi was forced to confront the reality of his position. He committed suicide.

"In line with the old warrior tradition of our people, Kurunmi, himself an Aare Ona Kakanfo, could not contemplate inevitable capture by Ibadan and a life of disgrace.

"In life, he had opposed the Alaafin, the symbol and head of our ancient Yoruba Empire. In death, he was true to the heroic tradition of our people. Despite his faults in life, Kurunmi personified the Oyo martial spirit. And I can say that he gained more honor in his death than he did in the many battles he had fought in his life. He chose death and honor over a life of disgrace."

Ogunmola now told the story of how Kurunmi, before his death, had made his attendants promise that his burial place would be kept a secret. He did not want the vengeful Ibadans to desecrate his body.

"After he died, Abogunrin, his head attendant, took two of Kurunmi's most loyal slaves with him to dig a grave for their master in the forests outside Ijaiye beneath an *iroko* tree. After digging the grave, Abogunrin killed the two slaves and buried them with Kurunmi's body so that no one would live to tell where the great warrior was buried.

"But somehow the secret leaked out. The Alaafin from Oyo sent his men to dig up the body. The head of Kurumi was cut off from the body. It was taken to the shrine of Sango in Oyo, where the skulls of all former Aare Ona Kakanfos, including Afonja's, are kept."

It was Ogunmola's opinion that Kurunmi's attributes as a man and leader had been overrated. After he died, he believed that Kurunmi's life story was embellished in the popular imagination by exaggerated chronicles of his exploits put out by his admirers. According to Ogunmola, this was what elevated him to hero status.

Ogunmola said wistfully, "Kurunmi is now revered like a god all over Yorubaland."

Kurunmi was Ogunmola's contemporary. The Ibadan warlord felt that he knew him better than most men. Ogunmola made it clear to Solesi that he did not care for Kurunmi's arrogance, his lust for power, and his insolence toward a reigning Alaafin. His cruelty to his chieftains was something else too. And in particular, Ogunmola thought that Kurunmi's unbounded appetite for war and booty, especially for slaves and women, was something to be condemned, not praised.

To illustrate this aspect of the character of Kurunmi, Ogunmola told Solesi a story of Kurunmi at the height of his power. It was in the aftermath of a military campaign that Ijaiye soldiers waged on Sabe, one of the original seven city-states of Yorubaland founded by the sons and grandsons of Oduduwa.

In that war, Ijaiye warriors under their Balogun, Akiola, completely overpowered this ancient town, caring little for its ancient pedigree. After they had made short work of Sabe, the Ijaiye men returned home with many captives. Among these was a beautiful young maiden called Ifawunmi.

As Balogun, Akiola had first pick of the female captives on the field of battle. So he chose the beautiful Ifawunmi. And he spent many delightful nights with her on the way home.

Unfortunately for the Balogun, when they got back to Ijaiye, Kurunmi insisted on his own selection of the war booty. He chose this same maiden, Ifawunmi, who everybody, including the trembling Akiola, assured him was a virgin.

Kurunmi had the girl washed, adorned, and brought to his bedchamber that same night. But the joy of possession turned into the bitterness of the cuckold when he discovered that Ifawunmi was no longer a virgin. The girl confessed to him that she had been despoiled by no less a person than Balogun Akiola. In a rage, Kurunmi ordered the death by strangulation of the brave Akiola.

Ogunmola explained to Solesi that this was just one example of the heartless and vengeful nature of Kurunmi.

These traits of cruelty and avariciousness, in Ogunmola's opinion, greatly diminished Kurunmi's achievements as a leader and war captain. Kurunmi was a bloodthirsty despot, he said, one who was unfit for the high office of Aare Ona Kakanfo, which his friend Alaafin Atiba had unwisely bestowed on him.

Ogunmola admitted that Kurunmi was a great general in his own right, perhaps one of the best of his generation. But he thought part of the reason that Kurunmi lost the war with Ibadan was because he had killed all the capable military commanders that he had in Ijaiye, like Balogun Akiola.

"He got rid of them because he was jealous that they would outshine or supplant him. Kurunmi was suspicious, imperious, and harsh toward his men," said Ogunmola.

"He was more cruel to his own *baloguns* than he ever was to his enemies. Thus, when the conflict came with us, his former comrades in Ibadan, Kurunmi had no experienced *balogun* or captain to lead his men."

According to Ogunmola, the Ijaiye men were individually very brave. They fought well, but they were essentially leaderless.

Ogunmola also pointed out that the war could have been avoided if Kurunmi had agreed to the compromise offered him by Ibadan. Many of the war commanders in Ibadan, especially Balogun Ibikunle, were reluctant to go to war against their old comrade. They, therefore, tried to give Kurunmi many chances to save face and avoid war.

"But Kurunmi's arrogance led him on. He believed he was fated to always triumph over his foes. This was why, in the war with Ibadan, Kurunmi refused all talk of compromise. He belittled us, his opponents and former comrades.

"Rather, he placed great stock in his own personal valor. He believed in the aura of the unconquerable Aare Ona Kakanfo, which, to me, is a myth of the past. He also overestimated the strength and number of the allies who had come to his aid. And to the very end, he put total faith in the fabled might of Ijaiye, which he called his *ilu jagun-jagun*, 'the city of warriors.'

"Thus, when the war with Ibadan started, Kurunmi told everyone who cared to listen that he had never lost a battle during his illustrious career as a warrior. 'Why should this happen now?' he asked them, beating his chest with his clenched fist."

Ogunmola continued his assessment. "I believe that Kurunmi went into that war blinded by his own bloated sense of invincibility. And it was this belief in a divinely bestowed destiny, rather than common sense, that, in the end, led to his downfall.

"Some people say that the gods of Ijaiye deserted Kurunmi. They forget that it was his arrogance and stubbornness that made him defy the authority of the Alaafin and the might of Ibadan. It was a misplaced trust in his own strength and those of his allies that led Kurunmi to fight on, leading to the total destruction of Ijaiye, his vaunted citadel and city of warriors.

"After the sack and plunder of the town, an edict, which I had nothing to do with, was proclaimed by the leaders of Oyo and Ibadan. It decreed that the town of Ijaiye was not to be rebuilt ever again as a place of human habitation.

"The effect of this edict, which today looms large in the stories and legends of our people, remains to this day. But to me, it is a curse on our land and a reproach on us Yorubas as a just and unvengeful race.

"But what could I have done? For the Alaafin, *igbakeji orisha*, *iku baba yeye*, supported this edict. And what the Alaafin says must be carried out. So today only wild beasts prowl and vultures hover around the once-crowded marketplace in the center of Ijaiye.

"As for the uprooted refugees from Ijaiye who managed to escape slaughter or capture, they were eventually given a place of refuge among the Egbas in their new town of Abeokuta. They named their settlement Ago-Ijaiye. This is where the remnants of the Ijaiye people reside to this day."

Ogunmola concluded that a lesson must be learned from the life and death of Kurunmi of Ijaiye. A good leader among our people should subsume his personal pride and willfulness to the good of his people. This was a principle that he, Ogunmola, tried to exemplify despite his admitted shortcomings.

Indeed, Solesi could see that despite the wildness of his younger days and his well-known imperiousness and penchant for self-promotion, Ogunmola was a far different kind of leader from Kurunmi. Where Kurunmi of Ijaiye was capricious, cruel, and vindictive, Ogunmola, as Bashorun in Ibadan, was reasonable, benevolent, and forgiving.

From what other people in Ibadan told him and from what he himself observed, Solesi could say that Ogunmola, on his elevation to the position of Bashorun, ceased to be a warlord and became a statesman.

Under Ogunmola's rule as Bashorun, Ibadan became a city governed by laws. The brigandage of the time of Oluyole, where a thief in the market would dispute the ownership of property with the owner, became a thing of the past. No longer could their detractors say the following about the people of Ibadan:

Ibadan, nile Oluyole,
nibi ole ti njare onihun.

Ibadan, the home of Oluyole,
where a thief would dispute ownership
of a stolen property with the owner.

Public brawls, *ija igboro*, among armed gangs of young men, that once bedeviled the city, decreased significantly after Ogunmola became Bashorun. The city of Ibadan became richer and safer. There was peace on its streets and security of life and property for its citizens. The influx of commerce that this state of affairs encouraged increased its population rapidly during the time of Ogunmola until Ibadan became the largest city in Yorubaland.

Another thing that Ogunmola explained to Solesi was that during the Ijaiye War, white missionaries and colonial administrators in Ibadan and Lagos supported the Alaafin. These *oyinbo* men wanted the new Oyo kingdom to remain peaceful and united under the Alaafin.

Their reasoning was that a unified authority under the Alaafin, the most important oba in Yorubaland, would promote peace and enhance the movement of goods and people throughout Yorubaland. It was these white people who convinced the people of Remo to supply Ibadan with food and allow guns and ammunition to pass to them from Lagos through Remo territory, even though their kinsmen from Ijebu-Ode were opposed to Ibadan.

Ogunmola explained to Solesi that this help from Remo contributed in no small way to the eventual victory of Ibadan in the Ijaiye War. This was why he, Ogunmola, and Balogun Ibikunle, had come to the defense of Remo at Iperu when it was attacked by the Egbas.

Ogunmola also told Solesi that after the Ijaiye War, the Awujale and his Ijebu chiefs were so incensed with the British that they forbade any white man or any non-Ijebu, for that matter, from entering Ijebuland or passing through its territory without permission.

Not to be outdone, the Egbas expelled all the white men, mostly missionaries, then living in their capital city of Abeokuta. For good measure, they burnt down the building that contained the printing press owned by the most prominent white man in the town, the Reverend Henry Townsend. It was he who published the first Yoruba-language newspaper in Yorubaland, *Iwe Irohin*.

According to Ogunmola, the Egbas wanted to punish Remo for allowing supplies and guns to get to Ibadan during the conflict. This was why they attacked the Remo towns of Ishara, Ipara, and Ode Remo—an action that led to the Iperu war in which Solesi had taken part.

"What a turn of events," Solesi said to himself ruefully. "If the Ibadans had not won the Ijaiye War, the Egbas would not have attacked Remo. There would have been no Iperu war. And I would not be here now in Ibadan, an exile from my homeland!"

*　　*　　*　　*　　*

Solesi's time in Ibadan was the epochal period of his life, just as it was for his father, Solaru, whose brief stay in that metropolis—his going to war in Oshogbo and his marriage to Aarin—dominated all the subsequent events in his life.

Just as in his father's time, the Ibadan that Solesi knew was a town of soldiers and refugees of war. It was also a town run by slaves. It did not take long for Solesi to find out that his master, Ogunmola, had a large retinue of servants and that most of these were slaves. Everyone knew that Ogunmola had become wealthy due to the success of his farms, which were mostly run by slaves.

Solesi estimated that slaves comprised about two-thirds of the population of Ibadan when he was there. Even the vaunted Ibadan army had a large proportion of slaves among its fighting men. Each warlord or chieftain brought his own men to battle. Many of these were slaves, whom the warlord trained and furnished with weapons at his own expense.

So who were these slaves, and how were they treated? Why didn't they try to escape?

Solesi discovered that the majority of the slaves in Ibadan were captives in war. War, in those troubled times, was a profitable business. Warlords increased their wealth and expanded their household by means of war booty, mainly in the form of captives who were sold or turned into domestic slaves.

But he also found that many of those persons designated as slaves in Ibadan were actually indentured servants whose families owed a debt they could not repay. Such persons had to stay with their master for a certain number of years, until the debt was paid, or until the person could redeem himself. Solesi was told of instances where men actually sold themselves to become slaves by reason of poverty and to avoid starvation in a time of war and famine. Therefore, only a small number of the slaves in any Ibadan household were actually bought from a slave market either in Ibadan or elsewhere.

From Solesi's observation, most of these slaves, who lived in the houses of great chieftains of Ibadan like Ogunmola, were treated like members of the family. They were generally well cared for, clothed, and fed by their masters. They were almost never resold. Most of them had the freedom to go and come as they wished. They ran errands for their masters, sold his goods in the market, and went to war with him.

Most slaves called the chieftain who owned them *iba*, "father," just like his own children. They chose to stay with their masters because, often, they enjoyed a better life with him than they had previously known.

Slaves were often given a share of the proceeds if they sold goods for their masters, or from war booty if they were soldiers. With their savings, many slaves were able to redeem themselves, take wives, or even go into business. Slaves were allowed to marry fellow slaves or even freeborn citizens of Ibadan, sometimes with funds provided by their masters.

Many masters took a fancy to their female slaves, took them to bed, and had children by them. It was agreed that once a slave woman was taken to wife, she automatically became a free citizen.

All the children born from the union of a freeman and a slave were free. They were not treated differently from the other children in the household. And they could aspire to a high position within the family and the town.

*   *   *   *   *

Life in exile was not bad for Solesi. He was not servant or a slave. Nor was he treated like one. Still, he was not a freeman. He longed for his home in Ikenne beside the sacred river. He missed his father and mother, his playmates, and the young maidens of Ikenne with whom he frolicked by the river. He often wondered if they also missed him.

"Wouldn't they have forgotten me? And would my friends and family still recognize me?" he often asked himself.

From the moment that Solesi was brought to Ibadan on the back of Ogunmola's horse, he had dreamt of escaping. But after some time, he began to say to himself, "Even if I were to get out of Ibadan, how would I find my way to Ikenne?"

Solesi became Ogunmola's favorite war boy because the Bashorun had lost his only son. This promising young man, named Ogunwole, died during a military campaign against the Ekitis.

Ogunwole was captured in an ambush by the Ekitis, who killed him instead of exchanging him as a war captive, as the custom was for such a highborn captive. Such was the hatred the Ekitis bore toward his father, Ogunmola.

And because Ogunmola no longer had a son—he had three daughters—his enemies, before a battle, would have their drummers beat out this song to taunt him:

> *Ogunmola o lomo;*
> *Awon omo Ibadan*
> *lo fe run.*

> *Ogunmola has no son.*
> *It is other people's children in Ibadan*
> *that he wants to destroy.*

Hearing this, Ogunmola's men would reply with their own drumming and singing.

> *Tani so pe a ko ni baba?*
> *Kai, a ni baba.*
> *Ogunmola ni baba wa*
> *Kai, a ni baba.*

> *Who says we have no father?*
> *Yes, we have a father.*
> *Ogunmola is our father,*
> *Yes, we have a father.*

Solesi also learned that Ogunmola had a fetish for tribal marks. He, Solesi, was not the only person whose cheeks were adorned with tribal marks on the orders of Ogunmola.

Once, Ogunmola captured some Egba war chiefs, whom he never forgave for their treachery for fighting on the side of Kurunmi during the Ijaiye War. Instead of killing these men, demanding ransom in exchange for their heads, or harming them in some other way, he had their faces branded with the peculiar tribal marks of the Tapa. Everyone knew this was a great insult to the proud Egba chieftains.

He later explained this exploit thus, "Mo so Egba di Tapa." *I turned the proud Egbas into Tapa.*

Though they were released and not killed, those Egba chiefs would bear the mark of their disgrace among their people for the rest of their lives. Ogunmola considered this a fate worse than death.

There was also the story of Ogedengbe, a warrior from Ijeshaland who, when he was young, had come to Ibadan to learn the art of war. Ogunmola took a fancy to him. He took Ogedengbe under his wing and personally supervised his training. But Ogedengbe returned to Ilesha to fight beside his countrymen in their rebellion to free their land and people from under the yoke of Ibadan. But he was captured in battle.

When Ogedengbe was brought back to Ibadan in fetters, the Ibadans regarded him as a traitor, not just an enemy combatant. They saw him as a former comrade whom they had fed and trained in Ibadan, but who had turned against them.

Ogedengbe was sentenced to death. He was being led away to the shrine of Ogun to be beheaded when Ogunmola intervened and pardoned him. But the great Ibadan chieftain wanted to teach Ogedengbe a lesson. He ordered that the young Ogedengbe should have *O'Bunu* tribal marks carved on his face. Ogunmola reasoned that this indelible mark would make Ogedengbe think twice before taking up arms in the future against Ibadan.

But Ogunmola was proved wrong in this act of magnanimity. For after Ogedengbe went back to Ijeshaland, he became a great war leader of his people in their fight against Ibadan. And he remained a painful thorn in the side of Ibadan until the end of that sixteen-year conflict known as the Kiriji War.

Solesi listened to his master as he raged over the perfidy of the Ijesha warlord Ogedengbe, whom Ogunmola himself had trained and whose life he had spared.

Ogunmola hated the Ijeshas and Ekitis with a passion. He never forgave them for the murder of his son. Besides, he saw them as traitors to the Yoruba cause. This was because at one time, they had aligned their forces with Ilorin, whose emir had promised to help them regain their lands from Ibadan.

Solesi accompanied Ogunmola on many of his military campaigns, including his brutal suppression of the Ekitis and Ijeshas. In one of the battles that the Ibadans waged against the Ijeshas, so many warriors were slaughtered on both sides that the river around which the battle was fought ran red with the blood of the slain for days afterward.

The Ibadan warriors referred to that battle as *ija feje boju*—the battle where you washed your face with blood. This was because for days after that battle, when people tried to wash their faces with water from the stream, they only succeeded in covering their faces with blood instead of water.

Ogunmola maintained a retinue of drummers and praise singers who woke him up every morning. They followed him everywhere he went as he made his rounds to see the Balogun and other chieftains of Ibadan. These drummers followed Ogunmola to his farms, where his servants and slaves raised yam, corn, and cassava and harvested the fruit of the *oro* tree.

They also followed him to war.

Thus, the sound that Solesi would later associate most with his time in Ibadan was that of war drums played for Ogunmola. He never forgot how his heart would quicken at the sound of those drums as he and other Ibadan warriors crouched with aching muscles as they prepared to make the mad dash into the open to attack the enemy.

In the middle of that mad cacophony of war, Solesi's palpitating heart would beat fast, and his skin would tingle. He would strain his ears to hear the beat of the *omele*, the small drum that was beaten by an Ibadan war boy even younger than himself. How could he ever forget the rapid beat of that drum that he himself had carried into battle at Iperu? And Solesi's heart would race even more when, in accompaniment to those drums, he heard the crier stationed behind the battle line sing out in a high falsetto the finely worded phrases in praise of their commander, Ogunmola, the war chief of Ibadan who never lost a battle.

Ogunmola, oko Foluke
Jagun jagun to fi ilu Iwo sile
Lati di ara Ibadan.
Baba mi, Ogunmola,
Igbakeji Alaafin ni Oyo ile,
O Jagun lo s'oke odo.
O molu pada was s'ile,
Bashorun ilu Oluyole
Iwo ni olokun esin
to so ilu Ibadan ro!
Jagun Jagun ke nile
Awon ota re nsubu loko!

Ogunmola, husband of Foluke,
The warrior who left
the town of Iwo
to become a great chieftain in Ibadan;
My father, Ogunmola,
second only to the Alaafin in Oyo.
It is you who carried war
up the hill above the river,
and conquered the foe
in the valley below;
Great Bashorun of the city of Oluyole,
You hold the reins of many horses
that keep Ibadan strong and unvanquished.
You are the chief who cries out
while resting in your tent
and your enemies are overthrown
in the field!

Solesi came to fear and love the beat of those war drums. Even when he was back at home, far from any battlefield, his heart would race when he heard the sound of drums as a troupe of drummers passed by in the street outside. And if he recognized the rapid beat of the *omele*, it stirred his blood and rattled his nerves as nothing on earth ever could.

"Where is my *omele* now?" he would ask himself.

Was it lost somewhere in the bush in Iperu? Or had it been taken back to Ikenne by his comrades to be presented to his parents as a testament to his death or capture?

*   *   *   *   *

Solesi loved to go around the different quarters of the city of Ibadan on visits with his master and on errands on his own. He came to know the names of the many *adugbos* and *agboles* inside the city. To his imaginative mind, those places were like colorful pieces in a highly intriguing tapestry.

He wandered through the narrow streets of Inalende, where refugees settled after their town burnt down in a fire set by raiding warlords. And Elekuro, a grove of palm trees which during Solesi's time in Ibadan, had become a famous market for the sale of palm kernel. His favorite place to visit, just to gape and look, was Oritamefa, where six different roads from six different directions met just outside the city gate.

Ibadan, as Solesi saw it, was the metropolis of Yorubaland, the melting pot where all manner of men and women came and were accepted. It was the place where anything was possible, where any plan or ambition was welcomed, nourished, and fulfilled.

On any single day on the streets of Ibadan, Solesi could hear every accent and dialect spoken in every part of Yorubaland. He saw palm readers, stargazers, and mullahs from as far away as Ilorin and Kabba. Traders and tricksters, farmers and fortune seekers, soldiers and warlords, travelers and merchants, slave traders and refugees—all jostled and bumped into one another. They crowded the narrow streets and colorfully named markets of Ibadan.

As he went around the town, Solesi marveled at the different tribal marks on people's faces, which spoke of their myriad places of origin. He saw people from Shaki, Igboho, and Ogbomosho, those ancient outposts on the fringes of the old Oyo Empire. He learned to recognize the facial marks of people from Ekiti, Ondo, Akure, and Owo; and of those that came from outside Yorubaland. They were Tapa, Bariba, and Igbira, even itinerant Hausa preachers of the Moslem faith. The latter combined proselytization in the name of Allah with trading in *tiras* and amulets to ward off evil.

There was even a handful of white-skinned Christian missionaries who had no tribal marks. Solesi was told that they were building their place of worship on Oke Kudeti under the leadership of their *alufa*, Reverend Hinderer.

Solesi noticed that very few Egbas and Ijebus lived in Ibadan when he was there. This was due to widespread resentment in Ibadan toward people from those two city-states following the recent wars.

Solesi discovered that the town of Ibadan was built in the midst of a hilly country. It was the proverbial city on seven hills. Its many high grounds were called *okes*, each with its own special name—Oke Mapo, Oke Are, and Oke Kudeti. The low-lying areas were called *isales*. With names like Isale Igbeti, Isale Odo, and Isale Idimu, they were situated in valleys that surrounded rivers and streams. These low-lying areas often became inundated with floods when the rivers—Ogunpa, Kudeti, and Odo Ona—overflowed their banks during the rainy season.

One of these *isales* in particular intrigued Solesi. It was Isale Ijebu, the valley of Ijebu, which he came to one day after going down the hill from Oja Oba and Oke Mapo. But he saw few people with the Ijebu tribal marks of three vertical lines on both cheeks. He knew of course that after the Ijaiye War, most of the Ijebu population, as well as the Egbas, had left the city.

Solesi listened to children playing in the street. He smiled at one of their songs.

> *Isale Ijebu ni ile Iyalode*
> *O di ile Adebisi*
> *Sunke—gbakere!*

> *Isale Ijebu is the home of the Iyalode*
> *Let's go to the house of Adebisi.*

He tried to imagine the Iyalode in that song as a rich and important Ijebu lady who had made good in Ibadan. But what did anyone know of this Iyalode except that her name was Adebisi? What had happened to her?

Solesi came to love the Ibadan dialect, which was very different from that of Remo. And he learned to speak it like a native. He loved the use of pun, which was unique to the people of Ibadan. He enjoyed their biting sarcasm, which he tried to copy, and the witty retorts and verbal dexterity with which the people of Ibadan spiced every conversation.

The people Solesi knew in Ibadan, including his master, Bashorun Ogunmola, believed that they spoke the standard dialect of the Yoruba tongue. This attitude was reflected in the works of the Christian missionaries based in Ibadan who had published the first Yoruba dictionary and book of grammar some years before Solesi came to live in the city.

In their translations, these missionaries used the Ibadan dialect, which was itself derived from the Yoruba spoken in Oyo. In later years, many people believed that it was the influence of those books printed by *onigbagbo* missionaries that led to the dominance, throughout Yorubaland, of the Oyo-Ibadan version of Yoruba in its written and spoken form.

For our people no longer just spoke their language. Now they could read it or have it read to them. But Solesi himself could not read or write. He did not have much contact with *oyinbo* missionaries or their native-born converts during his stay in Ibadan.

His master, Ogunmola, had no time for the adherents of the strange new religion of the *onigbagbo*, whether they were oyinbo or Yoruba. He only knew that these *onigbagbo* priests sometimes mediated disputes between warring factions and that they brought in food and aid to the wounded and displaced in the many wars of that time of troubles—conflicts started by warlords like him.

*   *   *   *   *

Solesi would stay in Ibadan for six years before he had the chance to get back to his native Ikenne.

One day, Ogunmola fell sick. Solesi was not allowed to see his master. But the hushed whispers in that stricken household soon became rumors that flew around the town—that the Bashorun was afflicted by the disease brought on by the god Shopona. Many noted *babalawos* and *oniseguns* from Ibadan and beyond were brought in. But their ministrations were of no avail.

One morning, Solesi woke up to the loud sound of repetitive gunfire. The sounds came from the main market, Oja Oba, which was not far from the Bashorun's compound.

Solesi rushed outside. What he had heard were volleys of *saka bula* musket shots that were being ceremoniously fired into the air by somber-looking Ibadan warriors arrayed in ranks. They were announcing the death of the great Bashorun.

With the death of his master and protector, Bashorun Ogunmola, Solesi knew his position in Ibadan had become dangerous. Ogunmola had made many enemies in his turbulent career. Now that he was gone, many of his foes would love to get back at his family and those he loved, including the exiled Remo boy. They might seize Solesi and sell him into slavery. After all, he was technically a war captive.

In the years since Solesi had been brought to Ibadan on the back of Ogunmola's horse, he had grown in size, strength, and wisdom. And he had become comfortable in his new town. But he continued to miss the place of his birth. He yearned to be back in Ikenne. He wanted to grow old among his own people. He would like to take a wife and have children who would speak the Remo tongue.

Solesi began to revive his old plans for escape. He added new refinements and memorized the route of his escape. By now, he knew the byways and quarters of Ibadan like a native. More importantly, he had a fair idea of the route to Remo. He would head south toward the hamlets of Ogunmakin and Abanla and then to the Remo border towns of Ipara, Ishara, and Ogere. From there, it was a short distance to Iperu and Ilishan, then Ikenne.

He was no longer the young and naïve drummer boy who had left his hometown to go to war in Iperu. He would return to his native town a fully grown young man. He was a warrior and hero who had been tested in many battles.

Solesi's chance came one night during a thunderstorm. Lightning flashed as Sango's ancient voice rolled down from the heavens in booms of thunder that made men shudder. Roofs were blown away, and there was flooding in the narrow muddy lanes that separated the houses in Isale Ijebu and other low-lying districts of Ibadan. Families cowered indoors in their huts. Women sat up on their raffia mats and hushed their crying children. They whispered in low tones ancient prayers and incantations to placate the god Sango.

Solesi took the saddlebag he had packed beforehand. Stealthily, he stepped out of doors, careful not be heard or seen. He made for the horses' stables, which belonged to the late Bashorun. They were not guarded.

He untethered Ogunmola's favorite warhorse, Mapo. Gently, he led the great horse out. He placed the bit in her mouth and the saddle on her back.

Solesi thought he knew what to do and where he was going. He had memorized his route. He would ride south on Mapo out of the city gates and keep going south.

But before mounting the mare, Solesi looked across the stables into the distance, one hand cupped over his brows. But he could not see much in the driving rain. Suddenly, the dark night was lit by a bolt of lightning, which startled the horse and made her jump. Then the thunder came. It was deep, growling, and menacing—making the earth and the heavens tremble. But to Solesi, it was an omen that all would be well. That flash of lightning had revealed to him clearly all that he needed to know.

Solesi knew the horse very well. For Mapo was the same horse on which Ogunmola had brought Solesi back to Ibadan from Iperu. And unbeknownst to Solesi, she was a descendant of Jagun, the warhorse that his father, the Warrior from Ife, had captured from the Fulani at Osogbo and brought to Ikenne.

Solesi mounted the horse. He pointed her nose southward and patted her flanks. The horse neighed in anticipation. By a strange telepathy between man and horse, Mapo knew her rider's intentions. She knew this would be no ordinary ride—not on this dark morning in the hour before dawn, with furious winds blowing about her ears in the raging storm.

But the brave mare was unafraid. She was prepared for this hour. She sensed the tension and desperation in her rider. And she knew what was expected of her. Since she had come back from the Iperu campaign, Mapo had never gone south out of Ibadan. But by a voiceless communication between man and beast, the horse understood the urgency and import of the occasion. It would be a wild ride to freedom out of the city boundaries to that land from whence she had borne Solesi into exile. Now she would take him back to his people.

Solesi dug his spurs into the horse's flanks. Mapo gave a great leap forward, and they were on their way. The horse followed that same route taken three decades earlier by her ancestor Jagun and the rider's father, the Warrior from Ife. They went out of Ibadan territory through Ijebuland and southeast to Remo. Solesi kept the horse to old unused forest paths. In this way, he rode without rest for three days, until he came to a stream he knew. It was the Uren.

Solesi heard muttering nearby. It was early morning. There were two women gathering firewood. They greeted him. And he answered them in the beloved Remo dialect he was glad he had not forgotten.

He jumped down from the horse. He stooped and scooped up some earth. He held out the red-brown clay in his open palm. He held it close to his face and smelled it. Solesi's face became damp with tears.

It was the texture and smell of that soft red earth that was part of his childhood and which he had not forgotten. He was in Ikenne by the side of the sacred river.

He was home. The war boy had come back as he knew he would.

CHAPTER 5

Ęweso, Solesi
Ǫmǫ Solaru
Jagunjagun Ile-Ife
Omo oba Akarigbo
Ǫmǫ Ijebu to kola Ibadan
Ǫmǫ orisa odo Uren
Omi ti ko ni gbę lailai.
Ǫmǫ ǫba nrin
Ilę nmi titi
Arin gbere bi eni egbe ndun
Egbe o dun rara,
Awǫn egbe re ni o fe ki.

Greetings, Solesi
Son of Solaru,
The old warrior from Ife,
Prince of Akarigbo in Shagamu,
The Ijebu boy with facial marks of Ibadan
Son of Uren, the sacred river
whose water will never run dry.
The king's son walks
and the earth shakes.
He feigns a limp when he walks
as if his side hurts.
But he is not in pain,
He just does not want to acknowledge
the greetings of his companions.

Solesi of Ikenne

I N HIS HOMETOWN of Ikenne, the war boy Solesi was mourned as dead after the Iperu war. Everyone in the town gave up hope of ever seeing him again. Surely, those dastardly Egbas had either killed him, offered him for sacrifice to propitiate their infamous *oro* deity, or sold him into slavery in exchange for guns.

Both his parents mourned him. But it was his father who took it the hardest. If only his father had known that Solesi had been taken to Ibadan, and by no less a person than his old friend Ogunmola, he would have sent a message to Ibadan and had him returned home.

But the gods would not have it so. Heartbroken, Adeuja, the former warrior from Ife, fell ill. He lingered for six years, but everyone saw that he had lost the will to live. He rarely ate or drank. He refused the concoctions ordered by the *babalawo* and *onisegun*. These specialists, who were called in by his wife and friends, came in, consulted their oracles, and declared that there was little anyone could do for him. At least, they were honest and did not deceive his family with unnecessary remedies and false promises.

And so it was that the Warrior from Ife declined slowly but steadily with no sign of remission or abatement of his illness. After some time, it became clear to all around him that he had given up on this world. His spirit was ready to be with his ancestors on the other side of that sacred stream that separated the living from the dead.

In his last days, Adeuja drifted in and out consciousness. In his delirium, he could be heard murmuring the names of his son, Solesi, who he thought was dead. And of Aarin, his former bride who had become a priestess. People heard him hold conversations with his aunt Tiwalewa, and his "baba" Osogbesan from Ile-Ife. He also talked to Osolarin, the dead father he never knew.

In the end, the Warrior from Ife died in his sleep exactly six years after his son had gone to war in Iperu and did not return.

Ironically, he breathed his last at that very moment that his son, Solesi, was setting forth from Ibadan on the back of the war horse,

Mapo, on his way home to his native town by the banks of the sacred Uren.

*　　*　　*　　*　　*

After he came home and learned of his father's recent death, the young Solesi was inconsolable. He would not eat or drink. The Ifa priest was called. The priest threw his ritual kola nuts on the mat spread on the floor and consulted his cowry shells for an omen. He muttered to his god Orunmila and spoke in wise old Yoruba proverbs. These he alternated with dreadful-sounding incantations that made those present shudder and move back. Then he drew himself up. He had a grave but not unpleasant countenance on his face.

The priest called for Solesi's mother, Efupitan, daughter of the Akarigbo of Shagamu. She knelt down before him. The look on her face was a mixture of fear and hopeful expectation. She waited for the dreaded will of the god Orunmila to be delivered through the mouth of his priest.

But Orunmila's priest smiled gravely at the widow, Efupitan. He declared that her boy would not die. He was destined to live very long on this earth. He would be a great chief like his father, and he would find favor from all quarters.

But after Solesi recovered, he was a changed man. He did not want to play with his old friends. People whispered that perhaps the Ibadans had bewitched him. He had become much older than his years.

Solesi himself had never felt better or stronger in his life. Physically, his body was fit, young, and healthy. But within him, he nursed a great bitterness. For his god had deceived him. Orisanla, that most favored avatar of Eledumare, had made to him an unfulfilled promise. He had prayed to the god that he would return home to his father and mother. And this had not happened.

Obstinate and bitter, Solesi no longer talked to Orisanla or visited his shrine. He refused to offer sacrifices to that deity. And then, he began to have nightmares.

Once, his nightmare woke him in the middle of the night. Solesi sat bolt upright on his mat. His breathing came in deep gasps. He could feel his heart beat loudly in his chest. His body glistened with sweat,

OLADELE OLUSANYA

though the night was cool. Through his delirium, his mind spun and whirled until his fired-up imagination took on a life of its own.

Solesi's body, borne on the wings of his imagination, took flight. It soared toward the bright orb of the sun, for it was no longer midnight, but midday. But though the light was very bright, shining directly into his eyes, he could see very well.

Solesi found himself in a strange land populated by figures from the myths and legends of his people. It was a place he knew from the stories of his childhood. He had come to the communal resting place of the heroes of his people—warriors and kings who had fallen in battle.

In this dream, Solesi himself was injured in battle and had died. As his eyes closed, he was carried aloft by three young maidens. They were clad in white girdles that exposed their upper torso. He looked closely at them. With a shock, he saw that each of these maidens had only one breast. Some had the breast on the right side, and some on the left. But always, each bosom was a single, round mound.

Solesi recognized these women. They were the female warriors of Dahomey known as the *ahosi*—the same warlike race of women of whom he had heard so much from his older comrades when he marched with them to the battle of Iperu. Instinctively, he called them in his Remo dialect "ewen yemi," *my mothers,* even though they were young maidens, no older than him. But he never found out where these "ahosi" were taking him. For just as they took him in their arms and soared aloft, he woke.

These dreams came often. Even when he was awake, they bothered him. He began to worry about deep spiritual questions that had never troubled him in the past. He pondered the mystery of life and death, and if something continued after men took their last breath. He thought about his dead father. *Where was the Warrior from Ife now?*

"Do we live on somewhere after we die?" he asked.

"If that is so, why hasn't my father reached out to talk to me. Or is it that those who have gone to that place of rest are forbidden to commune with those they have left behind on earth?"

He talked to his mother, then the priest of Orunmila, about these questions. But he was not satisfied. What they told him was difficult for him to accept. For he had begun to doubt the truth of those stories of the origin of men and their fate in the afterlife that he had heard from his childhood.

Thus it was that Solesi, a youth of seventeen, grew old before his time. He became saddled with the questions and doubts that should trouble an old man, not a young man in his prime of life.

*　*　*　*　*

As predicted by Orunmila's priest, Solesi recovered from his illness. He prospered in his hometown of Ikenne. He took over his father's farms and enlarged their boundaries. Soon he had more than forty slaves and servants working for him.

But more than his success as a farmer, what made Solesi famous as he grew into manhood, was his preeminence in the cultural life of Ikenne. He became a music impresario.

Solesi reorganized the drummers and musicians of the town into one large group. Under his leadership, his group revived old songs and practiced new ones. They performed their songs for chiefs and commoners alike. And so it was that Solesi's troupe of musicians and singers became a regular feature at religious festivals and social celebrations such as the installation of kings, not only in Ikenne, but all over Remo.

Perhaps the people of Remo remembered that he was the son of a princess of Shagamu. Whatever it was, they honored him for his musical creativity and high social position. They praised him for his revival of the traditional music of Remo.

Solesi became a confidant and favorite of the oba of Ikenne. Soon, he was invited to join the *awo eegun*, the high council of the leading *egungun* societies in Ikenne. In this capacity, he came to know many of the cults and secret societies of his town. One of these was the *eluku,* the most secret cult in Remo.

The mysterious men of the *eluku* came out by day or at night, but no one who was not an initiate was permitted to see them. People stayed in their homes and listened to the pronouncements of the *eluku* from behind closed doors.

The men of the *eluku* were not *egungun*. They did not dress in colorful strips of linen and raffia. And they did not hide their faces behind fearsome masks. The role of the *eluku* in the community was to single out persons perceived to have done wrong or behaved badly. The *eluku* would go in front of the house of the person so indicted. In lyrics and song, they would describe the alleged malfeasance. Then they would prescribe *etutu,* remedies that had to be carried out before the wrong-doer could be readmitted into the good graces of society.

Then there was the *oro* cult. The *oro* deity lived deep in the forest outside Ikenne where it was worshipped by its high priest with deep and sacred rituals. The ceremonies of the *oro* were meant to cleanse the town of Ikenne after epidemics and misfortunes. It was at such times that the men of *oro* would come out. They carried long flexible wands made of cane. Tied to each wand was a length of string ending in a small wooden carving in the shape of a fish. This was the symbol of the *oro*.

The *oro* worshippers produced unearthly sounds with these wands. When these piercing, high-pitched sounds were heard by the terrified townspeople, the *oro* was said to cry.

"*Oro nke*" people said, and they would cower inside their houses.

But the secret society in Solesi's time that captured the imagination more than any other cult, invoking fear in the ordinary people of Ikenne and other Ijebu-Remo towns, was the *agemo*. Solesi was told that the first *agemo* came from Ijebu-Ode. The *agemo* was viewed with great fear by the people of Ikenne. For everyone knew it could strike people dead from a distance.

When at last Solesi found himself for the first time a participant in an *agemo* procession, it was a strange, mystifying spectacle that met his eye. In the center of the packed group of men was a single rolled-up raffia mat. What was wondrous was that this mat managed to stay erect without anyone being inside it. So powerful was its magic that women were not allowed to see the *agemo*. Any woman who spied on the *agemo* would die instantly.

Solesi became acquainted with the rituals practiced by these secret societies of Ikenne. But he never developed a deep spiritual connection with those mysteries. He did not advance to a higher metaphysical plane. On the contrary, his sense of spirituality remained earth-bound. He remained troubled by those questions that had troubled him during his illness on his return from Ibadan. And he still had no answers to them.

Where do we come from? What happens to us when we die? But he no longer worried so much about these questions. He knew now that he would never be able to find answers to them. The truth of it came to him gradually. The gods had not given him the gift to read the minds of men, or to curse and prophesy. What he was meant to do was to change people's lives through the power of his music.

He had been invited to join those esoteric societies in Ikenne because he was a sociable man with a great life story. Everyone loved to have him in their group, for he was a hero of the war with the Egbas and a protégé of the *oba* of Ikenne. His presence in any group meant that the group would find favor with the people of Ikenne and their monarch, the Alakenne.

Through his father, the Warrior from Ife, and his mother, a daughter of the Akarigbo, Solesi's family was already well-known and respected in Ikenne. But now, by his own rights, he became quite important in the social life of his town.

His farms were productive and he was reasonably wealthy. He moved in the high social circles of his town. The *oriki* singers, who sang of the achievement of the great men of Ikenne, were patronized by him. He came in and out of the *afin,* the oba's palace, as if he lived there.

Thus, it was inevitable that though he was already a prince of Remo through his mother, the Alakenne made Solesi a chief. He became the *seriki* of Ikenne. This was in recognition of his prowess as a former child warrior and his skills with the horse. Solesi was the first to be given that title in Ikenne. By virtue of this office, he became a member of the *osugbo,* the council of chiefs that advised the *oba.*

Later, when he had become an old man and had been conferred with more chieftaincy titles than he could count, Solesi would relate to his listeners the events of that day of his installation as *seriki* of Ikenne. He put his memory into a song, using his skills as a former *egungun* troupe leader.

> *Aiye ye mi lojo yen*
> *Ti mo di oloye n'ilu Ikenne,*
> *Mo wewu oye*
> *Mo wo bata ileke;*
> *Oba wa fi ewe akoko*
> *si egbe eti mi!*

> *Life was sweet for me on that day*
> *When I became a chief of Ikenne;*
> *I wore a robe of honor*

and on my feet were sandals
decorated with costly beads.
And 'twas the king himself
who placed the "akoko" leaves
around my ears!

Not just in Remo but throughout Yorubaland, the *akoko* leaf was the symbol of chieftaincy. On that day of his chieftaincy investiture as *seriki* of Ikenne, Solesi wore his *akoko* leaves tucked inside his *abeti aja* cap with pride.

Solesi knew that the people expected something dramatic and entertaining from him. So he paraded Mapo, his white horse. He put the horse to a gallop, then stopped suddenly, causing the horse to rear up and bring its great hooves crashing down on the ground to the delight of the crowd.

He pranced around on the horse, showing off many carefully-rehearsed antics that the horse executed flawlessly. Then he dismounted, and asked the groom to take the horse back to the stable.

After this, Solesi joined his friends who had come to celebrate with him. After having a few draughts from a gourd of palm wine, Solesi stepped out in front of the group. His *bata* drummer saw him. Sensing his intention, the drummer moved close to Solesi. He began to strike with his two hands the tightly-stretched skin made from the skin of a kid goat on both sides of the two-faced drum.

Solesi responded. As he moved to the synchronized beat of the *bata*, he stamped his feet in measured steps. He held his head up while his upper body barely moved. And when the beat quickened, he bent his body and moved with passion to the rhythm. He allowed his arms to swing as he ceremoniously swished the skirts of his voluminous *gbariye* back and forth.

As this newest and youngest chief in Ikenne danced to the stately beat of the *bata*, an *akewi* appeared as if out of nowhere. And as he began to sing out Solesi's praises, the mellifluous voice of this praise singer gradually supplanted the deep thumps of the *bata* drum. After some time, the *bata* drummer beat a few dramatic flourishes on his drum. Then he raised his arms up in the air and withdrew to the cheers of the crowd. But before he had given his *bata* drum one last resounding thump, another drummer stepped up.

This was Baba Lati, who had already become the greatest practitioner of the talking drum the town of Ikenne would ever know. Baba Lati beckoned to his companions, and his full troupe of *dundun* drummers joined him.

"*Gbadi-gba-ngba-di, gbadi-gba-ngba-di,*" the voices of the talking drums said as they conversed with each other.

The *akewi* had to strain to make his thin, high voice heard above the heavy thuds of the talking drums.

> *Solesi, omo Adeuja*
> *Omoba lofin ni Shagamu*
> *Omo oba nrin, ile nmi titi*
> *Omo akenugbo,*
> *ki eru ba ero ona.*
> *Akeredolu,*
> *oko omoge mefa*
> *Ma gbadun ni tire*
> *Ti nba j'obirin,*
> *Solesi ni mba fe.*
> *Iru aso wo l'oloye wo*
> *Aso ofi ni -*
> *To ba wo dudu l'aro*
> *A wo funfun lojo ale.*

> *Solesi, son of Adeuja*
> *Prince of the palace in Shagamu*
> *The prince walks and the earth trembles.*
> *Is it not he who cries in the forest*
> *And people in the town quake with fear?*
> *Akeredolu, lover of six maidens,*
> *Life is meant to be enjoyed by you*
> *If I were a woman, it is Solesi*
> *I would want for a husband.*
> *What kind of cloth does the chief wear?*
> *It is a rich "ofi" cloth.*
> *He wears a dark blue color in the morning,*
> *But by evening time,*
> *he has changed to dazzling white.*

OLADELE OLUSANYA

Solesi turned to the crowd and laughed at these exaggerated praises. Still, he danced on. But after some time, overwhelmed perhaps by the heat of the afternoon sun and the energy of his own antics, Solesi stopped dancing.

Seeing this, the singer turned to the drummers and exclaimed,

Ko ma ro,
enyin egbe mi.
Mo le se bayi d'ola
nitori ore mi Solesi,
Omo Jagun Jagun Ife,
Omo olukun esin
to so ilu Ikenne ro.

Let your drums roll,
My good men.
I can sing like this till tomorrow
Because of my friend Solesi,
Son of the Warrior from Ife.
He is the owner of the horse's bridle,
the very rope that binds
the town of Ikenne together.

For years afterward, stories were told in Ikenne of the feasting, drumming, and dancing that went on that day of Solesi's installation as *seriki* of Ikenne.

It was not until dusk fell that people dispersed to their homes. The fear of darkness and the maleficent forces that ruled the night were still entrenched deep in the psyche of the people. But as they went to their homes, people said to each other that Solesi was the youngest person they could remember in Ikenne to be made a member of the *osugbo*.

Soon after this, Solesi became the head of all the *egungun* and drumming troupes in Ikenne. And when his *egungun* came out to perform, the two most singular spectacles that the people of Ikenne came to watch were the ancestral spirits of Obara, the hunter who founded Ikenne, and Ogbodo, the priest of Orunmila who chose the site of the town.

* * * * *

It was the day of the festival to mark the jubilee of the Akarigbo in Shagamu. The Akarigbo was the paramount monarch of Remo, and all the great chiefs from all over Remo jostled to be seated near him.

People came from every town and village of Remo. Performing groups had been invited from Ipara, Ishara, Ode Remo, Ikenne, and Ilishan. All these towns and hamlets, even small Ogere, sent their troupes to pay homage to the king of all Remo. But what everyone came to see in particular was the troupe from Ikenne led by Solesi, who himself was a prince of Shagamu.

As Solesi watched his drummers come out, he was proud of them. He could feel their excitement go through him. It was like the force he felt when he was in the shrine of a god. Indeed, it was a strange and mystical experience beyond the understanding of other men. He and his musicians were a tightly-knit, esoteric group with uncommon skills. And the work they produced together was very powerful indeed.

And now, as his group began to test their drums with well-practiced beats, Solesi warmed to the sound of each drum. He knew that what the crowd most wanted to hear was the *ilu dundun,* the set of drums that could be made to "talk" to imitate the pattern of human speech.

The *iya-ilu,* which dangled at hip level, was the mother of all the talking drums. This, Solesi reserved for himself. Then there was the *gangan*, the most adaptable of the talking drums. It was tucked under the armpit and was played by the best drummer in the troupe.

The smallest drum in this ensemble, the *omele,* was also held by the arm beneath the armpit. Its rapid staccato beat provided a steady percussion rhythm for the heavier, deep-toned drums. It was struck with a small curved drumstick by a younger member of the group. This was the same drum Solesi carried when he marched off to war to fight the Egba years earlier. But he had hung his own *omele* around his neck to allow him more freedom with his hands.

The music from the drums that Solesi's troupe presented that afternoon was the foundation for the complex polyrhythmic sound that would make Yoruba music so much appreciated by a later generation.

Taken by slaves from Yorubaland across the great ocean to the New World, it would form the basis of modern music from jazz and reggae to salsa.

But in Yorubaland in the nineteenth century, it was a small group of men like Solesi who revived the ancient drumming of our people and ensured that the tradition would be preserved for future generations.

As the civil wars across Yorubaland came to a close, people began to brighten their lives with scenes of religious festivals and family celebrations such as *isomo-loruko*, *igbeyawo*, and *ifijoye*. Music at these occasions of merry-making was provided by a plethora of dance troupes, each with its own master drummer, singer, and impresario.

This phenomenon went on all over Remo and Yorubaland. What made Solesi stand out was his integration of an array of other musical instruments with his "talking" drums to create a sound that was unknown in an earlier age. Solesi was one of the pioneers of the traditional Yoruba music later known as *agidigbo*.

And just as he had been versatile in learning the use of many different weapons when he went to war as a war boy, Solesi now acquired the skills necessary for the mastery of the many different musical instruments available in that day in Remo.

First, he established the *shekere* as the basic rhythm that set the pace for his drummers. The *shekere*, in Solesi's time, was a gourd covered with a net to which were attached small cowry shells that produced a swishing sound when shaken—basically it was a rattle. With the *shekere*, Solesi could slow or hasten the pace of his music by varying the rapidity at which that instrument was shaken or beaten against the palm of his hand.

Among his many skills, Solesi learned to play the stringed instrument known as *goje*. Most people believed that the *goje* came from the Hausa and Fulani soldiers who invaded Yorubaland at the time of the Ilorin incursion that culminated in the Battle of Osogbo. Solesi credited his family with introducing the *goje* to Ikenne when his father, the Warrior from Ife, brought a *goje* with him from Ibadan in 1840 during his flight on the famous horse Jagun with his young bride Aarin. It was Aarin, after she had become a priestess, after the Warrior from Ife had died, who gave the *goje* to Solesi.

But the crown jewel of Solesi's musical collection was the *molo*. It was a simple sounding box made of light wood. In the middle of this box was a large hole on the edge of which were attached five pieces of aluminum that were plucked to produce graduated pitches of sound.

The *molo* was usually laid on a stool in front of the musician, who strummed it with the fingers of both hands. But Solesi made a leather strap for his *molo* by which he hung the instrument from his neck. Solesi played this instrument with exceptional virtuosity. He even introduced an extra percussion beat to the *molo* by beating the side of the wooden box with his left thumb on which he wore a brass ring.

The *molo* that Solesi played that day before the Akarigbo was bought in Ikenne from an itinerary trader from Ekiti. By this time, the *molo* had become a musical instrument of the Ijebus as much as that of the Ekitis. And when, years later, it was exported to the island of Eko, it became an essential part of the popular *agidigbo* music. Many people even began to refer to the *molo* as the *agidigbo* itself.

Thus, when Solesi's troupe came out that day in the courtyard of the king's palace in Shagamu, it was a sophisticated ensemble of instruments, drummers, and singers that entertained the monarch of Remo and his guests.

First to perform were the royal *gbedu* drummers. Seated before their big drums, they beat out a stately symphony in honor of the king of Remo.

After this prelude, the maestro stepped forward. Solesi's sonorous voice rang out as he delivered this exhortation not just to his troupe, but to the eager audience:

> *Jelenke la o jo o*
> *Onilu mi fi lu si;*
> *To ba ti fi lu si*
> *A o ma bere gbe*
> *A o di jelenke.*
> *Nitori tani ma ba gari ja*
> *To ma ni iyanrin*
> *lo dun fohun lati je?*
>
> *It is a gentle beat*
> *that we must dance,*
> *My drummers,*
> *play your drums.*

OLADELE OLUSANYA

Once we start the beat,
let the audience join in chorus
And we will create a mellow symphony.
For who would quarrel with gari
and say that sand is
good for him to eat?

Solesi made a signal with a snap of his fingers and stepped back. Instantly, a sole *gangan* drummer stepped out. This man went boldly before the Akarigbo. He prostrated with his full length on the ground in homage to the king of Remo and the gathered chieftains. Then he stood up and dusted his *dashiki*. Tucking his *gangan* under his left armpit, he proceeded to shower praises on the king with his talking drum.

This was the famous Baba Lati. He had been trained by Solesi himself. But his skill now outshone that of his mentor. No voice of accompaniment was raised as Baba Lati sang the king's *oriki* with his sole talking drum.

After Baba Lati's virtuoso performance, Lanipekun, the famed *akewi* stepped forward. He was accompanied by several drummers carrying the full complement of *dundun* drums. The big *iya ilu* led the way, followed by the *gangan*, *gudugudu*, and the small *omele*. These drums serenaded the monarch and his chieftains with their deep, medium, and high notes. And as they played, they modulated their beats to the voice of the akewi.

Lanipekun was renowned and beloved all over Remo, but he was not a native of Ikenne. He hailed from Aiyepe. Many years earlier, Solesi had made a long journey to lure Lanipekun from his village on the edge of the lagoon. Under Solesi's tutelage, Lanipekun came into his own as the best praise singer in all Remo.

And today, despite the efforts of the *dundun* drummers to drown him out, Lanipekun did not disappoint. And when he appeared to be exhausted and his voice lagged, it was the Akarigbo himself who reached into a goatskin bag and threw money at him. It was a shower of *owo eyo*, cowry shells that Lanipeku stooped to pick from the ground without missing a note.

But today, Solesi kept the best till the last. People were beginning to say that there could be nothing better than the mellifluous voice of Lanipekun weaving in and out of those ancient drumbeats, when men and boys bearing several musical instruments, *shekere, seli, goje,* and *kakaki* stepped into the clearing.

Solesi had brought in a young boy no older than nine years of age, whose sole contribution was to strike a special bronze *agogo* with a thin metal rod that lent a plaintive tinkling voice to the symphony. He also had another young musician beat out a rapid rhythm with a thin wooden stick on a tiny hand-held *sakara* drum.

"*Ko-ko. Ko-ko-ko,*" it sounded, as the *shekere* swished and followed the harmony. And not to be outdone, the *kakaki* blower threatened to destroy the hearing of the crowd with his bugle.

It was then that the *egunguns* came out. The spirits of the founding ancestors of towns and villages all over Remo were represented on that day in full voice and regalia.

From Ikenne came the ancestral spirits of Obara and Ogbodo. They were followed by the founding spirits of Shagamu. Sabindu and Somoye were the two most fearsome *egunguns* in Shagamu. They were said to be so combative that the two were not allowed to come out together.

It was Sabintu who came out that day. His entry was as dramatic as the expectation of the people demanded. A hush came over the crowd and people pointed. On the roof of a nearby house, a figure could be seen. People gasped. They held their breath and looked more closely at the figure from the underworld. It was said that it would be a bad day for everyone if Sabintu wore red.

There was a sigh of relief. For on this day of the king's jubilee, Sabindu was dressed in multicolored strips of black, blue, and green.

Sabindu jumped from the roof to the ground. And as his criers and handlers scattered everyone before him, he appeared before the seated obas. In the guttural tones of the other world, he greeted and prayed for the monarchs and chiefs of Remo.

The last *egungun* to come out was the spirit of Koyelu, the great Akarigbo whose followers had founded many of the towns of Remo. The current Akarigbo stood up and bowed to the spirit of his famous ancestor. The *egungun* Koyelu appeared only once every five years or so, and few in the crowd had ever seen him. Tales of the exploits of the famed Koyelu only came from old men late in the evening after they had had several gourds of palm wine.

From Koyelu's head, a thin wispy spiral of smoke issued from a coal furnace that lay deep in that fearsome head.

At the sight of this apparition, women and children in the crowd panicked and scattered in all directions. But everyone knew that they would be back. The allure of those ancient drums, the eerie tones of the *akewi* and the antics of the criers that attended the *egungun*, would be too much of a spectacle to miss, even for the most timid of women.

At this time, many in the crowd may have noticed that Solesi was no longer to be seen among his troupe of drummers. Perhaps, some in the audience looked at a particular *egungun* from Ikenne and thought they detected a resemblance in this spirit-dancer to Solesi's gait and bearing. But if they did, they kept this to themselves.

Now, everyone in the audience knew that the drum *egunguns* liked to dance to was the *bata*. It was the large, two-faced drum that Solesi had danced to at his installation as chief in Ikenne.

The *bata* was beaten with both hands at both ends. Its rhythm was irregular. And it was with grave, measured steps that the *bata* dancer interpreted its beat. Like an opera, each dance of the *bata* that the Akarigbo and the crowd saw that day in Shagamu told a story that the crowd understood and related to. The dancers enacted different stories from the collective memory of the people of Remo. They also told in dance fables involving the deeds of animals and birds.

The *egunguns* moved aside. Dancers and performers who were skilled in the interpretation of the bata now came forward to entertain the crowd. Experts among them simulated the movements of great beasts like the elephant, crocodile, or leopard. When the eyes of the spectators grew tired, it seemed to them that the men had miraculously transformed into the very beasts they portrayed. Who were these beings dancing before them? Were they men, or were they beasts from the forest?

After the performance of the *bata* dancers, Solesi appeared once again in the middle of his troupe of performers. He could now be seen directing his drummers and exhorting his singers, while handling the *iyalu* of the *dundun* himself. Then, he put down his big talking drum and found a wooden stool. Someone handed him his *molo*.

Solesi sat down and strummed the *molo*. He knew that as a master performer, he was the cynosure of all eyes. Many in the crowd had come to the festival just to see Solesi play his *molo*. He did not disappoint them.

At last, the performance came to an end. Solesi, exhausted but happy, removed the *molo* from around his neck and put the instrument down. He held both his arms up in the air and waved them from side to side as he acknowledged the cheers from the crowd.

The overwhelming success of the festival into which he had put much effort gave Solesi great satisfaction. Over the previous week, he had supervised every aspect of the project, starting from the making of the drums.

Everyone in Ikenne knew that when a goat or a sheep, or in rare circumstances, a cow, was killed, some part of the hide was given to Desalu, the drum maker. This occupation of drum making had been in Desalu's family as long as everyone could remember.

Desalu was also the unofficial historian of the town. He could recite the names of the town's founding fathers who had come with Yawa from Ife. And he would tell stories of Ogbodo and Obara, the founders of the town as if he had been there with them. He knew the names and *orikis* of all the rulers of Ikenne right from the time the goddess Uren gave her name to the sacred river.

Desalu had been Solesi's friend since their early childhood. This was before Solesi went off to fight as a war boy in Iperu and did not come back for six long years. Desalu would not undertake the making of any great drum without first consulting Solesi. He would ask his friend to test the sound and pitch of each drum so he could perfect it. The big *iyalu* that Solesi beat that evening was one of Desalu's latest creations.

Solesi was exhausted. But he was not done. He felt his body vibrate with a new energy. He knew that something even more exciting awaited him that evening. And his senses sharpened with anticipation.

* * * * *

When the great festival of the Akarigbo in Shagamu ended, Solesi's drum and dance troupe prepared to go back to Ikenne. But Solesi was not with his men. He had another business to attend to.

During the festivities, a beautiful young maiden in the crowd had attracted Solesi's roving but practiced eye. Solesi knew he had made an impression on her, for the girl kept looking at him. He wasted no time in finding out who she was. He was lucky. She was a young woman from Shagamu who had recently become widowed. Solesi managed to get next to this maiden during an interval when another troupe, the one from Ipara, was performing. He worked his well-practiced charms on her. He found out that her name was Moyeni.

Solesi complimented himself on his eye for the female form. And as he now appraised this girl at close quarters, he was not disappointed. She had a dark, oval, smooth face, with large, deep brown eyes and long eyelashes that turned up and fluttered when she spoke. Her voice was low and husky. Her body was slim and lithe, like one of the reeds on the banks of a slow-moving stream in Remo.

Moyeni was taller than Solesi. He noticed that, as he talked to her, she frequently dropped her head to catch what he was saying. He was surprised when she told him that she was twenty-seven years old. He had thought she was much younger, at most eighteen years of age. Now he was going to spend some pleasant hours in the company of this young woman in her home. He had told her he wanted to continue their conversation. He would answer in more detail her questions regarding the *bata* and other drums.

Solesi knew he had to be discrete. Moyeni told him she would be home alone that night in her late husband's house. Her whole household consisted of her dead husband's aged mother, her servant, and a young man, a married relative who lived with his wife and two children with them and played the part of the man of the house. But they had all traveled to Ode Remo to visit a sick relative. They would be away for five days.

Moyeni lived in a quiet part of Shagamu where an inquisitive neighbor or prying relative would not be a distraction. The pleasurable conversation between Solesi and this young woman, which he promised to continue in the quiet intimacy of her dwelling, would not be interrupted.

When Solesi went to Moyeni's house later that night, it was already dark. But a half moon lighted his way. He remembered the directions she had given him. As he got to the path that went past the house that she had described carefully to him, he felt a sharp thrill of anticipation.

But though Solesi did not know it, Moyeni had been anticipating their meeting for a long time. She had known Solesi for many years from a distance. Though they lived in different towns, she had developed a secret yearning for him since she was a girl of nine, borne on his fame as a warrior and *egungun* leader, and his charming good looks.

All her childhood friends knew about Moyeni's infatuation for the famous former child warrior whose Ibadan tribal marks had not distracted from his good looks. In fact, most of Moyeni's childhood friends were also infatuated with Solesi. They would go to watch his troupe whenever they came to their town to perform, if they could get permission from their parents.

Soon, Moyeni grew into puberty. Her body filled out, showing her to the world as a very presentable beauty in her own right. But her infatuation continued. Secretly, she wished that Solesi would notice her. She fantasized and dreamt that his family would one day turn up at her father's door in Shagamu. They would lay at his astonished feet the large bride price they had brought for her hand in marriage.

This miracle never happened. She ended up marrying Idowu, her husband, who died in an accident on his farm after six years of marriage. They never had any child. But so besotted was Idowu with her, he never sought to take another wife.

She had been widowed now for six months. She had submerged her sorrow in the routine domestic activities of her home and her trade. She dyed clothes for a living.

So, when she heard that Solesi was coming to her town as the star of the festivities to honor the Akarigbo on his jubilee, she quickly made her plans. This would be her opportunity after all these years. She made sure she would be alone at home. She gave an excuse to the other members of her household when they departed for Ode Remo. She said she had some work to do with her dyeing.

On the morning of the festival, Moyeni bathed with water and soap using a *kanyinkanyin* sponge in her backyard. She inspected her body, which was firm and shapely like that of a *wundia*. She was glad she had never had a child. She kneaded her breasts and felt the tips harden. Her body yearned for Solesi and it was still a painful feeling after all these years. Her infatuation for him had never let up even during the six years of her marriage to Idowu.

This is my chance, she told herself grimly. *It is now or never.*

After drying herself, she came inside the house and entered her *iyewu*. Alone in her bedroom, she oiled her skin and prepared to put on her clothes. She laid her clothes carefully out on her bed, which was a narrow wooden palette with a hard mattress filled with dried grass and unsorted cotton wool. The cotton seeds had not been separated from the wool, and sometimes they dug into her back, making her wince when she turned in bed at night.

For her underwear, she chose a *yeri,* which was a short underskirt, rather than the *tobi,* a fuller wrapper that was tied round the waist. She usually wore the *tobi* underneath her outer clothes when she went to the market. It was the string tied to the top edge of the *tobi* that she often used to wrap her money, a bunch of cowries, in a small cloth bag.

For her undergarment top, she chose an *agbeko,* a sleeveless gown that was like a "shimmy," which was what later generations of Yoruba women would call it. It was above these, the *yeri* and *agbeko,* that she now wore her *buba,* the loose-necked, full-sleeved formal blouse that was standard for going out for a woman of her age and social position.

She had not dressed as carefully as this since the day she got married to Idowu. She wondered if perhaps she was overdoing it. But she was determined to look her best. Around her lower body, she wrapped an *iro,* which she tied long with the lower border ending just above her ankles. Since this was a formal public occasion, she tied around her hip, on top of the *iro,* an *oja* of maroon *ofi* cloth to match her *gele* of the same color and material.

After this, she inserted her *yeri* in her pierced ear lobes and placed a single *ileke* of red coral around her neck to hang low between her breasts. Lipstick was unknown among her people. Moyeni's only makeup was a dark powdery pigment which she applied to both her upper eyelids. She also darkened her eyebrows.

She remembered the word *faari* which she and her friends used when they came of age. The girl who engaged in *faari* went all out to make people notice her dressing and demeanor. The person making "faari" had to carry herself in a certain way. Moyeni knew she was engaging in *faari* that afternoon. She knew that her people, the Ijebus, were the greatest practitioners of *faari* among the Yorubas. Since she was fifteen years old, Moyeni had been able to carry her *faari* to a height that was envied and admired by her peers.

Moyeni carefully planned her strategy for the afternoon's festivities. She made sure she did not go with any of her friends or relatives. Then, she placed herself in the crowd in such a way that Solesi would be certain to see her. Any time he looked in her general direction, which he did several times, she smiled and rearranged her *gele* to draw his attention even more.

At the end, she almost swooned when he, not knowing of her plans and desires for him, approached her and introduced himself.

She looked innocently into his face and congratulated him on his performance. She curtseyed and called him *"Oloye."*

She could see that he was doing all he could to impress and charm her. She told herself, smiling, that he need not have bothered. She was aware of his reputation with the maidens of Ikenne and other towns all over Remo. But she did not care.

*　　*　　*　　*　　*

So, when Solesi came to Moyeni's house later that night, she quickly let him in. They had barely exchanged their "We so o," before she quickly went back to the doorway. She leaned out and looked sharply up and down the dirt lane that led to her house. Then just as quickly, she shut and latched her front door.

She now went on both knees to greet him effusively. After all, young though he was, Solesi was a chief and prince of Remo. She welcomed him with all the niceties her woman's wiles could muster.

Those conversations that Solesi promised to continue with this young woman lasted three long days and nights, interrupted only by her getting up to cook for them and get water for him. When she cooked for him, she went into her backyard, with Solesi staying indoors so that no prying eye would see him alone with her in her house.

She peeled some ripe plantains, *ogede agbagba*, and in a clay pot of hot palm oil, *epo pupa*, over a wood fire, she fried *dodo* for him.

"My *dodo* is ripe and sweet," she told him without any attempt at irony.

And he found then and in the next three days, that her plantains were indeed very sweet. Solesi was pleased, even inspired, by her devotion and ministrations to his desires and needs.

Solesi, a careful and experienced observer of the human form, discovered something unique in Moyeni while he was with her. Taking careful note, he marveled at the changes that took over the face of the young woman when she talked—at one moment laughing at one of his stories, and the next, expressing disdain at a particularly heinous behavior of a character in his story.

Moyeni's face was indeed beautiful, pliable, and very expressive. And her hands and fingers, not to be outdone, did not stay idle either. When Moyeni talked, an uncommon animation took over, not just her face, but her limbs. Her eyes rolled, her eyebrows moved up and down, and her lips puckered. Lines of mirth, surprise, perplexity, and anger formed all over that remarkable visage. They disappeared and reformed around her eyes, her forehead, and her lips as her mood and reaction changed from one topic to the other.

And her slim fingers, clever-looking hands, and delicate wrists adorned with jangling bracelets, even her hips, played along with her facial expressions. As Solesi watched, fascinated, Moyeni's limbs kept up this happy rhythm of a great symphony. It was a well-tuned accompaniment to her soft but lively voice that complemented the endless repertoire of her animated facial expressions.

Meanwhile, Solesi's ever-present creative genius was a spirit that tiptoed around them. It gestured to him, mouthing words and phrases that he strained to hear above the idle chatter of their talk which had now become intimate and amorous. Insistent on being heard and not willing to be denied, this phantom burst into wisps of a song that Solesi could no longer ignore.

It was this refrain that Solesi now repeated and whispered into Moyeni's attentive ears. And as he sang this ditty softly to her, first their hands, then their bodies touched and would not let go. It was the coming together of two strangers destined to meet. For Moyeni, it was the realization of the dream of a patient maiden who had waited a lifetime for her moment of discovery and enlightenment.

And when at last they retired to the *iyewu* for the consummation of that act that had been set in motion by the sweet whisperings of the muse in his ears, Solesi saw, to his wonder and delight, that Moyeni's body, not just her face and her hands, displayed the same dexterity of art in motion. Like a delicate musical instrument, her body responded with an astonishing range of mode, pitch, and tone to the manipulations of his masterful hands. It was as fine an instrument as Solesi had ever handled.

As for Moyeni, she found in this impresario from Ikenne the skilled performance of an artful master that more than fulfilled her high expectations. As Solesi probed, touched, and manipulated the core of her being, the many silent drums and sonorous, tinkling cymbals within her came alive. His mastery brought forth from her a music of an ecstasy that she never thought possible.

All Solesi's art was called into play as he practiced his skills on this delicate new instrument that had come his way. Artist and instrument complemented each other in a happy concert that was carried, sighing, and moaning, from the confines of that small and narrow room, to the highest heaven of the gods.

It was three days and nights of bliss that came to an end too soon. Moyeni clung to Solesi and did not want him to leave. But in the end, she thanked him and let him go.

As he stood by the door, ready to leave, she said, "Oloye mi, O dabo. O di gbere." *Goodbye, my chief.*

Moyeni sensed that she would never see Solesi again. He was not hers to keep. But she reasoned that three days in the clouds with the gods compensated for the many years of mundane ordinariness in her life.

And indeed, those three days with Solesi sustained Moyeni's need for sensual expiation for years afterward. At night, as she lay on her hard bed while her household slept and snored in their rooms next to hers, she would close her eyes. She would feel Solesi's hands touch her and bring brought forth once again the exquisite music from her delicate instruments. Pleasure and contentment would come to her. And with a smile on her face, she would go to sleep.

As for Solesi, Moyeni became the inspiration for the growth and expansion of his music. He had long ago discovered that the creative energy for his songs came in bursts. The songs came to him fully formed, often after a dream. After his encounter with Moyeni, the inspiring dreams for his songs became more frequent and more intense.

He had wide-awake visions in the middle of the afternoon. He experienced erotic dreams while he slept at night. And he dreamt of the gods and fetishes of Remo, who asked him to worship them with his music, his drums, and the esoteric dances of his *egungun*.

He dreamt of events that would happen to him in a world that was yet to be—of lovers laughing, panting and clinging to one another as they frolicked in pleasurable abandon. He dreamt of the children of many mothers playing in the compound of a great chief. And he dreamt of one-breasted maidens who bore him aloft to the clouds while he slept, and of the exquisite music that soothed him when he came back to earth.

He saw visions of his departed ancestors. For those ancient heroes of Ile-Ife, Oyo and Remo loitered around still. They spoke to him, assuring him that they would stay with him and his people. They would help him make his music. They would guide him on a journey of discovery and redemption to atone for the exile and displacement of the past. And they would transform the disquiet in the soul of his people into the happy rhythm of a time of peace.

But the creative spirit that had guided and inspired Solesi for so long was no longer content to act alone. His music needed a muse, an *awokose* in the flesh.

Thus it was that Moyeni became his *awokose*. And long after his amorous encounter with this maiden, even though he would never again see or touch her, Moyeni, the young widow of Shagamu, continued to inspire Solesi's music.

And this effect of Moyeni, his *awokose*, on Solesi, started from the moment he left her house. As Solesi made his way back to Ikenne that afternoon, something within him stirred and awakened. Starting to form in his brain were strains of a new song that he would compose for his troupe when he got back to Ikenne. It was the completion of the ditty that his amorous spirit had whispered in his ears while he was with Moyeni.

The song was about a damsel who was celebrated all over Remo for her beauty and her charms. But he changed Moyeni's name to Mojisola. In that way, he thought, no one would catch on.

Mojisola oreke
Oreke l'ewa
Elehin 'ju ege
Omoge eleyin menu gun
Bebe idi re etike

Omoge Mojisola,
awokose mi
Sere fun mi jowo,
O ya, je kajo jo
Omoge, jo si ilu mi

Nitori mo fe je dodo re
pelu itelorun,
Omo, jowo bami dele
Ki nfi e s'aya

Dainty Mojisola
Blessed with grace and beauty
The girl with delicate eyeballs,
You are the damsel with teeth
that make the mouth
straight and regular.
You movements are so graceful
with those enticing beads on your hips.

Mojisola, my sweet maiden,
Play with me
And let us dance together.
Dance to my drum,
I want to eat your sweet plantain.
Child, come home with me
and let me make you my wife.

Solesi and Moyeni were lucky they were not interrupted during those three days of their blissful communication. But despite their precautions, a neighbor saw Solesi leave the house of the young widow, and word spread of their dalliance.

*   *   *   *   *

Even though he was now a chief and an important man in the town of Ikenne, Solesi was still unmarried. It was not as if he did not desire women. In fact, rumors of his dalliance with several maidens of Ikenne and neighboring towns had become commonplace. These stories were shared by many people in the town. One of these women was said to be a young widow in Shagamu.

People also talked about how, years earlier, a farmer in Ilishan had sent his young bride packing, to be returned back to her parent's home, because it was said that she had confessed to having been touched before her marriage by a young Solesi, who was then still a teenager.

These stories threatened to become a scandal. And soon, they came to the ears of Solesi's good friend and mentor, the Alakenne, monarch of Ikenne. The Alakenne called Solesi one evening to the palace.

The king's message, which he disguised as an advice, was clear. Solesi was either to get married or the Alakenne would choose a wife for him. And he was not going to pick from among the comeliest maidens of Remo, of the type that Solesi's selective eye was known to favor.

So it was that Solesi approached the father of one of the town's beauties in his bid to marry his first wife. This maiden's father, Chief Awopeju had given her the name Iyekunbi—*Motherhood brings fullness to the family*. Everyone called her Yekunbi.

Yekunbi had grown up to be a very beautiful maiden, with soft, round cheeks and a light coppery complexion. People around her in Ikenne looked at her and they were happy. They felt that they were blessed that the gods had chosen to place one of the favored daughters of heaven in their midst.

It is not to be assumed however that the process of Solesi looking for and finding a wife was rushed or precipitate. Solesi took his time to go through all the required steps according to the traditions of his people.

First, Solesi promised himself that he would get the most beautiful maiden in the town. Then he started to inquire and look around. It was during this *igba ifojusode*, which was what his friends called this period of "looking around" for a mate, that Solesi heard about Yekunbi, the sixteen-year-old daughter of Chief Awopeju. Solesi took his time to observe the girl and to make inquiries about her family. Satisfied with what he saw and heard, he quickly made his choice.

Even in those days, it was not the practice among our people to marry off girls too early. The usual age for marriage for girls was after the age of sixteen. Yekunbi was sixteen and therefore ready for marriage. And Yekunbi was not only very beautiful, she was mature for her age. Everyone that spoke about her to Solesi and his friends commented on her gentleness and the uncommon wisdom she possessed for someone so young.

The Alakenne was very happy about his protégé's choice. Not willing to give Solesi the chance to change his mind, the *oba* went straight to the Ifa priest, who dutifully consulted his oracle and gave the approval of Orunmila.

"Ifa f'ore," was what he said.

It was after this that the family of the girl was approached and the consent of the girl herself sought. This was called the *isihun*, literally, releasing the voice of the bride to be. This particular *isihun* was not difficult to obtain. For Yekunbi herself was already thoroughly infatuated with the young, dashing, and rich Solesi who she had learned was making inquiries about her.

The *itoro iyawo* that followed was a festive occasion when all Solesi's relatives followed him to ask formally for Yekunbi's hand from her father and family. This was quickly followed by the *idana*, when both families were formally introduced. This of course was another excuse for more feasting and drinking of palm wine. It was only after this that the day of the *igbeyawo* was fixed.

Thus it was that at the ripe age of sixteen, Yekunbi was betrothed to the most prominent young chief of her town, Solesi, the leader of the *egungun* cults and close confidant of the *oba*.

For their formal union, no ceremonies were left out. Nuptial festivities in Yorubaland had not changed much since the time of Solaru, the Warrior from Ife. But the clothes worn by Solesi and Yekunbi that day in Ikenne were richer than those of Solaru and Aarin in Ibadan a generation earlier in a time of war.

Solesi and his bride stepped out in *alari* woven cloth of the finest quality. He wore an *abeti aja* cap. She was resplendent in ivory and coral beaded earrings, necklaces and bracelets that threatened to weigh her down. Indeed, the jewelry worn by the bride on that day was splendid to behold. But all those heavy clothes and jewelry made Yekunbi feel hot and stuffy. She waved about her face a fan made of ostrich's feathers. It had been brought from the Colony in Lagos by a merchant friend of her father.

Even though she was young, Yekunbi was aware that she was the acclaimed beauty of the town. She possessed that easy self-assurance of the young female who was used, from an early age, to the compliments and deference that beauty, as much as age, commanded among our people.

Yekunbi therefore listened with familiar amusement as the praise singers paid by her father shook their *shekere* and extolled her beauty, the softness of her skin, and the allure of her fluttering eyelashes.

"Eyin fun jowo," they said of her. For indeed, her teeth were whiter than cowries.

Solesi himself drew admiring glances from the gathered women. Everyone complimented the beauty of the couple. And quite a few maidens who watched the ceremony cast envious eyes at Yekunbi for having made the catch of the town.

There was no false modesty among the Ijebu people of that time. Girls and boys ran naked until they were about twelve years of age. They only started to put on clothes when they reached puberty. This was the time that breasts jutted out and there was a suggestive darkening of the skin of the pubis and armpits with pubescent hair.

Even children knew the anatomy of those parts described as private. They knew the proper names for these parts and knew what they were for. The male organ was *oko*, the female *obo*. There was even a song among the children about how *obo* was lonely and wanted *oko* to keep her company.

But despite this familiarity with body parts and their functions, premarital sex was not common in Ikenne. Indeed, it was frowned upon. To ensure this desirable state of female chastity, once a girl reached puberty, she stopped playing with boys. She would be married off as soon as the father could get a suitable bride price. It was a shame on her family if a girl was not a *wundia,* or virgin, at the time of the *ilo si ile oko,* when she was taken to her husband's house.

So, Yekunbi knew about the sex act, the body parts involved, and where children came from. And she had often overheard the older women in her household talk coarsely and loosely as they pounded the corn with mortar and pestle in the back of the compound to make *ogi*.

Men did horrible and painful things to women, these women said. All that men cared about was their own pleasure which was rarely shared by the women. Essentially, men were beasts. But they were the masters. What could women do but go along with the coarse demands of their men?

Polygamy was common, especially among the well-to-do. A rich man could have up to four wives. Once a woman was past her prime, she was put aside, to be replaced by a younger maiden barely past puberty.

As for the carnal act itself, it was important to women only as the necessary prelude to procreation. A woman had to have babies, in order to secure a foothold in her husband's polygamous household. The lot of the childless woman was abandonment to loneliness and poverty if her husband died. As for enjoying the act itself that led to procreation, there was little agreement on the facts.

The old women whispered to the younger ones their stories of horror at the intimate and painful things that men did to women. The best thing they whispered to these uninitiated young ones was to lay back and bear the pain.

Even the Remo word for a man taking a woman for wife *ne,* meant owning her, possessing her.

"Eranko ni awon okunrin. Men are beasts," one of these women told Yekunbi. "But they are the masters."

And of course, these elder matrons had to be right, thought Yekunbi. They were older and wiser. They had gone through the ordeal.

Thus, Yekunbi was a bit frightened on the evening of her marriage. But she was also excited. She genuinely admired the intriguing young chieftain of Ikenne who had chosen her, and she looked forward to being with him. Solesi was one of the most sought-after young men in town.

Her good spirits were also due to the effect on her of the ceremony itself. It was simple but impressive. Her father's prayers, admonitions and blessings calmed, but also animated her.

Mo nlo sile oko, she told herself. She was going to her husband's house and would leave her parents forever. Her eyes glowed with tears. She would miss her mother and her siblings.

But Yekunbi's innate wisdom overcame her fears, and she began to reassure herself. She told herself firmly and with some conviction that Solesi could not be a beast like other men. He was a kind and gentle man. It would be different with her and this young man who had caught her eye, with whom she had been infatuated for some time, who would now be her husband, her lord and master, the one to take away her virginhood.

He could be my master. But he would not be a beast, Yekunbi said to herself.

While she said this, she was walking slowly in the middle of a throng of women who danced and clapped around her. She was being taken to her husband's house.

"A nmu 'yawo rele oko," the women around her chanted.

And it was at that moment that Yekunbi's fears and trepidations for the terrors of that night's fateful appointment finally abated. She made up her mind. She was going to make sure she pleased her husband, the handsome and desirable Akeredolu Solesi.

Meanwhile, Solesi was in the midst of a palm wine-fueled celebration with his friends. They were a jovial band of old comrades. Any time one of them took a wife, tradition demanded that they would celebrate, but they would also tease the lucky man mercilessly.

That evening, after the nuptial festivities were over and he prepared to receive his bride, Solesi drank palm wine with his friends from the *egungun* fraternity. He became tipsy. His voice rose as he recounted his war stories from Iperu and Ibadan. His friends had heard most of it before. Still, they never tired of those stirring tales of Bashorun Ogunmola, Kurunmi and Mr. Pettiford.

But tonight, they quickly changed the subject and teased him about his coming task for the night.

"Akeredolu, are you sure you are ready?" his best friend, Awolesi asked him. He dug an elbow into Solesi's ribs, and there was a knowing twinkle in his eyes.

With your small stature, ae you sure, Solesi, that you are the right size in that important area? This was the insinuation.

Solesi knew which part of his body Awolesi was referring to. And his usual confidence, which did not desert him even on this night, came to the fore. He assured his friends that he had already proved himself to be above reproach in that area of manly endeavor.

And as if to lend weight to this assertion, Solesi drew himself to his full height and pounded his chest. On the spur of the moment, his *awokose* or creative spirit, had come upon him. His friends knew the signs. They grew quiet, the better to hear the latest creation from their bard.

Still on his feet, his voice full of authority and poetic cadence, Solesi began a chant the rhythm of a great *ewi*. But tonight, Solesi seemed to be addressing the lines of his *ewi* to himself rather than to the other persons present in that small and intimate gathering of friends.

I am Solesi,
son of the great Warrior from Ife
who drove the "imale"
Fulani from Oshogbo.
Behold the son of Solaru,
master of the war horse Jagun;
I am the grandson of mighty Adeuja,
Akarigbo of all Remo
who conversed with lions
in his palace in Ofin in Shagamu.
He was the great prince
Who built a fire in his backyard
That burnt his enemies in the forest.

My great grandfather
Was an eso of the Alafin
A guardian of the rope.
Yes! That same horse bridle
that kept Oyo safe
for a thousand years.

I am the Ijebu warrior
who bears the facial marks of Ibadan,
I have dined with Bashorun Ogunmola
And I am familiar with the byways
of the city of Oluyole
From Isale Ijebu to Oke Aare
In the town where horsemen ride
In broad daylight
To demand loot from their owners.

When we want to see the elephant
We search in the forest,
To find the leopard
A hunter must go to the savannah,
And before a maiden finds a man like me,
She would climb seven mountains
and cross seven seas.

OLADELE OLUSANYA

Solesi chanted these spontaneous lines, using classic *ewi* measures that he timed to the beat of an invisible *gangan*. And as his voice rang out, it assumed the classic Yoruba intonation of Ibadan rather than the familiar dialect of Remo.

His friends looked at him, and they were impressed. For they knew that Solesi had composed this ditty on the spur of the moment. They remained quiet for a minute. Then they loosened up and shouted their approval, egging him on.

Solesi now changed his voice pattern to the guttural sounds of the Remo *egungun*, as he continued his chant. At this, his friends laughed and slapped their hands together in awe and appreciation.

But just as suddenly as he had started, Solesi stopped his chanting. His friends watched as he sat down. He had become very quiet. All of a sudden, it appeared to them that Solesi remembered the task that awaited him that night.

And despite all his earlier bravado, Solesi indeed had become nervous. He looked uncharacteristically subdued. He reached for the gourd of palm wine. He filled a small calabash from which he drank slowly, savoring the sweet fermented liquid.

After this, without another word either of encouragement or jest, Solesi was allowed to go in to his bride. His friends knew he had an important job in hand.

It was the age-old ritual of the taking of a young woman's maidenhead as ordained by the rites of marriage.

*   *   *   *   *

Unlike his father Solaru, Solesi was prepared for his marriage night. He was knowledgeable, skilled, and experienced in the ways of a man with a maid. He had never had problems in this regard, even when he was very young. The knowledge of what went on between a man and a woman came naturally to him, without instruction or training.

When he was no older than six years of age, he was already aware of the allure of the other sex. He knew he was *ako*, male and *they* were *abo*, female. There was something in girls that was different. But that difference complimented him. He knew he liked being with girls just as much as he loved to play war games with his male friends.

Before he went off to war as a drummer boy, there was a girl he had a soft spot for who was a year older than him. They would arrange to meet in secret places—behind the abandoned Olokun shrine, in a small cave in the woods, or behind the shed in her father's house where yams were kept.

She allowed him to touch her breasts which were just beginning to bud. They assured each other earnestly that they would marry each other when they grew up. But when Solesi came back from Ibadan, she was gone. She had been married to a young trader from Shagamu.

And it was at this time after he came back from the war that Solesi had an encounter with an older girl that was the real thing. She was eighteen years old, a distant relation from Ilishan who was staying with them because both her parents were dead. Her name was Aduke.

Solesi remembered how it started. It was when he was ill after his return from Ibadan to find that his father had died. He had not gone out for three months. He was recovering and barely moved beyond the threshold of the house.

One day, he woke up in the middle of the morning and realized he was not alone at home. There was someone in the dark passage outside his room.

"Le si yen wa?" he called out. *Who is that?*

"Emi ni. Aduke," came a thin, girlish voice he recognized as that of their house guest.

Then she came in. There was a strange look on her face as she watched him intently.

"Le si wanule?" she asked, wanting to know if there was anyone else at home.

It suddenly occurred to him that she wanted them to be alone. She giggled and moved nearer to him. As he made to stand up, half reclining on his elbows, she put out her hand. She pushed him down and giggled again.

Solesi looked carefully at the girl. Aduke seemed excited. Her pupils were dilated. And she was breathing fast, her bosom straining against her *oja* as she moved closer still to him.

He became conscious of her feminity. It was in the soft allure of her voice which was low and seductive, and the musky smell that came from her body, which threatened to overcome him like the smoke from a smoldering wood fire in a small hut with shuttered windows. This

OLADELE OLUSANYA

fume was so powerful, he thought he might choke. It was a strange new feeling, and he felt confused.

But he reached out and touched her. Then his arm was around her waist. He drew her slowly, gently, and shyly, almost with deference, to himself. Suddenly, she was on the mat beside him, cuddling her head on his chest.

"Ummh," she murmured

She untied her *oja*, uncovered her breasts and pressed her body close to him. Her naked breasts were tantalizingly close to his face. He had never been so close to a female in his life. And he could smell her now even more. It was that strange adult smell that he would later associate with lust and longing.

Without a word, she put her hand inside the loose waist band of his *sokoto* and tugged at him. With another deft movement, she removed her *iro* and threw it aside. There was nothing on her body now except a string of *ileke* around her hips. She grabbed him firmly and murmured something he could not hear, but readily understood.

He was amazed as his own body came alive. A sensation he had never known before came over him, and he found himself pressing down on her. With one hand, he freed himself. And without quite knowing how, he found himself thrusting deep into a place that was warm and moist. It was over in a minute. A wave rushed over him, and he felt his vision go dark. He shuddered, and suddenly all was quiet and still.

He had not spoken a word to her. Aduke did not say anything. She got up, wrapped her *iro* around her slim body, wound the *oja* tightly around her breasts, and quietly left the room. But as she went out, she threw a shy smile back at him.

After this, they contrived to be at home when no one was around. And Solesi was instructed by this maiden as no pupil ever was. She was a dedicated and innovative leader and teacher. She instructed him in the many parts of a woman's body that had been made by the gods for the pleasure of men. He was an avid pupil and soon learned the secrets of those hidden places.

She was always serious afterward. She would get up without a word. And she would leave quickly, hastily tying her *iro* and arranging her hair, but not before giving clear instructions as to when the next lesson would take place.

But barely three months after their first tryst, Aduke left the Solesi family house. She had been betrothed by her family, her parents being dead, to a farmer in Ilishan.

Later, Solesi heard that there was some talk about the farmer returning Aduke to her family because she was not intact on their wedding night. But her family had refused to return the bride price. Aduke went back to her husband, and over the years, had five children for him, all in quick succession.

But would it be different tonight? Solesi now asked himself as he went to his wife.

He could not answer his own question. Guilt of old actions and the anticipation of new pleasures whirled around in his brain. He remembered Aduke, his young instructor, and Moyeni, the young widow in Shagamu.

That was in the past, he told himself. He would focus his mind now on pleasing this young and innocent maiden, his betrothed wife.

Would it be a raw physical act as it had been with Aduke?

"No", he reassured himself. "This is my wife, not an *ale*."

In Yorubaland, though premarital sex was frowned upon as bringing disgrace on a girl and her family, with men, it was different. Men were allowed not only to have many wives, but to acquire concubines and mistresses who were called "ale." Moyeni was his *ale* and had little claim on him.

Solesi made up his mind. He would be a good husband to Yekunbi. He would be unselfish in his devotion to her needs, starting from tonight. He felt an inner softness toward her, this maiden he barely knew. His thoughts were loving, caring, and gentle, almost paternal, as he prepared to go in to his bride.

For Solesi, as it was for his father Solaru before him, this was the moment of truth for a man and his young bride.

"The way of a man with his betrothed must be different from his action and behavior with others in his life," Solesi said to himself.

With his love for games and competition, he imagined this encounter as a contest, but a strange one in which two combatants would both lose and win. Like his father and countless men before him, he would lose his individual liberty. But he would win an enduring companionship.

The Yoruba people were not known for the practice of kissing with the lips to express affection between the sexes. But that night, as Solesi and Yekunbi were joined in the flesh, many uses were discovered for many different parts of their bodies which revealed their functions in the conjugal bonding of man and woman.

And what did Yekunbi learn? She now knew what the secret recesses in her body were made for. She learned that the body parts of a woman and her man were like a lock and its key, which when inserted and turned, opened up many secret chambers filled with wondrous delights.

As she lay beside her husband, Yekunbi discovered a new power she would have over this desirable young chieftain and former warrior. It was the secret weapon of her sex that she had never known existed till that moment.

Her discovery led to knowledge. But that knowledge had only come through pain. It was a deep throbbing pain that was interrupted by brief exquisite moments of pleasure.

"Ye mi" *My mother*, she cried. Then, *"Mo ku."* *I am dead.*

"Pele," he said.

Solesi whispered to his betrothed. He calmed her and reassured her that he would not hurt her.

But the climax, despite his experience, came too quickly. Perhaps what came over him was guilt of past escapades and the strange realization that each woman was different. This for him also, was truth and knowledge. His body went limp and he fell asleep.

He had his old dream again. The three one-breasted maidens bore him aloft from beside his sleeping bride to a place high above the clouds. It was the abode of Eledumare and the gods. He saw Yemoja and Olokun, even Orisanla. But who were these misshapen forms with faces of animals and birds, *iwins* with no heads and reptile-like *anjonu* with their tails wrapped around their bellies? He saw that he had his old *omele* drum hanging down for his neck. He beat a rapid staccato on the drum with his drumsticks, and the apparitions disappeared.

He had conquered his demons. He knew then that his union with Yekunbi was a good thing. It had been sanctioned by the gods.

Solesi awoke. His loins stirred, and he turned to his bride. He pressed his body against her. She moved lazily against him, but she was asleep.

The last thought Solesi had before he again drifted to sleep brought a smile to his face. He was happy. He remembered the crude jokes of his friends earlier that evening. Because many families in Ijebu did not circumcise their daughters, their clitoris was compared to the trigger of a gun.

"*Ijebu onibon ndi,*" he remembered. He murmured softly to himself, then went back to sleep.

*   *   *   *   *

After Solesi received his third chieftaincy title, *Bobagunwa* of Ikenne, he met and married his third wife.

Even in a household of beautiful women, Oreneye stood out. She was slim and straight, and seemed to walk without moving the top half of her body. She was light skinned, with high cheekbones like her husband Solesi. His friends could not stop telling him how much they complimented each other.

The most remarkable thing about Oreneye, however, was not her beauty. It was her laugh, which bubbled like the water of the Uren at a place where it tumbled over a small cataract. It reminded one of that enchanted place in the river where the water flowed through a narrow space into a pebbled pool that was calm, transparent and clean.

Soon, Oreneye became Solesi's favorite wife. And it was not long before she became pregnant and had a child. It was a girl, who was named Efunyemi. Right from her birth, everyone remarked how much this girl looked like her grandfather, the Warrior from Ife.

Solesi would go on to marry five wives who gave him twenty-two children. Later, when he grew old, people would ask him why he had had so many women.

His answer came readily. "I like women. And I take pleasure in their company."

And indeed, there were many things that attracted Solesi to women. He liked their soft skin. And he liked the natural aroma of women that was amplified by the strange scents and perfumes they used under their armpits and behind their ears and necks. He also admitted to himself that he liked to touch the tattoos in the shapes of lizards, triangles, and diamonds with which the young women of that age decorated their bellies and arms. He loved the sway of their hips, the jangle of wrist bracelets and their soft giggles as they moved in idle chatter from one gossipy subject to another.

Solesi enjoyed the domestic tranquility and contentment which women brought to his household. He loved the murmur of their voices and the sounds of activity in the backyard which signified that the afternoon meal was being prepared.

Even when he was busy on his farm on a hot afternoon, digging up cassava roots to store in his barn, Solesi would recall with pleasure the sights and sounds of home. It was the sound of pestle on mortar, and the sensation of raw, red pepper ground on a rock *olo* that made the eyes smart and the throat to itch.

And after the cooking was done, and everyone had had their fill, he loved to hear the patter of little feet as children ran about in the yard and called to each other in their innocent childish games.

Solesi was happy he had many children. He knew that they too would have their own children. His grandchildren and great-grandchildren, long after he was gone from this world, would continue his line. He had visions of his progeny traveling to far places unknown to him and his Remo people. Generations hence, his seed would be carried to the far reaches of the earth.

When Efunyemi was older, Solesi would get his "Dane" gun and ask his daughter to go hunting with him. Even though she was a girl, he showed her the burrows and hiding places of bush rats, rabbits and other rodents like the *okete* that the people of Ikenne hunted for food.

At such times, Solesi lamented to his daughter Efunyemi the fact that the big beasts—leopards and elephants—that roamed the wild forest in the days of Obari were long gone. For meat, he and other families in Ikenne contented themselves with the small game that they trapped or shot in the bush.

They also partook of the flesh of sheep and goats that were penned at the back of many houses in the town. It was only during big feasts such as the death of a great chief that the people of Ikenne in the late nineteenth century could delight in the slaughter, skinning, and cutting up of an ox, *malu*, be it a cow or a bull.

*   *   *   *   *

With time, Solesi became versed in all the ceremonies and religious festivals of Ikenne. He became the expert in all aspects of the traditional culture of his town.

He was conversant with the drumming, dances, and rites of the *agemo*, and the ceremonial details that attended the coronation of a new Alakenne. He became a member of all the known sacred cults of Ikenne--*Balufon, oro, eluku, agemo,* and *egungun.* Even the *agere,* those exotic dancers on stilt, came within his purview. Not a single one of the sacred societies of Ikenne escaped Solesi's interest, scrutiny and participation.

In his capacity as patron and grand master of *egungun* in Ikenne and a skilled performer in his own rights, Solesi went everywhere. He knew everyone and was invited to every social event that people celebrated. He was even credited with helping to establish and celebrate the first *"eyo"* festival in the town of Iperu. This was before this masquerade was exported from Remo to Eko.

Music and drumming came naturally to Solesi. It was a gift given to him by the gods from the time he was a child. Now, it was he who taught the young men of Ikenne to play the drums—*bata, gbedu, akuba,* and *dundun*—that defined the Yoruba music of his day.

He taught his acolytes and apprentices to convert the sounds of their drum into phrases and short songs, the better to remember them.

> *Ona fun ko gbe gungun eja.*
> *Ma gbe mi!*

> The throat cannot accommodate a fish bone.
> Don't swallow it!

> *Ninu ikoko dudu*
> *Lati nsebe.*

> It is from inside the black pot
> that we cook the delicious stew.

Solesi knew that there could be no music without dancing. He taught his pupils that their dancing was an extension of drumming.

"Your drum talks to you. You should dance to it as a way of continuing the conversation."

"Dancing," he told them, "should be as easy as breathing or walking." Or, as he once put it once, when he was in a light mood, as natural and pleasurable as lying with a maid.

"Drumming and dancing are skills that come naturally to our people. For we are a people who love music and gaiety."

But as Solesi would come to know, there was more than music and gaiety in the culture and religion of his people. There was a dark side that was not openly discussed.

In Ikenne and other towns in Ijebu, the most important ceremonies of the *egunguns* and other cults were performed at night. And women and children were not allowed to be present.

Why was this?

For most people, what went on in the shrines and meeting places of the cults and secret societies in Ikenne could only be guessed at. Most preferred not to know. But in the morning, after a night in which their sleep was disturbed by the songs and imprecations of initiates of a cult marching through the streets in the dead of night, people would whisper tales that sent shivers through their bodies.

They repeated stories they had heard of spirits of the dead appearing among the initiates of the cults, feasting, and cavorting with them. Some said that cult worshippers drank blood and sipped palm wine from the skulls of dead acolytes. It was said that when a cult member died, his head was cut off. The heart and liver were removed, to be consumed at initiation ceremonies for new members.

Solesi heard these stories too. And after he became a member of many of those cults, he came to know which of these macabre tales were fanciful and which were real. But he never discussed what he saw or knew with any of his wives or children.

Thus, Solesi spared his family the gruesome details of his knowledge of the practices of the occult in Ijebu-Remo.

*   *   *   *   *

Solesi was present when a cowering, shivering Ifagbemi was brought to the *osugbo* secret council one night, having been caught fishing from a canoe in the Uren in the middle of the night.

This Fagbemi, as everyone called him, was not a native of Ikenne. He had emigrated from Ijebu-Esure where his father was a priest of Orunmila.

Everyone said he should have known better, being the son of a priest. But Fagbemi was a greedy man. He was forever thinking up schemes to make more money in the shape of bags of cowry shells to enlarge his barns and purchase more wives.

Fagbemi was one of the richest men in Ikenne. He already had five wives. But he boasted to his friends that he was not done. His eyes had lighted upon Serifa, the sixteen-year-old daughter of the town blacksmith, and he was determined to have her as his latest spouse.

Serifa's father, Latifu, who was one of the few Moslems in Ikenne, sized Fagbemi up and decided he too could become rich. He demanded a large bride price for his daughter which most other men would have refused. They would have opened their mouths in disbelief, shaken their heads and gone on their way.

But Fagbemi was determined to prove that he could afford anything, even when it necessitated his incurring a large debt. To pay this off, he would need to make a lot of money fast.

But where would he get the money?

Fagbemi knew that there was a large fish market in Iperu. The fish had to be brought from the lagoon at Makun or Ikorodu. By the time the fish got to the market, the price had gone up. Worse still, the fish was spoilt and smelly.

Fagbemi told himself he could make a lot of money selling fish at the Iperu market. If only he could get his fish close by. He would bring it fresh to the market, and he would make a killing.

That was when Fagbemi hit on the scheme of getting his fish right in his backyard. He would get his fish from the river Uren.

Of course, Fagbemi had lived long enough in Ikenne to know of the ancient taboo against fishing in the sacred river. But to a bold and desperate man with greed in his eyes, this knowledge was no deterrence.

Fagbemi made his plans. Secretly, he bought a canoe at Aiyepe. He had it brought to Ikenne at night by paid couriers who were not from Ikenne. By day, he hid the canoe in a cave covered with palm fronds. By night, he brought it out. Using pole and paddle, he maneuvered it to the middle of the river at a place that was least frequented by the people of the town. Keeping his eyes and ears alert for intruders, he cast his net into the river and brought in fish by the score.

He sold his fresh fish in the market. Nobody asked him how he got them, and he became even richer. But after repaying his debt, he did not stop. He continued his nightly escapades for several months until two suspicious young men trailed him to the spot on the riverbank where he pushed in his canoe to cast his nets. They caught him as he was bringing his haul back to shore.

Thus it was that as a member of the traditional council known as the *osugbo* in Ikenne, Solesi took part in the sentencing to death of Fagbemi.

After a short deliberation that included the testimony of the two young men who had caught Fagbemi in the act and the confession of the accused man himself, the culprit was found guilty of violating the ancient sanctity of the Uren. Very swiftly and without a single dissenting voice, the ancient sanction was imposed. Fagbemi would forfeit his life for his crime against the goddess of the river.

Fagbemi was taken outside in the dark. He was bound hand and foot. His mouth was gagged with a piece of wood attached to ropes that were tied very tightly at the back of his head. His eyes were covered with a tight blindfold of black cloth.

Curiously, Fagbemi still had his cap on, a stylish *origi* that was cocked to one side over the left ear. And as a statement of his wealth, Fagbemi had had this cap embroidered around the crown with bronze-colored threading.

Of what use to him now is his expensive "onide" cap? Solesi thought to himself with a strange but perverse sagacity.

Two young, muscular acolytes held the struggling Fagbemi as the old but sprightly Uren priestess stepped up behind him. Carrying a heavy *olugbogboro*, an ugly, knobby club that she had to wield with both hands, she bludgeoned him from the back, bashing his skull in with a single blow. Fagbemi never knew what hit him. He fell like an ox.

The two young acolytes laid him gently on the ground as the priestess stepped forward and examined the still figure to make sure he was dead. Later, the body was carried away by six young priests from six different cults, accompanied by the priestess of Uren. They made their way rapidly toward the river. For there was one last ceremony to be performed by the banks of the river to appease the goddess

At the river, the six young *baba olorisha* bowed their heads and murmured *"Ase"* at intervals as the priestess chanted softly the propitiation to her deity. No sound or movement came from the forest to interrupt this macabre scene. Later, the body was cut into pieces and dumped into the river. The outraged goddess had been avenged.

But when everyone went home afterward, they were troubled and shaken. Not one of the participants slept that night. For no one could remember this having ever happened in the history of Ikenne. They turned on their sleeping mats and shook their heads. But they knew that the wise old men of the *osugbo,* who had found Fagbemi guilty, were right. They had done their duty to protect the whole town from the action of one man. Better that Fagbemi die than the whole town be subject to the fury of an angered goddess.

And Solesi, contemplating the ways of belief of his people, thought of the rightness of their actions in serving the will of the gods. But still, he could not answer those questions that had bothered him since he came back from Ibadan as a young man.

Where do we come from? And where do we go after we die?

*   *   *   *   *

The years went by. Solesi grew older. Children in Ikenne came to know the slight, light-complexioned old man with Ibadan facial marks, who rode his white horse, Mapo at festivals. When they passed him in the streets, he would greet them with the words, *"Alafia fun nyin* o."

Older people pointed to him. They spoke about his prowess as a child warrior who had fought the Egbas at Iperu. Solesi himself acknowledged the recognition and fame that had come to him at the end of his long and eventful life.

As he looked back, Solesi remembered those who had shown him love and devotion. He thought of his parents, his women, his horse Mapo, and even Ogunmola, the controversial Ibadan warlord who had adopted him as a son. He knew he bore a lucky trait. At all stages of his life, he had found favor among friends and strangers. He prayed to Orisanla that his own children and grandchildren would receive favor as they moved out of Ikenne into the many strange lands that beckoned to them.

And because Solesi came to have twenty-two children from his five wives, the *akewis* and praise singers in Ikenne, Shagamu, and other Remo towns had a busy time keeping up. When they chanted his *oriki*, as he sat under a colorful umbrella at some important occasion of state, the praise singers were always ready with additional lines to his *oriki*.

> *Omo o de kile kun*
> *Okun dede teru teru*
> *Omo a kenigbo*
> *K'eru ba ara ona*
> *Bi labalaba ba fara we eiye, a te*
> *Bi ina ba wole, okunkun a parade*
> *Oloye Solesi ko lafiye*
> *Nilu Ikenne*

> *Oloye agba Solesi,*
> *yoju siwa o,*
> *Omo jagunjagun ilu Ife,*
> *Omo Aremo Ofin,*
> *Ore Akarigbo*
> *Baba oloye gbogbo Remo*
> *Jagunlabi, a bi ila Ibadan*
> *To le Egba kuro nilu Iperu.*
> *Akeredolu, omo Adeuja*
> *Alagba Ikenne.*

> *He who comes home*
> *And the house is filled to the brim,*
> *It is a household of many children and possessions.*
> *He is the chief who cries out in the forest*
> *and fear strikes the heart of the town dweller.*
> *The butterfly that tries to imitate the dove*
> *will come to shame;*
> *When light comes in, darkness vanishes.*
> *Chief Solesi, you have no equal*
> *in all Ikenne.*

> *Solesi, come out to greet us,*

Son of the Warrior of Ife
Prince of the Ofin palace
Friend of the Akarigbo,
Chieftain of all Remo
The warlord with Ibadan facial marks
Who chased the Egba out of Iperu,
Akeredolu, son of Adeuja
You are a respected elder of Ikenne.

Solesi was happy in his old age. He was blessed with good health, reasonable wealth and the companionship of his wives, friends, and family. Apart from his illness when he returned from Ibadan and found that his father, the Warrior from Ife had died, he never had a day of infirmity in his life.

When anyone asked old Solesi the secret of his good health and longevity, he would reply, "*Agidigbo* music, and a daily gourd of palm wine by the best tapper in Ikenne."

Sometimes, he would add, "And the love and company of women."

But Solesi grew old to see the old ways of his people pass away. White men from Lagos and Ibadan came to Ikenne with their agents, teachers, clerks, priests, and administrators. They took over the running of his town. The Alakenne and his chiefs became rubber stamps to the Native Authority administration, a new contraption that was run by the *oyinbo* "resident" in Shagamu. The colonial courts and the Native Authority police with their red *kepi* caps and brown khaki shorts were the new powers of the day. It was a new and bewildering world that suddenly sprung up all around him.

The old religion of the Ijebus that he, Solesi had followed all his life, was rapidly sidelined. He saw the children of notable high priests of Ogun, Sango, and Orishanla abandon their father's shrines. They studied the white man's language at the *ile-iwe* set up by the *oyinbo* missionaries. They converted to the sect of the *onigbagbo*. And when they were baptized, they took strange names from the white man's holy book.

Solesi witnessed the building of the first *onigbagbo* church in Ikenne, the St. Savior's Church. It was erected on the hill crest where the old Orunmila shrine had stood for ages. This was the same shrine that was built centuries earlier by Ogbodo, the Ifa priest who founded Ikenne.

To be sure, Solesi, a member of the *osugbo* and former *olori* of the *egungun* masquerades, was not happy that the *oyinbos* were blatantly taking over his town, pushing aside the old gods of the land. But one of the younger men explained to Solesi that it was the consequence of a treaty the Yoruba *obas* had signed with the white man, which he, Solesi, a chief in the backwater of Ikenne, had known little about.

Solesi was told that a *Gesi* army, with the help of Hausa mercenaries, had defeated Ijebu-Ode at a village called Imagbon, and that the old authority of the Awujale was a thing of the past.

*   *   *   *   *

One day, Solesi went to Shagamu to see his old friend, Ojajagba, who had gone to the Iperu war with him. He had to walk because his horse Mapo had been dead for many years after being bitten by the tsetse fly. Thinking of his beloved horse, Solesi could not help saying to himself that the stalwart old ways of the Ijebus were dying all around him.

Or were the old ways already dead, like his horse Mapo?

He knew there were no horses in town anymore. He saw with disgust that young men, even farmers and palm wine tappers, now rode a contraption called a *keke*. Those with more knowledge of *Gesi* called it a "baisi-kulu."

But what he heard when he got to his friend's house near the market square in Shagamu surprised and shocked him.

Ojajagba, his friend, who was an *ogboni* high priest in Shagamu and a member of the Akarigbo's traditional council, told Solesi that he had become a Christian, an *onigbagbo*. He was going to be baptized very soon.

The question that Solesi put to Ojajagba was, "What is the *awo ogboni* in Shagamu going to do about your abandoning them?"

Ojajagba looked at his friend Solesi. He said sadly, "They say I'm no longer a chief."

This traditional council, which advised the Akarigbo, had stripped Ojajagba of his chieftaincy tiles. He was no longer allowed to wear the animal skin that was worn over the left shoulder by great chiefs on festivals and other great occasions.

The head of the *ogboni* cult had also sent a message to warn Ojajagba to keep his mouth shut. In no uncertain terms, he had been told what would happen to him if he divulged to his new friends, the *onigbagbo* missionaries, any of the rituals of his old cult. And the *oro* had come out just a week earlier to utter its dread voice outside his compound as a direct threat to him and his family.

Solesi shuddered and expressed words of sympathy. Then he asked his old friend to tell him more about this new religion.

"What is it really like," Solesi asked, "this strange worship of the *onigbagbo*?"

Ojajagba's face lighted up. He told Solesi of the lack of coercion, the absence of secrecy, and the complete lack of intimidating oaths and rituals in the religion of the *onigbagbo*. All he had to do was to say he believed in *omo Olorun*, the child of God called *Jesu*. And he was accepted. He had become a believer.

A light shone in Ojajagba's eyes as he spoke to Solesi that evening in his front parlor in Shagamu that spoke of the transcendental power of his conversion.

Ojajagba also informed Solesi that he would not only be baptized, he was going to be "confirmed" in the new faith.

"Confirmation" was a word that Ojajagba, like everyone else, pronounced with difficulty. It was a *Gesi* word which had no translation in the Ijebu language. Because Ojajagba could not read or write, to prepare for this ceremony, he memorized the whole catechism in Yoruba with the help of a man called "Lerida."

At the urging of this lay reader, Ojajagba chose the Christian name, John. Then the day of the confirmation came. The *oyinbo* bishop came all the way from Lagos.

"Kini oruko re?" *What is your name?*

The white *alufa,* Bishop Leslie Vining, asked Ojajagba this question in Yoruba.

But the *oyinbo* bishop's Yoruba was delivered in a nasal English accent that sounded strange to an Ijebu ear. And at first, Ojajagba did not understand what the bishop asked him. Then he remembered the responses from the Yoruba book of *Katikisimu* which he had studiously memorized over the previous four months.

"Joonu," he stoutly replied. There was a note of pride, even defiance, in his voice.

"Tani fi oruko yi fun o?" *Who gave you this name?* The bishop, now more confident, went on.

Again, Ojajagba remembered the response from the catechism he had memorized.

"Awọn baba mi nipa ti Olorun. *My father in the Lord—my godfather,*" was his reply.

Ojajagba did not think it odd that his "godfather" was a young man no older than his youngest son.

If he had any fears about the repercussions of his apostasy in turning against his old cult, Ojajagba did not let anyone know. When he saw his friend after his baptism, Ojajagba told Solesi that he was not afraid of any retaliation from his former comrades in the *ogboni* cult.

"Those Ijebu gods are false," he said, lowering his voice, as if he was fearful that he might be overheard in his own home.

"There is only one god, Olorun, Owner of Heaven."

The *lerida* in his church and the *alufa* had assured Ojajagba that Olorun, this supreme god, did not reside in any graven image of wood or stone.

"*Emi ni Olorun.* God is a spirit," they had told him. And he believed.

But strangely, he had also been told that this god had made human beings in his image, and he had a son.

After this talk with his apostate friend, Solesi himself began to think more and more of those questions that had troubled him after he came back from Ibadan as a young man.

Where did we come from? What happens to men when they die? Solesi looked at the great changes around him brought by the coming of the white man. Surely the god of such a people must be very powerful indeed. Could the answers to those questions he sought be found in the religion of the *oyinbo*?

Solesi was perplexed by many of the changes around him, including the new center of authority in the form of the colonial government, and the irrelevance of the *oba* and the old council of chiefs. And he did not know what to make of the new taxes imposed on everyone. It was not paid to the Alakenne. It was an *owo ori* that was paid to the agents of the white man.

But gradually, Solesi's way of thinking began to change. He thought of the cataclysmic events that had shaped his own life, and the wars between brethren that had destroyed the old ways of his people. He began to question the wisdom of much of what he had been taught as a child before he went to war. He found himself doubting the rightness of the old ways, and his people's reliance on the gods of Ijebuland.

Those deities should have been able to fight for their people. Instead, they had allowed Ijebu to be defeated by the white man and his Hausa underlings at the Battle of Imagbon.

He also questioned the harshness of the practices of his people, such as the putting to death of Fagbemi, who, after all, had merely been caught fishing in a river.

And indeed, belief in the old Yoruba gods died rapidly in Ikenne and other towns of Ijebuland in the last few decades of Solesi's life. Many people contemplated the relative simplicity of the new belief in a single deity, and they chose the new god. The hearts of these people, even old men like Ojajagba and Solesi, were ripe for turning. The ground had been prepared by the disillusionment that followed the time of troubles, when men betrayed their comrades and warlords sold women and children into slavery.

Solesi could see why the new religion of the *oyinbos* made sense to his people. Many of them were tired of the macabre practices of the secretive Ijebu cults. And they were disillusioned with a way of faith that permitted human sacrifice and slavery, atrocities which the white man's religion resolutely stood against. Solesi's own intimate experiences with the *egungun* and other cults in Ikenne had revealed to him the trickery and sleight of hand that often stood for divine intervention.

So, when the time came, the people of Remo did not ask, "Where did these *oyinbo* men come from to take away from us the beliefs of our fathers?" And they did not ask, "What do they want from us?"

They knew that the *oyinbo* priest and his native-born catechist wanted their soul. Willingly they gave it to them.

The *onigbagbo* missions were allowed to set up their churches and schools, which rapidly spread to all the towns of Ijebuland.

And it was not just the cult of the *onigbagbo* that the people of Remo turned to. Many families that Solesi knew in Ikenne had also become Moslems.

This religion of the *imale* appeared to be even more aligned than Christianity with the traditional beliefs of our people. It allowed the marrying of many wives. And the concept of curses, predetermined

OLADELE OLUSANYA

destiny, and use of *tira* and charms to ward off evil, which were taught by Moslem *alfas*, were similar to the practices of the old *babalawos*.

Solesi watched as the ancient polytheism of the Yorubas withered and died in Ikenne amongst former devotees of Olokun, Sango, and Orunmila. These old gods were merged into a single *Olorun Olodumare*, who was explained to Solesi as a spirit that could not be seen or touched.

A visiting *oyinbo* priest was brought one evening to Solesi's house by the catechist in Ikenne. This *alufa* explained to Solesi, through his interpreter, that *orun alakeji*, the former heaven of the pagan gods, was a place where good people were rewarded after their life on earth. This was after they had gone through the judgment of heaven, known as *idajo orun*. But there was another place, *Orun ina*, the place of fire, where those who did bad things on earth would endure suffering and torture.

All these new ideas made sense to old Solesi. He said to the *oyinbo* priest with a laugh that he himself would be equally at ease in an Olokun shrine, a Moslem mosque or a Christian church.

But after he was taken to the *ile esin* of the *onigbagbo*s in Ikenne to witness their service, Solesi admitted to himself that he liked the atmosphere of the Christian church the best. The quiet dignity of the *onigbagbo* songs and prayers impressed him more than the colorful but disjointed pageantry of his *egungun* shrine. And he discovered with surprise that his beloved drums and *shekere* had been co-opted for use in the music of the *ile-esin* of the *onigbagbo*.

By this time, Solesi no longer believed in the infallibility of the old ways. It was a personal metamorphosis that led to his own conversion, late in life, to the *esin* of the *onigbagbo*.

*　　*　　*　　*　　*

Solesi's friend Ojajagba died a few years later. Solesi heard the whisperings among the old cult members that his friend had been taken away by the god Orisa-ile as vengeance for his apostasy. Some said he was cursed or poisoned by the powerful head of the *ogboni* in Shagamu.

Whatever it was, the death and burial of his old friend became a pivotal moment in Solesi's own conversion. For after Solesi witnessed Ojajagba's Christian burial, he boldly decided to become a Christian himself. He wanted to be dressed and robed in white at his own funeral.

He was struck by the quiet grandeur of the Christian ceremony for the dead. He contrasted what he saw at his friend's Christian burial with what usually happened after the death of a member of any of the traditional secret societies in Remo.

Solesi shuddered as he remembered the inner sanctum of the *ogboni* shrine in Ikenne. Rows of human skulls, which had been taken off the bodies of dead cult members, were arranged on low shelves along a wall in an inner recess of the shrine. He tried not to think of the gruesome scene of the cutting off of the head of the dead acolyte and the disembowelment that followed, with the heart and liver cut out to be preserved.

But Ojajagba and Solesi should have known that the cults would have the last say in these matters. For that very night following Ojajagba's Christian burial, twelve silent men descended on the burial ground behind the CMS church in Shagamu. They were clothed in white robes tied ceremonially at their waists. Their upper bodies were bare. They came equipped with diggers, hoes, and axes. And in their hearts was a grim resolve to do the bidding of the head of their *ogboni* cult.

There was a heap of fresh red earth above the newly dug grave of Ojajagba, marking the site for their grim work of reclamation. The men went swiftly to work. The wooden coffin was soon exposed. Working with quiet efficiency, with not a word exchanged between them, the white robed men hoisted the box to the surface with a rope passed under its base. The flimsy wood was split open with a single blow of the ax. The body, still clothed in its now soiled white robe, was taken out of the gaping box and maneuvered into a long linen bag, which had been brought for the purpose.

The bag came with a rope at the neck which was twisted and tied in a tight knot. It was loaded into a small low cart, an *omolanke,* that was pushed along by two of the men, who, taking a back path through the forest, made swiftly for their shrine.

The men had to hurry. The head of the cult was waiting for them, as well as a full gathering of the adepts of the *ogboni*. There was a lot of work ahead. Rituals had to be performed on the body of Ojajagba.

Notwithstanding the wishes of their renegade comrade and the plans of the apostate Christian sect that had seduced him, his brothers knew that Ojajagba's foolish idea of abandoning the cult of his fathers had only been a delusion. Ojajagba, like all of them, had been consecrated with an unbreakable oath to the *ogboni* cult. Every one of them knew that the promise made at their initiation was a debt that would be paid in full.

By reclaiming the body of Ojajagba, his comrades had only done what they had to do. The deity had reclaimed its own. Their own time would come when it would.

*　*　*　*　*

Solesi lived to the age of one hundred and five years before he died in his hometown of Ikenne-Remo. The last of the "war boys," he was a survivor of that turbulent era of the Yoruba civil wars of the nineteenth century that had only ended with imposition of the white man's "protectorate" over his people.

Apart from his strange illness after the death of his father, Solesi had never been ill in his life. No one in his family, not even his children including my grandmother, Efunyemi, could remember their patriarch ever being confined to bed for any length of time.

But death came at last for the former war boy. His sudden illness and swift death in his house in Ikenne, surrounded by relatives and friends, was just what he would have wished for. Those who knew of his meticulous ways in the planning of festivals said Solesi must have planned this ahead.

The people of Ikenne would remember for years the songs, elegies and rites at Solesi's funeral that took place in that year 1954. Eyewitnesses to the deeply moving performances by the town's drummers, dancers and *akewis*, masked *egunguns*, *alagemos,* and *ageres* on stilts, talked about these for a long time afterward until their stories became part of a lore that reached us, his great-grandchildren.

Old drum and dance troupes all over Remo dusted off their moldy costumes and rusty skills. To honor their old leader and patron, they descended on the sleepy town of Ikenne.

Like an occupying army, they camped out for days in the square in front of the oba's palace. They even spilled into the courtyard of St. Savior's Church. This they did, despite the protestations from the Christians, who said it was a sacrilege to have to share their holy space with unrepentant *keferis*.

The choristers of the Anglican church practiced for days. Then, they came out in full force in their red and white robes and flat-topped hats to sing at his funeral. For they also claimed Solesi as their own.

And who could forget the songs and dances composed and performed by the women folk of Ikenne? The ancient *Balufon* dance was performed. Young maidens with bare breasts waved *irukere,* fly whisks, in the air and shook their seductive hips covered with multicolored beads.

Not many realized it at the time. But the burial rites of old Solesi would be the last pagan display of such magnitude and proportion in Ikenne, before the complete dominance by the Christian faith and the Moslem religion over the old ways of faith would banish forever the licentiousness and free-spiritedness of the past.

After this, no longer would young maidens of Ikenne dance and sing in public with only beads around their hips to cover from public view their natural endowments. No longer would young men gape at young naked breasts that hung like ripe low-lying fruit on an easy-to-reach branch of a mango tree.

And it is true that those young breasts had been depicted in sculptures of Yoruba maidens kneeling in supplication, calabash in hand, for hundreds of years before the coming of the white man. They could well be the metaphor for the one-thousand-year culture of our people. Brave, wild-spirited, and unencumbered, the uncovered bosoms of these winsome maidens swung free in their pride and innocence. But as symbols of the ancient culture of the Yoruba people, they faced a crisis with the coming of the white man. For they were enticing targets for greedy, predatory hands that would seize and violate them.

Still, the old cult of the *osugbo* had the last say at the burial rites of old Solesi of Ikenne. At the culmination of the ceremony, the aged head of the *osugbo* stepped forward.

The old man's creaky voice struggled to find the strength of youth for this one last duty in the service of a comrade. Everyone listened as he intoned slowly this ancient dirge to his friend, Solesi of Ikenne.

Ko si eni ti iku ko le pa
O di arinako, o di oju ala.
Solesi, ti o ba de ajule orun,
ma jokun, ma je ekolo.

OLADELE OLUSANYA

Ohun ti nwon ba nje lohun
ni ki o ma ba won je.
Solesi, omo Adeuja,
Omo Akarigbo,
Odigbose.
Sun re o.

There is no one that death will not claim.
Till we meet by chance or in the realm of dreams.
Solesi, when you get to that abode in the Sky,
Do not eat centipedes or earthworms,
It is what they eat in Heaven
that you should eat.
Solesi, son of Adeuja
Son of Akarigbo,
Farewell forever.
Sleep well.

CHAPTER 6

Ję ki n sǫ ìtàn mi pelu ibanuję
Fun ipadanu awǫn ǫmǫ Obanta.
Egungun kigbe,
oro na ke nita losan gangan;
Ṣugbǫn a ko le fi abo bo awǫn ibatan wa
"Bo o lo, ya fun mi"
ni a nke bi a ti nsalǫ kuro loju ogun.
Àwǫn ębǫ wa ni a ṣe lásán
niwaju Sigidi leti odo Yemoji.
Ṣugbǫn bi o tile ję pe
ogun na padanu
a ri aami fun alaafia fun ojo iwaju
ti o duro de wa ni oko Mamu.

Let me tell my tale of woe
For the loss of Obanta's sons
The egungun cried, and the oro wailed,
But we could not save our kin
from the white man's guns.
"If you can't run, make way!" we cried
as we fled the battlefield in terror.
Our sacrifices had been made in vain
To Esu and Shigidi at Itokin;
But though the war was lost
we found a token of peace waiting for us
at a farm in Mamu.

War comes to Ijebu

AROUND THE TIME that Solesi was born to the Warrior from Ife in Ikenne, another male child was born to a prominent family in Shagamu, another Remo town a quarter of a day's journey away.

Shagamu at this time was the largest and most prominent town of the Remos, a branch of the Ijebus who had carved out their separate identity as farmers and traders. The Remos were not known for the warlike proclivities that distinguished their more belligerent brethren in Ijebu-Ode.

Now, while it may be true that the sacred Uren river of Ikenne did not flow through Shagamu, Shagamu had its own river, the Ibu. This gentle stream flowed along the eastern edge of the town. It provided the town with its drinking water and afforded its grateful fishermen an ample livelihood. The Ibu had flowed beside the town of Shagamu as long as anyone could remember.

Like the Uren, the Ibu river was dedicated to a deity who protected the town. But in Shagamu unlike in Ikenne, there were no taboos attached to fishing in the river. Men could go out in canoes to catch fish in its waters.

*   *   *   *   *

This newborn child was the son of the Akarigbo, the *oba* of Shagamu and paramount ruler of all Remo. On the eighth day of his birth, as custom and the ancient tradition of his people demanded, the boy had his *isomo loruko* or child-naming ceremony. The child was named Adedoyin, meaning "the crown becomes as sweet as honey."

Now, it happened that a few years before the birth of this child, his father, the Akarigbo, in his capacity as chief judge of Remo, had given judgment against a certain priest or *abore* of the town.

This *abore*, named Ifayomi, had been accused of taking a goat from a supplicant without delivering the potion he had promised to his client. The evidence was clear against him. Several trustworthy witnesses supported the supplicant's story.

The Akarigbo ordered Ifayomi to repay the cost of the goat apart from giving the plaintive two rolls of white cotton and a bag of salt, expensive items in those days. In addition, he was removed from his position in the *osugbo*, the traditional council of priests and high chiefs who advised the oba.

For the miscreant, Ifayomi, this fall from grace, and the ignominy and shame that befell him and his family after this judgment, would never be forgiven. From that day on, Ifayomi bore the Akarigbo a deep grudge that would never go away, although the Akarigbo himself thought little about that case. The monarch could not even remember afterward the name of the errant priest.

Ifayomi had expected the ruler of his town as head of the judicial council to take his side as he was one of the *osugbo*. He vowed to get his revenge. This deep-seated hatred and quest for revenge consumed Ifayomi's waking hours. He was a very patient and vindictive man. And after many years of planning and waiting, he had his opportunity.

The child Adedoyin was now eight years ago. On market days, which was every five days, he was taken by Ajao, one of the servants from the palace to the market in Shagamu.

Ajao had been assigned to take care of Adedoyin since the boy was a toddler. He had become quite attached to the boy and doted on him. These trips to the market which were meant for Ajao to purchase household supplies for his mistress, Adedoyin's mother, had become a fun-filled excursion for the boy.

The young Adedoyin loved this weekly adventure. In between these visits, he did nothing but look forward to the next chance of getting out of the confines of the palace.

The scenes he witnessed in that busy market, and the fact that he was allowed to partake in what he regarded as an adult pastime, made Adedoyin feel important and mature. This trip outside the palace on market days became the most important event in his young life. It was what he lived for from week to week.

The main market in Shagamu at that time was served by one main thoroughfare passing through its center. This wide lane was lined on both sides with stalls, booths and great quantities of produce and wares arranged in baskets, mats, and leaves spread on mats on the ground.

It was the place where friends met and exchanged warm and elaborate greetings. Long-time enemies would also meet in the space between the stalls. But as they searched for wares and bargains, they would look in the other direction from each other and pretend not to have seen one another.

This was the place where kinsmen and old acquaintances from far off hamlets and villages, who had not seen one another for months or years, gasped in astonishment and grasped each other's hands in effusive greeting and slapped each other's backs with joy.

On any day in this market, one would see youngsters prostrating and kneeling in the dust when they met older relatives and were rewarded with cowry shells placed in their grateful hands. These boys and girls would then dash off to purchase treats such as *epa*, roasted groundnuts or *wara*, a native cheese made from goat's milk.

The market was also the place where a bold young man could surreptitiously arrange to meet and talk with a shy young maiden from his village who had caught his fancy.

On these market days, Adedoyin would ask for treats. Ajao always indulged him, buying him fresh fruits like mangoes, pineapples known as *ope oyinbo,* and the ripe yellow-skinned pawpaw bought from farmers who came from surrounding farms. Sometimes, it was a scoop of honey known as *oyin.*

Adedoyin loved the open-air performers who came to the market to delight the crowd. He loved the drummers, acrobats, singers, and dancers who entertained marketgoers for handfuls of cowry shells thrown at their feet. Once, Adedoyin laughed at the antics of a performing monkey who leapt from the shoulder of its master to grab a banana from a passing hawker of fruits who had tempted the animal with her uncovered basket balanced delicately on her head.

These were the scenes that would be forever and indelibly etched in Adedoyin's mind.

On this particular day, an *ikoko,* hyena, was displayed by a traveling troupe of acrobats. These performers came from *ile oke,* that mysterious place up country in the Yoruba hinterland. *Ile-oke* was the term used by the supercilious Ijebus for any place north of Remo, even if it was as close as Ibadan or as far away as Ilorin. People gathered around and threw cowry shells at the animal's handlers. Adedoyin clapped his small hands together and hooted for joy.

But soon, it was time to go home. But Adedoyin persuaded the servant that they should stop by the river on their way home. This was not the big Ibu river, but a tributary stream that led, a few miles downstream, into the main river. This stream was known as Eruwuru by the people of Shagamu.

Going to this stream instead of directly home was a detour that added at least an hour to their homeward journey. But Adedoyin wanted to wet his feet in the shallow waters of the "ilu-wulu," as he called it. He loved seeing the tiny crabs on the sandy riverbank scurry around as he tried to catch them with his hands.

Ajao protested that they would be late getting home. He might get a whipping from the head slave at the palace if he did not bring the boy home in time. But the ready tears that stood at the corners of the boy's eyes won him over.

Thus, instead of heading directly home along the busy street that led directly from the market to the *afin,* Ajao held the boy's hand in his as they took a narrow bush path down a slope that led to the stream. Today being a market day, they did not encounter anyone, not even the young women who normally walked along the narrow path to fetch water in the stream.

They came at last to the stream. The place Ajao looked for was a pool formed by a flat depression in the course of the slow-moving stream. This was where people would stand knee deep in the clear water and scrub themselves and their clothes with soft, black native soap.

Today, the pool was deserted. Ajao and the boy found themselves quite alone. And as Ajao watched the boy jump excitedly up and down the water's edge splashing his clothes with water, he was not worried. Still, he made a mental note to himself that they should not stay too long in this deserted place. They should be making their way home very soon.

It was then that Ajao felt a pressure in his bowels. And as the young boy joyfully pranced about and stamped his feet in the shallow water, scattering the fish and the crabs, Ajao went behind a large tree in the bush to relieve himself. But it was exactly at that moment when he was barely out of view of the boy, that a group of tough looking young men, with a masked *egungun* in their midst, came out of the bush on the other side of the path and grabbed the boy.

The astonished Ajao, who had just pulled down his *sokoto* to relieve himself behind the tree, heard the noise. He turned, sprang up from his crouching position and yelled the boy's name.

"Adedoyin!" he shouted.

As Ajao hastily pulled up his *sokoto*, he whipped out a long thin knife which he kept in the waist band of his *sokoto.* He ran back toward the stream, ready to do battle. But he was struck on the crown of the head with a large club, an *olugbogboro,* and he went down like a log.

When Ajao came to, he felt a huge aching lump above his right ear, but the child was gone. He ran blindly back and forth, first along the deserted bush path, then into the thick bush, where the undergrowth caused him to trip and fall in his wild frenzy. And as he yelled and cried out the child's name, tears of rage and terror blinded him.

It was too late, and he knew it. After half an hour of this fruitless venture, Ajao could barely see through his tears as he made his way back to the palace to tell the terrible news.

The young prince had been abducted.

*   *   *   *   *

Adedoyin had been kidnapped by a traveling band of *egungun* performers who went from town to town all over Remo performing on market days. They had been suborned for this dastardly act by the scheming Ifayomi who had given them several bags of cowry shells.

They were to take the child deep into the forest and murder him, digging a shallow grave for him that would be no barrier for hyenas and other scavengers of the forest. The body would never be recovered, and no news would reach the palace of the Akarigbo of what had happened to their prince.

However, Ojuwoye, the leader of the *egunguns,* did not want blood on his hands. He took pity on the boy. He decided that he would hide him, then take him far away from Shagamu.

The boy was kept hidden in the bush for three months. He was treated rather well. He was well fed. But someone was always there to keep watch on him while the rest of the troupe went to the surrounding villages to perform their *egungun* act on market days.

It was at this time that the leader of the *egungun* troupe was contracted to perform for a chief in Ijebu-Ode. Ojuwoye and his men left their forest lair near Shagamu and took the boy Adedoyin with them. And it was in Ijebu-Ode, the metropolis that was the chief town of Ijebuland, that they thereafter made their home.

As time went on, Adedoyin became attached to and inseparable from Ojuwoye, the leader of the troupe, whom he called "Baba." By this time, after the passage of several years, he was no longer a captive, but he did not try to escape.

For as Adedoyin grew older, these men were the only friends or family he knew. He became an active and favored member of the *egungun* group. Memories of his old home in the palace at Shagamu grew dim. He was never to see his birthplace again. He now called Ijebu-Ode home.

Before he reached sixteen years of age, Adedoyin stopped touring and performing with the *egunguns*. Ojuwoye, the leader of the troupe who he called *Baba* died, and Adedoyin found himself alone in the world.

By now, Adedoyin considered himself not only a native of Ijebu-Ode, but a patriot. This was how, as a teenager, Adedoyin became a warrior in the service of the Awujale, the monarch of Ijebu-Ode and paramount ruler of Ijebuland. He rose in rank, and as a favorite of the king, he was made *olori* or captain of the palace guard. When the time came, Adedoyin married a maiden chosen for him from the household of the Awujale himself.

In 1876, his first son, also named Adedoyin, who would later call himself Odusanya, was born in Ijebu-Ode. The younger Adedoyin grew up to be a hot-headed youth. He chafed under the authority of his father, who in his later years, had become quite a disciplinarian and tyrant over his household.

One day, when he was thirteen years old, this heady youth ran away from home after he was castigated and flogged by his father for a minor infraction.

The runaway wandered into a forest, the *Igbo Odu,* which was on the road to Ijebu-Igbo. There, according to the stories of our family, he fell into the hands of members of a cult that made that forest their home. This was how the young Adedoyin, the grandson of an Akarigbo of Shagamu, was forced to become an acolyte of the Odu cult, an organization of outlaws who lived in the forest near the town of Ijebu-Ode.

At this time in the history of Ijebu-Ode, the ancient religion of the Ijebus was not was it used to be. Many of the priests of the various shrines were dedicated, not to the honest service of their god, but to their own pecuniary advancement. To achieve these selfish ends, no means was too evil.

These wayward priests and their cults kidnapped men, women and children who were either sold as slaves or used as human sacrifices in macabre rituals. Slaves or residents of Ijebu-Ode who came from foreign parts were in particular danger. They could be seized anytime without warning to become victims of human sacrifice to one of the two hundred deities worshipped in the town.

This was a dark time indeed for Ijebuland, when the activities of secretive cults made Ijebu-Ode a fearful place to live, especially for foreigners. A saying of the time captured the mood.

> *Ilu Ijebu, ajeji ko le wo be*
> *O wole laaro,*
> *o di ebo lale*

> *A stranger dares not come into Ijebu.*
> *For if he enters the town on his two feet in the morning,*
> *By evening, he may end up in a sacrificial bowl.*

And of all the cults and *abores* in Ijebuland at that time, none was more feared than the Odu cult into whose hands young Adedoyin had fallen.

Within a few weeks of being among them, Adedoyin realized that half of the cultists who lived in *Igbo Odu* were crazed zealots. The other half were common criminals, thieves, and murderers—all of them outlaws from society. They were opportunists who found an excuse for their social deviancy in the apparent adherence to a religious deity.

Members of this *odu* cult made their living from kidnapping men, women, and children. They sent messages to the relatives of their captives demanding a ransom in exchange for their lives. Those of their captives who did not have anyone to ransom them were killed in cruel orgies of human sacrifice to their god, Esu. Veterans among these men of the forest told their young captive, Adedoyin, that Esu gave them physical strength and supernatural powers when they drank the blood of their victims.

And indeed, Adedoyin had spent barely a month in their company when he was made to hold the bound feet and legs of one such unransomed victim, whose throat was slit, and his blood drained into a ritual calabash. Adedoyin was told that the heart and liver of the victim would be cut out and eaten by the *abore* and his inner circle.

Adedoyin detested the outlaw existence he was forced to endure. And he hated even more the horrifying and dubious religious rites that the *odu* cult forced him to participate in the service of a deity he neither understood nor desired to follow.

But Adedoyin wanted to survive. He knew he had to be crafty not to let the other cult members know his true feelings. Somehow, he would find a way to escape. So he swore the oath that was administered to him by the leader of the cult. He knew he would owe his life to feigning acceptance of the evil ways of his captive cult.

But he could not always hide his repugnance and lack of enthusiasm for the tasks set out for him. Thus, his comrades were suspicious of him. Wherever he went and whatever he did, someone always watched and guarded him.

Adedoyin knew that the last thing this murderous cult wanted on its hands was a traitor or runaway who would divulge its secrets to the outside world. He feared that they might do away with him if they thought he became too dangerous or was too much of a burden to keep.

But Adedoyin was cunning and resourceful. He planned his escape carefully and bided his time. He made friends with some of the cult members. He took part with feigned relish in their revolting rites. And after twelve months, he found his opportunity.

One morning, the man left to guard Adedoyin thought he was asleep and went behind a tree to relieve himself. Adedoyin had already planned his escape and had memorized all the secret paths he knew in the forest.

His guard had barely turned his back when Adedoyin, who was feigning sleep, sprang up and took to his heels. Fear lent him wings, and he flew like a madman. He ran in the direction he had calculated to be the boundary of the Odu Forest. But he did not have much of a head start, for his guard immediately raised the hue and cry.

Soon, the entire gang was in pursuit of the fleeing Adedoyin. He could hear their loud noises behind him. Besides, they had two hunting dogs who joined in the chase. Adedoyin's heart pounded with panic and the fear of the death which his capture would most certainly entail. As he ran, he dared not look behind him. But he could hear the baying and yelping of the dogs become louder as his pursuers closed in on him.

It was at this moment that the man who would play a great and important role in Adedoyin's life came on the scene.

*　*　*　*　*

At that time in Ijebu-Ode, there was a certain chieftain who was descended from one of the great families who had ruled the town from ancient times. His name was Kuku. He was a close ally and counselor to the Awujale, and he was a man destined to play a great role in the story of Ijebu-Ode in that turbulent nineteenth century.

Kuku was a descendant of Sungbon, the daughter of Osotimi, the great inventor and military strategist of ancient times. Our stories tell us that this Sungbon was the first female to serve as a counselor to an Awujale in Ijebu-Ode. It was no surprise therefore that her family's tradition and skills as counselors to the monarch of Ijebu-Ode continued up to Kuku's time.

Kuku was a warrior, but one who had become tired of taking part in the incessant wars that Ijebu-Ode fought at that time against its neighbor, Ibadan. So, at the time of this story, Kuku had hung up his weapons and had become a merchant. He had discovered a knack for making money, and he was now very prosperous in trade and commerce.

At this time in the history of Ijebu-Ode, many of Kuku friends and kinsmen were doing the same thing. They bought farm produce from Owo and Ikire and took them to Ikorodu, Ebute Meta and Eko on the coast where they found foreign ships waiting to buy them at great profit. From Lagos Island, Kuku and his fellow Ijebu merchants returned with guns and ammunition, which they sold to the warring chieftains in the Yoruba hinterland.

It had not taken long for the Ijebus of Kuku's generation to realize that with wars raging incessantly among the Yoruba tribes to the north and west of them, they were in a lucrative position. They became middlemen between the Yoruba hinterland and the coast.

Working in the favor of these Ijebu middlemen was that no one who was not Ijebu—trader, soldier, or merchant—was allowed to pass through Ijebuland at that time without paying a heavy toll. Kuku and his friends were the agents responsible for the collection of this tariff, from which they extracted a heavy commission.

Kuku was one of the most astute and discerning men of his generation in Ijebuland. To bolster his position, he learned *Gesi,* the English language, after taking a prolonged trip to Lagos, where he apprenticed himself as a sales-clerk to a white man who was known as Mr. John. This *oyinbo* was the agent of a trading firm, Messrs. G. Goldsmith and Sons from Bristol, who had built a warehouse on the wharf on Lagos Island.

Kuku learned more than rudimentary English from this Englishman. He studied arithmetic and accounting. He became adept at keeping ledgers and balancing accounts. He was among the very first of that breed of men who made the Ijebus preeminent in trade and commerce in that century of turmoil and change.

It was this Chief Kuku who, by a stroke of fate, came on the scene as Adedoyin's pursuers closed in on him on the outskirts of the Odu forest.

*   *   *   *   *

Mounted on his bay mare, Kuku was surrounded by an entourage of fifteen trusted servants, who were all armed with cutlasses and "Dane" guns. These firearms were muzzle-loading muskets purchased from white traders at the coast. The Ijebus had learned to use these firearms with great skill during the Ijaiye War.

Kuku and his men were on their way to meet one of his produce agents in Mamu, a hamlet not far from Ijebu-Ode. They had taken a short cut using an obscure bush path that went across a portion of the Igbo Odu. It was this same portion of the forest that Adedoyin was heading for as he tried to outrun his pursuers.

Adedoyin would later call this lucky event the intersection of his prayers with the wishes of the gods. Kuku, for his part, said it was a happy coincidence.

One minute, a relaxed and pensive Kuku was thinking of the calabash of fresh water and the bowl of kola nuts that Lateju, the produce agent was certain to present to him when he got to Mamu. The next instant, his horse suddenly reared up on its hindfeet as it tried not to trample underfoot a frightened looking young man who had appeared suddenly in the middle of the path.

OLADELE OLUSANYA

It was Adedoyin, who was as astonished as the entourage that now stared at him. Instantly, he recognized that they were not part of the Odu gang in that evil forest. The look and bearing of the leader on horseback told him he could not be part of that outlaw cult.

Quickly, Adedoyin found his wits. He knew that his life, and indeed his future, lay with this man. But as he quickly knelt in the roadway pleading for help and succor from the obviously important personage that sat on his high horse, his pursuers burst onto the road.

Chief Kuku did not wait for further explanation. He, as a chieftain of Ijebu-Ode, was aware of the activities of these outlaws of the forest. From what he heard, they were brigands and hoodlums who were accused of myriad crimes from kidnapping and murder to human sacrifice. Besides, he hated with a passion the bogus and inhuman religious practices perpetrated by this cult, which had given his native Ijebuland a bad name.

Instantly, Kuku lifted his left arm and shouted an order to his men. They drew their weapons and ran at the outlaws who had closed in on the kneeling youngster in the roadway. Trained warriors that they were, Chief Kuku's men proceeded to give the cult members short thrift. The outlaws, armed only with knives and machetes, stood no chance against the disciplined and trained fighting men who were the bodyguard of Chief Kuku.

Before Adedoyin could blink, two of the outlaws fell dead on the spot. One was shot through the heart at point-blank range by one of Kuku's men carrying a musket. The other was cut down with a saber wielded by the leader on horseback as he foolishly tried to attack the chief himself. The rest of the Odu gang turned and fled. They knew when the odds were against them.

It was only then that a grateful Adedoyin told the incredulous Kuku his story. Kuku believed him. Without a word, he hoisted Adedoyin behind him on his horse, and took him along on his trip to Mamu.

Chief Kuku's entourage spent five days in the hamlet of Mamu. And when they returned to Ijebu-Ode, they took a longer route that avoided that corner of the Odu forest. When they got back to town, Chief Kuku helped Adedoyin to make inquiries about his home and family.

It was then that Adedoyin learned that he had no home to go back to. His father, the elder Adedoyin, had died during his son's sojourn in the evil forest. His mother had died earlier. And his only surviving sibling, a half-sister, had gone away to live with her mother's family.

Adedoyin was now alone in the world. He sat down in the street outside his father's house and wept. With no other options, Kuku took Adedoyin home into his own household.

When Adedoyin saw Chief Kuku's house in Ijebu-Ode for the first time after his rescue from the Odu forest, he thought it was the palace of the Awujale. For the house that Chief Kuku called home was a great and impressive edifice indeed.

It was a large compound, one of the most skillfully built in Ijebu-Ode in the late nineteenth century. What Adedoyin saw from the street was a sprawling one-story building which, as he approached, revealed a gap in the middle. This was a great arched entrance way that led to an inner courtyard surrounded on all sides by buildings which cut off this open space completely from the outside.

To the right and left as he entered this courtyard were two small *oro* trees. They were symmetrically placed and had obviously been planted by design. Facing him was a grove of three big mango trees that cast a shade in the center of the courtyard. There was a shed thatched with dried grass at the far end of the compound. Adedoyin surmised that this contained a shrine. On both sides of this shrine, forming a U-shaped enclosure, were two long buildings which were attached to the main building facing the road, with no gap in between. Adedoyin later found that these attachments contained rooms for the wives and servants of the head of the household.

When Adedoyin went through that archway for the first time into the compound, he stood transfixed for several minutes. He held his mouth open and gaped. But he was jarred out of his reverie by a servant who tapped him on the shoulder and took him into a small room to the left of the main building.

He was told to remove his clothes which were worn, dirty, and tattered. Then he was brought back into the open courtyard where he washed himself with water poured over his body from an earthenware jug while his skin was raked with *koinkoin* and *ose dudu*. He was given new clothes to wear, then he was fed.

Adedoyin ate his meal of *eba* and *ewedu*, using his fingers, on a wooden bench in that great courtyard underneath one of the mango trees. It was only after this that he was taken to the front parlor to see the great chief himself, who now told Adedoyin that this was his home.

And for the next few years, Chief Kuku's household, in the Ita Ntebo quarters of Ijebu-Ode, became the home the orphaned Adedoyin no longer had. Chief Kuku treated him like a son. With Kuku's suggestion, Adedoyin changed his name. In remembrance of his sojourn in the Odu forest and his rescue by Chief Kuku, he chose Odusanya as his new name. It meant "Odu has repaid my suffering."

Over the next few months, Chief Kuku told Odusanya his own story and that of his famous family.

*   *   *   *   *

Kuku was the son of a great chief of Ijebu-Ode who, in his time, commanded the Awujale's cavalry. Apart from being great counselors and chieftains, the ancestors of Chief Kuku's clan were noted warriors of Ijebu-Ode. Many members of his family had served as *Baloguns* and war chiefs of the Ijebus since their family story began to be recorded by the *arokens* in the *afin*.

These oral records tell us that they were descended from Sungbon, the famed daughter of Osotimi, who was a descendant of Osolanke, the patriarch who came with Obanta from Ile-Ife. It was this Osolanke who established the Ntebo quarters of Ijebu-Ode, where their family had lived ever since.

Kuku's own mother was a daughter of an Awujale. And his paternal grandfather, a Balogun of the Ijebus, had distinguished himself in that war during which the Ijebus joined the Ifes and Oyos to forcefully remove the Owu people from their ancestral homeland. In the process, they succeeded in wiping out the ancient city of Owu.

Kuku himself, an *otun Balogun* in his time, had taken part in several campaigns on behalf of the Ijebu king to help their one-time ally, Ibadan, push back Moslem marauders who came out of their base in Ilorin to devastate Yoruba towns in the forestland around Ibadan, Ile-Ife and Osogbo. But at the time of Kuku's rescue of the young Odusanya, the Ijebus were on the opposing side of Ibadan, their former ally. This was in the prolonged conflict that would later be known as *ogun odun merindinlogu,* the sixteen-year war.

But though Ijebu-Ode and Ibadan were now on opposing sides, Kuku continued to have warm relationships with Ibadan. He alone among the Ijebu chiefs continued friendly terms with many of the warriors from Ibadan that he had known from his early years. Those young warriors were now *baloguns* and *olori oguns*, warlords leading Ibadan forces.

When Kuku was still a young man, a Yoruba book of grammar was published by a white Christian missionary, the Reverend Hinderer, who had established the first Christian mission in the Yoruba hinterland in Abeokuta before going on to settle in Ibadan. Kuku obtained a copy of this book through his friends in Ibadan, and with it, he taught himself to read and write in the Yoruba language. Later, he learned *Gesi*, the white man's tongue, during his apprentice to Mr. John Oliver on Lagos Island.

After learning the English language, Kuku read the King James Bible from cover to cover. He also read the simplified editions of several English novels and books of poetry. He memorized phrases from these books and learned to repeat them. He discovered that he had a knack for poetry, and he began to write verses of his own.

With his love of poetry, Kuku learned to write in a flowery, high sounding prose. He once wrote these lines in a letter to his friend, the Reverend Hinderer in Ibadan:

"My good friend, I am pleased to relate to you that I have removed my war tunic, donned the robe of commerce, and remade my image to that of a lover of Peace and benefactor of Mankind."

No longer a man of war, Kuku had grown tired of armed conflict, and of the incessant shifts of alliances among the Yoruba chieftains and warlords of those uncertain times.

Kuku was one of the few men in Ijebuland in his time to speak and write fluently in the white man's tongue. He liked to repeat English phrases and quotations to himself. Many of these were adapted and paraphrased from the books he read. After all, he reminded himself, he had learned to read and write *Gesi* under the tutelage of a real Englishman.

By the time Odusanya came into his household, Kuku had secured for himself an enviable position in the *afin* in Ijebu-Ode. He was a special emissary of the Awujale. He communicated, on the king's behalf, with *Gesi* administrators of the Lagos Colony. He also wrote missives in

Yoruba to powerful potentates all over Yorubaland. These included *obas* and chiefs of the Egbas, Ibadans, Ijeshas, Ekitis, and on one occasion, the Ooni in Ile-Ife.

With the backing of the Awujale, Kuku became a leading member of the council of chiefs, the *osugbo* in Ijebu-Ode. This was how he came to be involved with the signing of the treaty to end the Kiriji War.

*　*　*　*　*

At this time in our story, when Odusanya became a protégé of Chief Kuku in Ijebu-Ode, events were shaping up in other parts of Yorubaland that would touch the lives of both Kuku and Odusanya.

For to the north of Ijebu-Ode, lay Ibadan. The former war camp of Lagelu had become a great city with a population that rivaled that of Ijebu-Ode and other ancient city-states of Yorubaland. And Ibadan warlords, flush with their success in driving back the Fulani invader at Oshogbo and in keeping the Egbas at bay following the Ijaiye War, had begun to entertain ideas of grandeur.

It helped that the new Alaafin in the new capital at Ago d'Oyo recognized Ibadan as the linchpin in the new realignment of power after the fall of old Oyo. For Ibadan war chiefs saw themselves as heirs to the *esos* of old Oyo. The Aare ona Kakanfo and Bashorun titles, which were traditionally awarded by the Alafin to his greatest war captain and prime minister respectively, were now given to Ibadan chieftains.

The Ibadan war captain, mounted on his war horse with his feet firmly in the stirrups, was now the new leader of the Yorubas. He maintained this primacy by force of arms. And he could say with pride and truth that his rank-and-file warriors from Ibadan were the most disciplined in all Yorubaland. His city-state of Ibadan had never been defeated in war. He saw himself as the paragon of Yoruba military valor. He and his fellow *olori ogun* from Ibadan were the new guardians of the ancient war-fighting ethos of the *eso*. Therefore, he could dream of a revival of the Oyo Empire, with his upstart city at the head.

Ibadan warlords had already humiliated the Egbas, who they had sent into permanent exile in Abeokuta. The lands of the Owos, Ekitis, Ijesha, and Ondo had also come under their control. Even Ile-Ife, the spiritual capital of the Yorubas, was now under the suzerainty of the Baale of Ibadan.

But it did not take long before the ambition of the Ibadan warlords came to be resented and opposed by the other Yoruba city-states. The Ijeshas, Ekitis, and Ondos were the first to rebel. They were encouraged by Ile-Ife, whose Ooni chafed at finding himself, spiritual head of the Yorubas, paying tribute to his erstwhile subjects, the Ibadans and Oyos. The Ooni was also peeved that Ibadan saw fit to support Modakeke in its quarrel with Ile-Ife after that town was created by war chiefs and refugees from Oyo after the old empire collapsed.

Thus, before long, Ibadan found itself alone, fighting the Ilorin in the north, the Ekitis, Ijesha, and Ondo in the east and the Egbas in the southwest.

The Awujale of Ijebuland, egged on by a group of young chiefs who held sway over the *osugbo,* also joined this coalition that had ganged up against his old ally. The Ijebus now joined the Ekiti-Parapo, which was the name adopted by the northern alliance comprising Ekiti, Ilesha, Ondo, and Ife, against Ibadan.

Kuku, a man of peace, watched with dismay as young men in Ijebu-Ode lined up and marched off to war to the sound of drums. In their naivete, those fresh-faced young warriors thought the war would last a few months. After all, how could Ibadan, brave and capable though its warriors and commanders may be, fight off the whole of Yorubaland?

But this war was to last much longer than anyone expected. *Ogun odun merindinlogun*—the sixteen-year war—was what the Ijebus and other Yorubas came to call it.

The chroniclers in the English and Yoruba newspapers in Abeokuta and Lagos at that time called it the "Kiriji" war. This made Kuku laugh. He explained to Odusanya that there was no town or place in Yorubaland called Kiriji. The name was given to the war as an imitation of the sounds of the heavy guns and rockets that were used incessantly on both sides—*krrj krrj krrj.*

Kuku explained to Odusanya that this was the first modern war in Yorubaland—fought with big, powerful guns and cannons imported from Europe, along with the new breach-loading rifles which were replacing the muskets and "Dane" guns of the past.

"This is not the battle of Oshogbo," Kuku said to his protégé. He shook his wise old head, which had now turned gray.

In the end, everyone, even the stubborn Ijebus, became tired of a war that had failed to produce a clear victor, even after sixteen years of ruinous fighting. The soldiers on all sides were ready to go home. They wanted to return to their farms, their wives and their children. But each side needed to save face. No one wanted to be the first to pack up his weapons, break up his war camp and go home.

Luckily, even though the young guns, the *odo,* in the *osugbo* in Ijebu-Ode continued to push the Awujale to continue the conflict on the side of the northern allies, voices of reason and moderation like those of Chief Kuku prevailed. Also playing a part were Christian missionaries based in Lagos and Ibadan who sent a peace delegation to all parties to stop the fighting. They were assisted by European traders and native middlemen whose livelihood was adversely affected by the war.

In addition, the British administrators in the new Colony of Lagos wanted an end to a war that was stifling trade and starving the local population. British merchants could not sell goods to a poor or dying populace.

Thus, with the help of Christian missionaries, some British and many native-born, a truce was mediated between the warring parties. Kuku, who knew some of these missionaries, told Odusanya about some of the personalities involved. He told stories of the Reverend Samuel Johnson, a descendant of Alaafin Abiodun of the old Oyo Empire. And he spoke highly of an Englishman, who was his friend and mentor. This was Rev. David Hinderer, who headed the CMS mission in Ibadan and had a lot of clout with the warlords in that city.

"This white man, Reverend Hinderer, is my good friend," Kuku said to Odusanya.

"He is a good man who wants prosperity to return to Ibadan and other Yoruba towns. He understands, as people like me do, that this will not occur if peace is not established.

"Only then would farmers be able to return to their fields and traders feel safe to supply the war-afflicted towns with food, clothing and other needs."

Due to his friendliness with the Europeans and the Ibadans, Chief Kuku was chosen by the Awujale to be the head of the Ijebu delegation to attend the signing of the peace treaty at Kiriji.

Odusanya could see that the older man, who he called "Baba," was excited and pleased at this turn of events. So much so that, as he told Odusanya the news, his mentor's voice bubbled with hope and excitement. It sounded to Odusanya like a pot of okra soup simmering over a wood fire. Kuku said he was glad that the sixteen-year war was coming to an end at last.

Kuku went on, "Warfare is not a fit occupation for good and just men. It is the ordinary people caught up in war who suffer the most. They, not the soldiers or their commandeers, are the ones who have to confront the overwhelming disaster that war brings into their lives.

"But war pays for the war leaders and *baloguns*. They raise money from illegal taxation that they extort from people in times of war. They seize property and lands belonging to others in the name of conquest. They take captives on whom ransoms have to be paid for their release. They also make money by selling many of their captives as slaves.

"This is why many men in power continue to promote and prosecute wars. They gain wealth, position and fame.

"But men of peace like me must always oppose war."

* * * * *

Thus it was that young Odusanya found himself traveling on horseback, perched behind Chief Kuku, as he accompanied his mentor to the signing of the great peace treaty that would take place on the Kiriji battlefield.

Although the journey took them less than a week, Odusanya would always remember it like a pilgrimage of several months. It was the same route taken by Obanta, traveling in the opposite direction, when he set off from Ile-Ife on his epic journey to find Ijebu-Ode. It was the first time that Odusanya had ever left his hometown of Ijebu-Ode. He was very excited. He was a young man having his first taste of travel.

Kuku made sure they did not go through Ibadan. For Ijebu and Ibadan were technically still at war. Kuku did not want to be detained in Ibadan or be taken as a prisoner of war, even though he had many personal friends among the Ibadan high chiefs.

So they went north and east through Ijebu-Igbo. From there, they followed the left bank of the Osun river. They used that ancient river as a guide until they reached the tiny hamlet of Gbabefo.

When they arrived at Gbabefo, they found that the village had recently being evacuated by the Ijesha army. All around them were signs of recent fighting. They saw empty, roofless dwellings and blackened corn farms which had been put to the torch by the retreating Ijeshas to deny the Ibadans any source of food or comfort.

Kuku paid a canoe-man two cowries to row them across the Osun river on his river ferry. From the other side, they went due east facing the morning sun, through Ikire, Gbongon and Ile-Ife. Then, skirting just north of the town of Ilesha, they arrived at a series of hills just outside Ijebu-Ijesa.

Here, Odusanya noticed a long, straggling column of the local people. They were mostly women and children, who filed past them going in the opposite direction toward Ilesha.

It was a motley group. Women balanced baskets on their heads. Many had babies on their backs and dragged toddlers along by the arm. The bundles they carried were odd, sad and assorted—tattered old clothing, children's playthings and dried food such as yam flour and smoked meat called *eran igbe*. This food would perhaps last several days until they reached the next town where they could stop and rest. These odds and ends were all that remained of their life possessions.

An elderly woman, who was so bent she could barely walk, led a famished-looking goat on a leash. Two older children walked listlessly beside their mother, who appeared to be so weak and tired, she barely dragged her legs along as she strove to keep up with her boys. It was obvious they hadn't eaten for days. Their eyes were hopeless, tired and defeated, revealing to an uncaring world the sad faces of the ultimate victims of war.

Odusanya noticed that one of the women carried a small wooden mortar and pestle balanced precariously on her head. She stumbled along stoically. Odusanya looked intently at her. She did not look back at him.

Oblivious of his gaze, her eyes looked straight ahead. No words issued from her closed lips. But her stoic demeanor sent a message to Odusanya that was as clear as if she had spoken to him. What she seemed to say to him was this:

This old mortar and pestle would be used again one day. It would be filled with boiled yam, which would be pounded into "iyan" to feed an Ijesha family of husband, wife and three little children. And this family would eat their evening meal in their own home after a fruitful day on the farm in a time of peace.

Amid all the hopelessness and loss among the people, not only of Ijeshaland, but all over the land of *karo o jire*, there was at least in one person a desire and a hope for a new beginning.

Kuku leaned down from his horse.

"What place is this?" he asked one of the refugees, a young woman with a bundle on her head. She had a sleeping baby strapped to her back.

"Oke Mesi," she replied.

Kuku told Odusanya that they had reached their destination. They had arrived at the southern edge of the Kiriji battlefield.

And true enough, as they rode along, they could now see and hear different groups of armed men encamped all around the rock-strewn, hilly countryside. Different dialects and accents of Yoruba, many of which he could barely understand, came to Odusanya's ears. But here and there, he caught reassuring snippets of conversation in the familiar Ijebu dialect.

Kuku seemed to know his way quite well. He was careful to stay on the side of the allied forces arrayed against Ibadan, whose fighting men occupied the western approaches to the famous battlefield.

But before they went to the Ijebu camp, Kuku took Odusanya to see someone who he said was very important. He was the paramount war chief of the Ijeshas, and his name was Ogedengbe. Since the Ijebus had entered the conflict as an ally of the Ekiti-Parapo confederation, of which the Ijeshas were the major contingent, Ogedengbe was the nominal commander in chief of all the allied forces, including the Ijebu contingent.

At the mention of Ogedengbe, Odusanya felt a surge of excitement run through him. Was he actually going to meet this formidable war leader whose fame had traveled from the hills of his native Ilesha throughout Yorubaland until it reached even Ijebu-Ode? Odusanya had heard many stories of this warrior who was said to be invincible in battle.

Soon, they accosted a group of young-looking Ijesha guards. Some of them could not have been more than sixteen years of age, for they looked no older than Odusanya. But despite their youth, it was clear that they were no greenhorns. Odusanya was impressed by their fierce looks and warlike accoutrements. Especially impressive to Odusanya was the outlandish variety of their war tunics, which were festooned with charms and amulets.

Most of these young warriors wore short swords and daggers strapped around their waists. But quite a few carried muskets with a power horn slung around their necks. On confirming the identity of Chief Kuku, two of the men led them to the tent of their great warlord.

Odusanya thought he would die with anticipation. Was he actually going to meet the great Ogedengbe, the most celebrated warrior chief in Yorubaland, savior of Ijeshaland and terror of the Ibadans?

But when they were ushered into the presence of the great man, Odusanya could hardly hide his disappointment. He had expected a giant of a man, a demigod, whose head would touch the sky or at least the top of the tent. And if, like Sango, fire issued from his mouth when he talked, Odusanya would not have been surprised.

But it was an ordinary-looking Ogedengbe who waited for them at the entrance of his tent. As they bowed low to enter through the aperture in the flaps of the canvas that an orderly held apart for them, their host turned around to precede them. He indicated, without speaking, by a movement of his hand, that they should follow.

It was only when they were inside the tent that the great man they had come to see turned around. He shook Kuku's hand vigorously, in the fashion of white men.

He said, "E kabo. Se dada le de?"

Ogedengbe was a thin man in late middle age. He had a dark, much-lined face that made him look older than his years. But he also displayed a mischievous, sardonic smile that lightened up his features and presented to the observer an odd hint of youth.

As Odusanya studied this face carefully, he noticed the prominent *O'Bunu* tribal marks that stood out like sentinels on the right cheek of the famous warrior. This was strange, for Odusanya knew that the O'bunu marks were not used by the Ijesha. Later, Kuku told him the story of how Ogedengbe received those marks.

One time, Ogedengbe was captured by the Ibadans, and Ogunmola, the famous Ibadan warlord, had Ogedengbe given those marks in exchange for his life.

Unlike the ferocious-looking young warriors who stood watch outside his tent, Ogedengbe did not look fearsome, warlike, or dangerous. Although the evening was warm, he wore a full *aso-ofi* dashiki with matching jumpers that reached just below his knees. His feet were bare. He had an *abeti aja* cap of the same *aso ofi* hue on his head. Odusanya could see that the hair on his head was sparse and gray.

By Ogedengbe's side was a great big black dog, a sleek-haired mongrel that appeared to be his constant companion. It was said that this dog ran errands for Ogedengbe, with notes tied to its tail. This dog, like his master, had become a legend of the time.

According to the stories that went around the Ijesha war camps, the favorite food that this dog, whose name was "Adu," would eat was fish, fried goat-meat and boiled okra, which he shared with his master. The only food Adu did not eat or share with Ogedengbe was pounded yam, which made many Ijesha patriots doubt if this canine companion of their famed warlord was a true Ijesha dog.

"The dog, Adu, has been spoilt by Ogedengbe," many of the Ijesha people, who heard this fable, said.

Those on the other side of the conflict who also heard the stories of Ogedengbe and his dog, shrugged their shoulders and said they were not surprised. They had always known that the Ijesha warlord, who had spent many years of his youth in Ibadan, was pompous and a bit mad.

After he had exchanged greetings with them, Ogedengbe offered them seats. This was on the floor, on a wide multicolored raffia mat that occupied a large portion of the tent. Ogedengbe himself sat next to Kuku. And all the time, his faithful dog was by his side, like a treasured assistant.

The dog Adu seemed to be taking careful notes of all the proceedings between the two humans with his black eyes and attentive ears. His tail twitched from time to time, especially when the voice of his master rose. He did not appear to be bored, and never went to sleep. He squatted on his haunches, watchful, friendly, alert—and, to Odusanya, slightly menacing.

What is a speechless dog doing in a council of men? Odusanya asked himself.

But his master appeared to be quite pleased with the close watch provided by his canine friend and bodyguard. From this watchful and protected position, Ogedengbe reached for a bag filled with tobacco, which he offered his visitors. He called it *taba*.

"Se e fe taba?" he asked.

Kuku politely declined. Odusanya knew that his mentor did not touch the stuff. He hated the smell of tobacco.

Ogedengbe then proceeded to fill the bowl of his pipe. He lit it with a long match tipped with sulfur, of European manufacture, which he scratched against the side of a wooden block, which was used as a stool, on the floor next to him.

Then he sat back and immediately started an animated discussion with Kuku on the rightness of the Ijesha cause against Ibadan.

Kuku delicately but firmly shifted the discussion in the direction of the treaty to be signed the next day. Finally, he got a firm assurance from Ogedengbe that he would be at the signing of the treaty in the morning. Ogedengbe told Kuku that his men would lay down their arms once the treaty was signed.

Having accomplished his mission, Kuku got up. He almost stepped on the dog as he made his way out of the tent. With Odusanya walking beside him, the Ijebu chief made his way quietly to the Ijebu camp.

Both the travelers were tired. Odusanya rubbed his eyes to keep them open and to see his way ahead in the darkness. While they were talking in Ogedengbe's tent, night had enveloped the allied war camps. This time, they did not ride. Kuku's horse had been given to one of the Ijesha grooms to water and get ready for them the next morning.

Near the Ijebu camps, they were recognized by the sentries who had been apprised of their coming. They were therefore received with happy shouts of "E k abo" —Welcome, and "E weso," in the Ijebu dialect.

Later, after they had been welcomed and feasted by the Ijebu commander who was an old friend of Kuku, they were taken to the tent where they would spend the night. They settled down and tried to make themselves comfortable in the darkness. The Ijebu Balogun would not permit any lighted lamp in the war camps for fear of fire or attracting the attention of the enemy.

It was there in the dark, that night before the signing of the great treaty of Kiriji, that Kuku told Odusanya all he knew about Ogedengbe.

The Ijesha warlord's real name was Orisarayibi Ogundamola. He had acquired the nickname Ogedengbe, which meant "stand alone" from his prowess in war. When he was born, in the small hamlet of Itorin near Ilesha, it was said that a *babalawo* foretold that he would be the savior of his people.

As a young man, he was rascally and uncouth, given to wild ways and dubious company. But when the Ijesha people had their lands seized by the Ibadans and their independence curtailed, the ruler of their city-state, the Owa Obokun, Oba Oponlese, called on all able-bodied Ijesha men to fight for their land.

Orisayabi, who had received military training in Ibadan, heeded the call. He soon distinguished himself and became a war hero. He was skilled—and equally at ease—with the sword, the spear and the bow and arrow. And with the rifle, he was a true master. Many of his contemporaries considered him to be the best shot in Yorubaland. He proved his mettle as a military commander. And before long, he had helped the Ijeshas and their neighbors the Ekitis, recover most of the territory that had been seized by Ibadan.

People began to talk of the brilliance of Ogedengbe's military strategy against the Ibadans, which liberated Efon Alaiye, Ita Awure, and Oke Mesi. He restored the grateful Owa Obokun of Ijeshaland to his former independent rule.

Combining bravery and cunning on the battlefield with the sagacity of a diplomat, Ogedengbe was able to forge an agreement between many of the city-states opposed to Ibadan to form a strong union dedicated to the liberation of all their respective lands. He was the impetus behind the formation of the Ekiti-Parapo confederation, which comprised Ilesha, Ondo, and all the Ekiti states, as well as Akure and Owo.

At this time in the Kiriji War, Ogedengbe was regarded as the most accomplished general on both sides of the conflict. He was a folk hero to his people, who celebrated him throughout Ijeshaland as "the great timber that cannot be moved." Already, songs composed for him were being sung at the Obokun festival in their capital town of Ilesha.

Many of the stories told about Ogedengbe at that time also spoke of his reputed magical powers that would allow him to escape the battlefield unscathed when his life was in danger. He was said to be able to unleash destruction on his enemies from a distance, even from the safety of his home.

Many of the stories about his life at that time also told of his fondness for tobacco snuff and his friendship with his famous black dog, Adu. These were all aspects of the great warrior that were witnessed by the young Odusanya.

* * * * *

Morning came, and the two travelers awoke. They ate a hasty breakfast of roasted corn, which was all they could get in that zone of war. Then, Kuku put on his chief's cloak, a richly embroidered *gbariye* of the finest Ijebu woven cloth, which he had carefully packed inside a saddle bag tied to the side of his horse.

Then he went outside their tent, mounted his horse, and with Odusanya once more riding behind him, made for the scene for the signing of the treaty, which was the battleground itself.

As Odusanya would remember for years afterward, it had rained during the night. The air was cool, even breezy. In the clear morning light, Odusanya could see that this was a different country from the dense forests of Ijebuland. Indeed, it was an eye-pleasing grassy terrain, with rocks and boulders that broke the monotony of the undulating hills. The brushes and tall grasses on the plain below, where the Ijebu camps were located, were spotted with mud due to the recent rain. But the color of the leaves on the trees, when Odusanya looked up to admire them, was a splendid deep green.

The sky was a delicate light blue color that had no description in the Yoruba language. Chief Kuku might have called it "azure" in English. There were a few lazy clouds drifting slowly toward the north, silhouetted delicately against the morning sun. The green and brown foliage of the surrounding hills stood out sharp and poignant, contrasting with the multicolored jumble of the soldiers and onlookers who had massed in rows on the hillside to witness the historic ceremony.

Odusanya remarked to himself that there must have been at least ten thousand warriors and common people gathered that morning on those hills. He had never seen, nor would he ever see again, so many men gathered in one place in his entire life.

He did not notice, however, the sad bare patches on the ground where the bodies of fallen warriors on both sides had lain barely a day earlier before they were moved from the battlefield in time for this ceremony. Both sides had agreed to sign the peace treaty on the same bloodied field where just a few days earlier they were shooting at each other with muskets and canons, and were hacking each other to death with swords and bayonets.

To the philosophical mind of Chief Kuku, the scene must have evoked a sense of pathos and regret at the futility and pointlessness of human conflict. But he kept his thoughts to himself and said nothing to the boy beside him.

As for Odusanya, what stuck out in his young eyes was the colorful pageantry of the chieftains with their traditional caps, great robes and regalia of office. He admired the fierce looking warlords on horseback who tried to control their skittish mounts. And he looked around in wonder at the thousands of warriors from the various factions, arrayed in ranks with their war cloaks festooned with amulets, cowry shells, and the bleached skulls of small animals. They all carried their long guns and short swords at the ready. Apparently, no one was ready to fully trust the other side until the treaty was fully signed and observed.

Odusanya's youthful heart quickened and stirred at the sound of the bugles, the boom of the seven-gun salute, and the singing of "God save the Queen" by the missionaries and oyinbo officers.

He saw white men for the first time in his life. He met the famous Rev. Samuel Johnson who was greeted by his mentor Chief Kuku as "Ajose." This was the way the Ijebus had reduced the European name Johnson. From Johnson it had been at first *A-Johnson*, and from there, it was but a small step to *A-Josin,* then *Ajose.*

As it had always been for our people, names were changed, corrupted and modified to suit the tongue of the speaker. Johnson or Ajose. To the Yorubas, what did it matter? They were the same thing. "Omi eko, eko ni," they would say. Ajose himself addressed Kuku simply as *"Oloye."* Chief.

That day of the signing of the great treaty on the Kiriji battlefield, where he saw more white men than he ever thought possible on this earth, and shook hands with the famous "Ajose," was to remain for Odusanya the most memorable spectacle of his life.

At the end, when all the great chiefs—from Ondo, Ijesha, Ekiti, Ibadan, Ife, Ijebu, and Modakeke—had come out one by one to put their marks on the long roll of parchment, the warriors and ordinary folks watching from the heights overlooking the battlefield raised loud cheers at the sound of the cannon that announced that peace had come at last to their land.

A group of Ijesha women approached the stage. Those who recognized them said to the person standing next to them that they were the royal singers from the *afin* of the Owa Obokun himself.

The women came before the kings and chiefs. Kneeling, all of them with their arms raised high, they sang joyfully of the coming peace.

Yoruba duro sinsin
Ogun omo iya ti re koja.
Gbogbo irokerodo ati ote ilu
Ti yi pada titi lailai.

Yoruba, stand firm,
The war among brothers is at an end.
The forced dislocation and civil strife
Are gone from our lives forever.

For indeed, what all the soldiers wanted to do now was go back to their children and their wives. And the common people yearned for their farms, their village festivals, and their neglected gods.

After the women had stopped singing, a group of drummers and praise singers appeared on the scene. They accosted the departing kings and war chiefs, singing their praise names and *orikis* to the accompaniment of talking drums, as they in turn were showered with cowry shells.

An elderly-looking musician with a small talking drum tucked under his left armpit approached Kuku. He had recognized the great Ijebu chief and seemed to know him well. Timing his vocal rhythm with the staccato beats of his *gangan*, he greeted the chief thus:

Oloye Kuku
Omo oba Fugbajoye
Fugbajowe Awujale
Ni ilu Ijebu Ode,
To fi Ita Ntebo sile
Lo joye nibadan
O de ilu Oluyole tan,
O kole ola,
o fa faranda si!

Chief Kuku
Grandson of Fugbajoye Awujale

in the town of Ijebu-Ode;
He who left Ita Ntebo
To flourish in Ibadan.
But he had not settled down
in the town of Oluyole
before he built a mansion of riches
adorned with a wide verandah!

Later that day, the sounds of drums, singing, and celebratory gunfire faded away. The great and important chieftains, warlords, and dignitaries departed. And the war tents were brought down and folded, to be carried away by servants on horseback.

But before they went to sleep in the tent prepared for them with the Ijebu contingent, Kuku showed his young protégé a rolled piece of paper which he brought out of the goatskin bag he carried. He had brought it all the way from Ijebu-Ode.

It was a white man's calendar. Kuku unfolded it and showed the boy a date circled in ink.

"Mark this day," Kuku said to the boy, rather sternly.

Odusanya looked. He squinted and tried to decipher what it said. But of course, he could not read. He saw figures and letterings but he could not tell what they meant.

Chief Kuku interpreted them for him. He told the boy that those marks showed the days and months of the year. It was the twenty-third day of September. The year was 1886.

Odusanya marked the day in his memory, and he remembered. And years later, after he too had learned to read and write in the white man's tongue, he began to mark the passage of time in his own life, the days, months, and years, by this new method of the white man, dated from the birth of a god that was nailed on two crossed pieces of wood.

* * * * *

From days and evenings spent listening to Kuku, Odusanya came to learn the history of his people, the Ijebus. Odusanya knew vaguely that his own father was a prince of Remo. But he had never cared much about the history of Ijebu-Ode, though this was the town he called home.

All this now changed. For Odusanya now learned the stories of Ijebu-Ode from the mouth of Kuku, a proud son of Ijebu-Ode who had risen to a position of privilege and power in the town of his birth. From Kuku, Odusanya learned about Olu-iwa, the first ruler of Ijebu-Ode and of the coming of Obanta to begin the reign of the Awujales.

Kuku's mother, Shewa was a great storyteller. In this, she was like many of the great matriarchs of our people who helped to pass our oral tradition from one generation to the next. She was the one who told Kuku most of the stories that he now related to Odusanya.

One day, Kuku mentioned to Odusanya that the Ijebus had been allies of Ile-Ife during the Owu war. Kuku's grandfather, Fugbajoye, was Awujale during that conflict, which ended with the Owu people being driven from their ancestral homeland by a combined army of Ile-Ife, Oyo, and Ijebu-Ode.

"Who are the Owus?" Odusanya asked. "And why did we Ijebus go to their land to fight them?"

"I thought we Ijebus are a just people. We were taught as children that we have to be law-abiding and fair. Or else, the *agemos* who administer justice in our land and the spirits of the Awujales will not be on our side."

His mentor concurred, "Yes, it is true that we Ijebus do not take other people's possessions without justification. And we do not fight unjust wars. But sometimes, things do happen in war that we as a people are not proud of afterward."

It was then that Kuku told Odusanya the story of Owu as he had heard it told by his own mother.

"The people of Owu lived to the northeast of the town we now call Ibadan, but which did not exist at the time this story began.

"The Owus are kin to the Egbas. And the Olowu, king of Owu, had always been an ally of the Alaafin. Their town of Owu was one of the most ancient city-states of Yorubaland. It had been in existence since the time the grandchildren of Oduduwa set out of Ile-Ife to establish their many ancient city-states.

"During the conflict between Oyo and Ilorin at the time of Afonja, many people from Oyo were uprooted from their land by the disturbances. They came south to settle in towns outside the territory of Oyo proper."

As Kuku explained to Odusanya, one of the consequences of that social dislocation was that most of these towns in the south, and the roads and bush-paths leading to them, became filled with refugees. Renegade warriors made bold by the lawless times began to carry out slave raids against those refugees in the very towns and villages where they had sought a safe haven.

"Reports came back to the Alaafin in Oyo that many of his people were being captured and sold as slaves.

"The Alafin, outraged, asked his ally, the Olowu of Owu to help him put an end to this practice. The Olowu of Owu, in obedience to the Alafin, ordered his warriors to free any Oyo man, woman or child that was put up for sale as a slave in any town or village in the Yoruba hinterland."

Based on what he heard from his mother, Kuku told Odusanya that the Owus were a brave and stubborn people. As warriors, their preferred mode of combat was fighting at close quarters with their *agedengbe*, which was a short sword, and their *ada*, cutlass.

"They wielded these weapons with such ferocity and skill that they were feared by all who ventured to go to war against them. And just as they were brave in war, they were equally merciless in victory.

"These fierce soldiers from Owu began to attack and destroy many towns that engaged in the slave trade. The chief market for the slave traders in those days was in Apomu. This town was overwhelmed and sacked by warriors from Owu.

"The notorious slave market in the town of Apomu was destroyed. But as so often happens when warriors are allowed to go on a rampage, the homes of many innocent people in Apomu, who had nothing to do with the slave market, were ransacked and looted.

"Thus it was that the Owus earned the enmity of Ile-Ife, in whose territory many of these towns were located, especially the market town of Apomu."

In retaliation, the Ooni of Ife sent a military force to attack Owu and bring its leaders to heel. He wanted to teach the Owu people, who he considered disrespectful upstarts, a lesson.

"So, at first, the conflict was between Ile-Ife and Owu. But soon, we Ijebus became involved."

"And how did this happen?" Odusanya wanted to know.

Kuku continued the story as his protégé listened with rapt attention.

"At that time, many of our Ijebu people were already showing their prowess in trade and commerce. They left Ijebu-Ode to trade as far north as Bida in the land of the Tapa. Some even went into the lands of the Hausa beyond the great Odo Oya.

"They took with them produce from our fertile farmlands and lengths of our traditional Ijebu cloth for sale in those distant markets. They brought back leatherwork, kola nuts, and groundnuts that were produced in great quantities in those northern lands.

"The most successful of these traders came back to Ijebu-Ode laden with riches. They led a life of splendor never before seen in our town. Some of them built opulent mansions with the help of Portuguese architects they brought from Eko.

"When Owu soldiers attacked Apomu, the trade of many of these Ijebu merchants was destroyed and their livelihood brought to an end. In the eyes of these merchants, who did not much concern themselves with political matters, it was an unjustified and unprovoked attack against them by warriors from Owu.

"These traders came back to Ijebu-Ode with tales of outrage and woe. The anger of their relatives and friends was kindled until it reached the ears of the Awujale. So it was that Ijebu also declared war on Owu."

Kuku continued the story.

"At first, Ile-Ife tried to bring Owu to heel on its own. But its army was defeated in ignominious fashion on three different occasions. So superior in skill and bravery were the undaunted Owus.

"It was at this time that we Ijebus came into the war on the side of Ile-Ife. We Ijebus were then the only Yoruba fighting men to be overwhelmingly equipped with guns, which our traders purchased from the island of Eko from Portuguese and other *oyinbo* merchants and sea captains."

According to Kuku, a former Ijebu war leader who knew about such matters, these guns were the flintlock muzzle-loading muskets known as "Dane guns." They were employed, not just for war, but for hunting. The noise these guns made when they were cocked, *sha ka*, and fired, *bu la*, gave them the name *shaka-bula*.

Brave though they were, the Owu warriors proved no match for the musket-bearing Ijebu army when it entered the field on the side of Ile-Ife.

When Owu warriors, displaying their customary bravery, dashed out of cover, cutlass in hand, to strike down the enemy, a careful order was given by the Ijebu *Balogun* to his men.

The front line of the Ijebus, who were equipped with bows and arrows and the short sword common to all Yoruba fighting men at the time, went on their knees. This allowed the second line, who were armed with muskets, to shoot down the astonished Owu warriors. The Owu had never encountered in battle an enemy equipped with firearms. The effect was devastating, and their morale was broken.

"That tactic, devised by our Ijebu *Balogun,* based on the possession of muskets by his men, proved too much an obstacle for the Owu defenders," Chief Kuku told Odusanya.

"To complicate matters for the Owus, the Ijebu warriors and their Ife allies were now joined by renegade warriors from Oyo, whose slave raids on innocent refugees had started the conflict in the first place.

"It was true that the Olowu was an ally and friend of the Alaafin, but the Oyo emperor had no control over these renegades. Also at this time in our story, the Alaafin had his hands full with its own problem with Ilorin, where a rebellion started by Afonja had been going on for several years.

"Swiftly pushing back the outmatched Owu defenders, the allies advanced until they reached the town wall of Owu itself. Their plan was to quickly overwhelm Owu after encircling it in a tight siege."

But the swift victory which the Ijebus, Ifes, and Oyo renegades hoped for proved elusive. The siege of Owu would last for five bitter years, marked by minor skirmishes and a few major battles now and then. But the outcome was never conclusive for either side to claim victory

For the Olowu had sent for help from his kinsmen, the Egbas, who at that time, lived in various towns and hamlets in the surrounding country south of the Oyo boundary and west of Ile-Ife. These intrepid Egbas managed to find a route to relieve Owu despite the ring of hostile warriors that encompassed the town.

Thus it was that the besieged town of Owu was helped in its hour of need by Egba mercenaries, many of whom were skilled in the use of the musket, thus countering the advantage of the Ijebus. These mercenaries were led by one of the most famous sharpshooters of his day. He was an Egba warrior named Sakula.

"According to my mother, this Sakula had learned the use of the musket from us Ijebus. And even among our proud Ijebu warriors, he was acclaimed to be the best shot with a musket on both sides of that conflict.

"Thus it was that the Ijebu and Ife attackers now faced a daunting obstacle when they tried to breach the walls of the besieged town. Sakula had positioned himself at the top of one of the high ramparts that loomed over the town wall. From his high vantage position, Sakula picked off allied warriors anytime they tried to scale the town wall of Owu.

"It soon became clear to the Ijebus that they could not hope to take the town of Owu if Sakula was not neutralized. So the Ijebu *Balogun*, a wily warrior and veteran of many battles, devised another plan. At the next attack, he ordered every Ijebu warrior carrying a gun to direct his fire at one target and one target only, Sakula."

In this way was Sakula, the great Egba marksman and hero, brought down at last, his body riddled with musket shot fired by scores of Ijebu marksmen.

And when the Ijebu, Ife, and Oyo attackers saw Sakula's body topple from that high rampart, from which he had killed or maimed many of their comrades, they raised a shout of triumph.

"Muso, muso," they shouted as they rushed in to pull down the walls of Owu and overcome its dispirited defenders.

In sad tones, Kuku now described to Odusanya the savage reprisals that followed the fall of Owu.

"The attackers pillaged and killed as they overran one defensive position after another. They killed every defender, sparing neither those who resisted nor those who threw down their weapons in surrender.

"The Ijebus and their allies were implacable in victory as few Yoruba armies before or after had ever been. Blind with rage, they sought revenge for their own losses at the hand of the marksman, Sakula.

"And so terrible was the orgy of blood and destruction unleashed that day that when it was all over, the attackers had completely destroyed the town of Orile-Owu. The dwellings were set on fire and the whole town destroyed in a massive conflagration.

"And in a final unprecedented act of vindictiveness, the victorious allied commanders and their *obas* decreed that the town of Owu was never to be rebuilt again for human habitation. That edict remains to this day.

"Ikija, a neighboring town that had offered help to the Owus during the conflict, was also attacked and destroyed."

Kuku now spoke sadly of the aftermath of the Owu war, as a rapt and shocked Odusanya listened.

"The remaining people of Owu, those who were not killed or sold into slavery, fled to a place of refuge many weeks march to the south along the Ogun River. There they live to this day in a section of a new town that they named after their ancient homeland of Owu. It is on a hill in a place they call Oke Ago-Owu."

Kuku told Odusanya that from his own calculation, based on the stories of his mother, daughter of Awujale Fugbajoye, that battle that destroyed the ancient town of Owu must have taken place between 1822 and 1825 by the white man's calendar.

He also told Odusanya how, after the defeat and destruction of Orile-Owu, many of the Oyo, Ife and Ijebu warriors who had taken part in the battle proceeded to the nearby lands where the Egbas lived.

The victors confronted the Alake, leader of the Ake clan of the Egba people. They were not happy that the Egbas had supported the Owus during the war. From this time forward, the Egba people who had lived for centuries in that area south of Oyo proper that would later become the settlement of Ibadan, were subjected to attacks and intimidation until eventually they had to leave their ancestral homeland.

Kuku went on, "Years later, the Alake and his people would find their place of refuge in a hilly rock-strewn country near the Ogun River. These Egba refugees called their new home Ake after the place they had fled from.

"At this time, refugees from Owu were already settled nearby. So also were the Egba Osile and Egba Agura who had settled at Oke-Ona and Gbagura respectively. Each group gave its new settlement the name of the ancestral home from which its people had fled."

Kuku told Odusanya that these different Egba groups came together later to form a unified city that would be strong enough to repel any enemy. From his estimation, this must have been around the year 1830. The Egbas called their new town "Abe Okuta"—the place beneath the rocks. And indeed, this city of refuge was guarded on all sides by majestic rock formations that would for years daunt any attacker.

"My son," for that was what Kuku called Odusanya, "I feel keenly the weight of that tragedy that befell the ancient town of Orile-Owu, even though I was not there when it happened.

"It is as if I was present at that savage assault when brave Sakula was killed and one of the most ancient towns of Yorubaland was burned to the ground. For I have seen with my own eyes that very place, now a desolate field, that was the site of ancient Owu.

"A few years ago when I visited Ibadan, my friend, the Englishman Revered Hinderer, took me to a lonely farmland just outside the northern city gate of Ibadan. 'Here, half a century ago, amidst these corn fields,' he told me, using the words of a Biblical passage that was familiar to him, 'the blood of the mighty Owus was vilely cast away.'"

Thus did Kuku conclude his strange and sad story of the destruction of Owu and the dispersal of the Egba people.

To Odusanya, this story of the siege of Owu and the brutal exile of its people showed the senselessness and horror of war. Even though his side, the Ijebus won, he did not think there was much glory in any victory gained from war. The consequence to the losing side was too harsh for his sensibilities as a human being

Kuku said he agreed with Odusanya that wars were senseless and cruel. That was the reason, he said, that he had told the story of Owu to Odusanya in such detail. And this was why he, Kuku, a former warrior, was now a merchant and peacemaker.

"Making money," he declared, "suits my conscience better than making war."

And not only was he now a man of commerce, Kuku had become a passionate advocate of diplomacy and reconciliation. He had already demonstrated this by the part he played in the treaty of peace that ended the recent Kiriji War.

"A wise leader should take his people into war only when his cause is just and all else has failed," he said.

"Only fools rush to war."

*   *   *   *   *

The *odo,* the brash young men who dominated the traditional council of the *osugbo* in Ijebu-Ode, were not happy with the cessation of hostilities with Ibadan following the treaty signed on the Kiriji battlefield. The power and wealth of their faction depended on the economic blockage they had enforced on Ibadan since the start of that sixteen-year conflict.

This faction, composed of the most hot-headed and belligerent young men in Ijebu-Ode, had managed to wrest control of the most important and powerful political and religious groups in the town. They kept the Awujale under their thumb. And they contrived to put the whole town in an atmosphere of paranoia and war fever based on the fear and loathing of foreigners.

In reality, what this group feared was that their prestige, livelihood, and grip on the economic and political hierarchy in Ijebu-Ode would be undermined if Ijebuland was to be opened to foreigners, who would then be able to trade and engage in commerce in direct competition with them. This war-mongering faction in Ijebu-Ode had become rich and powerful due to the economic blockade. They were not about to give up their means of livelihood and income, which would be threatened if peace prevailed with Ibadan. It was in their interest to continue their monopoly and trade embargo.

Apart from their detestation of Ibadan, the *odo* faction hated the British in Lagos even more. They blamed the government of the Colony in Lagos for interfering in their war designs and for favoring Ibadan during the Ijaiye and Kiriji wars. What they wanted most dearly, therefore, was to be able to strike a blow that would damage the interests of their two foes.

Apart from the *odo*, many cultists in the *osugbo* and secret societies feared that the religious practices of Ijebu-Ode, and the cults from which they derived their membership, would disappear if they had to compete with Christian missionaries from Lagos and Ibadan. These *onigbagbo* would pour in into Ijebuland once the blockade was lifted.

The priests and cultists feared that the Ijebu people would not be able to resist the black robed priests bearing the message of the white man's god. Had those missionaries not already shown how easily they could sway the minds of other Yoruba people in Lagos, Abeokuta, and Ibadan? If this was allowed to happen in Ijebuland, the native gods would be abandoned and the ways of faith of their ancestors would die out.

Thus it was that the *odo,* the belligerent "young guns" in Ijebu-Ode, who were essentially war profiteers, joined forces with the cultists, priests and the *osugbo*, who saw themselves as guardians of the ancient culture and religious traditions of Ijebuland.

These two factions combined their forces and ideas. They began to look for an excuse for another quarrel with Ibadan, so that they could resume hostilities. But first, they had to get rid of those who opposed their hardline ideas.

Chief Kuku, who was the *seriki* of Ijebu-Ode at that time, was the most prominent man in Ijebu who favored warm relations with both Ibadan and the white colonial administrators in Lagos. Trumped up charges were brought against him, and the war faction succeeded in having him sent into exile in Ibadan.

After this, an incident soon presented itself to aid the belligerent factions in Ijebu-Ode in their planned collision course with the British colonial government in Lagos and its ally, Ibadan.

A shipment of goods passed through Ijebu territory from Lagos to Ibadan. The Awujale did not know about it. Apparently, corrugated iron sheets were transported from the coast to Ibadan. This material was meant for the roofing of a new building to house the CMS. Mission at Oke Kudeti in Ibadan. The Ijebus claimed that it was an illegal shipment of guns to the Ibadan warlords, who they had vowed would be denied the purchase of firearms.

The Awujale demanded from the Ibadan Baale, and also the white missionaries involved, an apology and the payment of a fine. When these were not forthcoming, the Awujale demanded the head of Rev. Olubi, the Yoruba CMS priest who the Ijebus accused of arranging the deal. For good measure, the Awujale also asked for the head of Rev. Harding, the English head of the CMS mission in Ibadan.

The Ibadans at this time were in no position to enter into another protracted military conflict with anyone, especially the Ijebus, who they knew were armed with guns.

The incessant wars Ibadan had fought for three decades with other Yoruba city-states had only recently stopped following the peace treaty signed on the Kiriji battlefield. The Ibadan war purse was depleted. And with the Ijebu embargo stifling trade with the coast, the leaders in Ibadan knew they were in dire economic straits. They could not get their farm produce to the lucrative markets in Lagos. And they found it difficult to equip and supply their fighting men. They could not get firearms because, at that time, they were also blockaded on the western route to the coast by their perennial foes, the Egbas.

To reach the coast, Ibadan merchants had to use a long and costly road that skirted west of Egba territory to Badagry and Port Novo before they could get to Lagos.

Besides, the Ilorins, under the control of the Fulani caliphate, were still conducting raids into Ibadan territory. The Ibadan war chiefs wanted to concentrate their attention to the existential threat posed by the marauding jihadists from the north. They wanted to stop Ilorin once and for all. They had no stomach for opening up another military front against the Ijebus in the south.

The Ibadan Baale and his chieftains therefore swallowed their pride. They sent emissaries to Ijebu-Ode to plead with the Awujale to drop his demand for the heads of those two reverend gentlemen who were loved and respected by the people of Ibadan. This would be in return for certain gifts to be sent to His Majesty by the Baale and chiefs of Ibadan.

It was said that the Awujale, after making the emissaries from Ibadan cool their heels in his outer courtyard for two days before deigning to receive them, now made known his demands in return for lifting the death sentence he had imposed on the two erring missionaries.

Twenty-one fully grown sheep, seven horses, six hundred cowries, and a large number of young men and women, all slaves, were to be delivered to the palace at Ijebu-Ode by a certain date. The Ibadans, pushed to a corner, acceded to all the demands of the Awujale.

So, it came to pass that later that month, another Ibadan delegation came to Ijebu-Ode leading a caravan of sheep and horses. This was followed by a long line of young male and female slaves, all healthy and in the prime of life.

In addition to what the Ijebu king had demanded, a personal gift of six *eyele,* six drums of *epo pupa*, palm oil, and a hundred *owo eyo* or cowries were added to this peace offering by Seriki Kuku from his exile in Ibadan. He intended this gift as a mark of the new friendship between the Ijebus and the Ibadans, and undoubtedly, to help smoothen his own return to his native land.

The Ijebus had asked for two hundred young men and women, but this number was cut in half during negotiations. And of the fifty male and fifty female slaves sent to the Awujale's compound on that day, one in particular is worthy of mention, having been specially requested by the king's emissaries.

This was a young, smooth-limbed maiden from Bida in the Nupe country. Her father, a Tapa warlord, had forfeited her along with most of his goods and property when the Fulani from Ilorin overran his domain twelve years earlier. This was in exchange for his life which otherwise was forfeit by the rules of war.

At that time, this girl was only seven years old. She was placed in the household of the famous merchant and slave dealer, Mualimi, in Ilorin. This Mualimi was no ordinary dealer in slaves. He specialized in grooming promising young females for the *harim* of the emir himself. The girl, whose name was Bintu, was one of the ones chosen.

For seven years, Bintu was fed, clothed, pampered, and groomed while the other slaves were either sold off or put to work on neighboring farms in Offa, Okene, and Iseyin. The strong males amongst them were driven, chained and frightfully abused, on the brutal journey south to be sold at the central Yoruba slave market of Ipomu.

Bintu's education was painstaking and thorough. Put in the care of Limotu, an old concubine of the emir, she was taught the art of pleasing men. Her clients would be highborn princes with a taste for beautiful dark eyes ringed with *kohl*, young shapely breasts, slim hips, and firm buttocks that did not sag or jut out promiscuously.

Bintu learned to apply to her cheeks and eyelids the sophisticated makeup of the day. She used an indigo dye to make patterns on the skin of her belly, her thighs, and her breasts. She learned how to delicately string together multicolored beads to make the *bebe* that was worn around her slim waist and hips. These beads were obtained at great cost from traders who braved the dangerous highway to the coast to trade with Europeans in Lagos, Porto-Novo, and Badagry.

She learned the art of coquetry, to cast her eyes downward with a look of demure innocence, while the language of a pouting lip or jutting hips was designed to provoke a man's desire. She learned to talk softly and to tease gently.

She was then placed under the tutelage of a *mullah* who taught her to read and write. She learned to write the *jalimi* script in Hausa and Arabic on a wooden board with white chalk, and to chant aloud verses from the holy book, the Koran. She was also taught the Yoruba language that was close to her native Tapa. For it was not just any man that she was being trained to please. She was promised for the *harim* of the emir himself, Alimi the Great.

Bintu was thirteen years old when Alimi sent for her. We do not know how much the emir paid Mualimi for this exchange. But stories were told in the courtyards and markets of Ilorin of a shipment of salt and bags of silver coins delivered to the house of Mualimi.

Luckily, the years of training spent on Bintu had not been in vain. Her master was pleased. She quickly became the monarch's favorite. It is true that the emir was a devout Moslem and follower of the Prophet. But in those days, those scholars versed in the Koran and the Hadith followed the traditions of the Middle Ages handed down by the early Moslem caliphates in Arabia, Syria, and Baghdad. They fully enjoyed the pleasures of life. The only thing forbidden in the household of Emir Alimi was alcohol. After all, he convinced himself, the pleasures of nubile maidens were one of the pleasures promised to the brave martyrs of God in Paradise. So why not get some practice here on earth?

With Bintu, Emir Alimi partook of the pleasures of his paradise on earth. However, he had to part with her after three years, trading her in a diplomatic exchange during a delicate negotiation with the Balogun of Ibadan over the disputed territory of Offa which was later ceded to Ilorin.

This was how Bintu found herself as part of the retinue of gifts sent to the Awujale from Ibadan on this mild day in the harmattan season, to assuage Ijebu greed and pride. And indeed, Bintu's fame had preceded her. Her special skills were brought to the attention of the Awujale by his emissaries.

Anticipation of the enjoyment of his gift pleased the Awujale exceedingly. For he was a man in his prime, and justifiably renowned for his concupiscence.

Despite having six wives, the Awujale kept, in his *harim*, a company of not less than fifteen concubines at any one time. Many of them were freeborn women who were given to him by his chiefs and subjects who wanted a favor from him. But some were slave women, won as trophies of war or bought in the marketplace in Lagos. They were all purposed for the pleasure of the monarch and jealously guarded for his entertainment only. Death was the lot of any man who dared to tamper with any of the king's women.

Therefore, that same night when the exchange had been made and all the messengers had gone to their quarters, we find this young courtesan, then eighteen years old, prepare to do her duty and please her new lord.

She had been placed in a small apartment inside the king's palace. She had washed herself thoroughly with water drawn from the palace well. She was assisted by two old servants specially assigned to her.

The Awujale's orders to his palace staff were explicit. He wanted to enjoy his new acquisition that very night. So Bintu found herself alone in her small room which opened to the main passage of the Oba's palace.

She sat down on a low stool and carefully removed her robe, a richly hewn dark-blue *alare* of superior quality that had been brought to impress the king. She inspected her young unblemished skin. She kneaded her firm breasts and massaged her hips and buttocks until the skin warmed to the touch. Then, she oiled her skin slowly and gently, paying attention to her breasts, buttocks, and shoulders. She applied a smooth dark-blue pigment to the skin around her eyes. It was a special *kohl* obtained at great cost by Mualimi from Zaria.

After this, she wound a white turban around her head, her forehead highlighted by a shiny gem of superior quality. It was a deep lucent green, the color of her religion. A band of the silky linen of her headband was left hanging to cover her left ear. She then put on a short sleeveless coat of maroon-red satin that contrasted sharply with the white of her turban. The coat was short and barely reached her midriff. It had buttons in front which she carefully left unfastened.

She had no mirror to survey herself. But she knew she was beautiful, young, and desirable. Now stepping up, one leg at a time, she slipped her favorite beads around her hips. Finally, she clasped a copper necklace around her neck, and her dressing was complete. She had nothing on beneath the vest but the *bebe* below the waist. A sliver of dark hair peeped above the beads, and her belly button was a small knoll in a plain of well-toned abdominal muscle.

Then, Bintu rubbed perfume under her armpits, and squatting, in between her thighs and under and above the *bebe*. The sweet-smelling unguent came in a white alabaster jar sold to her master years ago by an itinerant Arab *mu'allam* who said he had come all the way from Kanem Bornu on the shore of Lake Chad.

Appropriately enough, on the vial was printed in Arabic script the legend, *Bint el-Sudan*, Sudanese maiden.

It was only then that Bintu walked along the short private passage until she got to the entrance to the king's chamber. She had been shown where it was, and she knew exactly what to do. The king would be waiting for her.

Gently, she pushed aside the screen made of raffia strands that partially blocked the doorway. For the door to the chamber was open, an invitation just for her.

She stepped in and approached the couch on which the Awujale lay, half reclining and eager with expectation. She came near him. And they were so close, he could smell her scent and that ancient allure that was as old as the earth.

The Awujale wanted to rise and grab the girl, the special gift brought from Ibadan for his sole pleasure. But he held himself in check as blood rushed to his brain, his ears, and his eyes. He felt giddy, as if he was about to swoon.

The girl knelt before him in obeisance.

"Kabiyesi," she whispered.

Her voice low and husky. Her northern accent was barely noticeable as she spoke in Yoruba.

Kabiyesi's loins stirred. He felt his body quicken and harden as the blood rushed to his veins. He cried out in a voice he himself could hardly recognize.

"Maa bo. Wa s'odo baba. *Come to Baba*," the voice said. He was not sure it was coming from him, so hoarse was this voice with pain and desire.

"Je ki Baba toju e," he said finally.

Then he reached for the beads around the girl's hips as she leaned forward toward him.

Bintu stayed in the king's chamber for five days and nights, during which time the monarch attended to no other business. Bintu for her part, lived up to her reputation. There were no details of her art that were not called into play. She swooned with rapture as Kabiyesi gasped and puffed, smothering her small lithe body with his overfed body.

"Yemi o," he cried, calling for his mother.

"*Mo ku*. I am dead!" she exclaimed in Yoruba, matching his ardor.

And when he stopped, gasping for breath, exhausted and limp, she brought him to life with a skillful application of oil applied to his most delicate parts. She crouched over him and let him push his head and lips into her soft bosom. He was like a child in her arms.

The Awujale was a leader who had led his men into battle in his day. He knew that in war, as in love, there were few rules, and all methods were permitted. There were only victors and the vanquished. And to the victor belonged the spoils. The conquered did not dictate terms. He recognized when to give in to a superior force and sue for terms.

But what a sweet surrender this was for the vanquished Awujale! Never had defeat in battle come with fairer terms, with a graceful foe embracing the enemy, lifting him up and carrying him with a song in his ears to the high altar of pleasure and lasciviousness in the mutual worship of victor and vanquished.

But then, this was a battlefield like no other. This was the calculated campaign of a practiced courtesan, and Kabiyesi was conquered at the first charge of battle.

*   *   *   *   *

The young guns in Ijebu-Ode were not satisfied that the Ibadan Baale had acceded so easily to their demands. Some now said they should have asked for more. They were a hot-headed, greedy, and stubborn group.

They soon found a different excuse for another quarrel with the colonial authorities in Lagos, the main supporter of their foe, Ibadan. And this time, they would outdo themselves in their audacity.

They directly insulted the British colonial power in Lagos when an English CMS minister traveled from Lagos to Ijebu-Ode to seek an audience with the Awujale. His sooth was for the Ijebu monarch to allow him enter Ijebu territory to preach the gospel.

While he was waiting in the palace courtyard for his appointment with the Awujale, this reverend gentleman was accosted by a group of young men, some from the oba's palace itself.

These ruffians rained verbal insults in Yoruba and broken English on the person of this minister sent by the governor in Lagos and by extension the queen of England. They ridiculed him and pushed him around roughly. They even threatened his life, forcing the gentleman of the cloth to leave Ijebu-Ode in a hurry without being allowed to see the Awujale. His personal letter of introduction from the governor was taken roughly from him and torn into pieces.

When he got back to Lagos with his tale of woe, his treatment was regarded by one and all as a great and deliberate insult. It was an affront to the power and prestige of Great Britain. In short, it was a not very subtle invitation to war.

Since they had already got rid of Chief Kuku by having him sent into exile in Ibadan, the hotheads in the *osugbo* advising the Awujale did not have any cool heads that would have allowed reason to prevail.

By this time too, the people of Ijebu-Ode, who largely supported the *odo* and the other warmongers, seemed to have become so confident in the perceived military prowess of their ancient town and in the power of their *oro* and *agemo* fetishes, that they believed that no power, not even the *Gesi* in Lagos, could overwhelm them.

Their leaders boasted that should the British in Lagos attempt to attack Ijebuland, the white officers and their mercenary Hausa soldiers would be captured and sacrificed to Orisanla, or sold as slaves.

They pointed out that Ijebu-Ode had never been defeated in battle. Nor had the city ever fallen into the hands of any invader during the seven hundred years of its existence. Ozolua's brief incursion did not count, or had been deleted from the collective memory of the Ijebus. And those in the palace who knew this history, the wise old women and the *aroken*, reasoned that Ozolua had not defeated Ijebu-Ode militarily or destroyed the city. He had used a cowardly and dastardly ruse to have his son installed as Awujale.

But still, they tried to protect their flank. The Ijebus sent emissaries to the Egbas, who they reasoned would be eager to make common cause with them against the British and their old foe, Ibadan. The Awujale's high-powered delegation to Abeokuta was led by no less a person than his eldest son, Adejobi, the Aremo.

They were immediately given audience by the Alake, Oba Osokalu. The Egba monarch had his own reasons for wanting to confront the British. The establishment of the British Colony in Lagos thirty years earlier irked him and other Egba chiefs. Not only was access now blocked to the slave port of Lagos, the British had also seized the port and slave market at Badagry.

Thus, the lucrative commerce of slave-dealing, on which many of the Egba chiefs relied to maintain their lavish lifestyle, had been taken away from them.

In addition, their own domestic slaves from Abeokuta were now regularly running away to the freedom promised them in the Colony in Lagos. These runaway slaves were welcomed in Lagos, where they were taken in by local missionaries and abolitionists who ensured that they would never be returned to their masters. They were clothed, fed and put to work as domestic servants, and in some instances sent to school and educated.

The Egbas had already arranged a meeting with a delegation from the French consulate in Porto-Novo. They had been promised that in return for signing a treaty with the French, they would be secured a route to the coast in Frecnh-controlled territory that would allow them to continue the lucrative slave trade.

The Ijebu delegation told the Alake that they were confident that they could defeat the British. All they wanted was an agreement that if the conflict dragged on for more than three months, the Egbas would come to their aid.

So confident were the Ijebus in the coming fight with the British that they dismissed the offer from the Egba chieftains of an immediate military alliance that would jointly confront the British, possibly with the aid of the French.

In doing so, the Ijebus were confident that they had neutralized Ibadan. They had seized certain dispatches sent by the colonial governor in Lagos to the Ibadan Baale asking him to attack the Ijebus from the rear when the British launched their attack from the coast. The messengers sent to Ibadan by the governor were captured by Ijebu spies and summarily executed. The Ibadans never received those messages.

The Ijebus were now confident that they had secured their southern flank so that they could focus on the British coming through the creeks and lagoons of the Ijebu waterside.

*   *   *   *   *

Meanwhile, the Governor of the Lagos Colony, Sir Gilbert Thomas Carter, Knight Commander of the Grand Order of St. Michael and St. George, waited, bided his time and planned.

This highborn representative of Her Majesty's Government was not going to allow an open defiance and affront on British honor and prestige to go unanswered or unpunished. The Ijebus had to be brought to heel. Or else, other groups such as the Egbas who were also blocking trade routes between Lagos and the interior, might follow Ijebu's intransigence.

Besides, the Colonial Office in London had a grand strategy for the whole Guinea coast, as West Africa was called in those days. This was, after all, the height of colonial domination of the dark continent, euphemistically referred to as the "scramble for Africa."

The British were the leading contender for the rights for ownership of the riches and people of the continent. So this might just be the chance they needed to put the whole of Yorubaland under a common rule controlled from Whitehall. They would, with the same bold stroke, strike a permanent blow to halt the annoying French expansion in this part of Africa.

The plans for the defeat of Ijebu-Ode were drawn up by the high brass in the War Office in Whitehall, but the fine details were left to Lagos.

Governor Carter was nothing if not a patient man. He knew he could not afford to fail. With careful planning and meticulous detail, he brought in extra men to augment his already formidable military garrison in Lagos.

Colonel Francis Scott was brought in from the Gold Coast as commander of the expedition. Captain Campbell of the Lagos Constabulary was put in charge of both the West Indian troops and the Ibadan irregulars. Campbell was a descendant of that Royal Navy officer of the same name who had sent dispatches to England from Elmina Castle following the Battle of Atakpamé more than a century earlier.

Captain Richard Bower, a young dashing subaltern who had recently been promoted to captain of the King's Royal Rifles, was chosen to lead the Hausa infantry. The Hausas were a well-trained and battle-hardened unit who had seen action in the Gold Coast. They were famous for their bravery in the face of enemy fire and their deadly accuracy with the rifle.

Colonel Scott and the other officers were to report directly to the governor. Their orders were clear:

Teach the Ijebus a lesson,
But do not harm their king.

As a believer in the natural right of kings, expressed absolutely in the person of Her Britannic Majesty and Empress of India, Queen Alexandrina Victoria, Governor Carter believed that even native rulers such as the Awujale, should be granted royal prerogatives.

The plan was not to dethrone any of the *obas* of Yorubaland such as the Awujale, but to use this opportunity to pacify the warring tribes in the hinterland and bring the whole of Yorubaland under the benevolent protection of the Queen. This Pax Britannia, enforced by force of arms if necessary, would allow British missionaries to win the hearts and minds of the restive natives so that British merchants could move in to make money in relative peace.

This was a grand imperial plan worthy of the history books. And Governor Carter liked to think of himself in bold, heroic terms. He was a man of destiny, brought to this part of the world to extend over the natives the benevolent and civilizing influence of the great British Empire on which "the sun never set."

Carter was sure that a kind history would see fit to write about him in later generations, not perhaps in the mold of Wellington who had defeated Napoleon or Gordon of Khartoum, but in the honored ranks of British soldiers who had defeated the Boers, conquered the Zulus, and by careful diplomacy and military maneuvering, united under the Union Jack the quarreling princes in the subcontinent of India.

The Colonial Office had told the governor quite clearly that the British would not be able to keep the French at bay in Dahomey and the Upper Volta if they could not pacify their own frontiers in this important outpost of British West Africa. He, Gilbert Thomas Carter would prove himself equal to the task. And the first act would be to bring the unruly Ijebus to heel.

It was not long before the Awujale in Ijebu-Ode got wind of the war plans of the governor in Lagos against his kingdom. After all, he had his own spies close to the British camp in Lagos. These were traders from Ijebu-Ode, and even clerks, translators, and orderlies working for the government of the Colony.

The Awujale did not stay idle. He consulted his high chiefs, the *osugbo* traditional council, his priests and his war commanders. It said a lot about the confidence and arrogance of the Ijebus that they were confident they would handily defeat the British.

"What in the name of Sango is this British colonial military force but a few overfed *oyinbo* officers from Lagos leading ignorant Hausas trying to look smart in ill-fitting khaki uniforms?"

This was a much-quoted statement from one of the Ijebu-Ode high chiefs at one of the meetings of the *osugbo* to discuss the coming war.

The other Ijebu chiefs and warlords laughed. And they repeated this piece of wisdom to each other as they reviewed their advantages and contemplated the coming fight.

For how could lowly paid Hausa soldiers who had strayed far from their native country north of the great river know how to fight in Ijebuland, with its creeks, marshes and secret forest paths? Clearly, they would be no match for Ijebu warriors.

"You certainly need more than a khaki uniform and a shiny brass bugle to fight in Ijebu, the land of Obanta." This was said loudly by another chief in the hearing of the king.

"And how can those Christian white men with their feeble religion defeat the mighty *juju* of the land of Ijebus?"

"Our powerful *egunguns* and *alagemos* will drown them in the marshes of our Ijebu waterside."

This was the reasoning of the high priests, who indeed agreed with the civil and military chieftains advising the king.

The Awujale would not learn the error in this kind of reasoning until it was too late. He did not have the benefit of the counsel of his old companion and adviser, Seriki Kuku, who was still in exile, after being banished two years earlier by his enemies who had the better ear of the king. Kuku was clearly too friendly with Ibadan and Lagos, and was not to be brought back to Ijebu-Ode at this time, even if he was one of the best war commanders the Ijebus had.

Chief Kuku therefore languished in exile in Ibadan, where true to his skills as a resourceful entrepreneur, he flourished. He even built a great new mansion for himself in the Ita Oba quarters of Ibadan.

*　*　*　*　*

As soon as the Ijebu spies reported that British soldiers were on the move from Lagos, the Ijebu commander in chief, the Balogun, moved his forces to meet them at the village of Itokin.

This waterside hamlet was also known as Ito-iken based on the Ijebu word "iken" or "ikin" for the lush river grass abundant in that part of Ijebuland. The Balogun hid his marksmen with their new Enfield rifles, and his bowmen with their arrows tipped in poison, in the long *ikin* grass of the Eluji valley by the banks of the creeks.

The plan of the Ijebus was simple. They would force the British army to cross the swollen creeks emptying into the lagoon near Itokin. There, they would cut them down with deadly volleys of arrows and gunfire from their vantage point under cover of the grass on their side of the creeks. The British soldiers would have to ford the muddy creeks carrying their weapons high above their heads. The water at that time of the year would reach up to their chests.

The Ijebus were also confident in the power of their *orisas* and their famed sixteen *agemos*. For hadn't the chief Sango priest in Ijebu-Ode been summoned by the Awujale, and having consulted the famous oracle at Porogun, predicted a great victory for the Ijebus over the *oyinbos?*

The Awujale stayed behind in his palace in Ijebu-Ode with a few household staff. Some whispered that he preferred to stay at home to enjoy the nightly comfort of his newly acquired slave paramour. His children, his wives, and the rest of his household were sent away to safety to Ijebu-Igbo.

Then the Balogun gave orders for sacrifices to be made. It was on everyone's lips that for the success of this great military venture, one of the greatest the Ijebus would face in their long history, a significant offering had to be made to propitiate the gods. According to the great and wise authorities of the day, this called for the human sacrifice of two slaves.

The two victims, male and female, who were captives from a recent raid on Ibadan territory, were brought to the banks of the creek. Completely naked, their hands and legs were tied together behind their backs.

The *abore* now came out of the bushes. He was a thin, surprisingly agile old man. Wearing a white cotton robe tied around his waist, he stepped quickly forward, knife in hand.

With a swift slash of his keen knife, the *abore* cut the throat of each slave, using one hand to push the head back on the neck to expose the throat. Each victim was swiftly beheaded and disemboweled. The body parts were thrown into the creek to propitiate Sigidi and Esu, those deities of revenge and retribution. The blood of the victims was smeared on the effigies of these gods which had been brought from their shrines in Ijebu-Ode.

With powerful incantations delivered in a high, thin voice, the *abore* called on Sigidi to wreak vengeance on the *oyinbo* and their minions who dared to invade the sanctity of Ijebu soil. Esu, as messenger of the war, was told to tell the gods in heaven to stand firm in their support of their favorite sons and daughters, the Ijebus, children of Obanta.

After this, priests of the major deities and cults of Ijebu came forward and surrounded the *abore*. They raised their voices high in curses and dreadful-sounding imprecations. They called down death upon any invader who would attempt to cross the creek, predicting that such persons "would not live to tell the tale or return home to eat from their mothers' pots."

Several of the dreaded Ijebu *agemos* were also present, lending fear and their ancient mystique to the proceedings, notably their chief, Tami from Odogbolu. The ancestral spirits of Ijebuland in the form of several masked and colorfully attired *egunguns* also added their powerful voices from the underworld against the invading British.

Then the Ijebu army waited, their marksmen hiding in the trees whose branches overhanged the expected crossing.

But the British colonel was crafty. Guessing the intention of the confident Ijebus, he took his men by the long route to Epe, where they disembarked from their boats under cover of darkness. Then they marched quickly and quietly with a plan to cross the Yemoji river in order to outflank the Ijebu army.

It was almost too late for the Ijebus by the time they realized this ruse. The Balogun had to act fast. He gave swift orders to break up camp at Itokin. His men now made a mad dash east across the marshes and creeks of that water-logged terrain in an effort to stop the British before they crossed the Yemoji river. If they failed, the Ijebu forces would be cut off from the rear and the British would be in Ijebu-Ode within a few days.

Fresh intelligence soon reached the Balogun that an advance column of the *oyinbo* enemy was already close to the river crossing near Imagbon. This was the place where the Yemoji river, meandering through the treacherous marshland, contracted to form a ford that could be used for crossing by the *Gesi* soldiers even loaded down as they were with their heavy weapons.

A column of Ijebu warriors ran ahead to try and cut off the *oyinbo* invaders. But despite a few bloody skirmishes that occurred over the next three days around the villages of Pobo and Erebo, located a few hours march north of Epe, the Ijebus were not able to stop the British from advancing steadily toward the river.

The main body of Ijebu warriors now arrived to set up camp just north of the swollen Yemoji. It was at a village called Imagbon. There, the exhausted Ijebu warriors prepared to man their new defensive positions. They moved their advance guard close to the riverbank, and placed their marksmen and bowmen in position to cover the river crossing. Then they boldly faced the direction from which the British were expected to come in their attempt to ford the river.

Soon the British arrived with an advance scout company of Hausa infantry and Ibadan irregulars. These latter, under their leader, Toyan, were mercenaries who had come to revenge their recent humiliation at the hands of the proud Ijebus. The Ijebus could now clearly see the British deploying on the other side of the swollen and muddy river.

The Ijebus were still somewhat disconcerted from their hasty and unplanned march from Itokin and the unsuccessful skirmishes which their advance guards had had with the British invaders. Still, their war captains harangued the men, telling them they should be ready for the coming fight to defend the sacred land of Ijebu. Then the Balogun gave the order, and the men set off a defiant volley of musket shots and arrows from their side of the river.

But the British commander had a secret weapon that the unsuspecting Ijebus knew nothing about. He had brought a brand-new Maxim, a machine gun which up to that time had never been used or tested in battle.

Delivered from England with the latest shipment of supplies from the HMS Southampton, only one or two of the men, apart from the quartermaster and Captain Campbell of the Lagos Constabulary, had seen the gun or practiced with it by firing a few rounds. The noise it made was horrific, and the governor did not want word leaking out about his secret weapon. He knew there were Ijebu spies in Lagos, even within his own administration.

The Maxim was, at that time, the most powerful repeating machine gun in the world. It had ben invented nine years earlier by the British inventor, Hiram Maxim, who developed the patent on behalf of the Vickers munitions factory. It was based on the mechanism of the first true recoil operated firing system in history. This allowed the recoil energy from the ejected bullet, acting on the breech block, to eject the spent cartridge and automatically insert the next one.

Reading the manual carefully, Captain Campbell, within a few weeks, taught himself to put apart the machine gun and reassemble it. Maxim's earliest designs had used a 360-degree rotating cam to reverse the movement of the block, but the specimen sent to Campbell had been simplified to a toggle lock to reverse the movement of the block. This made it vastly more efficient and less labor-intensive than the other rapid-firing guns then in use, like the Gatlin gun used by the Americans, which relied on mechanical cranking.

Maxim's design also decreased the gas build up in the barrel, allowing the gun to fire more bullets over an extended period without overheating. The gun design also required cooling by water, giving it the ability to maintain its rate of fire for a far longer time than earlier air-cooled machine guns.

Captain Campbell came to love this gun like a child. He called it, in his Cockney accent, "my beauty."

Trials conducted by the War Office in England had demonstrated that the Maxim could fire six hundred rounds a minute. And although it was rather heavy and awkward to maneuver and pull around, Campbell did not think this would matter. He knew that the Ijebus would launch frontal attacks. He would not need to wheel his heavy gun around.

Campbell had chosen five men, the smartest of the Hausas of the Frontier Force from the Gold Coast, for his machine gun team. He knew that apart from the gunner which would be himself, he needed a team of at least five trained men to reload, ready the ammunition and carry the cans of water to cool the machine gun. These men would also help him mount and move the heavy weapon.

History records that the Maxim gun in the late nineteenth century would become the deadliest weapon in the arsenal of the British forces as they pacified the native tribes in Africa from the Matabele and Zulu in South Africa to the Buganda in East Africa. But at that time, no one, least of all the Ijebus, knew anything of its potential.

Campbell's Hausa team mounted the Maxim in place on their own side of the Yemoji river directly across from the Ijebus who tried to pick them off with their carbines. These of course were largely inaccurate at that distance. Then, with a signal to his men, Captain Campbell ducked behind the protective flank in front of the gun. He positioned himself on a makeshift seat of sandbags. Then, he aimed his gun, held the trigger and pressed it down.

The front ranks of the Ijebu warriors on the other side of the river were blown away in a matter of minutes. Before their stunned comrades could regroup, most of the British officers and enlisted men had forded the river. The muddy water swirled around their chests as they pushed their way across.

The colonel positioned himself in midstream, directing the action while the Maxim maintained its hellish din, its fire now directed upward to avoid the British as they clambered up the far riverbank, shooting down at close range any Ijebu fighter still standing.

Young Captain Bower, who had only recently left Sandhurst and was promoted from subaltern just in time for this expedition, could be seen shouldering the ten-pounder howitzer, as men around him made their way across the river.

Under this uninterrupted barrage, the Ijebu warriors had no room for maneuver. Most of them had no time to reload and fire their Dane guns and muskets. They had a few Snider-Enfield breech-loading rifles. But without the sights which their agents had neglected to purchase, the Ijebus were limited to short range shots. They were therefore no match for the British and Hausa riflemen who were equipped with sights that enabled them to shoot down their quarry at two hundred yards. The British soldiers were also better trained in their use. After all, the Snider was a British-made weapon, which for several years had been standard issue for the British army in India and other colonial outposts.

The arrows, lances, and short swords of the Ijebu warriors were of no avail, as the Hausa soldiers with their British officers kept a safe distance while allowing the great gun to do its deadly work a hundred yards away.

The slaughter that day was merciless. The carnage was such that some of the British officers looked away in pity and horror. They saw before their very eyes, bodies of the enemy blown into the water, their butchered body parts thrown here and there. Arms and legs, even severed heads, were grotesquely smashed against the trunk of trees, darkening the green foliage scarlet with rich warm blood.

The horror of this apocalyptic day was further amplified by the decision of the colonel to order incendiary rockets to be fired high up into the trees. The branches and leaves caught fire, completing the atmosphere of fear and panic among the superstitious Ijebus.

"Igbo ti gbano—the forest has turned to fire!" they wailed.

Their eyes wide with fright and horror, the Ijebus turned and fled, many dropping their useless weapons. Those who were not cut down by the machine gun fire or drowned in the river were now shot down by the carbines of the British officers and the rifles of the well-trained Hausa infantry as they methodically aimed, shot and reloaded.

Captain Campbell had now succeeded in bringing the big gun across the river, a feat of strength and courage on the part of his men. The gun was quickly reassembled, remounted on its swiveling carriage, and its work of death resumed.

Shigidi's ancient power was clearly not in evidence on that fatal day by the banks of the Yemoji river. The immolations and sacrifices made in his name at Itokin had been useless and of no avail.

And perhaps, Olokun and Ogun, those wise and prudent deities of the Yorubas, refrained from intervening on the side of the Ijebu warlords since they had not bothered to propitiate them before embarking on their rash and reckless venture. These gods were clearly disgusted with their old protégés. They turned their eyes away as the British gun exacted its deadly toll.

The gods of war were on the side of those who had the Maxim gun. A British writer of the time put it wryly thus:

Whatever happens,
we have the Maxim gun,
and they have not.

CHAPTER 7

Oun jẹ enia to feran alaafia
O si ti ka iwe mimo awon onigbagbo
Bi o tile je wipe o feran obirin pupọ.
Ni igba kan, o wa ni idande ninu igbo Odu,
Sugbon o sá kuro lowo awọn olè
Lati ri iranlowo lati odo oloye Ijebu Ode
"Ṣe o lo si oju ogun Kiriji?"
awon enia pejọ lati beere lọwọ rẹ.
"Se oto ni pe o gba Oyinbo lowo?"
O dahun wipe,
"Gbogbo eyi ni mo ṣe,
Ṣugbọn ohun ti mo fẹ nisisiyi
Ni ki ngbadun oko mi ni Mamu
ati awọn iyawo mi atata."

He was a man of peace,
And though he had read the holy book,
he was a polygamist nonetheless.
Out of the forest of Odu
he fled the lair of thieves
to succor in a great chief's household.
"Were you at the battlefield at Kiriji?"
people gathered around and asked him.
"And is it true you shook
the hands of white men?"
"All this I did," he said,
"But now, I want to enjoy
my farm at Mamu,
and my many wives so dear to me."

Baba Mamu

ODUSANYA WAS ONE of those who fled following the British bombardment across the swollen Yemoji. His friend Musiliu was one of the first to fall. He was cut down, right next to the astonished Odusanya, his locally made musket flying out of his hands.

Blood from Musiliu's severed neck sprayed into Odusanya's eyes, blinding him. The blood found its way into his mouth, his nose and his throat. Horrified, Odusanya tasted a salty mixture of flesh, muscle, and hair-covered skin.

Odusanya turned and ran with the rest. The sight of his fallen comrades, their bodies cut to pieces by the Maxim gun, the spray of hot blood on his face, and the groans of the wounded and dying all around him, seared his vision, his ears and his senses. And yet, amidst this horror was the quiet silence of the dead, insensible to the noise of guns and rockers, and the clamor of fleeing men.

Odusanya jumped over countless bodies that blocked his path. Some lay quite still. But many thrashed about and moaned in the throes of a painful death. Smoke rose from the burning forest and black soot filled his eyes, making them water and obscuring his vision.

For a moment, he thought he was dead and was on the other side of that fatal river that separated the land of the living from the dead.

Was he in *orun alakeji?* Or was he in a bad dream? Like the one he used to have when he was in captivity in the forest with the *odu* cult, when he would dream at night that he was being chased by an army of *anjonu* and *iwin*.

Odusanya blinked and tried to keep his eyes open as he ran. No, he was not dead. He was a living man of flesh and blood in an apocalyptic world made mad by the insanity of war.

As he ran, something made him look up at the sky. Through the cloud of smoke and burning branches, he saw a massed group of vultures circling overhead. Those prognosticators of death had been drawn to the scene of war and human chaos by the promise of carrion.

Odusanya said grimly to himself, "The prospect of feasting on the bodies of the dead has those vultures excited."

He looked down and surveyed the scene around him. And the horror below was worse than the sight above of those winged scavengers of death.

> *Mi o ni ku loni;*
> *Gunugun ko ni je ara mi.*

> *I will not be a victim today;*
> *Vultures will not feed on my flesh.*

Odusanya shouted these words to himself as he ran. This refrain was his antidote to fear, the talisman that would vouchsafe his safety and survival. He repeated the lines over and over, like an *ofo*.

Those words spoken aloud to himself, combined with a desperate determination to live, gave him wings. And he flew like a madman. He knew he had to get as far away as he could from this place of death, away from the smell of exploding gunpowder, flaming trees and burning flesh.

Odusanya ran for hours, following the sounds of his comrades running beside him. He could hear them—as they fled—to his front, right, left, and back. And as he ran, tears of rage welled up in his eyes. They made his cheeks wet and blurred his vison. He could hardly see where he was going.

It was true he had become a warrior. But he was a boy, only sixteen years old. He now knew that in his heart, he hated war. Like his mentor, Kuku, he was a rational and peace-loving person who loved life, pleasure and learning. He was a man of peace. He did not want to die. He wanted a future that would stretch to full manhood, even to a ripe old age. It was a life that would be filled with the pleasures and comforts that money would bring.

So much, Odusanya said bitterly to himself, for the glory and camaraderie of war, which one of his commanders had blithely talked about in their camp two days earlier as they encamped outside the village of Itokin. That was a lie, as he could now see. It was an imposition on gullible young men eager to prove their manhood. Now, he knew the truth! War only led to grief. Its rewards were loss, tragedy, and death.

He had lost his best friend and companion, Musiliu as a result of a foolish and unnecessary war. And who knew how many had perished with him on that riverbank?

And how many boys of his age would die later that day as they were hunted down by the *oyinbo* and Hausa soldiers, who were now pursuing them with a careless and unfeeling arrogance?

He remembered Musiliu's laughter and his roguish ways. And the pranks he seemed to live on, as when he convinced Odusanya to go with him, sneaking into someone's farms to pilfer mangoes. They had climbed the big trees and wrenched ripe yellow fruits from their branches. He would never again go with Musiliu to fish in the river. Or see him laugh as he mocked and admired the firm, round breasts and swinging hips of passing maidens on their way to the stream.

As he ran, Odusanya railed at the incompetence and dishonorable conduct of the Ijebu leaders, who had pushed the Awujale into this conflict with the white man. Who did not know that the British possessed resources and powers that even the Ijebu gods could not match?

If only Kuku had been around to talk sense to the council of the osugbo?

Odusanya fumed as he remembered the glib, ignorant talk of the townsmen as they extolled the military prowess of Ijebu warriors, who, they said, had destroyed the might of the Owus, Ibadans and Egbas in countless battles. The occult magic of their *agemos*, they argued, would silence the guns of the white men. Those pale-skinned *Gesi*, who talked through their noses and sipped tea in small cups while they ordered their Hausa servants around, would not know what hit them.

Odusanya remembered with disgust the bellicose talk of the young men of Ijebu-Ode, and of the old men in the *osugbo* who chewed kola nut and put snuff in their nostrils as they contemplated the coming victory. They had all laughed complacently. Their war commanders talked of heroism and their duty to defend the sacred land of Olu-iwa.

Odusanya remembered having an uneasy feeling of foreboding when all this talk was going on. At the time, he thought it was because he missed the presence of his mentor, Chief Kuku. Now he knew his doubts were correct. If only "Baba" Kuku had stayed in Ijebu-Ode to talk the Awujale out of this madness, instead of allowing himself to be sent to exile in Ibadan!

Now he and the whole Ijebu army were being chased and hunted down like hares in the bush. And not on a foreign battlefield, but right here in their own Ijebu forests.

And why hadn't the deities of Ijebuland saved them from this tragedy?

As the depth of the humiliation of his people assailed him, belief in the cults of his Ijebu people and the potency of their *egungun* and *agemo*, whose powers he had been brought up to fear and trust, crumbled at his feet. And the dust of their decay was grounded into the earth of the forest floor by his feet and those of other fleeing warriors running behind him.

This debacle that had befallen his people was all too much for Odusanya, a boy of sixteen. He wept as he ran. And his thoughts turned to his own future and survival. He swore to himself that if he got out of this debacle alive, he would never again venture into war.

Before Kuku had been forced into exile, Odusanya had listened to passages from a well-worn copy of *Bibeli Mimo*, the Yoruba Bible, that Kuku often read aloud. The part he loved to hear most was called *Ifihan*. There was a passage in it that he loved to hear and to recite. Since he himself could not read, he had learned it completely by heart. Kuku told him that it was about the battle that would end the world.

> *Si kiyesi, esin rondonrondon kan,*
> *Oruko eniti o joko lori re ni Iku.*
> *Ipo-iku li o to o lehin.*
> *A si fi agbara fun won*
> *Lati pa pelu ida.*

> *I looked and saw a pale horse,*
> *And the name of he that sat on him was Death.*
> *And Hades followed him.*
> *Power was given unto them*
> *to kill with the sword.*

On that day of calamity and death, as he fled from that last battle of the Ijebus on the banks of the Yemoji river, Odusanya thought he had seen what that final war of the nations of the earth would be like.

* * * * *

When the British forces with their Hausa and West Indian infantry men entered Ijebu-Ode two days later, on May 20, 1892, they found the town deserted. They marched to the Awujale's palace, where they found him cowering in an inner chamber. He had been deserted by his attendants, his guards, his wives and his concubines. All had fled into the bush or the surrounding hamlets for safety.

The first thing the Awujale told the commanding British officer, after he had summoned courage to talk once he realized they were not going to kill him, were these words.

"I warned those 'boys' not to confront the *Gesi* Governor in Lagos. But they would not listen to me."

When the interpreter gave the white men this message, Colonel Scott winked at the other officers and nodded. Captain Bower tried to suppress a laugh.

The colonel told the Awujale they would take care of him and not harm him. Since he had only two servants of the royal household who had bravely stayed behind with him in the palace, the British commander gave orders for his own orderly to make sure everything was done to cater to the needs of the Awujale.

Then the colonel ordered the Hausa soldiers to look around the palace, for traps and hidden places that could conceal an ambush. The Hausas, for their part, were on the lookout for valuable items and treasures that could be looted or claimed as spoils of war. They had heard stories that this was the palace of a rich and powerful king of the *Yaraba*.

Left alone in the company of the British officers, the *oba* continued to complain bitterly that even his wives and children had deserted him. He kept telling the colonel in his broken English that he had not wanted the war, that the young "boys" in the *osugbo* were hot-headed and did not listen to him.

The British officers again nodded and winked at each other. They went outside to look for a well with drinkable water. They needed to water their horses.

*   *   *   *   *

As he fled toward Ijebu-Ode to escape the terrible carnage on the banks of the Yemoji, Odusanya noticed that two of his friends were with him. They were Taju and Fajimi, who he had known casually before they volunteered together at the outbreak of war to fight the *oyinbo*.

Now, his two friends ran beside him, their breaths coming in loud grunts that he could hear on both sides of him. In between his breaths, he called out to each by name. He had become close to these young men, who were his own age, since they had been conscripted into the same company of Ijebu-Ode irregulars under the same *ajagun* or commander.

Now, as they ran, the boys stayed together for safety and company. Odusanya looked to his left and his right. Besides Taju and Fajimi, running beside him were other warriors, mostly young men who panted and grunted as they ran between the trees, leapt over fallen tree trunks and dodged boulders and rocks.

They ran through farms where the maize harvest lay uncut. They waded through shallow streams in which the water came up to their thighs and hips. And they dashed through hamlets where a few old men and women looked at them with surprise and consternation.

Had they not heard there is a war on? Odusanya thought.

But after some time, the sounds of the British guns faded in the distance, and the forest around them became quiet. On a sudden whim, Odusanya motioned to his two friends running beside him to stop.

In between gasps, he told them that they had run enough. The battleground and that fatal river were far behind them. And it was doubtful if any British soldiers were in pursuit of them. They needed to rest and take their bearings.

Odusanya was now able to look closely at his two companions. Like him, both of them had lost their muskets. And Fajimi had an injured left arm that hung limply by his side. He had a bleeding wound which he had tied up with a piece of cloth, a vest taken off a dead Ijebu warrior.

The boys could see that they were in a valley beside a stream. They did not know it, but this was the farming settlement of Odogbolu. All the men had gone to war, and the place was deserted. Odusanya and his two comrades decided to take a rest and plan their route.

They sat down, laid Fajimi flat on the ground, and unwrapped the cloth around his bleeding arm. Odusanya and Taju inspected the wound. It was a deep flesh wound. They caught a glimpse of white bone in the depth of the wound, Odusanya held Fajimi's shoulder while Taju pulled on the elbow while they exposed and probed the wound. Fajimi winced with pain and gritted his teeth, and once or twice, he cried out in pain. But the bone did not appear to be broken. Odusanya and Taju helped their injured friend to wash the wound in the nearby stream. Then they tied up the wound with a bandage made by cutting up the *sokoto* Fajimi was wearing.

All three now took time to inspect themselves carefully. But other than a few grazes on the forehead, face and legs, Odusanya and Taju were unscathed.

They stood beside the stream, which reminded Odusanya of a coiled serpent as it wound its way through a valley of wild grass that lined both its banks. The view was very inviting, and suddenly they knew they were thirsty. So the three boys squatted beside the shallow water and drank their fill. They filled their mouths with the cool water with their cupped palms.

After this, they found bananas growing in a nearby grove. These they ate heartily. They made a rough sack from the remnants of Fajimi's trousers and wrapped in it the bananas they could not eat. These would be handy when they became hungry later. And by that time, they reasoned, they should have found a place of rest and safety.

Odusanya told his friends that they had to move on. But now, they found that all they could do was walk. For after they had stopped to rest, they found they were too winded to run even if they wanted to.

And as the tree boys prepared to continue their flight, they regained some of their youthful humor. They poked fun at each other. Their close brush with death seemed now so far away. They began to act and talk like young men would who were at an age when there should be no care in the world.

Odusanya and Taju pointed at Fajimi and laughed at his dirty cotton underwear, which in fact was little more than a loin cloth folded under his crotch and tied at the waist. It barely concealed his genitals. Fajimi had continued the journey since they left the stream clothed only in this makeshift underwear and a single upper garment, which was a short, blood-stained *dashiki* festooned with charms, the typical warrior's cloak of that age.

Putting their heads together, the boys now held a council of war. They decided it would not be safe or prudent to go to Ijebu-Ode. The victorious *Gesi* were certain to make for the capital city of Ijebuland in order to capture the Awujale and the rest of the *osugbo*, the king's advisory council, who had started this war. It was not safe staying where they were either.

They knew they had to move. But where could they go?

They all stood up. But still, they looked in the direction of Ijebu-Ode. They knew they had to hurry. If any British or Hausa soldiers found them, Odusanya and his three comrades would be treated as vanquished foe. If they were not killed immediately by a vengeful Hausa infantryman, they would be taken as prisoners of war. They might even be sold as slaves. Who knows what those heathen Hausa soldiers might do to them?

It was then that Odusanya remembered the forest lair where he had been held captive by the *odu* cult, and Chief Kuku's farm close by in Mamu. His two friends could come with him to hide out in this place in the bush near the hamlet of Mamu. They would hide there until it was safe to go back to their homes in Ijebu-Ode. On the farm, there would be food to eat and they would not starve.

Odusanya described to his friends the isolation of the farm and its advantages as a hideout. Taju and Fajimi readily agreed to come with him. After all, they had no other option or plan of their own.

After thinking carefully for a while, Odusanya began to map out in his mind how to get there. After fixing the directions firmly in his head, he got up and the others followed him.

Odusanya set off at a brisk walk, his two companions close behind him. He looked behind him from time to time to make sure they kept pace with him. But on taking another look at Fajimi, who still had not found a replacement for his trousers, Odusanya laughed with boyish glee. But he sobered quickly when he realized the seriousness of their position.

On this next phase of their flight, the boys skirted the northwestern boundaries of Ijebu-Ode. With Odusanya leading the way, they turned into a forest path he knew, and soon they were in Mamu.

He knew there would be a small hut on the abandoned farm. It was formerly a shed which Kuku had constructed years before to store a harvest of corn and yams.

Odusanya remembered that he and Kuku had filled in the open sides of the shed with a wall of compacted mud. They had left an opening in the front over which they placed a wooden contraption, planks nailed together to make a door to keep off the elements and stray animals. They had also made a small opening in the side for a window to let in air and light. Odusanya smiled to himself as he remembered the many occasions he had taken shelter in that hut when there was a rainstorm.

And it was into this small hut that Odusanya and his two comrades now crept. They were grateful that they had made it out of the jaws of death in that killing ground on the banks of the Yemoji River. They fell and prostrated on the earth floor of the hut and said prayers to Orisanla.

It was while they were thus engaged in this thankful devotion to the great god of their clan that they were surprised by a soft voice which said "Eweso" from the doorway.

*   *   *   *   *

The three boys stood up and turned to look. Staring at them was a strange figure that stood in the open doorway to the hut. It was a young maiden, who stood there nonplussed, regarding them with a look of amusement on her face.

This girl seemed to have recognized them for what they were— fearful boys running away from the horror of war. And she appeared not to be afraid of them, even though she was a lone female at the mercy of three lusty young men.

But she must have seen that they were tired, worn-out and hungry, and that one of them was wounded.

"They will do me no harm," the strange girl said to herself.

It was Bintu, the slave girl, concubine of the *oba*. She had also made her escape from the palace of the Awujale when war came to Ijebu-Ode. The other women in the palace would not take her with them as they fled to villages and farms outside Ijebu-Ode where they had relatives.

Having nowhere to go, Bintu had walked northward until she stumbled on this hut on the abandoned farm. She had been there now for two days, and had made herself at home. She had discovered a grove of fruit trees, and had gorged on bananas and guava until she felt sick. She had also found a stream nearby, from which she drank fresh water.

She did not know how long she would be able to stay in this lonely place undetected and unmolested. But she was determined to stay here until she could make her way back to Ijebu-Ode when it appeared the conflict was over.

Now, as she contemplated these newcomers, Bintu quickly assessed her situation. She surmised that they were boys escaping the war. They would need food and clothing, and the care and attention that only a woman could provide.

As a very practical person, Bintu decided that the presence of the three boys, who obviously were runaways like herself, would not interfere with her plans. In fact, the boys would protect her from older and more malicious human intruders and beastly predators that might otherwise menace her on this abandoned farm at the edge of a mysterious and dangerous forest.

So, Bintu spoke to the boys kindly. And in the end, they all agreed to make common cause to live on the farm until the war was over.

Thus it was that Bintu helped the three former warriors enjoy three languid months sampling the delights of their hideout and the attention of their friendly hostess.

Bintu was only a little older than the boys. The four of them got along like any teenagers would with no care in the world. Bintu spoke the archaic Yoruba of the northern tribes, which the boys at first found a little difficult to understand. But soon, they were able to teach her the fine points of their own Ijebu dialect.

And as they waited until news came of peace in Ijebu-Ode, the four young people became farmers. On a high ground next to the stream that was not too far from their hut, they found a resilient crop of wild maize that bore fruit within a month. They harvested this corn, and for days and weeks afterward, they roasted and boiled corn. They ate until their bellies almost burst.

Fajimi's torn arm healed. And soon, he was running around with the other two boys. Bintu watched the boys scamper about with delight and encouragement. She remembered vaguely her own brothers in Nupe country. The boys climbed trees, and sometimes stripping naked, they jumped in and swam in the small stream.

With Bintu to instruct them, the boys dug up roots of cocoyam, carrots and cassava. They plucked mangoes, pawpaw, guava and other fruits off the trees. In turn, the boys taught Bintu to join them in trapping small animals like the *okete*, and to bring down birds with a sling and a stone. In a very short time, they all grew fat, contented, and happy.

The boys would look away or go outside the hut whenever Bintu wanted to change her clothes or perform some other delicate part of her toiletry. And none of them laughed when Bintu, a devout Moslem, knelt in a corner of the hut several times a day, facing the east, and went through the motions of standing, bending, and kneeling to say her prayers.

Taju, whose parents were Moslem, joined her several times. But he made sure he knelt several paces away from Bintu since he remembered that it was *haram* for men and women to pray side by side. That of course did not prevent him from joining the other boys in frolicking around with her when it came to playing or foraging for food.

Bintu knew the alphabets in both Arabic and Yoruba. She could read and write simple phrases and sentences in both languages. She tried to teach the boys the alphabet in Arabic, which she knew better. But she gave up after a few recitations of *alif* and *ba*. The symbols would simply not sink into the boys' hard, illiterate skulls.

She made more headway with the Yoruba alphabet. She got the boys to recite their A, B, D up to GB. Having no slate, paper, or chalk, she used a twig that had fallen off a tree to draw the symbols in the earth outside the hut.

The boys would say later that this was the most restful, instructive, and idyllic period of their lives, made the more pleasurable by the presence of the girl, Bintu. The stories that came to us did not dwell, perhaps out of respect for delicate ears, on the frolics of a different nature that Bintu enjoyed with the boys during their period of exile.

All we can say is that Bintu did her part. On lazy afternoons, when the world stood still, and there were no more pranks left for them to practice on each other, she patiently recited to the boys lines from the Koran. She explained to them in Yoruba the meaning of the sonorous Arabic chants.

And at night, she lay with them on a single mat on the floor of the hut. She kept them warm on cold, rainy nights when the wild tropical storms of Ijebuland threatened to bring down on their heads the thatched roof of the hut.

Bintu was happy and fulfilled. She knew that the boys learned a great many things from her. And in the end, she accomplished what war had not succeeded in doing. She turned the three boys into men.

It would be three months before the four runaways came out of their hideout. This was after Odusanya and Taju made a surreptitious trip to the hamlet of Mamu. They learned that the war with the *oyinbo* had ended weeks earlier. Peace had been declared throughout Ijebuland. All former warriors from Ijebu-Ode were pardoned by the British. They could now return to their homes and families as long as they lay down their arms and caused no more trouble.

Joyfully, the two boys ran all the way back to the farm to tell the others that all was well. They could now go back to Ijebu-Ode.

"How time flies!" they said to each other as they took a last look at their place of exile and refuge.

*　　*　　*　　*　　*

It was a new reality that the boys found when they got back to Ijebu-Ode. Although the Awujale had been restored to his palace, the unfettered rule of the monarch of Ijebu-Ode was a thing of the past.

And the power of the *osugbo* had been broken. The boys learned that orders for the running of their ancient town were now issued, not by the Awujale, but by the *oyinbo* resident, who was part of the colonial administration appointed by the Governor of the Colony in Lagos.

When Odusanya got back, he was happy to learn that his mentor, Chief Kuku, had returned from exile in Ibadan. The old man was happy to receive Odusanya back into his household. When he had returned to Ijebu-Ode and heard no word of him, Kuku had mourned his protégé as being among the dead from that disastrous campaign at Imagbon.

Kuku told Odusanya that he was now the leader of a group of elders in charge of managing the peace. It was true that the bulk of the British army had departed. But they had left behind a contingent of Hausa soldiers under the command of a single *oyinbo* officer. These Hausa soldiers were to keep order on the streets of Ijebu-Ode. They occupied the house and compound of the former Balogun, who had fled and had not come back home. Some said he was hiding in exile in Ijebu-Igbo.

The Hausa soldiers had the run of the town. They made the palm wine tappers give them their ware for free. They drank this palm wine in public and with abandon, even though as Moslems, they were forbidden from touching alcohol. On one occasion, some of them became drunk, went on a rampage, and ravished a maiden. But no punishment was meted out to the culprits.

They entered people's farms and harvested their ripe *agbado, ogede*, and *gbaguda* with impunity. In short, they behaved like the victors and occupying army that they knew they were, to whom were due the spoils of war.

To be fair, the British could be said to have been magnanimous in victory in their treatment of the humiliated Awujale Tunwase. The Ijebu king was not imprisoned or sent into exile, as some in Lagos demanded he should. After all, in similar circumstances, in 1887, the British had exiled the powerful Jaja of Opobo.

As Kuku told Odusanya, this Jaja had refused to accept British trade hegemony in the territory of his city-state of Opobo, which he had founded decades earlier in the Niger delta. The British vice-consul, the cunning Henry Johnston, then tricked Jaja into attending a meeting to discuss their differences. But armed British naval ratings stationed at the meeting place arrested Jaja. He was sent into exile in St. Vincent in the British West Indies after a brief stay in England, where he was said to have met Queen Victoria.

And some years after the Ijebu Campaign, the British would exile Ovonramwen, the Oba of Benin, after a similar conflict when British forces inflicted a humiliating military defeat on the Benin Empire. It was said that Oba Ovonramwen bribed Ralph Moor, the British Consul General with many barrels of palm oil and hundreds of carved elephant tusks—a veritable king's ransom. But the crafty consul took the goods and still had Ovonramwen exiled to Calabar, where the deposed Benin monarch would spend the rest of his days. The Awujale therefore must have considered himself lucky.

Some weeks after the Battle of Imagbon, Governor Carter sent from Lagos a delegation which included the resident district officer and an interpreter, who explained to the Ijebu monarch the contents of a treaty the governor wanted him to sign.

This piece of paper would allow full access by all traders, merchants, priests and travelers into Ijebu territory. The Awujale would be required to enforce an end to the practice of slavery and of human sacrifice. And he must allow Christian missionaries to open their missions and establish schools anywhere they wanted throughout Ijebuland.

The final act of the treaty was that the young English officer, Captain Bower, who had led the assault across the Yemoji river with his Hausa infantrymen, would stay in Ijebu-Ode with a detachment of Hausa troops to keep the peace.

The Awujale had no choice but to acquiesce. So it was that the Ijebu king had blue ink rubbed on his right thumb, which he pressed on a piece of paper full of markings he did not understand.

The formal signing of the treaty was supervised by Governor Carter himself. A couple of colorfully-attired military attachés who had come down from Lagos with the governor put down their signatures as witnesses, as well as three chieftains of Ijebu-Ode who affixed their marks in the form of an *x*.

Thus came to an end the unquestioned rule of the Awujales which had held sway in Ijebu-Ode for six centuries. By agreeing to this treaty, the Awujale would enforce terms that effectively ended his own power.

Sleeping in his bed at night in the weeks and months after this, Awujale Tunwase no doubt yearned for the old days of absolute power. But at heart, he must have been glad that he no longer had to answer to the hot-headed *odo* in the *osugbo* who had pushed him and his people to war and disaster.

The signing of the treaty to end the Ijebu Campaign was given full prominence in the leading Lagos newspapers of the day. The *Lagos News* carried a daguerreotype of Governor Carter in full military regalia and colonial hat, his chest resplendent with medals won in action from many foreign battlefields, while a ceremonial sword swung at his side. There was also a photograph of Chief Kuku, who was described as "Balogun of the Ijebus." He had come to the palace at the invitation of the Awujale to receive His Excellency the Governor on behalf of the Ijebu monarch.

The birthday of Her Britannic Majesty, Victoria Regina, had occurred a few days earlier on May 24. This august occasion was celebrated with the pomp it demanded, to go along with the ceremony attending the signing of the treaty. The *oyinbo* officers stood at attention as bugles were blown and arms were presented by the Hausa soldiers.

After this, the white officers and administrators gave a lusty rendition of "God save the Queen." The Christian missionaries who were present, both Yoruba and *Gesi,* joined them.

The words they sang were strange and meaningless to Odusanya, who was there, standing behind Chief Kuku. But later, he would learn to sing this anthem when he himself became a subject of the British Crown.

> God save our gracious queen,
> Long live our noble queen,
> God save the Queen.
> Send her victorious,
> Happy and glorious,
> Long to reign over us,
> God save the Queen.
>
> O Lord our God arise,
> Scatter our enemies,
> And make them fall . . .

Had Odusanya understood the words then, no doubt he would have said to himself that the enemies of the queen of England were certainly falling and being put in their place. Surely, no one would want to be on the receiving end of the wrath of this happy and glorious monarch.

* * * * *

It had been a long road for Chief Kuku. On the day he returned to Ijebu-Ode a few months earlier, people said the old man looked sad. For indeed, he could not feel jubilant.

Kuku's predictions had come to pass. But he could not utter the words, "I told you so," as he ruminated on the fate of those who had not heeded his warning. He mourned the loss of the thousands of young men who had died in sacrifice to the foolishness of the *osugbo* and the *odo*, the brash "young guns" of Ijebu-Ode.

Following the signing of the treaty in the oba's palace, Kuku wasted no time in negotiating the terms of the new order with the British. He told himself that he had to do this in good faith, with the welfare of his Ijebu people at heart.

As a result of his efforts, the Awujale was granted a yearly pension of two hundred pounds. In return, the Awujale honored and enforced his side of the bargain. He opened the roads throughout Ijebuland to commerce, and he dismantled the toll at Konankonan on the southern border with Ibadan. Most importantly, he banned slavery and allowed Christian missionaries for the first time to enter Ijebuland.

The *onigbagbo* were now free to build their churches and schools in Ijebu-Ode and other Ijebu towns, and to preach their message of a god who died on the cross.

But having got their way following the victory at Imagbon, the British revealed their grand plan. They were not content with merely subduing Ijebu-Ode and making the Ijebus stop the practice of slavery and human sacrifice. This first act of the signing of the treaty with Ijebuland was simply the means to an end.

The colonial administrators in Lagos and London had drawn up an ambitious plan for a British "protectorate" over all the Yoruba city-states. This was similar to what had proved successful in other British colonies from Kenya to India. Using the example of Ijebu and the threat of force, the British governor in Lagos began to sign a series of treaties with all the major Yoruba *obas* and chiefs. It was in this way that over the next six years, the *oyinbos* succeed in creating a British Protectorate over the whole of Yorubaland.

But the governor found that he did not have enough soldiers and administrators to rule the vast land. So he and others after him, devised the concept of indirect rule. They used local chiefs and potentates to administer the new order and to enforce the will of the British queen over her new territories. One of these local chiefs was Chief Kuku of Ijebu-Ode.

Chief Kuku's voice now prevailed over that of any other person in Ijebu-Ode. He was the new Balogun of Ijebu-Ode. And it was his role to explain to his fellow Ijebu chiefs that they had to sign yet another treaty. This time, it would be to agree to live under a "protectorate" of the *oyinbo* queen across the sea.

Kuku himself was not sure exactly what this word "protectorate" meant. But he told his compatriots that they would be protected by the great and powerful Queen Victoria. Everyone knew that the Ijebu people as well as those living in every Yoruba city-state would be losing their ancient independence. But they had no choice. No one was ready to face once again the fury of the British Maxim gun.

So it was that for the second time in his lifetime, young Odusanya accompanied Chief Kuku to the signing of a great treaty involving the major Yoruba chiefs and obas. But this time, they traveled, not to Oke Mesi, but to Oyo.

Kuku explained to Odusanya that this Oyo was a new town, not the old capital city of the Yorubas in the grasslands near Odo Oya. Old Oyo had been burned down six decades earlier by the Fulanis from Ilorin.

And again, Odusanya had the honor of shaking hands with "Ajose," the Right Reverend Samuel Johnson, who said "A wa yu" to everyone.

Odusanya saw many white men, many in ceremonial military uniform. But now he had more fear and respect for these *oyinbo* men. He remembered the destruction they had wrought at Imagbon, where they had shown everyone what they were capable of. Armed with their repeating gun, mortar, and fiery rockets, they had killed Musiliu and many of his friends. But now, Chief Kuku told Odusanya that they would be his protectors.

Odusanya observed with a strange fascination how the white officers and priests talked to each other in their peculiar tongue. The sounds they made came out as if they had pinched their noses with thumb and finger. He noticed that the *Gesi* officers stood apart in their crisp khaki tunics and shorts. Their tall colonial pith helmets were pushed down low until it rested just above their eyebrows, but their chin straps were untied in the afternoon heat.

He heard these *oyinbo* officers bark orders to the Hausa soldiers who stood stiffly at attention, and saluted, or ran about to carry out the orders of the white men. Odusanya noticed that the blue tunics and red fez of the Hausa conscripted men contrasted sharply with the staid brown khaki of the *oyinbo* officers.

Kuku told Odusanya that these soldiers were there to keep order among the crowd. They would also keep the chiefs from bringing all their servants and attendants too near the special place reserved in front for the dignitaries and those who would sign the treaty.

Under Chief Kuku's tutelage, Odusanya's young mind had developed a sense of history. His eyes now took in the scene before him, and he tried to fix it in his mind so that he would remember it.

It was just like at the signing of the treaty on the battlefield at Kiriji. Odusanya basked once again in the pageantry of a great and portentous event that would be remembered in the annals of Yorubaland. And as he gawked at the gaudy outfits and colorful retinue of the great chiefs and obas gathered there, it gave him a feeling of excitement and awe to witness this grand display of the ancient culture and traditions of his people.

As Odusanya stood and walked around that field in front of the Alaafin's palace in Oyo-Atiba, what he saw was the largest collection ever in any one place of the crowned heads of Yorubaland. It was a magnificent and historic sight that he would always remember. So, he gaped in admiration at the colorful array of the elaborately attired *obas* and chieftains. Many of them were on horseback. The *obas* wore their richly woven beaded crowns, some with veils that covered their faces. Odusanya stared and tried to figure out who was who.

Who indeed was the Osemawe of Ondo? And where was the Owa Obokun of Ijeshaland?

Odusanya tried to remind himself that these tired-looking *obas* were the descendants of the ancient monarchs and deified heroes of his people. Their lines had ruled for centuries in their various city-stated after Oduduwa came to Ile-Ife and Oranmiyan established his dynasty in Oyo. As he gaped at them, Odusanya was conscious of being an eyewitness to the great legacy of the ancient glory of his Yoruba people. But on that day, though the young man did not fully grasp it, everyone else knew that this gallant spectacle was a show. What they had come to witness was the humbled majesty of a once-proud race.

The *obas* and chiefs were surrounded by their underlings, who all jostled for position and attention. Everyone wanted to be near the great stage now being set up, where the treaty would be signed.

Men bearing talking drums and *shekere*, accompanied by praise singers and dancers jostled in the crowd with chieftains, warriors and onlookers. Now and then, the voice of an *akewi* would rent the air as he chanted the *oriki* and praises of the Alafin or some other *oba* or chief, who, resplendent on a high horse, would smile down at the praise singer. Occasionally, the attendants of the *oba* or *oloye* would throw a fistful of cowry shells at the musician.

What made this scene so poignant was that all the adults present, especially Balogun Kuku, knew that these kings and chieftains were not there that day to enjoy the rights and privileges of their ancient heritage. They were gathered to relinquish their rule to the agents of a foreign power.

"Will the power and prestige of our Yoruba obas ever come back?" This was the question the Ijebu chieftain asked himself.

Aloud, Kuku said nothing. He held Odusanya by the arm. And from to time, he would pull the boy out of danger when he did not pay attention as a great horse raised its hooves over his head, threatening to trample him underfoot.

Odusanya, engrossed by the scene around him, paid little attention to his mentor. But when they prepared to move nearer to the great stage in order to have a view of the signing of the treaty, something made Odusanya look up at his mentor.

Kuku's face was as inscrutable as the bronze mask of an Ooni from Ile-Ife, as he and Odusanya watched as the Alafin and other Yoruba *obas* and chieftains affixed their thumb marks to a roll of parchment in the presence of the representatives of the queen from across the sea.

But what were Chief Kuku's actual thoughts at that moment? Although it saddened him, as Balogun of Ijebuland, to witness the sight of Yoruba *obas* signing away their ancient legacy, Kuku thought this moment was inevitable. His own opinion was that by their stubbornness, lack of foresight, and constant warring among themselves, these Yoruba leaders had proved that things would only worsen if they were allowed to hold on to the reins of power.

Kuku was a practical man. He knew that the days of the hegemony and power of the Yoruba city-states were at an end. That era had passed, and another had come to take its place.

He quoted softly to himself.

> *Igba kan nlo, igba kan nbo.*
> *Aiye nyi nlo bi orere.*

> *One era passes away;*
> *Another comes to take its place.*
> *The world spins on like a top.*

By the treaty signed on that day, the British now ruled and controlled all of Yorubaland. Joined with Lagos, the ancient land of Oduduwa was named the *Colony and Protectorate of Southern Nigeria*. Among other things, the document, which was translated into Yoruba and read aloud to all present, condemned and abolished the practice of slavery in all the territory of the protectorate.

It said, "Slavery is an evil practice that is abhorrent to all civilized nations on the face of the earth."

When he heard those words in Yoruba, Odusanya nodded his head, for he agreed with the assessment. Then he looked at Chief Kuku. The older man was nodding too.

*　　*　　*　　*　　*

The massacre of an estimated two thousand "native" warriors who died during the Ijebu Campaign spurred a debate later in the English Parliament. Several members of the House decried the brutality of using the Maxim machine gun against an ill-equipped native enemy.

This dissension against the policy of the Crown came from certain vocal back benchers of the opposition Liberal Party. These were the same radicals whose predecessors had pressed the British government to use its navy to forcefully stop the movement of slave ships of other nations on the high seas a generation earlier.

But the supporters, among the ruling Tory party, of the policy of using maximum force to advance the cause of empire, pointed out that the Maxim gun had saved the lives of British soldiers wherever it was used in the two years since it was deployed.

In the Ijebu Campaign, they pointed out, it allowed just twenty British officers and ninety-nine noncommissioned officers, leading 158 rank-and file-soldiers and 100 irregulars to force the defeat of an Ijebu army of ten thousand men, and to kill approximately two thousand of the native warriors.

Among this group was no less than an authority than Captain Frederick Lugard, who would later become the face of British imperialism in Nigeria. He was the brain behind the amalgamation that formed the Nigerian Federation in 1914.

"Pacification and empire building come with a price," he would write in his memoirs.

Apparently, the empire was all too ready to advance this philosophy. The price was paid with the blood of native warriors. In 1893, a year after the defeat of the Ijebus at Imagbon, using a single Maxim gun, a small British force of forty soldiers under Major Patrick Forbes destroyed a Matabele army of twenty thousand warriors in a battle fought on the South African veld near Bulawayo. This event paved the

OLADELE OLUSANYA

way for the colonization of that country, which was subsequently named Rhodesia, after Cecil Rhodes, the British businessman who bankrolled the expedition.

And what happened to Captain Bower, the dashing young *oyinbo* officer who shouldered the fifteen-pounder gun as the British forces forded the Yemoji River?

After being stationed in Ijebu-Ode for several months to maintain order with his Hausa soldiers, Bower returned to Lagos. He was then posted to Ibadan after the declaration of the Protectorate. He was the first *oyinbo* Resident of Ibadan. From his base in Agodi Hill, he oversaw the administration of several other former Yoruba city-states including Ondo, Ekiti, and Ilesha.

It was in his capacity as resident that Captain Bower masterminded the arrest and imprisonment of Kuku's old friend, the warrior Ogedengbe of Ilesha. The old warrior, now in his sixties, along with his war boys, had refused to lay down arms after peace had been declared by the British.

Ogedengbe and his war boys continued to terrorize the countryside around Ilesha. For several years, this band of former warriors behaved as if the old days of internecine war, rapine and disorder were not at an end. Perhaps Ogedengbe, who for most of his life, had known nothing but war, pined for the sound of those big guns at Kiriji. He, Ogedengbe, ever the old soldier, did not die, and did not want to fade away.

But at last, the day of reckoning came. Ogedengbe was chased, cornered and arrested by the native soldiers of Captain Bower, whose jurisdiction extended over Ijeshaland.

After a short time in detention in Ibadan, during which, no doubt, Bower made the old warrior acknowledge the might of British justice, Ogedengbe agreed to abide with the terms of the new peace.

He and his warriors were disarmed, and Ogedengbe returned at last to the peaceful life of a civilian. He went back to Ilesha to his wives and children. With the retirement of this symbol of the turbulent past, the age of the Yoruba warlords ended. A new era of peace and reconciliation began. The time of troubles that had devastated Yorubaland for a century was finally over.

And how about Bintu, the king's paramour?

Doubtless, she was set free like the rest of the slaves following the dictates of the new dispensation. There was a rumor amongst the warriors who fought at Imagbon that she was the female victim of that hideous sacrifice to Esu and Shigidi near the stream at Itokin. This was only a rumor however, as the king would not have given up his paramour for any Ijebu fetish.

The story that came down to us was that after her brief sojourn hiding out on the abandoned farm near Mamu with the three young war-deserters, Bintu was received back warmly at the *afin*. She stayed in Ijebu-Ode in the king's household as a favored concubine. She later gave birth to a child, a girl, who was raised by the king's own sister, who had no child of her own.

Another story had it that after she was set free after the coming of the British, Bintu sought the help of Hausa soldiers who had stayed behind to keep peace in Ijebu-Ode after the war. There was talk of her rendering some personal services to the head of the Hausa contingent.

Whatever it was, Bintu found her way back to her native Nupe country. There, she was honored and accepted by her people.

From the stories told in our family, it was not uncommon at the end of the nineteenth century in Ijebuland for many prominent Ijebu *obas* and chiefs to have children by their slaves. But the stigma of that old institution took a long time to die down.

Even late in the twentieth century, the sons and daughters of Odusanya, who knew of these stories from Ijebu-Ode, would point out some of their cousins and neighbors as children of slaves. Many of those so identified were members of prominent Ijebu families who now lived in Lagos. And they had made a name for themselves in the civil service, the professions or commerce.

The statement, made to sound like a question, would be in a low, conspiratorial voice.

"Nje e mo pe omo eru ni Mrs. Sowaja?" *Do you know that Mrs. Sowaja is the child of a slave?*

That phrase *omo eru,* child of a slave, was strange and alien to us, children of a new age. But the legacy and stigma of slavery, that peculiar institution of the nineteenth century, persisted well into our own time.

*   *   *   *   *

The proud and recalcitrant Ijebus soon found themselves being "civilized." This process occurred whether or not they wanted it.

At first, everyone said the stubborn Ijebu chiefs and their war boys would not acquiesce in this. But, against all predictions and expectations, the Ijebus adopted the white man's "civilization." And this proved to be to their great advantage.

Chief Kuku, Odusanya's mentor and protector, now became even more powerful and wealthy. The old gun runner became the master of new avenues of commerce thrown open to native-born entrepreneurs with the opening of the Ijebu trade corridor and the cessation of hostilities in the interior.

His business ventures expanded. They ranged from trading in timber, kola nut, and palm kernel to transportation. He bought native built canoes and motorboats imported from Germany. And for many years, he ran a lucrative ferry to Lagos from Epe and the Ijebu waterside. Then he brought in a Portuguese architect and engineer from Lagos who helped him design and build the first story building in Ijebuland.

Odusanya spent the first six months, after coming back from witnessing the signing of the great treaty of the Protectorate, learning and perfecting his grammar in English and Yoruba. This was at the insistence of Chief Kuku.

And it was Kuku's friend, the English missionary Reverend Pratt, one of the first to enter Ijebu-Ode after the ban on foreigners was lifted, who took Odusanya under his wings. Diligently, the white man taught the young Ijebu man to read and write in English and Yoruba.

Starting with the Yoruba alphabet, Odusanya spent hours saying aloud A—Aja, B—Bata, D—Doje. Then he switched to English. Odusanya tried his best to pronounce the "ch" sound without making it sound like "sh." But despite his diligence and persistence, the good reverend gentleman could not get Odusanya to pronounce his English words and phrases in the clipped tones of the Queen's English of his native Surrey. Try as he would, Odusanya retained his broad Ijebu dialect which spilled into his English.

The only book available to Odusanya for reference in the Yoruba language was given to him as a present by Rev. Hinderer, who had come from Oke Kudeti in Ibadan to visit Kuku. It was a well-thumbed copy of the Yoruba Bible translated years earlier by Ajayi Crowther, who Kuku said was a Saro from Lagos. On the thick black cover of this book were printed in bold gold letters the title, *Bibeli Mimo*.

Odusanya read the book daily. And he memorized words, phrases and whole passages. One of the phrases he liked best was from the book of Proverbs.

"Ogo lehin asiwere," it said. A rod for the fool's back. In Yoruba it sounded to Odusanya like *a rod on the back of the madman.*

The Ijebu dialect that Odusanya grew up with was not available in written form. Odusanya found to his chagrin that what he thought was his native tongue was much different from the Oyo Yoruba with which Rev. Ajayi Crowther had written his Yoruba Bible. Undoubtedly, by using the classic Yoruba dialect of the old Oyo Empire, Crowther wanted to simulate the high flown Elizabethan flourish of the King James English Bible.

Thus, Odusanya had to make an uneasy adjustment from Ijebu Yoruba to the Yoruba of Oyo and Ibadan. Still, he was thankful that Rev. Ajayi Crowther had translated the Bible into Yoruba half a century earlier in 1843. This gentleman had also published a small volume on Yoruba grammar.

Later in life, Odusanya would insist that his own children learn their Yoruba grammar by daily devotion to these two books. The advantage of this policy was that his children learned to write in their own language, and they learned their new religion too.

Odusanya also learned arithmetic and accounting. He spent many painful hours on fractions and compound interest. He learned how to keep a ledger. He wrote down credits and debits under their appropriate columns, and he balanced many real and fictitious accounts.

With his knowledge of *Gesi*, Odusanya was soon called upon to be a translator in the service of the Awujale and other prominent chiefs in Ijebu-Ode. He drafted many of the official letters, petitions, and missives sent between Ijebu-Ode and the colonial government in Lagos. Based on the way he was taught by the Englishman, Rev. Pratt, Odusanya always ended his correspondence, both official and personal, with the phrase:

I remain truly, Your most obedient servant, Emmanuel Jonathan Odusanya.

"Mo duro nihin," was how he wrote it in Yoruba.

Odusanya continued to live in Chief Kuku's house, for he was not married. He made the brief acquaintance of Captain Bower while that *oyinbo* officer was stationed in Ijebu-Ode. The dashing young

Englishman would ride by, tie his horse to a pillar at the front of the compound, then go into the house to discuss some problem of law and order with Chief Kuku.

Odusanya also got to know the Irishman, Mr. John McEwen. It was he who was brought in from Lagos to supervise the construction of the story building, which had been designed by the Portuguese architect, Pereira to replace Kuku's sprawling old compound in Ita Ntebo.

Odusanya would always remember the new additions to Kuku's *oriki* as his mentor became even more famous. Because of his influence and closeness to the few *oyinbo* men who lived in Ijebu-Ode or who passed through the town, Kuku was greeted by praise singers with the epithet, "A *ji b'oyinbo soro*." This meant he was the one who woke up in the morning to converse with white men.

Odusanya noted that power, in his native land, had shifted from the old traditional hierarchy to the hands of white men and their native-born subordinates. A local administration that answered to the British resident officer was now in place. It was called the Native Authority. It assumed all real legislative and administrative powers in Ijebu-Ode. This included levying taxes on market women and regulating the activity of local artisans.

Due to his position as translator, Odusanya became one of the agents of change that facilitated this transfer of power. For it was he who was sent for whenever the Awujale or some chief needed to communicate with a visitor from Lagos or any of the *oyinbo* army officers who were entrusted with training the local police force that would give muscle to the newly established Native Authority.

"E lo pe alakowe wa," the *oba* or chief would say.

Call the clerk.

And Odusanya would come. He kept his pen—a long polished piece of wood with a shiny metallic nib, not a feather quill that was still in use among the *Gesi* priests and educators of his day—along with his bottled ink, blotting paper and writing pad, in a small flat leather bag which he carried everywhere he went. He was paid well for his services as a translator and letter-writer.

A cooperative bank for farmers and traders was now open for business along Folagbade Street, the main thoroughfare in Ijebu-Ode that went from Ita Ntebo to Ita Afin and wound its way out of town toward Ijebu-Igbo. Odusanya opened an account at this bank at the first opportunity. He began to save his money in shillings and pence. He kept his blue bank "passbook" under his mattress when he slept at night. Odusanya knew that this small book was as good as the money it recorded, which was kept safely for him in a safe at the bank.

Wherever he went, everyone called him *Alakowe*. It was a word that, in Yoruba, went beyond mere acknowledgment of his status as a "clerk." "Alakowe" signified solidity and prestige, pointing Odusanya out as a member of the new educated class.

The Yoruba people had always paid attention to the power and meaning of words. Words were important when they were spoken. But they sounded even grander now that they could be read out from mysterious looking black print on a white piece of paper. Odusanya, the *alakowe* of Ijebu-Ode, was the possessor of *imo iwe* or book knowledge. As the *alakowe,* he was the person who owned the art of writing

It was during this time that Odusanya became a thinker. He began to think of the whys and hows of his existence. But as he did so, he began to lose his faith in the ways of belief of his fathers. The ruminations that agitated his mind during his flight from Imagbon came back again and again to him, and he realized that he had had these doubts about his beliefs for some time. The horror and calamity of that fateful day by the banks of Yemoji had only brought into focus the thoughts that had germinated in his mind, nourished by the radical ideas of his mentor, Chief Kuku.

From his exposure to the teachings and examples of Chief Kuku, Odusanya learned to be liberal and forward-looking in his social and religious views. As he looked around him in Ijebu-Ode, Odusanya could see that the old worship of his ancestors was dying out, largely replaced by two new religions, *esin igbagbo* and e*sin imale.* Both had been brought to Yorubaland by *ajeji*, foreigners.

Kuku told Odusanya that these two foreign sects originated from what *oyinbo* men called the Holy Land and Arabia. He said that this part of the world was not far, just across the Red Sea, from Nubia, the country where Oduduwa, the originator of Yoruba religion and traditions, was said to have been born.

Thus, in Kuku's view, the religion of the Yorubas came from the same source as those brought by the foreigners. But because these new ways of faith came with an impressive array of books, canons and tenets, they appealed to him, a man who loved knowledge and instruction.

Kuku was not alone in this preference. For the two foreign sects brought to Yorubaland by the *Oyinbo* and *Larubawa* people began to peel off converts at a rapid rate from among erstwhile worshippers of Orisanla and Orisa-oko. As the nineteenth century drew to a close, shrines of the ancient gods of Yorubaland were becoming a rare site in Ijebu-Ode.

Odusanya's mentor, Kuku, was a man whose ideas were advanced for his time. Often his thought processes proved too complex for Odusanya. This was how Kuku explained his thinking on religion to his protégé one afternoon.

"I have known too many priests. And I have seen too many wars." Kuku said this all of a sudden, looking up from his book.

Odusanya was trying to balance a ledger while his mentor read from a book in *Gesi*. He nodded without looking up from his ledger. He already knew that Kuku believed that everyone should be free to worship whatever deity he wanted to and by whatever means he choose.

But Kuku continued, "Most religious rites are the products of our desires and wishes as humans. They fulfill our desire for ceremony and symbols.

"But all too often, religious cremonies merely serve the interests of priests and leaders of sects who use them to maintain allegiance to the sect. Especially is this so with the traditional religion of our people."

Odusanya was not surprised when, not long after this, Chief Kuku completely abandoned any pretense of adhering to the worship of the traditional gods of Yorubaland. But he was surprised at the direction of his mentor's conversion.

For soon after the dawn of the new century, which was ushered in with prayers and fireworks in Ijebu-Ode following the example of Lagos, Kuku publicly declared his conversion to the Moslem faith. This was in 1903. It was said that Kuku's exile in Ibadan had put him in proximity with Hausa Moslem preachers who lived at Isale Gambari. It was their ideas, people said, that had influenced him.

When Odusanya asked his mentor about his choice, Kuku said, "I love the simplicity of Islam and the absence of priests in that religion."

"A true religion does not need priests," he explained.

The Moslem *imams,* he said, were scholars who were there to help people decipher the message of the Koran. Kuku also told Odusanya that he admired the commitment of the Moslem religion to the idea of the oneness of mankind. To him, Islam was the one true universal faith

"No race is superior to another. Therefore, there can only be one deity for all peoples," he said.

"And this universal god is a spirit, not a person. I cannot accept that this spirit resides in any sculpted figure of stone or wood. And certainly, it is not in a river or a tree, or somewhere in the sky."

"Best of all, there is no compulsion in Islam," Kuku added, quoting from their holy book.

As to the origin of Islam among our people, Kuku explained to Odusanya that Islam had been practiced in Yorubaland for a longer time that most people realized.

"Islam was brought to Yorubaland from the Mali Empire of Mansa Musa five hundred years ago. Over these centuries, it has been embraced by many Yoruba kings and chieftains. However, it did not become popular with the common people until the time of troubles came upon us a hundred years ago with the crisis involving Afonja and Alaafin Aole. This coincided with an influx of Hausa and Fulani Moslem preachers into Yorubaland from across *Odo Oya*.

"I have evidence that some of the Alaafins before the time of Abiodun, practiced Islam in the *afin*. But they continued to pay lip service to Ogun, Sango and the *egungun* cults that were popular among the people.

"Many of these rulers tried to combine the two religions. Thus, many *afins* in Yorubaland had a mosque within their walls alongside the shrines devoted to the ancient deities of our people. The first mosque here in Ijebu-Ode was built at the time of Awujale Fidipote when I was still a child."

Kuku went on. "Our people called this new religion *esin mali*, the religion from Mali. This was later corrupted to *esin imole*. It is certainly not *imo lile,* the hard religion, that some people wrongly interpret it to be.

"Some of the old priests of our traditional Yoruba religion even incorporated Arabic *suras* into Ifa theology. A whole Ifa *odu* was added in this way many centuries ago. It is known as *odu imale.* I know because I have studied it."

But despite the many fine and convincing arguments of his mentor, Odusanya did not follow Chief Kuku into the Moslem faith. When he was baptized as a Christian at the newly-built St. Savior's CMS church in a ceremony that was attended by Chief Kuku and the Awujale, Odusanya took the name Emmanuel.

The catechist had explained to him that his new name in Hebrew meant "*God is with us.*" To Odusanya, with his penchant for symbolism, it was the repudiation of his experience with the pagan Odu cult.

Odusanya loved reading the Old Testament, especially stories of the early kingdom of Judah. He identified with David, the low-born commoner who became king of Israel. And he wept at the death of Saul and his son Jonathan on Mount Gilboa. He memorized with poignant sadness that elegy composed by David for Saul and Jonathan.

> *Wo bi awon alagbara ti subu laarin ogun.*
> *Ha, Jonatani, iwo ti a pa ni oke giga re!*

> *See how mighty warriors fell in battle.*
> *O Jonathan, you were killed in your beloved hills!*

That story of the tragic defeat of Israel reminded Odusanya of the experience of his own Ijebu people fighting the British at Imagbon. Thus, it was to honor the memory of his friend Musiliu, who died on the riverbank of Yemoji, that Odusanya chose "Jonathan" as his second Christian name.

After he was baptized, Odusanya adopted as his personal prayer a psalm of David, which he said every night before he went to bed.

> *Emi yi o gbe ori mi si oke iwon ni.*
> *Niboni iranlowo mi yio ti wa?*

> *I will lift up my eyes to the hills.*
> *From where will my help come?*

Odusanya was not alone. All around him in Ijebu-Ode, practically everyone he knew, sooner or later, became baptized to the faith of the *onigbagbo*. It was a wave of conversion that depopulated the ranks of the traditionalists at the turn of the century, leaving only a few holdouts who stuck stubbornly to the old ways.

Borne on the wings of this massive conversion to Christianity, the fever to copy and to learn the white man's ways caught on all over Ijebuland. And from the beginning, education of children in the *onigbagbo* mission schools was used by missionaries in Ijebuland as a two-sided weapon. Young people learned to read and write in the white man's tongue. And they were converted to Christianity.

Moslem families who were wary of allowing their children to receive a Christian education, remained less educated as the years went by, and were disadvantaged in getting jobs. The few Moslem children who were admitted to mission schools were converted to Christianity. And they were given Christian names. Musa became Moses, and Moriama became Mary.

The conversion to Christianity of children whose parents were "keferi" or pagan was even easier. These children were allowed to keep the pagan last names of their fathers, such as Esubiyi, Sangobiyi or Osolanke. But their first names were picked from the Christian Bible—Isaac, John, and Ezekiel. These children never had the chance of knowing the old gods of their fathers. Many of them went home with an evangelical fervor. They destroyed the graven images and shrines of their fathers.

In Lagos, the first secondary school for boys, the CMS Grammar School, was established in 1857. After Ijebuland opened its towns and villages to Christian missions and schools after 1892, young men who could speak *Gesi* and who had been trained at the Grammar School in Lagos, moved to Ijebu-Ode to set up churches and schools.

These young, energetic teachers made such an impression on the people of Ijebu-Ode that even the Awujale sent his sons to study at the newly opened St. Savior's Primary School not far from Ita Afin in Ijebu-Ode.

*   *   *   *   *

After his stint as a clerk and translator for the Awujale, Odusanya decided to go into business. He wanted to be a farmer.

In the aftermath of the Imagbon War, young men in Ijebu-Ode could no longer follow the ancient pastime of war. Hunting was now taken up by many of these men, especially with the profusion of guns and muskets left over from the war. But this occupation was not to prove very profitable. For many would-be hunters found out that the habitat of big game like leopards and elephants that should bring them money, had disappeared from Ijebuland during their own lifetime.

This was partly a result of their own activities in hunting and killing these large mammals with their new improved firearms. But mostly, it was due to the widespread burning and clearing of ancient forests carried out by farmers cultivating the land. For farming became a very attractive and respectable livelihood for former warriors who did not mind toiling in the sun. It was this group that Odusanya hoped to join.

Odumosu explained his plan and rationale to his mentor, Kuku. "I know I can make a lot of money as a trader who is a farmer. The produce I will sell as a merchant would be what I grow on my own farm instead of something I will have to buy from someone else."

Odusanya knew that he did not even have to take his produce to the coast to sell to make a living as a farmer. For Ijebu-Ode had its own farm market. It was located on the edge of the town, near the old town walls where the farmlands began.

In this market, farmers sold their *gari, elubo, isu,* and *gbaguda.* The traders who bought their produce came from far and wide, not just from Ijebu-Ode. They bought *eja gbigbe, eran igbe, ogede,* and *agbado,* along with vegetables such as *ẹfọ-tẹtẹ, gbure, iṣapa, ila, apon* and *ewedu* which they took away in large quantities to sell elsewhere.

Luckily for Odusanya and other would-be farmers, Ijebu-Ode had for centuries being renowned for its metalwork. Freed from the need to manufacture war tools such as swords and spears, Ijebu blacksmiths began to make farm implements such as hoes, rakes, and cutlasses.

But to make decent money from farming, Odusanya also knew that he had to have a large farm. And very few young, first-time farmers like Odusanya had the means or the capital to acquire such big farms.

Subsistence farming was the norm for most farmers in Ijebu-Ode at that time. Land inherited from ancestors was shared among all the grown men in the family. No one had heard of hired labor. Each farmer used his children and wives to till the toil, plant the crops, and bring in the harvest. These relatives also helped him take the produce to the market. Thus the output from these small farms remained modest. Most of the harvest ended up being consumed by the family, and little cash was earned.

But from the start, Odusanya told himself that he wanted to be a rich farmer. Since he did not inherit land from his father, he would have to lease land from families who lived on arable land outside the town of Ijebu-Ode. And he would have to pay his landowner an annual rent, called *Iṣakọlẹ* or *Owo-Onilẹ*.

Kuku in his turn explained to Odusanya that to achieve his dream of great wealth from farming, he would need to grow what he called "cash" crops. He told his protégé stories of rich farmers who were paid a lot of money for these "cash" crops by *oyinbo* merchants and ship captains in Lagos who shipped these products to Europe. He explained that that was because people living in *oyinbo* countries far away across the sea had developed an insatiable appetite for delicacies such as chocolate which were made from agricultural produce grown in Yorubaland.

Indeed, palm kernel, kola nut, and tobacco were the first cash crops grown in Ijebuland to be exported to Europe in this way. But by the time Odusanya set his mind to become a farmer, a new crop, cocoa, was king.

Cocoa was said to have been introduced to Ijebuland many years before the Imagbon War. But very few people knew about this. Chief Kuku told Odusanya the story of how *igi koko*, the cocoa tree, came to Ijebuland.

"Dried cocoa fruits were first brought to Lagos from Brazil around 1850. After Lagos became a colony, trade in cocoa boomed. This was because the planting of cash crops like cocoa was promoted by the governor of the colony as an alternative to slave trading which had been banned.

"The planting of the first cocoa tree in Yorubaland took place around 1880 on a farm in Agege, an Awori village about half a day's journey north of Lagos Island.

"From what I heard, the first Yoruba to get hold of cocoa seeds for planting purchased them from a Brazilian ship captain. He was a Saro who had settled in Lagos after fighting for the *Gesi* on their warships. He is dead now. His name was Captain J. P. L. Davies."

Kuku continued, "Davies gave those seeds to another Saro named Coker, who had a farm in Agege. Coker was the president of the Agege Planters Union.

"Coker and his friends were determined to make money from growing and exporting cash crops. They were all educated expatriates from Sierra Leone. Many of them were the children of Yoruba slaves who had been set free from Portuguese slave ships by the British Navy."

According to Kuku, these men put aside their European clothes and went to work with a will.

"They seeded the rich soil of Agege with this new crop from Brazil. And they used new farming techniques of rotation, irrigation and fertilization which they had been taught by white men in their mission schools in Sierra Leone.

"Coker and his friends reaped the fruits of their labor. Within a few years, they were making a lot money from the farming of cocoa, which they exported through the port of Lagos."

But after some years, according to the story that Kuku told Odusanya, their intensive cultivation of cocoa exhausted the delicate soil of Agege.

But these men did not give up. They searched further afield, going north until they got to Ijebuland. To their joy, they found that the soil of Ijebu and Remo was even more suited for cocoa planting than their farms in Agege.

"This is how cocoa seeds were introduced to Ijebuland. Within a few years, our farms in Ijebu became the largest sites for cocoa cultivation in all Yorubaland."

Kuku said this with a light in his eyes that could only be ascribed to his well-known Ijebu patriotism. His enthusiasm was shared by his protégé. Odusanya made up his mind to join the ranks of the wealthy cocoa farmers of Ijebuland.

And as he began to look for land for what he knew would have to be a large farm, Odusanya remembered the abandoned farm near the hamlet of Mamu where he and his friends, Taju and Fajimi, had hidden after the Imagbon War.

Odusanya talked to Kuku about this land, which he thought the older man should remember. After all, he and Kuku had built on that farm a shed to store a harvest of corn.

And of course, Kuku remembered. He told Odusanya that he did not have any claim on that farm or the surrounding forestland. It was mostly a wild, virgin forest, untouched by the toil of men, which meant that no family laid claim to it.

Odusanya went to Mamu. He secured a large tract of the vast forest land around the abandoned farm of his wartime exile.

He worked hard. He cut down trees and cleared thick undergrowth. He loosened the thick black soil with his hoe. It was in this way that Odusanya planted his first crop of cocoa. He had obtained his seed through a business contact of Chief Kuku who lived in Ibadan.

And when the Baale of the nearby hamlet of Mamu learned that Odusanya was the *alakowe* who was a friend of the Awujale, he gave him no trouble. It was true that the abandoned farmland and the surrounding forest were under the jurisdiction of the Baale, but neither he nor his fellow villagers had any use for the land. The Baale gave Odusanya permission to have perpetual use of the land. As much land as he could prepare for planting was his for the taking.

After this, Odusanya went back to Ijebu-Ode. He returned to Mamu with several friends and relatives, who helped him to clear and burn more land. Odusanya was now able to plant more rows of his cocoa seed. But soon, it became clear to him and the people he brought with him from Ijebu-Ode that the work required to plant the land was too much for them to handle.

So, on the advice of Kuku, Odusanya went to Isale Ganbari in Ibadan. He brought back dozens of young, muscular Hausa men. Determined and focused, he turned these greenhorns into farmers within a few weeks.

This was how Odusanya became a prominent cocoa farmer in Ijebu-Ode. With his ability to read and write, he became secretary of the Cocoa Farmers' Cooperative Union of Western Nigeria, when a local chapter of that organization was established in Ijebu-Ode.

* * * * *

Everyone in Ijebu-Ode knew that a young man who owned a cocoa farm from which he was making a lot of money would soon be looking for a wife.

Thus it was that Odusanya took a fancy to the daughter of one of the leading families in Ijebu-Ode. Her name was Oku. She was only sixteen years old when Odusanya paid her father a substantial bride price in kola nut, yams, and palm oil, and took her to wife.

Their union was fruitful. The birth of his first-born son was the proudest day of Odusanya's life. And prouder still was he when he took his eight-day-old son to St. Saviour's CMS church to have the Anglican priest officiate his baptism. The child was named Daniel, after the great prophet of Judah. His second name was Folorunsho, which in Yoruba meant "placed in the care of God."

When his wife gave him his second child, also a boy, Odusanya also gave the child a Christian name, which the boy would reject when he grew up. For Odusanya's second son preferred his Yoruba name, which was Olubadejo. *God keeps company with the crown.*

When Badejo boy grew up and had gone to school and knew how to put words together in the Gesi tongue, he would say to people he met, "Truth is next to godliness." We are told that Badejo largely lived up to the name his father gave him by keeping close company with truth all his life.

The next child born by Oku to the now wealthy farmer of Mamu was a girl. She was named Adebowale, which meant "the crown comes home."

The use of *ade,* or "crown" as a prefix to a child's name in Yorubaland denoted origin from a royal family. For at this time, Odusanya remembered that he was the grandson of an Akarigbo of Shagamu. And indeed, Odusanya would give many of his children names with the *ade* prefix. And he made sure that his children knew the roots of their royal pedigree from the land of Remo.

The time came when Odusanya felt that he was wealthy enough to marry a second wife. He knew that the priests of his *onigbagbo* religion railed against the marrying of many wives. In their church sermons, these men of God called it a "pagan" practice. But many good Christians in Ijebu-Ode, like Odusanya, who regularly went to church, went against the teaching of their pastors in this regard.

Odusanya and others like him preferred to take their precepts from the Old Testament. From their reading of that ancient text, they pointed to the examples of Abraham, Jacob, David, and Solomon, who had many wives and hundreds of concubines, and still found favor in the sight of God.

For his second wife, Odusanya looked for another maiden from a prominent family in Ijebu-Ode. With his booming cocoa farm, Odusanya had indeed become very eligible. The family of his intended bride felt honored when Odusanya approached the head of the family and respectfully asked for the hand of their daughter.

This maiden was Morohunkeji. Her family was wealthy and famous, her grandfather having been a *seriki* of Ijebuland. Morohunkeji had three daughters for Odusanya, all of whom became highly educated and successful. Her only son, named Adeolu, was Odusanya's favorite child. His name in Yoruba told everyone that he was the "crown of the lord." It was said that Odusanya spoilt the boy Adeolu in a way that outraged even his mother.

Tragically, Adeolu died in young adulthood. But he left behind a daughter, named Morolahun, whose name meant "I have something of worth to hold on to."

It was at this time that many people in Ijebu-Ode, including his wives and children, began to call Odusanya "Baba Mamu." Odusanya now expanded his farm. He increased the number of his Hausa field hands who he continued to recruit from Isale Gambari in Ibadan.

And as a result of his frequent trips to Ibadan, Odusanya made the acquaintance of many businessmen in that bustling city, including the noted entrepreneur, Chief Ogunsola, with whom he shared a very profitable partnership in the cultivation of cocoa. For by this time, the old Ijebu antagonism against Ibadan had been forgotten.

As secretary of the Cocoa Farmers Union, Odusanya's reputation was established. His word was respected everywhere he went. Even the Awujale recognized his worth, and Odusanya was given the chieftaincy title of Olotu Ona of Ijebu-Ode. He continued to work hard as a farmer and trader. And when he was not on his farm in Mamu, he carried himself with the gravitas of a prosperous man about town.

He also enlarged his compound in Ita Ntebo and built a new house in Eti-tale. This area of Ijebu-Ode derived its name from its location at the edge of Ijebu-Ode's famous night market. Odusanya's house in Eti-tale was leased to visitors from out of town, mainly businessmen and *Gesi* priests from Ibadan and Lagos, who stayed there for weeks, even months.

Odusanya now convinced himself that he was ready for his third wife. In his now comfortable world of polygamy, the words of an English adage, which he knew from Kuku having said it so many times, seemed apt, "In for a penny, in for a pound."

For his third wife, Baba Mamu turned to the neighboring land of Remo. He sought the hand of a young widow from Ikenne. Her name was Efunyemi.

The betrothal of Efunyemi to Odusanya was a ceremony that was attended by no less than five great chiefs of Ijebu-Ode who represented the Awujale. They were matched by a large contingent from Ikenne. This included the bride's father, who Baba Mamu was told was a famous Remo warrior in his day. It was great Solesi himself.

Solesi brought with him three Ikenne chiefs of high rank who were prominent in the *osugbo* council of their town. He also brought his old troupe of drummers and singers who tried to make money from the other guests by singing the *oriki* and praises of anyone of importance they saw. Solesi did not bring his famous war horse, Mapo, although this beast was frequently alluded to in conversations with the men from Ikenne. This was the horse that was said to have once belonged to Ogunmola, the late Bashorun of Ibadan.

It was explained to Baba Mamu's family and friends that the *oba* of Ikenne could not attend. But the Alakenne sent his *akoda*, who brought the king's royal totem. This was a long pole about seven feet tall, which was decorated with colorful beads and crowned at the top by a shiny bronze eagle.

There was a small wrangle about the bride price. But everyone on both sides knew that this was not a serious disagreement. Even in those days, the "bride price" in Ijebuland was largely a symbolic amount. It was a token of faith to indicate that the husband valued his bride and would take care of her.

The traditional marriage ceremony that followed between Odusanya and Efunyemi was colorful and grand. Evocative of the old days, some new touches were added that bore witness to the new-found wealth of Ijebu-Ode. No expense was spared, and no ceremony was omitted to make this *igbeyaiwo* an event that would be remembered for years afterward.

The women of Ita Ntebo in particular had a field day. A group of elaborately dressed women from Baba Mamu's family, including Odusanya's two wives, approached the bride's family from Ikenne. Kneeling, they greeted them thus.

Eweso o, yemi
Eweso o, bami
Eweso o, dede ara adugbo

Greetings, my mothers
Greetings, my fathers
Greetings, all you neighbors and kinsmen

Then, these matrons of Ita Ntebo, still on their knees, formally asked the Ikenne group to allow their daughter Efunyemi to be taken in hand by Odusanya, her new husband.

Baba Mamu was all smiles as he and his young, new wife sat together on two elaborately carved wooden chairs under a colorful canopy.

It was a bright and cloudless day. The gods in heaven looked down with favor on the happy couple. A cool breeze blew across the open field where the ceremony took place. Scattered all over this open space were tents, canopies and large colorful umbrellas that shielded the celebrants and guests from the sun.

The evening air cooled the faces, bodies and necks of the participants and guests who had endured all morning and afternoon the stuffy heat made worse by their heavy *aso-ofi* outfits. And since it was now noticeably cooler, the bride had stopped waving across her face and neck the ceremonial fan that she delicately held in her right hand.

The groom and bride were made to taste food from the same dish together for the first time. It was a bowl of *ikokore*, considered by many to be the national dish of Ijebuland. It was a symbol of the life they would share together from that day on.

Husband and wife now looked at each other with relief and appreciation. For it was only then that the couple could appraise each other with any degree of focus or attention.

Baba Mamu admired his bride's attractive face and shapely body. He noted with approval the rich *aso-ofi buba, iro, ipele* and *gele*, and the *ilekes, egbas,* and *yeris*, necklaces, bracelets, and earrings that adorned her youthful body.

Under this appreciative gaze, Efunyemi, far from being embarrassed, beamed and smiled. Though she was tired, and her legs and arms ached, she was happy. She had also appraised Odusanya's tall, commanding figure and dignified, serious mien. She told herself that her father's choice of a husband for her could not be faulted. Despite the long travel from Ikenne, and the long prayers and ceremonies earlier that day which had made her tired and apprehensive, Efunyemi was relieved and happy that the rite of her *igbeyawo* would soon be over.

Thus it was that despite his open and honest embrace of the Christian faith, Baba Mamu, the well-to-do cocoa farmer and man about town in Ijebu-Ode, became an entrenched polygamist.

* * * * *

In the years ahead, Baba Mamu's household grew. His house in Ita Ntebo was always full of women and children. His three wives cooked, gossiped, laughed, and quarreled as women would who lived close together in the same home. And their numerous children played, laughed, and fought as would be expected of children in a large household, especially a polygamous one in Ijebu-Ode in the early years of the twentieth century.

Baba Mamu was kind and attentive to his wives and children. Apart from the area of their education, where he would brook no mention or thought of failure, he was no more strict or overbearing with his children than other fathers in Ijebu-Ode of that age. He rarely beat his children, especially the girls, even for the most serious infractions like lying or playing truant in school. He left their corporal chastening to their mothers.

And unlike many farmers of his day, Baba Mamu did not put his children to work on his farm. He sent them all to school. All Baba Mamu's children attended St. Savior's School, the CMS primary school in Ijebu-Ode. After this, the boys were sent to the boarding secondary school—the Ijebu-Ode Grammar School—a boys-only establishment fashioned on the English model which was opened by the CMS in 1913. There were no secondary schools for girls in Ijebu-Ode at that time.

Most of Baba Mamu's sons who attended the grammar school later joined the colonial civil service or worked for the Nigerian Railways, an occupation that took them to the north of the country where they lived and worked in Hausa and Fulani towns with names strange to the Ijebu ear—Zungeru, Kafanchan, and Kaura Namoda.

Baba Mamu himself had never lived outside Ijebuland. His experience with travel was limited to the two trips he had undertaken as a young man with his mentor Chief Kuku to the signing of the treaties at Kiriji and Oyo. This was apart from his short business trips to Ibadan. Thus, those towns with strange names in the North, where his sons lived and worked, seemed to Baba Mamu to be farther away from Yorubaland than the places Oranmiyan visited during his travels and conquests.

Baba Mamu's fame as a successful farmer and philanthropist of the church was now established throughout Ijebu-Ode. Although he spent most of his time on his farm at Mamu, he was well-known in his neighborhood of Ita Ntebo. He was also not infrequently seen at the *afin*.

This former warrior, who had spent time in a pagan cult in the *odu* forest, became a pillar of the CMS church. He contributed money for the renovation and beautification of St. Savior's Church, which later became the cathedral and seat of the bishop of the Ijebu diocese.

After he met Rev. Ransome-Kuti, the Egba principal of the grammar school, Baba Mamu, and the educator became good friends. Despite the difference in age, for the principal was born a year before the Imagbon War in which Baba Mamu fought as a teenage warrior, they found that they had many things in common.

The two men debated and argued about theology, the *oriki* of the ruling houses of Yorubaland, and the place of corporal punishment in the education of boys.

On the first, there was some disagreement, since Baba Mamu tended to favor the Old Testament to buttress some of his own habits including his adherence to the institution of polygamy. And he never fully understood the concept of the Holy Trinity.

"God is god. And he is one God," Baba Mamu would declare with stubborn exasperation.

He added for good effect that there was no mention of the Holy Trinity in the Old Testament. Ransome-Kuti retorted that this was the reason why there *was* a New Testament.

But on the issue of the education of boys, the views of the two men converged. The injunction from the Bible that said, "Spare the rod and spoil the child," was Ransome-Kuti's operating philosophy. It was an ethic that was fully shared and embraced by the other man. This was what made Baba Mamu promise that he would send all his sons to the good reverend's boarding school.

Baba Mamu liked in particular a story he heard about Ransome-Kuti. The principal was said to have punished one of the new boys in Form One at the grammar school by having him publicly caned during the morning assembly. The erring schoolboy, not used to the strict

OLADELE OLUSANYA

discipline of the grammar school, had broken bounds by sneaking out of the dormitory to go home. He wanted to eat *ikokore* prepared by his mother.

Though he himself rarely administered corporal punishment to his children, Baba Mamu approved this essential disciplinary practice when it was duly performed by a schoolmaster.

It was around this time, when he was cementing his great friendship with Rev. Ransome-Kuti, that Baba Mamu made a rare error of judgment that would cost him dear and lose him a close friend.

*   *   *   *   *

Chief Odugbesan was one of the most successful farmers in Ijebu-Ode. He was also a good friend of Odusanya with whom he shared a passion for the cultivation of cocoa as a cash crop. Odugbesan was well-known and popular around town. He was a cousin of the Awujale, with whom he shared a grandfather who had reigned as monarch of Ijebu-Ode before the time of the Imagbon War.

Chief Odugbesan was comfortable enough as a cocoa farmer. He fed his three wives and educated his children. He took care of his responsibilities to his extended family and as a chieftain on the Awujale's council, the *Ilamuren*. But he did not become very rich until by a stroke of fate, a young man was introduced to him by a good friend to work for him as a bookkeeper.

The young man's name was Ojo Madarikan. The friend who introduced him to Chief Odugbesan gave him good recommendations, saying that although Ojo was not from Ijebu, he knew his family in Ibadan, and that he came of good stock. His parents had died tragically when he was young. And the guardian who had brought him up and trained him in business vouched for him.

And indeed, Ojo proved his worth from the first week of going to work for Chief Odugbesan. He followed his employer to his farm at Oru. Assiduously, he made an inventory of all the stored seeds of cocoa and other produce on the farm that had been bagged waiting to be sent to the produce agent in Shagamu. He counted all the trees and even the seedlings that were still to be planted.

Within three months, Odugbesan's profit doubled due to the improved economy of management that Ojo introduced, not just to the farming side of the business, but to the transportation and selling of the cocoa pods. It was Ojo who talked personally and persuasively to the agent at Shagamu. He bargained with this man until Odugbesan obtained a better price per pound for his cash crop than the other farmers.

Of course, after this, Ojo got a raise. But Odugbesan came to regard this useful and efficient young man as a son. He gave Ojo a room in his own house at Ita Ntebo. And secretly, he started to debate with himself which of his three daughters might be suitable to be given in marriage, when the time came, to this fine young man.

For as my mother Adedotun who knew him in those days told us later, Ojo was a fine-looking young man. He had come several times to visit Baba Mamu in their house in Ita Ntebo in the company of Chief Odugbesan.

As Adedotun recalled, he was light-complexioned, slim of build, and of medium height. Everyone knew he was from Ibadan, but he had no facial marks. He had a laugh that was innocent and unguarded. It was a laugh that was natural, calming, and inviting, even to a child. It spoke of intimacy, forthrightness, and a lack of guile that was pleasant and disarming.

Adedotun could not help noticing his eyes. The two irises were of different colors. If one looked closely at that pleasant face, one saw that while one eye was light brown speckled with gray, the other was a homogenous, brooding light gray that was the color of the sky during the harmattan. Ojo also had an unconscious habit of blinking the left eye when he wanted to make a point. Women thought this tic made him even more charming and amiable. Ojo's easy but compelling charm captivated women especially. Every girl or woman that met him fell in love with him. Or they felt they should.

Perhaps the reason they felt that way was because Ojo was different from any other boy or man they knew. He was clean and fresh, handsome and intelligent. He was every girl's mother's dream. He was always dressed in the latest European style, a real *akowe*. To the people of Ijebu-Ode, he seemed the embodiment of the new educated class, the model for the future of our people.

When he spoke, people watched his lips and wanted their children, when they grew up, to speak like him. His English came out in clipped tones, like the way the *oyinbo* spoke. And his Yoruba was classic, as if a catechist trained at St Andrew's College in Oyo was reading *Iwe Ekisodu,* the Book of Exodus, from Ajayi Crowther's translation of the Yoruba Bible.

Ojo was always very courteous and polite to the three wives of Chief Odugbesan, now that he had come to live with them. He won them over by offering to help them with chores around the household, whenever he was around.

Who would chop up some firewood for Mama Olobi for her wood fire? Who would fill up the giant barrel of drinking water that was kept in the center of the backyard? And who bought a costly length of *ankara* print imported from Holland as he passed through the market at Shagamu while on a trip to the produce agent, to be presented as gifts to all the three women? It was Ojo.

In this way did Ojo worm his way onto the heart of Odugbesan's household. His pleasant and easy charm, directed at the womenfolk, captivated and ensnared them in his power. Chief Odugbesan's youngest wife in particular, the twenty-three-year-old Bosede, looked just once at Ojo, and she melted in adoration and desire of him.

Bosede was a slim and graceful girl, taller than her portly husband, with small breasts and narrow hips that were like those of a boy. She had large, dark impudent eyes that looked out at the world with a cool, slightly mocking appraisal. Her nervous, impatient hands seemed always to be searching for something to do. She yearned for love, adventure, or indeed, anything that would break the dull monotony of her life as the junior wife in a polygamous household.

The first time she was introduced to Ojo, Bosede had to look away from the young man, and run, confused to her room, giving some excuse about something she had to get for her child.

Back in her room, Bosede thought she was going to swoon. She found it difficult to breathe. She removed her clothes and lay on the iron bed, which her husband, to the envy and jealousy of the other wives, had bought for her soon after he had brought her to his home.

As she lay naked, dazed and dizzy on her bed, images of the convoluted cosmology of her Ijebu people filled Bosede's vision. Floating before her half-closed eyes were visions of gods and demigods that had been with her people from very old times. She saw *iwin, ebora, and anjonu,* maleficent spirits that swarmed out of dark secret chambers that men and women, to preserve their sanity, dared not peep into.

But the voices of these demons came to her, summoning her to follow them into their dark caves. And Bosede found that she could not resist them. She could only hearken and obey. She did not ask, "Where are you leading me?"

For a long time, Bosede did not get up from her bed, with its crumpled bedcover made out of an old *iro* and its thin, hard mattress filled with dried grass. She continued to lay there. For what she had seen in those dark caves frightened, but excited her. It was a vision of lust and forbidden desire.

A strange and heady feeling of wantonness came over her, confirming what she already knew when she staggered out of her husband's parlor. She had taken one look at that strange young man who she had never met before that day, and she *knew* she wanted him to possess her.

Bosede tried to be rational and to take stock. She was the young and beautiful wife of Chief Odugbesan, an important chieftain of Ijebu-Ode and close kinsman of the Awujale. She was a woman and a wife who should be the queen of her citadel. But she was weak and vulnerable. Her stronghold lay exposed, robbed of its defenses. The entrance to its secret vault lay open, unlocked by the keeper herself, for a handsome young pillager to despoil of its most valued treasure—her pride and wifely virtue.

And strangely, it gave her a perverse pleasure to know that she wanted her defenses to be overcome and her treasures pillaged. She wanted to be ravished and taken away by this young man to a a strange and far place where no one would ask questions.

Bosede felt for the first time in her life that she was a female who could be adored, worshipped, and caressed by someone like this masculine young man. Ojo was about her own age. She told herself that she was a maiden with as yet unsatisfied urges. She was married and had a child, and had experienced the burden, if not the pleasure, of her husband's body probing deep into hers. She knew this to be her duty, a wifely obligation in exchange for her position in that privileged household. But what she felt now was different. It was a naked, sheer desire, an ache and a longing that made her pant for breath.

Suddenly, she felt that her husband was too old for her. Her father should not have arranged the marriage in the first place, she told herself. He had been lured by greed and Odugbesan's wealth and high social position in Ijebu-Ode society, which her father thought would rub off on him. She remembered that the bride price paid for her had made people open their mouth in astonishment.

Bosede closed her eyes. She imagined that the young man was with her. She touched her naked body and imagined it was Ojo doing it to her. She felt his hands touch her buttocks and fondle her breasts, and as he lay beside her, tenderly probe her deep and secret places. Somewhere in a deep recess of her body, a muscle twitched. A warm feeling suffused her body. She felt drowsy and languorous, and she went to sleep.

*   *   *   *   *

Bosede was not the only female in Chief Odugbesan's household to have been seduced by Ojo's charms. The day came when Chief Odugbesan's fifteen-year-old daughter, Olusade, confessed to her mother that she had not had her monthly periods for three months. She said Ojo was responsible.

Apparently, she had been sneaking into Ojo's room every night for several months while the household was asleep, creeping stealthily out of the very room she shared with her mother, and tiptoeing silently down the dark corridor to slip into Ojo's bed. Ojo always had his door open for her.

Her mother was livid. How would the family bear this disgrace?

But Chief Odugbesan surprised everyone by being totally accommodating and forgiving with the young man. He was very practical in thinking of a solution to resolve the situation. The truth was that Odugbesan had secretly hoped he could give one of his daughters in marriage to this incomparable young man who he had begun to look upon as a son.

A betrothal was hastily arranged, and a small traditional engagement was celebrated. But one condition was stipulated at the insistence of the girl's mother, Aduke. Ojo had to leave Chief Odugbesan's house. Arrangement was made for him to rent a room in a house belonging to one of Odugbesan's acquaintances in Eti-tale.

Ojo agreed to leave the girl alone until she had her baby in her parents' house after which the full traditional marriage would be performed, and she would move in with Ojo. He was apologetic and respectful, and he agreed to accept all the old man's conditions and stipulations. He personally visited Chief Odugbesan late one evening, and in the presence of all the wives and the whole family, prostrated before the chief and asked for his forgiveness for violating his daughter against all traditional norms and protocol.

By this time, Odugbesan had come to trust the young man so much that he was now sending him on confidential errands to deposit money in the Cooperative Bank at Ijebu-Ode or to accompany consignments of farm produce to the agent in Shagamu. Ojo would collect the money and bring it back to Ijebu-Ode to be deposited in the bank.

Odugbesan was a chieftain of Ijebu-Ode with close connections to the *afin*, but he had little of the white man's education. So he allowed Ojo to complete and sign most of his paperwork. He permitted the young man, who he now trusted more than his own family, to have access to his bank account, to deposit and withdraw money on his behalf.

The arrangement with the bank was that Ojo could deposit any amount of money. But for withdrawals of more than five pounds, a written and signed instrument from Chief Odugbesan must be submitted. For this purpose, a sample of Chief Odugbesan's signature was obtained in duplicate and stored in a file in the bank. As Odugbesan's secretary and bookkeeper, this arrangement only seemed proper and convenient.

One day, Ojo was sent to take a consignment of cocoa and other produce to the agent in Shagamu. For weeks, the farm had amassed a great store of produce including hundreds of bags of cocoa pods that were stored in sheds on the farm at Oru.

Normally they sent these consignments to Shagamu every month, but Ojo had suggested to Odugbesan that they should wait four months so that his trip would be more cost effective. They would send a larger consignment at one time and would save money on transportation and other costs. Besides, the business had so much money in the bank at that time, there was no great need to sell any produce to raise more money. The farm, due to the efforts of Ojo, was making more money than it ever had.

Chief Odugbesan, like many businessmen, had borrowed a lot of money to start his business. He now wanted to start paying them back. But Ojo told him to wait. The interest rate was very low when he borrowed the money. Allowing the money to collect a higher interest now made more sense.

"Let the creditors wait," was the advice Ojo gave to Odugbesan. They would pay the creditors' money back later after they had made more money out of them. Odugbesan agreed with the sagacity of this business-minded line of thought.

The first inkling that Odugbesan had that something was wrong was when he woke up on Sunday to go to morning service at St. Savior's, and Ojo was not already in the front parlor, dressed in a neat shirt-and-trousers, his hymn book tucked under his arm, to accompany him to church. His own wives went to a different church, the Methodist church in Porogun.

Odugbesan and the young man always attended church together. They sat by each other on the same pew, as fellow congregants filed by, bowed low and allowed themselves to be greeted by Chief Odugbesan, who was considered an "elder" in the church. When it came to collection time, it was Ojo who put the envelope in the *igba ore* on behalf of Odugbesan.

Odugbesan knew that Ojo had gone to Shagamu with the consignment on Tuesday, but normally it took only two days for the round trip. And Ojo had been expected back on Friday night.

There had been a conclave of the *Ilamuren* chiefs in the *afin* that Saturday. Odugbesan had come in very late. He was tired and did not want to send a message to Ojo's house at that time because he thought his assistant would already be asleep. Now it was Sunday morning, and his wives and children told him that messages had been sent to Ojo's rented house. No one had seen Ojo since he left for Shagamu on Tuesday.

Immediately, Odugbesan became worried for the safety of the young man. Could he have fallen sick in Shagamu? Could he have had an accident on the way? Or could he have been waylaid by robbers and the money stolen?

When he got to church, Odugbesan sought out some of the other young churchgoers who he knew were close to Ojo.

"Yes," said one of them.

This was Luke, who was a son of one of Odugbesan's fellow chiefs in the Awujale's council.

Luke had seen Ojo on Friday afternoon on Folagbade Street. In fact, he had tried to hail him, but Ojo had hurried around a corner. He seemed to have been in a great rush.

Now Odugbesan began to be worried.

"Why would Ojo return to Ijebu-Ode and not go home at all?" he asked.

Was Luke sure that it was Ojo he had seen?

"Haba," Luke exclaimed. "Se mi o wa ni mo Ojo ni—*Are you saying I would not recognize my friend Ojo?*"

Odugbesan could not sleep that night. He could not make sense of this riddle. Why would Ojo come to town and not come and tell him at Ita Ntebo?

All inquiries to Ojo's landlord and fellow tenants had yielded the same answer, "A ari i—*We haven't seen him.*"

The next morning, Odugbesan went straight to the bank. It could not be said at this time that he panicked, but his heart sank when he saw the strange look given to him by the teller, a middle-aged Ondo man named Dawodu. Odugbesan asked for his ledger of accounts. Dawodu showed it to him.

The entries were in blue-black ink in a carefully looped cursive, the writing of a careful man of business and accounting. There was a long column for "credit" and another for "debit." Odugbesan's eyes followed Dawodu's finger as it went down to the last row. Under "Balance," there were exactly two pounds, five shillings and six pence.

It was then that the teller told Odugbesan that Ojo had come in on Friday afternoon. He had a signed note from Odugbesan asking to make a large withdrawal because there was a major project by their partner, Chief Ogunsola in Ibadan, in which Odugbesan wanted to invest. It was going to yield a huge and quick profit, an opportunity not to be missed, and all the money would be returned in two weeks.

The reason that Ojo had come alone by himself was that Chief Odugbesan had been ill and would not be able to leave his bed for at least the next five days or so. That was why the clerk had given Odugbesan such a strange look, seeing him looking so hale and hearty.

It took the clerk more than thirty minutes to explain to the now thoroughly confused Odugbesan that no one at the bank was to blame. The clerk had to give Odugbesan a chair to sit on so that the chief would not collapse on the floor. His legs were wobbly, and his vision failed him.

All the bank clerks and tellers gathered around the stricken and speechless Odugbesan. They made their explanations to show that they were not at fault. They produced a note, which they showed him, with Odugbesan's signature on it. Dawodu, the middle-aged teller, had checked with the manager. They had both carefully checked the signature on the note with the sample they had on record. They had matched.

It took a long time before the full gravity of the situation sank in for Odugbesan. He was ruined.

Not only had Ojo, the polite, smart young man who he had trusted with his life and who at that moment was practically his son-in-law, not failed to deposit the money he had obtained from the sale of four months of produce from the farm, he had cleared out all the balance in the bank, the total working capital for his business as well as the money owed to his creditors.

Odugbesan's mouth and lips moved, but no words came out.

"All the money that I have made from all these years of hard work, and which I deposited in the bank, is gone," he found himself repeating to himself.

Odugbesan sat very still on the chair that Dawodu got for him. Numb, he felt nothing. His eyes were wild. They stared, unfocused and unseeing. As Odugbesan tried to look at the bank clerk who stood in front of him, the figure was blurred. What he saw was a dark vision in the far distance, from another world and another time.

Dawodu started to talk. His manner was timid, hesitant, and apologetic. He cleared his throat.

"Chief, I did not want to tell you this before, sir. The bank has not been paid its fees for this large transaction. Mr. Ojo said it would be paid when the money was returned. In fact, we had to clear our safe when we paid out the money to him. We did not have enough money in hand. But fortunately, one of our other customers, Chief Odusanya, came in and deposited a large sum of money.

"Our fees are nineteen pounds and six shillings. Since your current balance will not cover this amount, you owe the bank seventeen pounds and six shillings. We will need to have this money as soon as possible."

Odugbesan continued to look at Dawodu with hollow, unseeing eyes. He tried to focus on the figure of the bank clerk in front of him who continued to try to explain the situation to him. But Odugbesan could see nothing but visions of ruin and loss, and a deep calamity that offered no hope of restitution or redemption.

"I hope you understand my position, sir," the bank teller continued. "I am only a teller here."

"I discussed it with our manager. And I took a risk, since you are one of our best customers, when I agreed to deduct the fees when the money was put back."

*　*　*　*　*

Back in Chief Odugbesan's house at Ita Ntebo, there was consternation, accompanied by wailing and weeping. The women of the household jumped up and threw themselves on the floor. They unloosed their *gele* and tore at their hair.

"Yeparipa!" someone cried. It was the old Yoruba wail of desolation and distress.

"Mo ti daran," Aduke, Odugbesan's second wife kept repeating to herself.

Tears streamed down her face. It was her daughter, Olusade, who had been made pregnant and was betrothed to Ojo. The girl was expecting her baby anytime.

In that stricken household, it was as if someone had died. And in fact, someone had. The third and youngest wife of Chief Odugbesan, Bosede, had died just three weeks earlier. It was a tragic loss that was still felt in the household. They still wore black in mourning for her.

Bose had suddenly fallen dreadfully sick with a mysterious woman's disease that caused her to have severe bleeding and excruciating abdominal pain. Despite prayers at the *Aladura* church and sacrifices at various shrines in town including the ministrations of a *babalawo* who had been called to give her poultices and *agunmus*, she had succumbed.

The dead Bosede's only child, a girl of three, had been taken away by her sister to live with her in Ago-Iwoye. The family had not recovered from this tragedy when this trouble with Ojo burst on them with a suddenness and violence that was difficult to grasp.

"What would become of us now?" The women mouthed this question as they looked desperately at each other for answers.

But no word came out of any one's mouth. The answer to this question was not to be found in the hopeless eyes and sorrowful looks that Chief Odugbesan's remaining wives cast at each other, a family at the end of its tethers.

In fact, the other wives felt that it was because Chief Odugbesan had been distracted by the loss of Bosede, who everyone knew he loved more than his two other wives, that he had lately allowed himself to entrust Ojo with so much of his business transactions.

The next morning, Aduke, the second wife of Chief Odugbesan, knocked on his door to wake him up.

Uncharacteristically, the door was locked from the inside. Aduke pounded again on her husband's door. When there was no answer, she called the eldest wife, Mama Olobi. Fearing the worst, they both rushed out to call in a neighbor who broke in the bedroom door. The lock was flimsy, and all it took was the broad shoulder of the young man from next door to push the door in.

They were too late. Odugbesan hung dead by the neck with a rope looped around a big twisted iron nail which had been left by the carpenters on the wooden rafter of the ceiling when the house was built. This was something that Odugbesan sometimes used to hang a hurricane lamp on.

This was how Baba Mamu, who was Chief Odugbesan's best friend and neighbor in Ita Ntebo, ended up taking in three of the dead man's children into his own household. One was a boy who Baba Mamu sent through school, paying for his education at the grammar school.

Two were girls, for whom Baba Mamu arranged suitable marriages when they came of age. Regarding the fifteen-year-old daughter who was pregnant with Ojo's baby and had been betrothed to him, she died during childbirth and her child, a boy, did not survive either.

Baba Mamu never forgave himself. For he was the friend who had recommended Ojo to Chief Odugbesan to be employed as a bookkeeper.

But how had this happened?

A year earlier, Odusanya had traveled to Ibadan to meet his partner, Chief Ogunsola, one of the first entrepreneurs in Yorubaland to recognize the great potential of cocoa as a cash crop. When he came back, he brought home a young man who he introduced immediately to all his wives. This was very strange to them because Baba Mamu rarely brought to his house the assistants, laborers, and servants who worked for him on his farm at Mamu.

"This is different," he told his family as his children peeped, behind their mothers, to have a look at the stranger he had brought with him. "His name is Ojo."

He told them that Ojo was the orphaned son of Chief Ogunsola's first partner who had drowned with his two wives when the Ogunpa river overflowed its banks fifteen years earlier and carried their house away in a terrible flood. This man, whose name was Madarikan, had built his house too close to that unpredictable and treacherous river.

Somehow, the boy Ojo had survived. He was found on a dry stretch of high ground the next day. And apart from being hungry and asking for food—*eko* and *moinmoin*—he did not have as much as a scratch on his body. Chief Ogunsola was called by one of Madarikan's neighbors whose own house had survived the flood. He knew about the great friendship between the two men.

Ogunsola picked the boy up, took him home, and gave him to his first wife, Atinuke, to feed. Ojo was then five years old.

Now he was twenty. He had been educated by Ogunsola at the St. James's School, Oke Bola, after which he had learned bookkeeping from the chief himself. On learning during this trip that Odusanya's business had grown so much that he may need a secretary and a bookkeeper, Chief Ogunsola had suggested that he should accept Ojo for this position and take him back to Ijebu-Ode with him.

However, Oku, Baba Mamu's first wife had a premonition. Without saying a word to Baba Mamu, she left the house and went to consult her "baba," an *alfa* who lived in Eti-tale.

When she came back, she called Baba Mamu to his room. She was adamant. He could not employ that young man, she told him firmly. The old man had said, after consulting his oracle, that this young man would ruin Baba Mamu and destroy his household if he employed him. He should let someone else have him.

And this was why Baba Mamu, rather than ask Ojo to return to Ibadan, had recommended him to his good friend, Chief Odugbesan, who needed a secretary and a bookkeeper more than Baba Mamu himself. For Odugbesan was practically an illiterate in the reading and writing of the *oyinbo* language, and this had affected his business.

Later, the full extent of Ojo's atrocities and despoilment of Chief Odugbesan's household came out in bits and pieces.

For soon after he had already impregnated the daughter, Ojo started to sleep with his employer's youngest wife. For Bosede, it was the actualization of her erotic fantasy. And she indulged herself with a wild and passionate abandon.

She would surreptitiously meet Ojo in his rented room in the middle of the afternoon while she was supposed to be tending her stall in the market. She arranged countless rendezvous with him in secret places—the back of an abandoned Native Authority building at night, at a friends' house just outside the city limits on the road to Ijebu-Igbo, and even on Odugbesan's farm at Oru when no one was there. She spent days holed up in his room while she told people she had gone to visit her sister in Ago-Iwoye.

Once they had a tryst in a schoolroom of the primary school in Ijasin on a Saturday afternoon when she was supposed to be in the market. Wisely, Ojo had suborned the caretaker, who betook himself elsewhere and guarded the entrance to the school compound from snooping intruders while they did what they had to do. She had brought a thick woven *iro,* which she lay on the rough cement floor while they frolicked and caressed.

Bosede laughed and giggled at the sheer audacity of their escapade, teaching each other new things about their bodies in a classroom for children.

Well, she said to herself happily, they were both young, and were little more than children themselves. They were playing a secret game which no one else had to know about.

The sheer voluptuousness of her lust and her total desire to please Ojo so enmeshed her that she abandoned all reason. In between their trysts, she could think only of his caresses and how soon she would marinate herself in his embrace as time and again, that wonder of that small miracle overcame her. A deep vault in her body opened its gates. Her muscles twitched, her eyes dilated, and a warm feeling overcame her, soothing her to sleep.

Nothing else mattered. She neglected her stall in the market, her household chores, even her daughter. But sometimes, a sliver of sanity and an Ijebu woman's common sense would penetrate her concupiscence-drenched obsession. Then, after he had lain with her, tears would well up in her eyes. She pestered him.

"What is going to happen to us?" she would ask him. "When are you going to marry me?"

He made solemn promises to her, swearing by all the gods and fetishes of his native Ibadan and the even more potent ones of Ijebu.

He told her that he only continued to work for Chief Odugbesan so that he could save enough money for both of them. Then he would take her out of Ijebu-Ode, to Ibadan, where he would marry her. They would have many children.

And through a mind that was besotted with infatuation and lust, she listened. Eagerly, she believed what all along she had wanted to believe. Bosede told herself that this was the happiest period of her young, previously unremarkable life. She had only wanted to be happy and fulfilled. And her wish had been granted beyond any earthly measure.

Outwardly, Bosede glowed. Her constant smile was something the other wives commented upon, not guessing its source. She bought exotic perfumes from Hausa traders in the market. She tied her *gele* in a score of different ways with skill and ingenuity. She went before her husband on her knees and asked for money to buy new clothes, new shoes, and a new set of earrings, necklace, and bangles. Her wrists and ankles jangled as she walked.

To please and entice her lover, she took to wearing a *bebe,* a string of beads that she wore on her hip and which she showed off to him, wiggling her waist, as one night, they lay naked on a mat outside in the open verandah of the small storehouse on Odugbesan's farm.

She pushed up her pelvis and pouted at him, a child waiting to be praised and rewarded. And not waiting for her prize to be given to her without effort, she reached eagerly for her reward, plucking it eagerly from the forbidden tree.

Shifting her position, she reached out to him. And delicately and expertly, for she had learned a lot from Ojo, she touched and caressed him until he was big and strong. Then her body shook and trembled as he completely filled her with his power, until like a juicy and overripe pawpaw, she burst open, joyful, and fulfilled.

Bosede knew of course that nobody could see them on this farm in the middle of the night as she indulged in her bold but secret liaison with her lover. But the very thought of doing these forbidden things under the stars on her husband's farm excited and stimulated her.

And it was true indeed that there were no human eyes watching them. But unseen by her, the *iwins* in the nearby forest, her lover's minions, crept nearer, leaving their lair in the bushes, and watched. They leered and peeped, grinned and applauded, as the couple came

OLADELE OLUSANYA

together, moved apart to rest and came together again—an exclusive and intimate performance for their eyes only.

The infinite variety of the young man's skills and techniques to make her gasp and moan, and to cry out in pain and pleasure, amazed Bosede. But she wondered, sometimes with dismay, why she could never be satisfied.

But of guilt and shame, she felt nothing. For he had stopped up all her avenues for remorse or any conscious thought of the pain or harm she would cause her husband, her family, or her young daughter if her adulterous escapades were to be discovered.

Bosede said to herself, "I don't care," as she gave way once more to her pleasure.

She kept going to this river to drink. And though temporarily satiated, she was never satisfied. She always wanted more from that font that she knew would never stop, so limitless and mysterious was its source. It was an unearthly addiction that she could not stop.

Gradually, she came to know she was in the presence of a master. Ojo's knowledge and skills were not of this world. And slowly but surely, she came to realize the extent of his power over her.

One day, after he had been with her, naked as the day she was born, she knelt before him and paid homage as to a deity. This magnificent being, in the form of this young man from Ibadan, was the god of her idolatry. And she worshipped gladly at his feet.

But although he might have been a god, demigod, or demon, who had come out of a dark infernal cave to lure, ensnare, and ravish her, and to help her fulfill her strange, overpowering, and self-centered desires, she had an earthly body. She could not long evade the rules of nature. For there are consequences, then, now, and always, for the actions of mortals on this earth, no matter if sometimes they are pushed and instigated by the whims and caprices of the indifferent gods.

Eventually, Bosede got pregnant. But when she told her lover of her missed periods, he told her to deal with it, or to tell her husband the truth. Desperate, she fell on her knees and begged him. She said she would abandon her husband and her child. She would run away with him to his town of Ibadan or anywhere he wanted to take her. She wanted him to take her away from her shame and the heavy sanctions of an outraged society.

But, unblinking, he told her to leave, telling her brusquely that he would never see her again. His eyes, when she looked up at him from where she knelt, were cold and distant. They were not those of the lover she knew. Those strange uneven-colored eyes stared at her with an unfamiliar disinterest that was a shock for her to see. She now saw them for what they were, alien and cruel, and full of great evil and malice.

She thought of the way he had used her body and played with her mind. He had incited her libido and had pushed her beyond the boundaries of reason, propriety, and shame.

She looked desperately into his eyes, trying to discern in them that look of love and amity that used to animate them. But the eyes that looked back at her were cold and friendless. And those shy, amiable tics of the lower eyelids were gone. His voice was stranger still. When he spoke to her, his tone was superior, mocking, and derisive.

She shuddered as the knowledge came to her. The veil lifted at last from her eyes, bringing light and instruction to her limited understanding. It was what she had seen in those dark caves that had now come to claim its due. It was a thing unknown and unknowable, from the dark side of creation, one of the grotesque beings of Obatala, warped, not in body but in mind. The young man who stood before Bosede was not only bad and dangerous for her to have known; he was evil incarnate.

Devastated by this bleak realization and the implacable hatred and rejection that confronted her as her lover sneered at her, Bosede collapsed on the floor.

Ojo stepped over her and entered his bedroom, locking the door. They had been talking in the sitting room of his rented "room and parlor."

Bosede made an attempt to rise and knock on the door. Maybe, just one more time, she might appeal to him. But she knew it was no use. The person she had given her body to was not human. She had allowed a demon to possess her. And now, her body, her life, and her soul were forfeit as a result of its dark embrace.

Her sorrow was overwhelming, but no tears came. And her eyes, if she could have looked into them, were red and bloodshot. They burned with pain and a deep shame. Her body lay crumpled on the floor, shaking with sobs. But after a while, she got up. She went away frightened, confused, and desperate. And it was an attempt to have an abortion that had caused her death from bleeding and infection.

The final chapter of this tragic story came a few weeks after Ojo's disappearance and Chief Odugbesan's death. Oku, Baba Mamu's first wife, went to see her "baba," the same one who had warned her not to let Baba Mamu employ the young man.

This is what "Baba" told Oku.

"I did not know the full extent of what we were dealing with when my oracle told me to tell your husband not to have anything to do with that young man. But now I know.

"He is not from this world. It is Agbako himself who took the earthly form of this young man to wreak his customary and wicked punishment on the people he has chosen to punish."

Everyone in Yorubaland knew of course that Agbako's sole reason for existence was to punish men and women.

Traditionally, he was depicted as carrying a bag of whips with which he flogged his victims. But the punishment that Agbako dishes out can take many forms. As "Baba" explained to a wide-mouthed Oku, the people he punishes do not need to have done anything to deserve his punishment. Agbako chooses his victims with an indiscriminate and perverse indifference.

The pleasant young man who everyone knew as Ojo, was from the spirit world. It was he, Agbako, who had destroyed the family of Chief Madarikan in the Ogunpa flood and had contrived to be discovered and recognized as the lone surviving child of that unfortunate family.

As for Bosede, this is what "Baba" said:

"So nfu lobo, A se-e, emi ren lo nwa."

She thought she merely gave her lover her body to possess. But what he wanted was her *emi*, her soul.

"Ojo would never be found because he is not of this world," concluded Baba.

"He has gone back to where he came from."

But as Agbako, he would be sure to be back, in another place and time, to wreak his familiar and destructive vengeance on the carefully contrived happiness of another human family.

"Olorun ma je a pade Agbako," Oku, Baba Mamu's first wife muttered. *May the Owner of Heaven never let us meet Agbako.*

Then she got up. She gave "Baba" a few coins for the consultation, and walked slowly to her home in Ita Ntebo.

*   *   *   *   *

Later in life, Baba Mamu came to face an enemy that was deadlier and more insidious than the cult worshippers of *Igbo Odu* or the British Maxim gun at Yemoji. He developed diabetes.

He discovered this when he saw that urinating on the ground on his farm at Mamu, ants would congregate on the spot. No viable treatment was available. As Baba Mamu tried to confront this implacable foe, he found that he had no suitable weapons to bring the enemy to heel.

Thus was Odusanya brought low by a strange and devastating illness. He, an Ijebu teenage warrior and friend of the great Chief Kuku, who had been to the Kiriji battlefield and had shaken hands with the Reverend Samuel Johnson.

As his diabetes got worse, Baba Mamu lost all sense of feeling in his extremities. Gradually, he found it difficult to walk. His vision became progressively blurry until he could no longer see anything more than five yards away. He retired from active farming in 1946, but he continued to go to Mamu to supervise his farm workers.

When he died in 1954, he had lived to see his children and grandchildren become civil servants, businessmen, lawyers, and physicians. He was an enlightened man of his age. Though a Christian by his own lights, he followed the traditions of his forefathers in being an inveterate polygamist to the end.

Many people would say that he had abandoned the worship of the gods of his people. But to Baba Mamu, the new God of the Christians, who had a son named Jesu, was the same paramount deity who had sent Obatala to create the earth at Ile-Ife. It was he who had protected his people since the coming of Oduduwa from the east.

Baba Mamu's world view was simple. His theology was unconvoluted, free from the dogma that came from too much reading of books. In this regard, he was no different from most people in his day.

From the few books he read, Baba Mamu knew that there were many stories told by people all over the earth about the origin of mankind and the action of the gods in directing the affairs of men. His own view was that the stories of his people, the Yorubas, were as valid as those of other races, even if those other people had white skin and wrote their stories down in a big black book.

He explained it thus to one of his friends who stubbornly followed the old pagan gods, "It is not an *oyinbo* god that I am serving when I say I am a Christian. Olorun is my god. He is your god too, and he is the ancient god of our Ijebu people."

Baba Mamu remembered to the end of his days the stirring stories of the founding of Ijebu-Ode that were related to him by Chief Kuku, and of the part his own ancestors had played in the heroic history of his town. Though he had embraced the new ways of the white man, he liked to think that he embodied the great traditions of Osogbesan, his ancestor who founded Ita Ntebo, and of Obanta, the first Awujale of Ijebu-Ode.

Baba Mamu was a man who embraced new ideas in his lifetime. But he also cherished the old ways of his people. He wanted to pass this ancient heroic legacy to his children and their children

Toward the end of his life, Baba Mamu had a dream in which he found himself perched on a high precipitous bridge. From this great height, he looked down. What he saw was a panoramic view that showed him the future abode of his people but also the ancient homesteads of his departed ancestors. He knew that the bridge on which he sat connected the days of the ancient Awujales to the modern hierarchy of the pen brought by the white man. The quintessential Ijebu way of life might change from one generation to the next, but it would never perish. He himself was the embodied metaphor of his dream—the bridge between old and new.

Baba Mamu married his last wife, Afusatu, in 1946. This was two years before his daughter Adedotun married a scion of another distinguished Ijebu royal line of Oremadegun from Odogbolu. From this last liaison, Baba Mamu had two more children, Oluyemi and Olusegun, both of whom went to live with Baba Mamu's first son, Daniel Folorunsho Odusanya in Idi-Oro, Lagos, where I, his grandson lived next door in a house which also belonged to Baba Idi-Oro with my grandmother Efunyemi, his third wife.

By 1954, many of Baba Mamu's children, including my mother Adedotun, had left the old family compound in Ita Ntebo for the bright lights of Lagos. They sought opportunities in civil service jobs in that bright new city which was the colonial seat of government. And from that old Portuguese slave port, some of them sought berths on merchant ships to sail to England, *ilu oyinbo*, in search of the "golden fleece."

So, when news came that year of the death of the patriarch, those of his children who were studying abroad in England booked a passage on the *MV Aureole* from Liverpool. They came back home to Ita Ntebo to join those who had made the shorter journey from Lagos and Ibadan and the few who had stayed behind in Ijebuland.

They were all glad to be back home. But the once familiar surroundings of Baba Mamu's house in Ita Ntebo had become strange to them. Their childhood home looked old, neglected, and decayed.

Still, the children of Baba Mamu killed half a dozen cows. They celebrated the passing of their father in the old tradition. They fed everyone in their neighborhood in Ita Ntebo. They also sent *eran malu* and *akara* to their kinsmen at the palace at Ita Afin.

Although they were there to celebrate the rites of passage of a traditional chief of Ijebu, Baba Mamu had a "Christian" burial. There were no pagan rituals at midnight or sacrificial animals buried in the dead man's courtyard to speed the soul of a former warrior to the abode of the gods.

Still, the old ways were not forgotten. Baba Mama's children and grandchildren nodded their heads in approval when a masked Ijebu masquerade made his appearance and recited the *oriki* of their famous father.

> *Omo Ita Ntebo Alaba meji*
> *Omo Jagun Aso*
> *Omo a nukan johun ekun*
> *Omo a yeye bi ero oja.*

> *Child of Ita Ntebo,*
> *He of the two homesteads,*
> *Owner of many grand clothes,*
> *To whom alone is bequeathed*
> *The dread voice of the leopard.*

After the funeral, those of Baba Mamu's children who returned to Lagos gathered to unpack their bags in the house on Daniel Street in Idi-Oro which had been built by Baba Mamu's first son, Daniel Folorunsho Odusanya.

Known as "Baba Idi-Oro," Daniel was now the patriarch of the family. Daniel Street in Alakara, Idi-Oro, where his house stood, had been named for him by the Lagos Mainland Town Council. He was one of the first persons to build a house in that desolate suburb of Yaba near the railway tracks on which the train ran between Loco in Yaba and Mushin, following a straight line from Iddo terminus to Agege. All his adult life, since the age of twenty-three years, Baba Idi-Oro had lived with the sound of railway engines in his ears. He woke to, and slept to that sound. So he had his house built next to a rail line.

Years later, I lived with my grandmother Efunyemi on that same street in another building also built by "Baba Idi-Oro." I looked up often at the inscription engraved in cement on the upstairs balcony of the house next door in which lived the landlord.

"Ntebo Lodge," the legend read.

Baba Mamu was gone. But his spirit lived on in the edifices built by his children. Far from his native Ita Ntebo, it lived in a house on a quiet street in a suburb of a new city ruled by *oyinbos* who had come from thousands of miles away to colonize his people.

Baba Mamu's children, like other Yorubas of their time, still lived in their land of *karo o'jire*. But it was a new, uneasy time for these descendants of ancient *esos*. For they lived under the aegis of a foreign power, whose dominance over their lives was not always benign. The age of Oonis, Alafins, and Awujales, as absolute rulers who held the power of life and death over their subjects, was gone. And what did these new children of Odudwa care for those ancient monarchs? Probably not a lot. But as the Odusanya clan went about their lives, the spirits of their ancestors stirred in them, reviving those stories of the golden age they were told as children.

"Would the days of glory ever come bac*k?*" they would ask.

Or had the proud spirit of their Yoruba people crumbled into the dust with the destruction wreaked by the British Maxim gun on the banks of the Yemoji river?

Had the hero ethos departed for good from the land of *karo o jire* with the passing of the generation of warriors like Solesi and Baba Mamu?

In that house in Idi-Oro, which looked strangely clean and modern after the decay they saw in Ijebu-Ode, the children of Baba Mamu contemplated these questions. But they were able to look toward the future with little perturbation.

For these inheritors of the one-thousand-year Yoruba legacy drew inspiration from the past—from the heroism and sacrifice of those who had gone before and the wisdom inherited with their ancient culture. This was manifested in the continuation of their *omoluwabi* ethos, penchant for diplomacy, elaborate dressing, and verbose, proverb-laden speech. And they had their traditional Yoruba music, the talking drum, *egungun* festivals, and *ewi,* their inimitable oral poetry.

Their resilience as a people had been proven in that previous century of *igba inira,* the time of troubles. Surviving that unhappy era ensured that they would continue to live in the land bestowed to their ancestors. New chapters beckoned in the story of the Yoruba people to be written by their generation and those coming after them.

So the children of Baba Mamu turned to each other and said, "This is not the end. It is a new beginning."

OLADELE OLUSANYA

ILLUSTRATIONS

Front Cover: *'Ajantala,'* Oladele Olusanya
Foreword: *'Yoruba slaves taken to Brazil,'* Dipo Alao
Chapter 1: *'Madam Tinubu,'* Dipo Alao
Chapter 2: *'Omo Eko,'* Dipo Alao
Chapter 3: *'Aarin and the Warrior from Ife,'* Dipo Alao
Chapter 4: *'War-boy,'* Dipo Alao
Chapter 5: *'Solesi of Ikenne,'* Dipo Alao
Chapter 6: *'Battle of Imagbon,'* Dipo Alao
Chapter 7: *'Baba Mamu on his cocoa farm,'* Dipo Alao
Back Cover: *'Battle of Osogbo,'* Oladele Olusanya

ACKNOWLEDGEMENTS

THE FRONT AND back cover of 'A time of troubles' were designed by Adebayo Akinde of Dallas, Texas, based on original art works, 'Ajantala' and 'Battle of Oshogbo,' acrylic on canvas paintings by the author, Dr. Oladele Olusanya.

The illustrations that precede each chapter are original pen and ink drawings on paper, specifically commissioned by the author for this book and drawn by Dipo Alao, a Yoruba artist of the 'Osogbo' school, based on sketches and ideas by the author.

All the chapter poems and quotations in verse attributed to the characters in the book, both in Yoruba and English, are the original, previously unpublished creation of the author except when otherwise stated as 'Traditional.'

THE "LEGEND" CONTINUES

The story of *A Time of Troubles* continues in
A new age, Book 3 of the *Itan: Legends of
the Golden Age* trilogy by Oladele Olusanya.

For more information, visit www.oladeleolusanya.net